Brides of
KENTUCKY

50 States of *Love*

Brides of

KENTUCKY

3-in-1 Historical Romance Collection

Lynn A. Coleman

BARBOUR BOOKS
An Imprint of Barbour Publishing, Inc.

Contents

Raining Fire

Dedication

To my grandson, Matthew, who's been slow to
speak but from whom I expect great things will come.

Chapter 1

November 1833
Cumberland Gap, Kentucky

Quinton!" Pam Danner screamed, tumbling down the steep road through the Cumberland Gap. Pinned by the wagon against a huge boulder, Quinton appeared lifeless. Again she tumbled, tripping over the hem of her dress. Her fine high-heeled boots were no match for this rugged terrain. *I should have listened to Quinton and purchased a pair of traveling boots.*

One large wheel sat in his lap and crushed his chest against the stone. "Quinton!" she screamed again, finally reaching him. His eyes fluttered open, then immediately closed. "Dear God, help me." She pulled at the wagon. It wouldn't budge. *Leverage.* She scanned the area. Spotting a large, fairly straight branch along the side of the trail, she retrieved it.

"Hang on, Quinton," she panted. His eyes barely moved under their lids. "Dear God, no. You can't take him away, too." Tears burned the corners of her eyes.

A small trickle of blood edged his pale lips.

She pushed and pulled at a small boulder to bring it close to the wagon. Even if she did manage to lift the wagon, she couldn't pull him out. "God, help me!" She wiped the tears from her cheeks, placed the oak branch under the wheel, and wedged it across the smaller boulder.

"Stop," a deep voice hollered from behind. She turned to discover a bear of a man dressed in leather with a Kentucky long rifle in his hand. "You'll kill him for certain."

Her hands released the pole as if it were on fire. He leaned his rifle beside the huge boulder and bent down to check Quinton's pulse. "He's alive but just barely. I'll lift the wagon; you grab him." He didn't wait for her reply.

She scurried into place.

He planted his feet. His face darkened as he lifted. "Now," he said in a strained voice.

She wrapped her arms under Quinton's and pulled him away from his trap.

The man released his hold on the corner of the uncovered wagon, and it immediately lunged forward. The iron-covered wheel scraped against the rock. The huge man bent over, maneuvering his hands around Quinton's still body. "Isn't good. He's busted up pretty bad. I suspect he's bleedin' on the inside. It isn't safe to move him. Whatever were you thinking, trying to drive a wagon over the gap?"

"We didn't. We took it apart and brought it over piece by piece. Quinton was working on the left wheel when it pinned him."

The man shook his head and stood up.

"You best make camp tonight. You aren't going anywhere." His gaze worked its way up and down the trail. "Where are your horses?"

"Quinton tethered them down a ways. He figured they could feed while he worked."

He nodded. Thick black hair spilled out of his coonskin cap. All the sketches she'd seen over the years of Daniel Boone and the other frontier men were rolled into this one man. "I'll fetch 'em, if they haven't been stolen."

"Stolen?"

"Bandits, ma'am." He grabbed his rifle and ran down the mountain.

Quinton groaned.

"Quint, Quint. Please don't die on me."

"Pamela. . ." His lips shaped her name more than she heard his voice. Trembling, she leaned over him, wanting to touch him but afraid to.

"Hurts bad," he gasped, his breathing ragged and labored.

Carefully, she wrapped her hand around his. His response was nonexistent. She squeezed a little tighter. "Quinton, fight it. I can't lose you. I can't. I just can't."

"The store," he coughed. Blood spilled over his lips. Her stomach knotted. *Dear God, don't do this. Not now, not again.*

"Remember," he wheezed.

Remember? How could she ever forget? She hadn't wanted to come. She'd fought God, fought her parents, and had even fought Quinton. In the end she'd ignored all the omens and came anyway.

Now look what's happened. Quinton lying by a rock in the middle of nowhere, dying. She should have made him see that her parents' death was a warning to stay away from this cursed land. Angus, the old house slave, had warned her how things would be if they chose to move west. He said the air didn't smell right, that trouble was in the wind. She'd never understood how Angus would know all these things, but somehow he'd always been right. Or at least it seemed he was right more times than not. Her parents hadn't believed in Angus, and look where it got them. Dead. Quinton hadn't heeded Angus's warnings. Now he was dying, too.

"The dream," he sputtered.

It wasn't her dream. She'd wanted to stay in Virginia. Stay among her friends, society. She had no interest in taming the wilderness.

He squeezed her hand ever so slightly.

"Quint, I can't. I don't want it like you and Mother and Father. I only came with you because you said I must. I can't go on without you."

His eyelids drifted shut. Slowly, he tried to raise them again.

"Quinton, please don't leave me." Tears dripped from her chin. Lovingly, she wiped them from Quinton's tortured face. She kissed his forehead and ran to the edge of the woods. "God, forgive me, I can't watch him die."

੩

Mac stroked the muzzle of the lead horse. Thankfully, they were still tethered where Quinton had left them. November brought far less traffic on the Wilderness Road. The drovers had come and gone earlier in the fall, taking the herds of livestock back East to sell.

Not much hope for the young man. Perhaps he'd make it through the night and they could ride him in the morning to Yellow Creek. Nearest doctor was in Barbourville, but Mac doubted he'd make it that far. The young couple could spend the night in their precious wagon. Their supplies hadn't been restocked. It certainly wasn't going anywhere lodged up against Indian Rock.

Christian duty required him to help these poor folks. The eight-point buck he'd had in his sights moments before the squealing broke the woodland silence had bolted. He preferred deer to elk. Both were plentiful, and that eight-point buck was large enough to have met all his winter needs. But now he had neither deer nor elk. Instead he had a mess on his hands.

He tied the horses loosely to the wagon. A soft, golden hue filled the sky, the setting sun a sharp reminder of how little time they had before darkness enveloped the gap.

Gathering some standing deadwood and small stones, he lit a fire. "Excuse me, ma'am," he called to the still distraught woman. "Sun's setting. We'll need to make camp."

She turned ever so slowly at the edge of the woods. Her golden hair hung haphazardly across her shoulders.

"We'll need to keep him warm." *Not that it would help much, other than provide the man a small bit of comfort,* he mused. *If he's aware of the heat at all.*

With deliberate steps, she plodded her way toward him.

"Let's make a bed in the wagon for you and your husband," he suggested.

She knitted her eyebrows, then nodded her head.

They really shouldn't move the injured man, Mac knew, but would it make any difference now?

"Pam," the wounded man moaned.

It was hard to figure why this woman didn't stay constantly by her husband's side. *It might be too painful,* he guessed.

She scuffled to her husband, bent over, and held his hand. Her hands trembled. Mac's gut tightened.

"Quinton!" The heart-wrenching plea echoed off the mountain.

Should he run to her rescue? Should he give them time alone? Uncertain, he sat on his haunches by the campfire he'd been making moments before.

She turned to Mac and motioned for him to come beside her. Tears slid down her cheeks. Mac obliged.

"Thank. . ." The young man coughed. His chest heaved from the heavy labor. "You," he finally managed to get out.

"No need, just doing what any good Christian would do."

The pale eyelids closed and opened again. *His agreement, no doubt.* The man's lips moved, but no words came. Mac bent down on one knee. Again the lips moved. Again, nothing.

Mac glanced over to the young woman who had buried her face in her hands, then leaned over again, his ear an inch from the dying man's mouth.

"Please, Pamela. . .safety. . ." The broken sentence whispered, then blazed a silent echo within his ears. *Take the woman to safety?* How could he argue with a dying man's request? He could take her as far as the Cumberland Ford Camp. She could work for one of the taverns. Or, he supposed, he could take her to Barbourville.

"Creelsboro." The word barely escaped.

Mac wanted to plead with the man to fight, fight harder. But he'd been in this situation before. He knew the dying person was far more aware of his passing than those who stood around.

"Help, please." Another labored whisper passed.

The man's hand clutched his.

To take a woman halfway across the state was a heap more to ask than for him to simply bring her to a nearby settlement or town. But he couldn't ignore a dying man's request. Not to mention, if his parents ever heard he'd failed to help a stranger, he'd be hauled off to the barn as if he were a child in need of correction from his father's broad leather strap. Nope, everything in Mac screamed to help, and everything in him feared lending a hand to this woman.

"I'll take her."

The waning clasp on his hand released. Quinton's gaze locked onto Mac's.

"I promise, her honor is safe with me," Mac reassured the dying man.

The man's lids opened and closed once more. Then the pale blue eyes focused past Mac toward the heavens. They widened, then immediately darkened. The final gasp of air escaped from his body. He was a young man who accepted death with a gentle peace, a calming peace. A peace that only God could give.

Mac reached over and closed the man's eyelids. *Father God, be with his widow,* he prayed.

&

Pamela prepared her brother's body for burial, washing his face and hands, combing his hair. Mac, as she'd learned the stranger's name was when they'd exchanged introductions, informed her they could take Quinton into Yellow Creek and bury him. Up here in the gap, solid rock lay six inches or less below the surface. She'd prepared her parents' bodies last year, a ritual all too familiar. She never would have dreamed she'd be doing the same for Quinton.

Darkness covered the mountain, a fitting end to Quinton's life. Mac, with his Daniel Boone attire, was a man of few words. Truthfully, she didn't feel like talking. She didn't want to eat, sleep, walk, or do anything. Getting Quinton's body ready for burial seemed logical, and doing something seemed far more practical than crying.

At least that's what she kept telling herself.

Mac said they'd put Quinton's wrapped body in the open wagon to protect it from the animals. She laid a cloth over Quinton's face.

"I'll carry him to the wagon," Mac whispered.

The gentle giant lifted the lifeless form of her brother. *What am I going to do now?* The thought of heading back East and the day-long prospect of carrying the wagon piece by piece over the gap again didn't interest her at all. But the dream of going farther west had never been hers. It had been the dream of her father, her brother, and even her mother, but never her own.

Mac returned to the fire and held a cup out for her. "Drink this."

"Thank you, but I'm not hungry."

"I don't blame you, but this tea will help you sleep tonight."

"What's in it?"

"Black cohash."

A female herb? What's this man doing traveling with that? Who is he? "Thank you." She reached for the cup and brought it to her lips. The tea leaves sat on the bottom of the cup as the warm liquid soothed her parched lips and mouth. She closed her eyes and sighed. Life. It didn't seem fair. Why was she alive and the rest of her family gone?

"Try not to think about it." Mac's gentle words broke her thoughts.

How could he know what I was thinking?

He sat down beside the fire.

"Why are you here?" she quietly asked.

A disarming grin creased his face. Several days' growth formed a shadowy beard. "I was hunting nearby and heard the accident."

"But why are you still here?"

"It wouldn't be right for a man to leave a woman alone, and I promised your husband I'd take you to Creelsboro."

"Quinton was. . ." Her words caught in her throat. Should she correct the man, or should she simply let him believe she was a widow? Posing as a grieving widow would give her a bit more safety with this stranger, she decided. "How? When?"

"Those were his dying words, ma'am."

She ran her finger across the rim of the tin cup. "I'm not certain I wish to go to Creelsboro."

"Why were you heading out there?"

"My father purchased a business a little over a year ago. Shortly after that, he passed on. Quinton was going to complete his dream."

He poked at the fire with a stick, stopped, then looked at her. Inhaling deeply, he continued. "I'm not one to disregard a dying man's wish, but if you don't want to go to Creelsboro, I'd be happy to escort you back East."

"I don't know if I want to return to Virginia, either." She rubbed her temples. The whole prospect of deciding one's future when your family, your past, had just died seemed pointless.

"Tomorrow we'll go to Yellow Creek and take care of your husband's burial. I'll leave you there for the night with some friends. I'll return the next day, and perhaps by then you'll have a clearer understanding of where you'd like to go. But for now, it's time to sleep."

He stood up and held out his hand. Did he wish for her to sleep with him? Fear crept down her spine. "I'm not ready for sleep." A yawn betrayed her words.

"I set a bedroll by the fire for you. It won't be as warm as your wagon, but you'll be safe by the fire."

She tilted her head slightly to the right and saw the laid-out bedroll of woolen blankets. She swallowed hard. "Where are you going to sleep?"

Chapter 2

Mac stood and stretched. As Mrs. Danner slept by the fire, he had kept watch throughout the night, taking in brief snippets of sleep. He gazed over at Indian Rock and groaned. What had he gotten himself into, making such a promise to a dying man? Fortunately he knew where Creelsboro was. His parents' farm was in Jamestown, a short distance north. Creelsboro was a boomtown of activity. Folks would load up on supplies there before they ventured farther west. He looked over to the sleeping Mrs. Danner and wondered what she could possibly do there, now that her husband was gone.

He rolled his shoulders. A man keeps his word, he resolved. He set his coonskin cap on his head and looked at the eastern horizon. A thin ribbon of pale yellow lit the saddle, the lowest part of the Cumberland Gap. He glanced back at Indian Rock. How many people had lost their lives due to this boulder? In years past, the Indians would hide behind it and ambush the parties coming over the saddle. Today, Indians hiding behind the rock weren't a problem. But who'd ever expect it to be a part of another man's death? He wagged his head and headed into the forest.

Bandits were a constant threat along the trail. He needed to be on his guard. A defenseless female alone on the trail would be an easy target.

Crack.

A small branch snapped. Mac knelt down behind a bush. He focused in the direction of the sound. He sniffed the air. Silence. *Too quiet,* he reasoned. He looked back at the small fire and saw the sleeping form of Mrs. Danner. Easing his gun off his shoulder, Mac readied it.

A small fawn came into view. Mac eased out a pent-up breath. The wind stirred the tops of the trees. *Father, keep me calm. We've got a long journey ahead of us. I'll need sleep.*

A sliver of the sun now radiated over the saddle of the mountain gap. He finished scouting the area and returned to camp. Perhaps he could get in an hour's sleep before the Widow Danner rose.

He went back to the fire and stirred the dying embers, putting on a pot for hot water and coffee.

Pamela sat upright and blinked. "Is it morning?"

"Getting there. There's a small spring to your right. It's not much, but it's enough to help you clean up."

She opened her mouth, then snapped it shut and nodded her head. Perhaps it wasn't right for a man to tell a woman she needed to clean up. Mac held down a grin, but the situation was humorous.

He watched her trek over to the pile of her belongings. Mac groaned. He'd have to pack the wagon. The Danners had more stuff than he'd ever seen anyone bring through the gap. It was probably a good thing they were traveling this late in the year. The mud would have slowed them down. Still, it would be a chore getting it over the Cumberland River around Flatlick. The crossing at Camp Ford wouldn't be too costly. That would be a blessing.

He surveyed their trunks and the mounds of items they had neatly packed on the side of the road. *How'd they ever get all of that in there?* he wondered. *Mrs. Danner will have to decide what comes and what stays.*

"Mr. Mac? What is your last name?" Pamela asked as she approached.

"MacKenneth. I go by Mac."

"Oh, I just assumed your first name was Mac."

"No, my first name is Nash, Nash Oakley MacKenneth, but everyone calls me Mac."

She nodded. "I'll fix us some breakfast. Shall we load the wagon after that?"

Mac sat down beside the fire. Widow Danner set a cast-iron frying pan on the hot coals. "I was just thinking about that. I'm not quite sure how you managed to get all of those items in that wagon. But some will have to remain behind."

She glanced back at the stockpile. "I wouldn't know where to begin. I suppose Quinton's chest could stay behind, although I'll want to take out his good suit for burial."

Mac scratched the nubs on his chin. *This could take all morning.*

A slab of ham sizzled in the hot skillet. Its fragrant aroma stirred his empty stomach.

She ran to a chest and removed a couple items wrapped in white linen. Upon her return, she flipped the ham over and produced a couple eggs that she proceeded to whip in a small bowl.

"You're traveling with eggs?"

"A farmer, a day's journey back, traded some fresh food for some of our supplies. They won't stay fresh much longer if I don't keep them in a cool stream at night. I forgot about them last night. . . ." Her words mumbled to an end.

"That's understandable."

She removed the slab of ham and set the whipped eggs in the pan, crumbling bits of cheese over them. He hadn't had a breakfast like this in months. *Perhaps taking her to Creelsboro won't be such a strain after all.* He fought back a grin.

"So, do you live around here?" she asked.

"I have a winter cabin a few miles south of the gap. During the spring and summer, I live in Jamestown and help my parents with their farm."

"I'm sorry, I don't know much about Kentucky. Is Jamestown close by?"

"Actually, it's close to Creelsboro, and that's halfway across the state."

"Oh." Her hand paused from forking the now-cooked eggs from the frying pan to his plate.

"Mrs. Danner, I promised your husband I'd take you there. You don't know me, and I can understand your fear, but with God as my witness, you can trust me."

She looked down at her lap, wringing her hands. "I shall try, Mr. MacKenneth. We should eat so we can get a move on this morning."

He took the offered plate from her. "Thank you." He bowed his head for prayer. "Father. . ." He heard her metal fork clank on the metal plate as if dropped. *She doesn't pray, Lord? Does she believe?* "Lord," he continued, "we ask for Your traveling mercies this morning, and I ask You to give Mrs. Danner peace during this time of grief. In Jesus' name. Amen."

"Amen," she whispered.

≈

Making breakfast for Mr. MacKenneth seemed like the logical thing to do. Eating, however, took all her willpower. And praying? She struggled down a piece of ham. Praying was useless. She glanced over at her rescuer gulping down his meal. Being alone with a stranger in the middle of nowhere didn't ease the growing knot in her stomach.

Just yesterday. Was it really only yesterday she and Quinton had been talking about all the plans they had for the store? Stopping at farmers' homes gave them a pretty good idea of the standard items needed by those living in the area. But Creelsboro was more of a town for those heading farther west. They both had agreed they didn't know enough about Creelsboro and the surrounding towns to decide if local items would help the store grow. But a certain amount of bartering with the local farmers would keep them fed. They wouldn't have time to tend to their own livestock. Perhaps a couple chickens, but a cow and other animals would take up valuable space that would be needed for storing supplies.

Quinton was gone now. All the choices and decisions would have to be made by her. If folks would let her. How many men would trust a woman as the owner of a general store? Not many, she feared. *Lord, I don't know what to do.*

Pamela left her half-eaten breakfast and went through her brother's belongings. She removed a couple mementoes she wanted to save as keepsakes and a few that had belonged to her father. Leaving Quinton's chest behind wasn't enough. She would have to give up something else.

"What did you decide?" Mac huffed, having returned for another crate to be placed in the wagon.

"His chest can stay behind. I'll place these things in mine. The rest of these are items for the store. I have no idea what I can afford to part with."

She eyed her father's chest. It held the linens and, hidden in the bottom, their entire family assets. Mac had asked her to trust him, but the amount of money in there could turn the most honest of men. No, she'd have to keep another secret from this man.

"What's in this one?" He pointed to a large crate.

"Plow blades."

"That can stay behind."

"But. . ." She wanted to protest. Didn't he know how much those things cost?

He scowled.

"Fine, it can stay behind. Since you already know what can and can't go, you decide. These three are a must." She pointed out which three items she was referring to.

"I know this is hard, and I know you're sacrificing a fair amount of income, but unless you want to drag your husband's body behind the wagon—"

"Don't you dare speak to me like that! Who do you think you are?" She planted her hands on her hips. "I may not be a frontier woman, but I certainly know what's right and wrong. You don't treat the dead—"

He raised his hands in surrender. "I'm sorry, you're right."

"Fine," she huffed and went to the wagon, where she started shoving the crates in the best order. Quinton had showed her how to disburse the weight more evenly for the horses.

A few hours later, they had the wagon loaded. Quinton's wrapped body lay on top of the crates, and a secured tarp covered all. They were slowly working their way down the mountain. Mac walked beside the horses, helping them resist the urge to run down the steep path. Pamela walked behind the wagon, easing the burden by a hundred pounds. The horses snorted under the strain of all the weight. Perhaps she should have left more items behind.

The cool autumn air blew past, a welcome relief to her overheated body. If nothing else, the silent trek down the mountain gave her time to think. It wasn't proper for a woman to travel alone with a man. Perhaps she could hire some folks to escort them. Although, Mac did say there were bandits in the area. Who could she trust?

The wagon jerked as a rear wheel went over a small outcropping of rocks. If only Quinton had believed her. The signs were all there, saying they shouldn't go. At least that's what Angus had said the tea leaves revealed. Quinton hadn't given much thought to tea leaves and the like. He'd even argued that she, by believing such things, was hindering her faith. But who was right now, Angus or Quinton?

"You know, Lord, I'm having trouble believing in You. Ever since Mother and Father died, it's been a struggle. Now You've gone and taken Quinton away. What do You want from me? Angus and the others say, 'You've got to help yourself. God is good, and all that. But you've got to be aware of the other forces in the world and pay attention to them.' Quinton didn't believe in such, and look where it got him. I guess I'm reaching out and asking You one more time, are You what the Bible says, or is faith what Angus speaks of?"

The Twenty-third Psalm drifted into her mind. *"Yea, though I walk. . ."* Pam groaned. *Do You have to take everything so literally, Lord? I'm trying, I'm honestly trying to believe, to have faith. I wouldn't be talking with You if I wasn't trying. But You're not making it easy, Lord. Just so You're aware how I feel, that's all that matters at the moment.*

Pam listened for any additional reminders from scripture and eased out her pent-up breath. "I'm walking, Lord, I'm walking."

❧

Mac heard Pamela mumbling, praying, he supposed. But where was her faith? Did she have one? She did say "amen" after their morning prayer over breakfast. Of course, some of the roughest men he knew would say amen while possessing less faith than an ant.

On the other hand, she could have simply been lost in her grief and not given the Lord much thought. He certainly had caught her crying more than once over the course of the morning. She claimed not to be a pioneer woman, and that was evident enough, but he sensed she could be a wild cougar guarding her young when pushed too far.

Whatever possessed me to say such cruel things about her husband's remains? And I'm questioning her relationship with God? No wonder she doesn't trust me. Lord, I promised a dying man, and You know I'm not one to go back on my word, but if You see fit to have me hook this gal up with a group heading west, please guide us to them.

He turned back and watched her stumble over the rough terrain. Roots and small washouts along the trail made for an uneven path. Hundreds of head of cattle, pigs, and sheep had tramped through this road months before. Herding animals didn't leave level paths. And her fancy eastern boots were for city life, not the frontier. For a reasonably intelligent woman, she definitely had some moments that made him wonder if anything worked in her pretty little head.

"Ugh," Mac groaned. What was he doing noticing her beauty? *She's a widow. You don't admire a widow. Or at least you shouldn't,* he reprimanded himself.

The team of horses snorted. "Whoa, boys. You're doing fine." He patted the white striped muzzle of the horse closest to him. "Fresh water is moments away." He couldn't blame the team; they were working hard. He'd need to brush them down and let them cool before they continued to Yellow Creek.

"What's the matter?" Pamela asked as she rounded the side of the wagon.

"The horses smell the fresh water. There's a nice spring down a hundred yards. They'll need a break. It's a good time for them. After they drink, we can ride and should make it to Yellow Creek by nightfall."

"I'll make you something to eat while the horses feed."

"Don't go to any trouble. I have some pemmican in my pack." He tapped the leather pouch on his hip.

"Pemmican?"

"It's dried meat and berries. Great for hunting trips."

"Oh." She stood for a moment and let the wagon proceed past her.

Maybe I should have taken her up on the offer, Lord. You know I'm not much good with people. You're going to have to help me here.

"Whoa." He brought the horses to a halt. Making quick work of releasing them from their rigging, he led them to the stream to drink and began rubbing them down.

Mrs. Danner stood by the stream with her hand on her hip, paused for a moment, then sat down on a boulder and lifted her face to the sun. Her blond hair spilled from her bonnet, her skin shimmering like fine china. She didn't belong here. She definitely belonged in a fancy house with servants.

She glanced back at him. "Do you really think they need to be rubbed down so soon?"

"They could probably walk to Yellow Creek without a problem, but why risk it? They worked hard."

"True." She got up and went to the back of the wagon, returning a moment later with a couple of horse brushes. Without saying a word, she went straight to work on the other horse. He neighed in agreement.

"How long before we reach Creelsboro?" she asked.

"If the weather holds, possibly eight or nine days. Were you planning on going by wagon the entire trip?"

"I believe so. Quinton had the journey pretty well mapped out in his head. Why do you ask?"

"We could make better time traveling by water for a portion of the trip."

"By steamboat?"

"Canoe." He glanced back at the wagon. "With this load, it probably isn't an option."

"Perhaps I can sell some of my wares to the folks in Yellow Creek."

"Perhaps." There was a very small group of farmers living in that area. "Camp Ford and Barbourville might hold better opportunities."

"I was told that this region of Kentucky was wilderness."

Mac chuckled. "What one man calls wilderness might be a metropolis to another. All depends on where a man's from and what he's used to. Me, I prefer far less souls. Too much like a city, if you ask me."

A horse neighed behind them. Mac reached for his rifle.

Chapter 3

Pamela's hands froze over the rib cage of her horse.

"Howdy," Mac called out to the unwelcome guest.

"That your stuff up on the road apiece?" the stranger asked.

She couldn't see who it was or how many. Could they be the bandits? Fear gripped her backbone like a vise, applying pressure to the point she feared the slightest move would cause her back to snap in two.

"Afraid so. I hope to retrieve it later tonight. Why do you ask?"

"No reason, just curious." Leather creaked as the man descended from his horse.

Mac laid his rifle across his left arm with his right hand poised over the trigger guard.

"Whoa, Mac, it's me, Jasper. Got hitched? I thought you were a loner." Pamela eyed the disheveled man. His stomach hung over his belt and jiggled as he walked.

"I am, but you know the long winter can be cold and lonely." Pam wasn't too pleased to hear Mac's insinuation, but she also noticed he hadn't let his guard down. His finger remained snug against the trigger. For whatever reason, this Jasper was a man Mac didn't trust.

"She's a pretty little thing. Where'd you find her? In church?"

"She was praying the first time I laid eyes on her," Mac acknowledged.

Pam had to admit that was true. And he hadn't lied about them being married. Jasper just assumed. Who was this burly mountain man? Could she trust him?

"Hate to call the visit short, Jasper, but I promised the missus I'd get her to Yellow Creek before nightfall."

"Ain't no tavern there."

"True."

"Be happy to escort you. I'm heading that way," Jasper offered.

"Well now, Jasper, that's a mighty fine offer, but me and the missus. . ." Mac glanced over to her and winked. "Well, you know."

Jasper looked Pamela up, then down. She wanted to jump in the creek and cleanse herself from his slimy gaze. He slapped Mac on the back. "Never thought I'd see you hitched. See ya in Yellow Creek."

Pam noticed the strange weapon attached to his belt. It looked like a short handgun with a small handle and a barrel that was definitely shorter than usual, yet wide and thick. *If he isn't a bandit, he sure looks like one,* she mused.

Mac held up his hand, silencing her. He listened intently for a moment, then waved to Jasper as the man passed by.

"Who was he?" Pam whispered when Jasper had rounded the corner down the path.

"Trouble with a capital 'T.' It's never been proven, but I suspect he's one of the bandits I spoke of."

"What kind of a gun was that?" She came up beside Mac, who continued to watch the wooded area above the trail.

"An Artemus Wheeler. He got it in the navy. Nasty weapon. Can shoot six shots without reloading. All he has to do is spin those six barrels."

Pamela started to shake. Mac reached out and held her shoulders, pulling her close to him. "There're men in the woods watching," he whispered. "Jasper believes you're my wife. Forgive me."

She looked up to the tower of a man. "I appreciate the comfort, and I noticed you didn't lie. Jasper just assumed. You didn't correct his misconception."

"Thank you. I'd been thinking I'd drop you off at the Turners' farm, but I'm not certain I should leave you alone now. I suspect Jasper will be watching us for a while."

"Why?"

"Why?" He helped her up onto the wagon. "Because a wagon this full is a temptation."

"Oh." She bit her lower lip to keep from exploding. *Why did life have to be so hard?*

Mac went straight to work hitching up the horses. *Hitched, what a rude term for marriage,* she thought.

The horses set, the wagon leaned to the right as Mac climbed aboard.

Late afternoon shadows darkened the trail. Lowering deeper into the valley, she remembered her brother's body lying in the wagon. She thought about his desire that she finish the dream—her parents' dream, her brother's dream, but never hers. Death circled around her like a vulture waiting for its next meal. Her gloom was compounded by fear—fear of the unknown, fear of the known, and fear that her relationship with

God was but a wave of a feather away from dying, too. *How can I endure this, Lord?*

Every once in a while she'd catch Mac scanning the hillsides. What did he see?

She wrapped her winter shawl over her shoulders and held it close to her chin.

"Yea, though I walk through the valley of the shadow of death, I will fear no evil," drummed in her head over and over with each passing hoofbeat. Quoting scripture couldn't hurt, could it?

❧

On his left, Mac spotted some activity in the underbrush of the trees. If he remembered correctly, they were about to turn a corner on the Wilderness Road. *A perfect place for an ambush,* he thought. He reached for his Kentucky long rifle.

Mrs. Danner seized his arm like a vise. "What's the matter?"

"Just being careful. I doubt anything will happen." *Please, Lord, keep us and her possessions safe.*

She nodded but continued clenching his arm. *Be awfully hard to shoot with her hanging on,* he mused. *Whoever was in the woods will be exposed soon. Or they'll stay behind,* he hoped. *It's more than likely Jasper's men continuing to keep watch.*

Mac scanned the western horizon. It would be nightfall by the time he and Mrs. Danner arrived at the Turners' farm. *Lord, prepare their hearts for our arrival.* They had a good barn and a large cabin. It would keep them safe from Jasper and anyone else who happened along. And Will Turner and his sons were none too shabby with their aim. Fact was, Will had been paid a few shillings for killing off some wolves in the early years of settling this part of Kentucky.

He caught a glimpse of Mrs. Danner nibbling her lower lip. "This here part of the Wilderness Road was first made by the Indians."

"Huh?"

"The Indians, they used to travel this part of the road for hunting. It's part of the original trail."

"Oh." She scanned the woods. "Are they gone?"

"The Indians are, and Jasper and his men soon will be. I think they're just watching, trying to decide if it's worth the trouble or not. You see, I have a small reputation in these parts."

She eyed him more cautiously.

"I'm a fair shot," he supplied for her benefit.

"Oh." She released her grasp of his arm. Hopefully he'd calmed her fears some and not created new ones. Perhaps he shouldn't have shared with her the thought that there might be danger. He could just as easily have said that black bears were known to be in the area. Which was true, and he wouldn't exactly be lying. He'd always prided himself on being a man of his word. How could one woman cause him to wonder if he shouldn't be quite so honest?

The wagon bounced over a small rock. "Sorry," he apologized. He wasn't used to driving a team of horses. His favorite modes of transportation were his feet and a canoe. As his backside began to protest his current form of travel, he felt certain he'd keep right on using those methods.

"I'm taking you to William Turner's place. They have a good-sized cabin and a barn."

"Will they put us up?"

"More than likely. Out here everyone kind of looks out for everyone else." *At least the ones who are settlers.* She'd already learned about the others. He prayed she wouldn't experience their evil firsthand.

"How much longer?"

"Not too much. A couple miles and we should be able to see Will's farm."

She nodded.

She must still be working through the shock of her loss, he presumed. Then there was the fact that they were strangers, compounded by his natural tendency to be a loner. This was going to be a mighty long trek across Kentucky. He snapped the reins. "Yah, come on, boys. Let's get there before the sun goes down. Fresh oats are on me." *Providing Will has planted oats again this year.*

The valley spread before them. "See that smoke?" Mac pointed in the direction of the Turners' farm. "That's where we're headed."

Will Turner and his family had been busy this summer. The rail fence extended farther along the edge of the road than the previous year. They hadn't turned more than twenty yards down the Turners' long path to their home when he spotted Will standing at the front door, rifle in hand.

"Howdy, Will. Mac here. I got a flatlander in need of a place to stay tonight."

Will set his rifle near the door and waved back. For a man in his early fifties, he stayed mighty fit. "You're always welcome, Mac."

"Whoa." He pulled back on the reins and brought the team to a halt.

Will's eyebrows rose, seeing a woman. "Hello, Miss..."

"Mrs. Danner," Mac introduced. "Her husband came by way of an accident. We'll need to bury him tomorrow."

"I'm sorry to hear of your loss, ma'am. You're welcome to stay in the house. I'll have my wife, Mary, make a bed up for you."

"I don't mean to be any trouble."

"No trouble at all." Will smiled. "Mac, pull the wagon to the barn and take care of the horses. I'll be out shortly and give you a hand. Did you folks put a feedbag on?"

"Not since lunch. My stomach's been gurgling for a mile, smelling Mary's fine cooking."

Will chuckled. "We'll have a couple plates warm for ya. Excuse me."

Mac turned toward Mrs. Danner. "They're good folks. I think you'll enjoy getting to know Mary Turner."

"Let's get the horses brushed down before we lose all daylight," she suggested.

Mac placed his hand on hers. "Go inside, Mrs. Danner. I'll take care of the horses. I'll even bring your small bag in for you."

She looked down at his hand. He removed it. What was he thinking? She gazed back into his eyes. "Thank you."

He assisted her graceful departure from the wagon. Mac swallowed hard. *She's beautiful, Lord. Guard me from any wayward thoughts.*

❧

Will and Mary Turner's home was simple but practical. The log cabin had several additions for each of their grown children and their wives. It was hard to believe all these people lived under one roof, but the house was set up in such a way that they each had their private spaces. A small room with a bed for guests made up Pamela's quarters. A wonderfully colored quilt covered the bed, and a fine feather pillow rested at its head. One wall was curtained with fabric. Behind it were all the canned vegetables the family had set up for winter. Even the small space under the bed doubled for storage.

A gentle knock on the doorframe caused Pamela to turn around. Mary Turner stood in the doorway.

"Are you all set, dear?"

"Yes, thank you. This is very kind of you."

"No trouble at all. As you can see, we always have room for one more." Mary's smile revealed small wrinkles around her eyes, showing her age.

She'd been the perfect hostess. She'd fed them, made them feel at home, and even provided Pamela with some water and soap to clean up with.

"Do you have guests often?"

"Not too much. Once in a while we have a drover stay as he's heading back. But for the most part, it's pretty quiet these days."

"What's a drover?" Pam eyed the bed. Should she sit down or continue to stand? Knowing what to do in a stranger's house always left her with questions.

"They're the men who drive the livestock back East for sale. The biggest use of the road these days is from that of drovers. Most folks heading west are using different routes."

"Quinton said we would be traveling by ourselves most of the time."

"How did your Quinton pass on, if you don't mind me asking?"

Pamela sat down on the bed. Obviously her hostess wanted to talk, and Pam was glad to have someone to talk with. But as the image of Quinton squashed against the rock flashed through her mind, her hands trembled. Her lips quivered.

Mary Turner sat down beside her and wrapped her in a protective embrace. Odd, the woman had more muscle on her arms than Quinton had on his. Must come from working the land in the middle of nowhere.

"I don't know how it happened. One minute he'd nearly finished putting the wagon back together, and the next he was pinned between Indian Rock and a wagon wheel."

"Oh my, how tragic. I'm sorry. Have you been married long?"

Did she dare tell Mary Turner the truth? Tears welled in her eyes. She bit down on her inner cheek.

"Forgive me." Mary rose. "How'd you like a nice warm bath? I imagine it's been awhile since you've had one."

Pamela fought the desire to check her armpits and make sure she didn't smell.

Shock and worry crossed Mary's face. "Oh no, child. I was thinking a warm bath comforts me. I don't get to take them often, mind you, but William built me a tub, and I've been spoiling myself every now and again. Might help relax you and work off some of the tension from traveling."

"It sounds heavenly, but I wouldn't want to put you to too much trouble."

"None at all. I'll get the menfolk to fill the tub." She winked.

Pamela had to admit she liked Mary Turner. Her kindness equaled her very practical spirit.

Thirty minutes later, Pam found herself neck deep in warm water. She leaned her head back against the wooden tub. William Turner had done a fine job. She traced the wood grain with her finger. *I wonder if he'll take a trade,* she mused. *Nope, Mary would never part with it.* And she couldn't blame the woman.

A soft sigh escaped her lips.

"Feels good, doesn't it?" Mary said from behind the partition they'd put up around the tub. It really was quite an imposition. The men had to move the table, set up the tub, and fill it while Mary poured in the hot water she'd boiled on the stove. They told her they only took baths once a month. A girl could get used to this kind of spoiling.

"Mac, what are you doing back in here?" Mary's voice called out.

"I need to ask a favor, Mary."

Pamela wanted to hide. She heard Mary cutting and preparing something.

"Come on, boy, spit it out."

"Can I leave Mrs. Danner with you?"

What? Pamela wanted to scream. *I thought he promised Quinton to take me to Creelsboro. Why has he changed his mind?* She couldn't stay here. The Turners were nice folk, and she could even see herself developing a friendship with them, but she wasn't a part of their family. She had no right to live here. *What is he thinking?*

"Does my Will know your reasons?"

Chapter 4

Yes." Mac heard water slosh from behind the divider. He still couldn't believe Mrs. Danner would be so brazen as to ask for a hot bath. He'd thought about not leaving her with the Turners for fear that she'd have them waiting on her. But if he was going to travel to Creelsboro, there were a few things he'd need for the journey back to his cabin.

"I'm fine with Mrs. Danner staying here if my Will is approving."

"Oh no, no. I didn't mean for her to stay a long time. I'll be gone for a day, two at the most. When I return, we'll continue on."

Mary nodded her head and wrung her hands off on a towel.

"Thank you." His gaze shifted from Mary to the folding partition. "Mrs. Danner, I'll be back to fetch you. Don't worry."

"All right." Her voice strained as if she wanted to say more. Their conversation had been limited. He'd given her space to grieve. He didn't know if fear of him or shock at her loss kept her tongue, but for a woman, she certainly used few words.

Mac set his coonskin cap on his head and left the farmhouse that had grown an additional room this past summer. Will was talking about building a new house with milled timber and two floors. He'd made a fair profit for the past two years and felt he could afford to have the chestnut trees on the back of his property milled.

Mac shook his head as he headed back down the Wilderness Road in a cloak of darkness. The moon was blanketed with a cloud of lace as it stood half full, dancing off the ridge of Cumberland Mountain. He had no doubt that Jasper and his men had made camp someplace along the road. Jasper would be expecting him to come back for the items they'd left at the saddle's ridge. Mac would have to remove some belongings and perhaps hide a chest or two in Gap Cave just north of the gap.

He kept an even pace that would allow him to run twenty miles in four hours. He'd make it home and still have enough time to rest before dawn.

The smell of a campfire alerted his senses. Someone was close by. Few camped these days, with all the folks who had opened their homes as taverns. So one had to be careful. He cocked his rifle and continued his pace. He had no objection to Jasper seeing him tonight. It would play well with the story he told.

A half mile past the campfire, Mac quieted his steps. His ability to blend in with the woodland areas gave him much success with hunting. Tonight it would serve him well in hearing if he had picked up a follower. He grinned. He'd picked up one man in relatively good shape. Mac kept his pace. This man wouldn't last long enough to make it up and over the gap. No, he was huffing too hard already. Mac would lose him before the gap, and his plan to store a chest in the cave would bode well for him. He'd open one chest and carry some of the clothing to his cabin. He prayed doing this would keep up the ruse for Jasper and his men.

Mac began the upward run toward the Cumberland Gap. His follower had slowed down considerably. When Mac arrived at Indian Rock, he found men's clothing hung haphazardly over the chests. Apparently Jasper and his men had already rummaged through them. He opened a large, sturdy shirt and piled other clothing on top of it. Using the arms and the tail of the shirt, he created a small bundle. He picked up the smallest chest and continued his run. Up and over the saddle, he worked his way and headed down the road. Just a little bit north was Gap Cave. After placing the chest in there, he strapped the clothing to his back and continued home. He prayed that his follower hadn't seen him working his way up to the cave. Thankfully the night sky shrouded him.

His undisturbed cabin greeted him as a welcome relief. He folded the clothing and placed it on a chair in his room. *Father, I hope this will convince Jasper.* Will Turner had agreed to take a couple of his boys and carry the remaining chests to his home. Mac rubbed the back of his neck. He hadn't asked Mrs. Danner if she minded his giving away her husband's belongings. But then again, he hadn't wanted to remind her of the loss.

He still couldn't believe the woman had asked for a bath. Of all the self-centered things to do. She obviously came from a well-to-do family. Her clothing and the amount of belongings they'd been carrying on their journey west were numerous.

He grabbed a kettle. Water slowly poured from the wooden barrel. A hollow sound echoed from it when he tapped the side. Nearly empty.

He'd have to fill it if he were staying. Their journey would take him two weeks if they met with no hazards. He could return within a week after that, he hoped. If they didn't have so much stuff for the store, they could make the trip in less time. He doubted she'd reduce any personal items. And how could he ask? Her family heritage was in that wagon, and she'd need all the comfort possible to keep her through the lonely nights of loss.

With the water heated on the woodstove, he made himself a cup of tea. "Lord, give me a good night's rest and help me understand this woman. You and I both know my history when it comes to the fairer sex, and I've come to terms with the fact that I'm meant to live alone. What I desire most from life is not what women want. And as pretty as Mrs. Danner is, I can't be having thoughts and feelings for her. She needs to mourn her husband's death. I'm certain there is another man out there who would like settling down and wearing fancy clothes." Mac yawned. "Forgive me, Lord, for carrying on here."

He finished off his tea and headed for bed.

His door rattled in its hinges.

❧

Pamela pulled the quilt up over her shoulders. It felt so good to sleep on a mattress again. For five days she'd been sleeping on the ground, dealing with bugs and vermin. *Goodness, Lord, why did Quinton insist on our going west? I know Father purchased the business in Creelsboro, but. . .* She rolled over and buried her head in the pillow. *No, I'm not going to think about this again. It's over. They're dead. Quinton's dead. Why do I have to go on to Creelsboro? Why do I have to go anywhere?*

Quinton's strained words came back. *"Remember the dream."*

She punched the pillow and closed her eyes tight. *It's not my dream. So why am I alive and not them?*

Reality stung.

❧

Sunlight streamed through the small window. It was morning, time to rise and time to face her brother's death. Today she would bury him. The Turners had given her permission to bury Quinton in their family plot.

Resolute, she flopped the covers off and dressed. It would take the better part of the morning for her to dig Quinton's grave.

"Good morning, Mary," she said to the kind woman with broad hips and broad shoulders standing at the stove.

"Morning, dear, have a seat. I'll serve you up some pancakes and eggs.

How do you like yours cooked?"

"I can cook. You don't need to go to any trouble."

Mary continued to work at the stove. "No trouble at all. I always fix a big breakfast. Everyone will be in from early morning chores in a minute."

Pamela's stomach rumbled as the scent of fresh bacon filled her nostrils. On the table she found a plate of sausages, home fries, a stack of pancakes, a loaf of fresh bread, some bowls of various jams, and a jar of canned peaches. *Is she feeding an army?*

"Set yourself down. They'll be here in a minute or two. You haven't told me which way you like your eggs."

It was no longer a question. "Any way. I like them the way you're serving them."

Mary nodded her head, grabbed two more eggs from a bowl, and cracked them open over a flat grill. This was a working farm. Pamela had never been on a farm early in the morning. Some friends back East had told her how much work they would have to do before they ate breakfast and before they left for school. She'd always thought they were exaggerating. *Perhaps not,* she mused.

Pamela sat down, then realized they probably had an order. "Is there a particular place I should be sitting?"

"Nope, first come, first served here. It's my job to fix the morning meal. Lunch, every man, woman, and child fends for themselves. At dinner, each of us women takes a night. Whoever cooks doesn't clean."

Pamela chuckled. "Sounds wonderful."

"You need order when blending four families under one roof. We're hoping to build a new house next spring. Will Jr. and his family will stay in this house, and the rest of us will move into the large farmhouse. Eventually each of the boys wants to build their own homes. We'll apply for a tavern license then and hope to use the rooms for travelers like yourself."

"Seems like a lot of work."

"Always is when you're trying to build a community. The Cumberland Ford settlement just up the road is doing well. But it's taken them a few years. Most folks don't stop here at Yellow Creek. They just head on up to Cumberland Ford. Of course, most folks aren't hauling a wagon like yourself."

"It's not the most comfortable road."

"Ain't built for wagons. You shouldn't have too much trouble crossing at Flatlick. I heard they moved the tollgate down there in 1830. You could try crossing other places to avoid the tolls. Depends on how low the river is and how mucky the shoreline."

"Great," Pamela mumbled.

"If you don't mind me asking, what are you taking to Creelsboro?"

"Mostly things for the store. There were a few pieces I left up on the gap—some lamps, small furniture pieces. Most of those were in the large trunk."

"Will said he and the boys were going to fetch your trunks today."

Why? she wondered.

"Mac said you ran into Jasper, and he told Jasper he was going to go back for 'em. So he and Will figured the best thing was to fetch 'em."

"Well, you and your family can keep whatever you want from the trunks. Quinton's clothing was left behind. Didn't figure I'd be needing that." Pamela bowed her head.

"Speaking of Quinton, the boys ought to have his grave dug before breakfast."

"I was going to do that. I don't want to impose."

Mary came beside her with a platter full of fried eggs and placed her hand on Pam's shoulder. "Now, dear, a woman shouldn't have to dig her husband's grave. It's been done, but my boys are strong, hardy men. They can do it in no time. You just rest. You've had quite a heap of trouble for one so young."

Pamela sighed. Mary didn't know the half of it.

The door flew open, and a team of people bustled into the room. Each grabbed a plate, filled it, and sat down. Pamela sat watching, holding her fork in midair. They weren't pushing or shoving, but they worked in pace with each other. A dance of sorts. A breakfast waltz. She shook her head. She'd been away from civilization too long, and it had only been five days.

The morning meal went by as quickly as it started. Pamela found herself alone at the table, the three other women standing at the sink, one washing, one drying, and one putting the dishes away. *Talk about an organized household.* The women chatted on and on about their plans for the day.

Mary came in from her private room with a clean housedress on. "Takes some getting used to, doesn't it?" she asked as she sat down beside Pamela.

Pamela stared down at her half-full plate. "I've never seen a meal eaten so quickly yet orderly at the same time."

Mary roared. "A couple hours of hard work drives a person to not waste time." She placed her hand on Pamela's. "When you're ready, we'll bury your husband. Will thought it'd be fittin' to read the Twenty-third Psalm."

How'd they know that psalm has been running through my head for days? On the other hand, it was the standard scripture to read at funerals. Even the preacher back home had read it at her parents' grave. Pamela cleared her throat. "That'll be fine."

"God's got big shoulders, dear. He understands our tears and our anger."

Pamela eyed Mary cautiously.

"It's been a few years, but I remember crying out to the Lord over the loss of my young ones."

"I'm sorry."

"It still hurts when their birthdays come around, but I remind myself of all the hard times we've gone through and relax in knowin' they never knew pain, hardship, and anguish. They've only been held in the Lord's bosom."

Pamela noticed the chatter of the three other women had ceased. She looked up, realizing each of them had their own losses to bear as well. *Why, oh why, do people willingly want to live in such wilderness?*

&

"Black Hawk, what are you doing here?" Mac opened the door wider and let his old Indian friend in.

"I am old. I wish to die with my ancestors." Black Hawk sat down on the bench by the table.

"But, if they catch you. . ."

"They will not catch me. See, I wear white man's clothes, and my hair is hidden under my cap."

Mac had never known Black Hawk to wear anything but his tribal clothing. He'd taken a risk to come back East. His people had been forced to move to Indian Territory years ago. But Black Hawk had always defied the "white man laws" and lived as he felt he should.

"My home is your home. I'm going to bed to rest. I'll be packing tomorrow, then heading west for a few weeks."

"What is this I hear about a woman?"

"You met up with Jasper?"

"No, I overheard them. Beware, my friend. His eyes are on you and your bride's wagon."

"She is not my bride." Mac's voice rose.

Black Hawk's eyebrows did likewise.

"Sorry. Jasper assumed she was my wife. She is a widow. Her husband died at Indian Rock two days ago."

"Ah, I saw the blood."

Mac had thought he'd cleaned the rock well enough. But for someone like Black Hawk, obviously not. "I promised her husband I would take her to Creelsboro before he died."

Black Hawk nodded. "Do as you must, but beware."

"I will, and before I leave I wish to have words with you."

"It will be my pleasure, Swift Deer." His leathery smile accented the deep wrinkles in his face. Black Hawk had taught Mac to hunt, to live off the land, and to identify plants that were helpful for medicine. He owed the man a debt of gratitude and a heap of prayers. As of yet, Black Hawk had not seen the white man's God as the answer. *If he's dying, this might be my last chance, Lord. Help me.*

"Good night," Mac said and smiled.

"You mean, 'good morning.'" Black Hawk chuckled under his breath.

"Yeah, nothing like being up most of the night. Let's get some rest, and we'll talk later."

"Swift Deer, your heart is still pure. It's your faith, I see it now."

Mac halted in his steps. He glanced back at Black Hawk. Unspoken words proclaimed the glory of eternity in the simple wink of an eye. Black Hawk had come to terms with the white man's God. *Thank You, Lord.*

After a gentle nod from Mac, Black Hawk laid a bedroll down in front of the woodstove, his movements stiff, his frame thin, thinner than it had been several years ago after he'd returned from Indian Territory. "Black Hawk, sleep in my bed tonight, please," Mac pleaded.

The old man looked down at the bedroll. "Thank you, my friend. My brother."

Mac swallowed a lump in his throat the size of a chestnut. He pulled a small pillow from the bench in the living room. His mother had made it for him last year. He stripped to the waist, removed his boots, and lay down on the hard floor. Black Hawk was a wise man and knew he was dying. *Father in heaven, forgive me. I don't want to fulfill a dying man's request. I'd rather stay by the side of my friend and help him exit his earthly home.*

Chapter 5

Quinton's wrapped body lay silent and still in the bottom of a filled pit. The last bit of hope that all of this had been some strange nightmare took flight. Oh, how Pamela prayed to wake up in her old bed. Mary's warm embrace helped, a little. Tears streamed down her face. Will's kind words gave little solace. Quinton was dead. She was alone and condemned to live a dream that others had created.

Pamela gripped her sides as she held back some of her emotions. These godly people would not take too kindly to her spitting words of anger out to God. Granted, Mary had mentioned that God could handle it. But it slammed into everything she'd been taught. In church you learned to respect God and accept what He gave in life, whether it be good or bad. Her slaves told her not to anger the gods, to tread lightly.

"We'll leave you be for a while, child," Mary whispered into her ear. The family of strangers who had opened their home knew her pain. And they claimed God could handle her grief, her anger, her questions. Was it possible? Or was this a new brand of religion? Wilderness religion.

She'd been told only a half dozen farmers lived in the region of Yellow Creek. Most folks were in Cumberland Ford, where they could find a traveling preacher some days. Will and his sons had offered to see if they could find one to do the service. But Pamela insisted they not extend themselves further.

"Thank you," she whispered. *How can I ever repay this family for their kindness?* she wondered.

She turned and looked at the freshly dug grave. A single tear plopped on the soil below. Her face felt swollen. Grief shook loose any restraints holding back the tears from the strangers around her. She could expend all her emotions now. Later, she'd be expected to be grown and mature, to have put the matter behind her. Hadn't that been what her father had always taught them with each death that overshadowed her family?

"God, why have You cursed us? What did my ancestors do to allow You to punish us for generations? When does it stop? When I'm dead and buried? Take me now, Lord. I don't want to go on. Why should I? It was never my dream. It was Yours. . .my parents. . .even Quinton's. But maybe he just felt it or thought it the best way to go.

"I know You don't care for those who speak with the spirit world. But Angus and the others said trouble would happen if we left Virginia. I'm sorry, God, if I'm not supposed to believe in such nonsense, but You've left me no choice. They were right. My family and their beliefs about You, about Your direction, were wrong. Look at them, they're all dead!"

Pamela's chest heaved. Her fist clenched, she raised it toward the sky. "Take me, God, take me now. I don't want to live without them. I'm alone. No one cares for me, not even You."

Fresh tears spilled down her cheeks.

A gentle breeze whispered across her heated flesh. A voice—no, the feeling of a Presence—swept over her, and the words from the Twenty-third Psalm passed through her mind. *"Yea, though I walk through the valley of the shadow of death, I will fear no evil: for thou art with me; thy rod and thy staff they comfort me."*

"Where are You, God? Where?" She looked around the expanse of the meadow, the rugged foothills climbing up to the mountains. "Are You up there? Down in the valley? Where are You, Lord? I can't see You. I can't feel You. I can't feel anything right now. I'm so empty, Lord. So completely empty."

Pamela crumpled to her knees, hunched over her brother's grave. *Evil is all around, Lord. Look at Jasper. And can I really trust that giant of a man, Mac?*

"Thy rod and thy staff they comfort me."

"Lord, I may not have paid attention as I should have in my church lessons, but isn't the rod used for discipline? For spanking children? I'm not a child," she huffed.

A man coughed. "Do you think it might be that it's because a parent loves his child that he disciplines him?"

Tear-soaked eyes blurred her vision. Pamela tried to focus on the image of Calvin Turner leaning against a shovel.

"Forgive me for overhearing, but if a young one keeps reaching for the hot stove, a parent needs to spank their hand to keep them from doing far worse damage to themselves. I know you're hurting, and your loss is great, but I've always found new life springs from death." He nodded and placed his molded woolen cap back on his head. "Fact is, bad things happen all the time. My young wife didn't deserve to die in childbirth, but she did. It wasn't God's fault. It wasn't my fault. It wasn't even my child's fault. Those things just happen from time to time. They hurt, they're unfortunate, but from her death new life came—my boy, Jason."

He bent down on one knee and picked up a small pebble. "She's still in my heart. I love her. I miss her. But God's also given me a new wife and a new child on the way. I'm not saying this is easy. Lord knows, I cried out to Him like you are doing on more than one occasion. I'm just saying that as bad as it feels right now, there will be a time when it won't ache as much. You might not understand all the reasons why, but you'll be comfortable with the fact that it's happened.

"Ma thought I might be able to help you deal with your anger, seein's how I'd been there, too."

Pamela swallowed hard. "I'm sorry for your loss." What else could she say?

He pointed to her left. "That's Catherine's grave."

"How long?" She wiped the tears from her eyes.

"Four years this past August. I ain't perfect. I still hurt. But as that psalm says, Thy rod and staff do comfort."

"What's God's staff?"

"To me it's like a staff a shepherd uses to tend the sheep. He'll nudge a lamb here and there with the tip to keep it on the right way, so as not to get caught in the briars or other things on the path. He also uses it to help him continue on the long miles of the journey. You know, somethin' to lean on. Just like this shovel." A lopsided grin slid up the right side of his face. His rugged chin and wayward hair showed he was content with who he was. He had no need to impress anyone. He simply lived his life out to the fullest.

Am I vain, Lord? she prayed. *Have I been trying to do it all my own way?*

❧

Mac woke to find Black Hawk reaching over him to the woodstove.

"Sorry, Swift Deer, I did not mean to wake you, but my old belly was in need of something warm. The wind blows from the northwest. It will be a cold winter, lots of snow."

Black Hawk had never been wrong on his weather predictions. *I'll have to chop more wood for the winter,* Mac mused. The window brought in the warm rays of sunshine. And for the first time, he noticed how the creases in his old friend's forehead and cheeks were deeper, the luster of his eyes gone. Only dull orbs remained. Mac sat up.

Black Hawk took a seat on the bench. "The time is close."

"I'll stay with you."

"What of this young woman who needs you?"

"I'll send word, hire someone else to take her."

"Ah." He leaned back and rested his elbows behind him on the table. "I do not want you to go back on your word, my friend. Not for an old man who's lived too many days."

"Nonsense. You're not that old."

Black Hawk roared with laughter that lapsed into a chest-rattling cough. "Older than you are aware, my son."

Mac clasped his hands in front of him, resting his elbows on his raised knees. "When did you make peace with the white man's God?"

"Six moons ago, when a preacher came to the reservation. You know how fired up I was about being there. Well, he spoke about God's people, the, how you say, Jews, and how they were taken from their land, used as slaves, and one day their God rescued them and brought them back to their Promised Land. This is my land, my promised land. Your God, my God, brought me back so I can die on my land. The land of my people. A gift, you might say."

Mac searched his memory to see if he'd ever told the story of Moses to Black Hawk. He thought perhaps he had, but found no definite recollection.

"You, my friend, were an example of the life your God, my God—I have to learn to keep saying that—wants people to live. There is a lot of evil in this world. I see it in white man, red man, black man, every man I've come across. They lie, they cheat, they kill. But you, my friend, never, never in all my days of knowing you, did. Why? I'd ask myself. Then I'd remember your words about your God. When this preacher came, I chose to come and listen. Then it made sense.

"I'm old. I'm tired of fighting. I want to have my spirit rest on the wings of God."

"This is why I should stay," Mac protested. "I should be with you."

"No, my friend, you must keep your word. How shall I continue to believe if you do not?"

Mac wasn't too sure how he liked his life being an example that a man based his entire faith from. He pinched the bridge of his nose. "Then come with me. I could use a chaperone."

Black Hawk chuckled. "I said I understand your God. I did not say I understand your women. Why is she not married to you right now?"

"Her husband just died." Mac swallowed hard.

"Exactly. A woman needs a new husband to feel complete, to feel loved. A warrior takes on a widow to keep her content, to give her children if she is without. This makes a woman happy."

"I do not understand women, either, so I'll just let someone else make her feel loved and give her a child."

Black Hawk wagged his head. "Is she not pleasing to behold?"

"She's beautiful. But you know my past. I could never. . ."

Black Hawk raised his hand and held it out toward Mac. "I once said I could never believe in the white man's God. I do not think *never* is a good word. It isn't true."

Mac opened his mouth, then closed it. How could he argue with that kind of logic?

"Go, take this woman to Creelsboro or wherever you said she must go. And if she pleases you, make her your wife. Don't think. Just do what your heart is telling you. Wonders are found in the arms of the woman you love."

"I shall take the woman to Creelsboro, but I will not take her as my wife. She is grieving. And I like living alone. I have no woman to tell me what to do every day."

"And no woman to warm your bed."

Mac's cheeks flamed.

"Ah, my young friend. Forgive. Anger only dries up the spirit of the white man's God who lives within."

Mac blinked at Black Hawk. How could he be so wise and have known the Lord for so little time? "Please come with me. I wish to spend these last days with you."

"I would like that, too. But I am to die here. It would be a risk for me to travel by day."

True, he'd be sent back to Indian Territory. Or be killed trying to resist capture. "All right then. You can make yourself comfortable in my home."

"Thank you, my friend." Black Hawk grinned. "Your soft bed is gentle on these old bones."

Reluctantly, Mac got up and prepared his pack for the long trip, knowing Black Hawk would not be there when he returned. *Into Your hands, Lord.*

For weapons he brought his Kentucky long rifle, his bow and arrows, and a knife he kept in the side of his boot. He packed a few pemmican cakes. He'd hunt on the trail and let Mrs. Danner barter for home-canned vegetables and fruit. He had to admit, her cooking on the open fire set with his stomach a lot better than the pemmican.

His throat thick, he embraced his old friend and left him with a final warning. "Be careful of Jasper. I expect he'll pay the cabin a visit."

"I may be old, but my ears still hear like a hawk." He winked.

"God bless you, my friend. I'll see you in glory."

Black Hawk's eyes watered. "I'll be there."

ॐ

Pamela appreciated the heart behind the words Calvin Turner had shared. Mary mentioned they had suffered losses similar to her own. She'd scream if one more person called Quinton her husband, but to tell them the truth would be to tell Mac the truth, and she couldn't trust him with that bit of information. In some small way it made sense to let him believe the lie. She felt safe. A recently widowed woman would be treated with respect by a God-fearing man. And Mac gave all indication that he was a God-fearing man. Someone like Jasper she should fear. Would she be safe in Creelsboro, owning and operating a store? Would the men in town let her do it? Nothing made sense anymore. Nothing.

She rummaged through the wagon and finally found the chest she'd been looking for. The one with fine linens. Mary and her family could use these. It seemed the perfect gift. It was practical and yet also fancy—something to decorate their tables. From another chest she pulled out a bolt of thick cotton cloth. Perfect for making shirts, dresses, and even some light trousers for the hot summer months, not that they'd wear them for a while.

Then the idea struck her to place the remaining linens in her trunk and her dresses and undergarments in the trunk with the money. Her task completed, she jumped down from the wagon, grabbed the items for the Turners, and headed for the house.

"Need a hand?" Mac strained a smile and stepped past her, placing a large pack in the back of the wagon.

"Oh, you're back." Pamela squelched her surprise. "Thank you. I'm giving these to Mary."

He nodded.

"Is something wrong?"

"Nothing." He took the two bundles from her arms and started toward the house. He stopped and turned back to look at her. "Anything else?"

"No." *Who are you, Mac? And what is so heavy on your heart?* Did he not want to take her to Creelsboro? Was he only doing it because of a promise to her brother? Should she hire someone else? *Perhaps Calvin. He could use some money with the new baby coming, couldn't he?*

"Thank you for asking them to bring Quinton's trunks down."

"You're welcome."

"I gave them to the Turners as well."

He raised an eyebrow.

"What? Should I have kept them?"

"No. You have no need for the items, and they can make use of some of them. It's practical."

"And by that you're implying that I'm not?"

He looked down at his feet.

"Look." She poked her finger into his chest. "I'll have you know I'm quite practical."

He glanced back at the wagon.

"What?"

He fumbled with the bolts of cloth. "Do you know how difficult it will be to take that wagon on the trail?"

"Some. But the trail's been used for years. It's a well-worn highway now."

Mac lowered his head but not fast enough. She saw his snicker.

"What are you telling me, or not telling me, as seems to be your way of communicating?"

He looked back at her, fire in his eyes. He opened his mouth, then promptly closed it. "Let's just say your concept of the trail has no basis in reality. You society folks always have a problem with that."

"Society folks? Oh, I get it. You think you're better than I am because you live off the land. You think that because I come from a place that has actual roads and rules, laws that are enforced, I have no logic? Let me tell you, you couldn't be farther from the truth. My logic works just fine. And when we arrive in Cumberland Ford, I'll find another who will take me to Creelsboro. Someone who doesn't feel so high and mighty about himself." She huffed and marched off to the house.

Just who does he think he is, telling me who I am and not knowing the first thing about me? I'll admit I picked the wrong traveling shoes. . . . But Quinton had led her to believe the road was like the streets in Virginia. Perhaps not cobblestone, but the ground would have been well trod and hardened from the many, many people traveling along it for the past fifty-seven years or so.

A high-pitched whistle whizzed past her ear. Mac grabbed her by the waist and pushed her to the ground. Wood splintered from the log siding of the house.

Chapter 6

"Stay down," Mac whispered. The shot had come from the foothills.

Will pulled open the front door, squatted down, and ran over to them. "Who was that? Jasper?"

"I don't know. Take Mrs. Danner inside. I'll find out."

"I'll be right behind you," Will informed him. "Not all of the children are in the house."

"I'll keep an eye out." Mac released the frightened woman. He had to admit she had spunk.

Mac crawled on his belly toward the barn. He didn't plan on beating Black Hawk to heaven. He worked a wide circle from behind the barn up to the edge of the trees. The shooter couldn't have gotten too far. He hadn't heard any rustle in the underbrush. Birds were beginning to sing again. Obviously, the person was lying low.

He turned and saw Will working his way around the barn. Hopefully, the children were playing in there.

Stealthily, he worked his way through the underbrush, careful not to make a sound. A mumbled whimpering caught his ears. He turned toward the southeast. *Crying? Someone was crying?*

"Hello," he called out.

The sobs increased. Mac picked up his pace. The voice of a young one. *Dear God, please let them be safe.*

He broke through the underbrush and came upon Jason, with a pistol lying at his feet. "Jason, are you all right?"

The large brown eyes stared back at him. Black smudges ran from side to side across his cheeks.

"Target practice?" Mac asked.

The boy nodded his head. Mac opened his arms, and he came running into them. "I didn't mean to shoot her. Is she alive?"

"You missed, thank the Lord. What were you aiming at?"

The child pointed to a tree about ninety degrees away from the house.

"I'm not your pa, but I think you're a bit too young to be shooting."

"Jason?" Will shouted, gasping for air.

"I'm sorry, Grandpa. I didn't mean to."

Will simply embraced the child and headed with him back to the house. Mac picked up the pistol, checked the barrel, and found it warped. *No wonder he hit the house.*

He heard Will send out a familiar whistle, a sound that let everyone know all was well. Soon, folks started coming out of the house. Mac felt certain Calvin would be taking Jason out behind the barn later. *But I think Jason will find that a welcome relief.* The fear of what might have happened in that boy's eyes sent a chill down his own spine.

One person hadn't emerged from the Turner home. Mrs. Danner. How had he gotten on the wrong foot with her two minutes after he returned? *And Black Hawk thinks I ought to marry her? He has no idea what this woman is really like. She's so self-consumed.*

Mac gnawed his inner cheek, reassessing that judgment. *She did willingly give the trunks to Will and his family.*

Mac took in a deep breath and let it out slowly. *Guess I need to go see if the widow is all right.* After a few minutes greeting the various members of the family, he entered the house. The living area was empty. The kitchen, too. *Where is she?* Then he saw her exit the room she'd slept in with a small carpetbag in tow. "And just where do you think you're going?"

"Cumberland Ford. There's a tavern I can stay at." She walked past him as if he weren't there.

"No, you're not." He reached out and grabbed her elbow.

She glared at his hand. Hot daggers of emotion singed his heart. He released his grasp.

☙

"I absolve you of my, my. . .of Quinton's dying wish." *Why can't I tell him he's my brother?* Pamela wondered. *What am I afraid of?*

"Absolve all you want, Mrs. Danner, but that doesn't change that I'm a man of my word." His voice remained tight but controlled.

Pamela shivered at the thought of this mountain of a man ever losing control.

"Mrs. Danner, perhaps we've gotten off on the wrong foot here. I wish to honor Mr. Danner's request to take you to Creelsboro. And I will try to not make judgments about your social upbringing. Truce?"

Pamela relaxed her shoulders. "I appreciate your concern, Mr. MacKenneth, but I think it best if I should try and find another traveling companion. You and I tend to be fire and ice."

"More like fire and gunpowder," he mumbled.

Pamela chuckled. "You may be right there. Seriously, though, I've been giving this a lot of thought, and I've concluded I should ask Calvin or one of the others to take me."

"Calvin, with his child due soon? You can't be serious."

"Yes, you're right. He'd need to stay by his wife. Perhaps one of the other brothers. I'm sure they could use the money."

"At the moment I think they're all rather busy discussing firearms and safety with all their children."

"Oh dear, I heard it was safe. What happened? I just assumed it was a stray bullet."

"Jason was target practicing without permission. Calvin will be quite busy with the boy for a while."

Pamela resisted the urge to rub her backside. On more than one occasion, she'd been the recipient of such instruction. Thankfully, her infractions had never revolved around a firearm.

"Mrs. Danner, I am the most logical choice to take you west. I have no family obligations, and I have no business that would need my attention."

"What do you do?"

"I'm a fur trader. But as I mentioned to you before, during the spring and summer I'm a farmer."

Pam sat down on a wooden chair. *Handmade,* she presumed. "I don't know, Mr. MacKenneth. The trip will be long and hard. I have enough grief dealing with Quinton's death, the loss of my parents, and. . ." She shook her head. He wouldn't understand how others had made plans on her behalf. A man like Mac lived his own life.

☙

Why am I fighting with her to continue the trip? She's right. She could find someone else. Even one of the Turner brothers would do a great job. Why am I insisting? Mac turned and walked over to the one window in the front of the log cabin.

There had been no further evidence that Jasper would pursue them. Even Black Hawk wouldn't fault him for letting the woman go with whomever she felt more comfortable. He pulled off his coonskin cap and wiped his brow.

He glanced back at the young widow. Fine yellow hair concealed Mrs. Danner's face, her head bent as if in prayer. Her fingers knit together. Water-filled blue orbs appeared and stared back at him.

"Mr. MacKenneth. . ."

"Mac," he corrected.

"Mac," she continued. "You'll probably think less of me than you do already, but you seem to be a bad omen. Every time you appear, something bad happens. And personally, I've faced enough hardships. I don't want to risk more."

Mac mentally picked his jaw up from the floor, clamping his mouth shut so he wouldn't speak a word out of turn.

"Quinton died shortly after you arrived. Jasper showed up on the trail; and since you've returned, I've been shot at. Don't you think that's more than coincidence?"

Lord, give me the right words here. I don't want to alienate this woman further. "There is another side to what you've presented."

"What's that?" Her eyes searched his as if longing to be proven wrong.

Slowly he made his way over to her as if approaching a fawn. "God may have had me there to help you just when you needed it."

She blinked.

"How would you have removed that wagon from Quinton?" He paused, letting the question penetrate. "How would you have dealt with Jasper if you had managed to get Quinton free and had continued on the road?"

A tear trickled down her right cheek. He raised a finger to remove it, then thought better. Scanning the room, he lowered his voice. "And if I hadn't been here, you might have been hit by Jason's bullet."

She opened her mouth a fraction to speak. For the first time, he noticed how perfect her lips were, the perfect shade of pink for her fair complexion, carefully riding the contours of her mouth. *Whoa!* Mac jumped up and retreated to the window. He kept his back toward her, his stance rigid. Where had those thoughts come from? It was all Black Hawk's fault. *If only he hadn't suggested I need a wife.* Who was he fooling? The woman was beautiful. He'd never seen anyone finer. He had to protect her. Glancing over his shoulder, he wondered how much he'd have to protect her from himself.

A knock at the doorway broke his wayward thoughts.

"Is it safe to come in now?" Mary smiled.

Mac felt the heat rise on the back of his neck. If he'd been wearing a four-in-hand, he'd be pulling at the collar of his shirt.

"Beggin' your pardon, Pamela, but you're a different woman around Mac. And, Mac, I've never seen you raise your voice at anyone before. To see you've done that to a widow. . . You should be ashamed of yourself." Mary put on her white linen apron and went straight to the kitchen.

They had been heard arguing. *Great.* He winced. "I apologize, Mary. I'll be in the barn if you change your mind, Mrs. Danner." He slipped on his cap and hiked over to the barn.

He examined the wagon. Why had he lost his temper with Mrs. Danner? What had caused them to blow up with each other in the first place? He tried to think back. Nothing. Then his words, *"It's practical,"* echoed through his mind. Mac leaned against the wagon and let his head bang against it. He was no good with women. Never had been. Why was he the one being dragged across the country with her? Surely God could have found a better man.

And perhaps that was the real problem. He was fighting God's choices for his life. Mac squeezed his eyes shut and rubbed his forehead with his thumb and first finger. *Why did You lead me down that road, Lord, at that particular time?* The answer that he was needed was too easy. Perhaps there was more to Mrs. Danner's situation than simply needing a guide to Creelsboro. Perhaps God had chosen to use this opportunity to teach Mac to trust Him on a new level.

Mac slid to the ground and sat with his knees to his chest. He'd always considered himself a Good Samaritan of sorts, willing to go the extra mile for others. Of course, his lifestyle limited the contact he had with others. He gnawed his lower lip.

"Heard ya hollerin' at Pamela Danner. What's that all about?" Will Jr. asked as he came in and towered over him.

"I've just been trying to figure it out myself."

Will Jr. tossed back his head and laughed. "Ya don't figure out women, my friend, ya only figure out how to live with them."

"I don't need to figure that out. I'm not *living* with her."

"You most certainly are if you're taking her halfway across the state." Will Jr. sat down beside him. "Tell me, what's the real problem ya have with her?"

"She's unbelievably impractical. Just look at the contents of this wagon. I can't imagine how we're going to get this across the river."

"Several trips?" Will Jr. quipped.

"That's the problem. A trip that would take maybe five days at a good run could take two weeks, perhaps more."

"I see. You think she should just run across the state like you?" Will Jr. narrowed his gaze, his bushy brown eyebrows knit together. "No one runs like you. I swear you're half Indian."

Mac was tempted to tell Will that Black Hawk was back in the area but decided against it. The fewer who knew, the safer his old friend would be. "I admit I'd rather run than ride."

"That's what I'm saying. You're more comfortable with that. Me, I prefer a horse. I get there quickly, and I'm not hot and sweaty."

Mac chuckled and nodded his head. "No, I'm not expecting the woman to run across the state. But couldn't she lighten the load some?"

"Aren't the contents of this wagon what she needs to run her business in Creelsboro?"

"I reckon. I think they would have been wise to ship it through a northern route or have it delivered shortly after they arrived."

"I see. Now you're a man who knows how to run a store."

"Don't go twisting my words, Will. I made no such boast. I'm just speaking logic, pure and simple logic."

"To you, yes. But what about the rest of us who don't live the way you do? I, for one, am pleased to have some of her husband's wares. I ain't seen much and, well, it's nice to get dressed up for the missus every once and again."

"I wouldn't know," Mac mumbled.

Will Jr. placed his hand on Mac's shoulder. "She's gone, Mac. Leave her in God's hands and stop thinking every woman is the same as Tilly."

"I should have known better. It's my fault."

"We've been over this ground before, my friend, and you know my feelings on the matter. I've said my piece. I'll leave ya to your thoughts."

Mac molded his beard with his hand. Had he been reacting as if Mrs. Danner were Tilly?

❧

Pamela looked down at the carpetbag on her lap. Heat rose on her cheeks. The entire Turner clan had heard them arguing. Pamela closed her eyes and tried to focus. Taking in a deep breath, she stood and walked into the kitchen area. "Mary, I'm sorry for my outburst."

Mary turned and motioned for her to sit down. Pam did.

"Pamela, what are you afraid of with Mac? He's a good and decent man. Generally he keeps to himself, but I've never heard a complaint from anyone. What did he do to you?"

"Nothing. . .everything. . .I don't know. From the moment we met, he's been telling me what to do and how poorly I've been doing everything else. I'd be the first to admit I made a poor selection in my shoes, but that does not give him the right to think of me as addlepated with no thoughts or feelings for anyone but myself."

"Ah." Mary poured two cups of tea.

"One minute he seems like the kindest and gentlest man I've ever known; the next he's carrying on like a bear denied his favorite honey tree."

Mary chuckled.

"What?"

"You're taken with him, aren't you?"

"No." Pamela, realizing her voice had risen, lowered it. "I mean, he's not a bad-looking man in a huge, bear kind of way, I reckon, but. . ."

"Quinton wasn't your husband, was he?"

Pamela buried her hands in her face. "No, he was my brother. How did you know?"

"No ring, dear. And you've not referred to him once as your husband. You're grieving, that's clear. But after Calvin spoke with you, I was certain of it." Mary reached over and placed her hand on Pamela's.

"Mac assumed we were married. I've simply not corrected the error. I figure I'm safer being single and alone with a stranger if he thinks I'm a new widow. And I do ache."

Mary sipped her tea. "This area is wilderness. Your life can be placed in danger very easily, and Mac is a man of his word. If he promised your brother that he'd take you to Creelsboro, then that is what he'll do. He'll probably continue to be hard on the realities of wilderness living. He, more than most others, knows what he's talkin' 'bout."

"What do you mean?" Pamela held the cup in her hand.

"That's for him to say, if the time is right. Just as you have your own secret. I wager the good Lord is none too pleased with you stretching the truth."

Thankfully, Mary hadn't called her a liar. Pam didn't need someone to spell it out. She sipped her tea to keep from justifying her actions. What could she say? She shouldn't let Mac believe the lie. On the other hand, he was just as guilty in letting Jasper believe she was Mac's wife. No, it was better that he be left with his misimpressions.

"You're welcome to spend the night here," Mary added. "It's late and will be dark before you reach Cumberland Ford. I wouldn't want you running into Jasper or any other bandit along the way."

Pamela rubbed her arms. For some reason she'd been hoping Jasper had moved on. "If he's that bad of a man, why don't you have him arrested?"

"Can't prove he's done anything." Mary rose from the table. "No one's survived. No one's seen him actually commit a crime. And the local law is in Barbourville. Cumberland Ford might be getting someone soon. Hard to say. Lawmen and preachers are in short supply in these parts. Folks don't plan long engagements. Once they hear a preacher is coming, they line up. Though that's been changing some with the one at the Ford settlement all the time."

Preachers and lawmen. Weren't they the cornerstone of a healthy community? How can people live like this, Lord? No law, no order? "Thanks for the tea. I'll speak with Mr. MacKenneth and see if he'd prefer to spend the night or not."

"Fair enough. Dinner will be ready shortly."

The scent of a hearty stew passed Pamela's nostrils. How could she have missed its fine aroma? *Because your mind was on something else,* she reprimanded herself.

She found Mac sitting on the barn floor, leaning against a wagon wheel. "Mac?"

He opened his eyes and turned to look at her. "I'm sorry," he apologized.

"I'm sorry, too. You're right. I don't know what came over me. You are the best choice to take me to Creelsboro."

He nodded.

"Mary would like to know if we'd like to leave tonight or wait until morning."

"If you're agreeable, tonight is fine. If we leave right away. However, if we wait another thirty minutes, it'd be best to wait until morning."

"Now is fine. It's hard to face everyone after having made such a fool of myself."

"We're both in that place, I reckon. Let's say our good-byes and be off, then."

"Fine." She tossed her carpetbag in the front of the wagon. It had been a pleasant visit with the Turners, but it was time to move on.

A black cat scurried past her. Pamela froze.

Chapter 7

"What's the matter?" Mac scanned the area, looking for danger.

"I think we should wait until tomorrow." She reached back to the wagon and grabbed her carpetbag.

"What's the matter?" He fought down his temper. What had she seen or heard to scare her? Wouldn't he have heard any real danger?

She stood resolute, shaking her head slightly.

He stepped up to her and placed his hands on her shoulders. "Mrs. Danner, Pamela, you need to trust me. Tell me what has frightened you."

Fresh tears filled her eyes. "You wouldn't understand."

"Try me." He brushed a wayward strand of gold from her eyes.

"I'd been warned before we left that this trip would be disastrous. And it has been that. Now that I've determined to go on to Creelsboro, the very next thing that happens is. . ." She broke her gaze and looked at the straw-covered floor. "You'll just think me foolish."

He placed his forefinger under her chin, prompting her to look at him. A strong desire to protect her coursed through his veins. "Trust me," he whispered.

"I know you'll think this is idle foolishness, but a black cat just crossed my path. It's another omen, a warning. I don't think we should leave tonight."

If it hadn't been for how frightened she'd become, he would have roared with laughter. No one should ever be frightened by Blacky. That animal barely caught the mice he was supposed to catch. Blacky was more skittish than any creature Mac had ever seen. He found it amazing Pamela had even seen the animal.

"I don't believe in omens. I believe God is stronger than anything we'll face and will protect us. However, if you'd prefer to wait till morning, we shall wait."

"Thank you." She sighed. "I'm sorry. I know most people find these things nonsense."

"Like I said, I don't believe in 'em, but I know folks who do."

He watched as calmness played across the tranquil blue of her eyes. A desire to wrap her in his arms and pull her toward him startled him. He released his hold on her shoulders. Heat rose on the back of his neck. There were blessings to having long hair, he mused.

"I'll let Mary know to expect two more for dinner." She slipped past him.

"Sounds good. I'll see if I can hunt down a wild turkey to help replenish what we've eaten."

Pamela paused and turned back toward him. "Oh my, I hadn't thought of that. I have some canned goods in the wagon. Should I fetch a couple items?"

"I've never seen a woman can or prepare more food than Mary. But they have a large family. What do you have that they might not?" Mac inquired.

"Sugar, what about sugar? Don't folks out here run low on that?" Pamela climbed up into the wagon and started to move crates.

"Tend to. I'm sure Mary would appreciate such a generous gift, but. . ." Mac rubbed the back of his neck. "Will Jr. said you've given them a lot already. They might be offended, with them just being neighborly and all. It's a fine line. I, on the other hand, haven't contributed anything."

Pamela sat down on a crate. "I don't want to give too much. Quinton always said I was too generous. He's the businessman, not me."

How would this woman survive running her husband's business? Would she give it all away? Would she know when to order, to restock? Did she understand what kinds of supplies were needed for folks heading west? *Lord, give this woman direction.* "I think you've given enough. Let me help you down from there."

"Do you think I can find a new pair of shoes in Cumberland Ford?"

"Not likely. Closest place would be Barbourville, but that's three days down the road."

She nodded. "We'll plan on buying me a pair of rugged boots then."

Maybe he had misjudged her. She definitely had problems with her faith, mixing it up with omens. But perhaps she wasn't as impractical as he'd first suspected. He helped her down and grabbed his cap. "Go tell Mary we're spending another night. I'll be back in an hour."

Mac set a quick pace and ran into the woods at the bottom of the mountain. Wild turkeys were plentiful in these hills and something he knew the Turner family enjoyed. He stopped and scanned the ground for tracks. Turkey tracks could be easily missed in this terrain, but Black

Hawk had trained him well. There, he spotted some. He worked his way deeper into the woods and placed an arrow on his bow. He spotted a flock and took aim. The gentle twang of the bowstring sent the arrow flying, hitting its mark. The remaining birds scattered as he picked up the gift and headed back.

The smell of a campfire caught his attention. He circled around and found it. The fire had been hastily put out, the camp abandoned. He looked around. Three men, possibly four, had spent a fair amount of time in this spot. Mac put more dirt on the dying embers and continued back to the Turners. Had Jasper given up his watch?

&

The next morning, Pam and Mac headed north toward the Cumberland Ford camp. They talked little. She'd been worrying all night if she'd made the right decision to continue the trip to Creelsboro. Her heart wasn't in running a business, certainly not in a community where no one stayed for long. From what she recalled her father saying about Creelsboro, it was one of the last stops for people heading west. Day in and day out, people arrived, spent a day or two, and left. It also occurred to her that a riverfront town probably had lots of taverns selling spirits. The prospect of being a woman alone in that kind of environment didn't excite her.

An hour into the trip she began to relax. The mountains seemed so peaceful. The winter branches seemed less threatening somehow. She imagined what they would be like in the spring when the trees bloomed.

"We're almost there," Mac said.

"We cross the Cumberland here, correct?"

"Yes, ma'am. We'll cross the river near the ford and try to avoid the toll. We'll see how high the water is. This time of year, it shouldn't be too bad. The wagon is heavy. We might have to unload and carry some items across, then take the wagon over."

Like when Quinton had to get the wagon across the gap. Her heart beat wildly. She stared straight ahead. Her hands clasped the bench seat of the wagon. "Pay the toll, cross at the ford," she ordered.

"What's wrong?" he asked.

"Nothing," she demurred.

He pulled back slightly on the reins, slowing down the pace of the horses. "Your knuckles are white. What's wrong?"

"I just thought of Quinton and. . .and the accident."

"I'm sorry. We'll cross at the ford."

"I've noticed you use rather strange terms." She needed to get her mind off Quinton and the accident as it replayed over and over again in her mind. "Like 'flank,' but you weren't talking about the flank of a horse. You were referring to the mountain."

"Has the same meaning—"side of." The houses flanked the north side of the mountain."

"Do folks heading west carry pemmican?"

"I can't say. I picked it up from my Indian friend Black Hawk."

Pamela's eyebrows rose. "I thought the Indians were gone. They still live here?"

"No, they've been moved to the reservation in Indian Territory. It's hard to have peace about our need for land and expansion while seeing the Indians moved out. I think it would have been better if we could have embraced them, learned from them, learned how to live with them. But our ways are very different from their ways. I don't have an answer for what's right. But somehow it doesn't seem fair that a group of people who have lived for many generations in an area have to be sent out to live somewhere else."

Pamela hadn't given the issue much thought. She'd only heard the stories of how the Indians had killed so many white people. She feared them, as many of her friends did. And yet this man beside her had befriended an Indian, perhaps more than one. If nothing else, this trip was teaching her about different people and their ways.

They spent the night at the Renfroes', finding the Colsons' tavern, where Mac had stayed during other journeys, already full. The next morning they traversed the ford. The river was quite low, and they crossed easily. Pamela paid a toll of sixty-three cents. "Highway robbery," Mac muttered.

"I hope to get us up to Flatlick by nightfall," Mac offered as they resumed their perch on the wagon's bench.

"What's in Flatlick?"

"Not much. It's one of the oldest settlements in the state. The horses will love it there—still plenty of salt for them to lick. Years ago hunters found it an easy way to hunt bison. The animals would come up to the lick, and the hunters would pick them off from behind the bushes."

Pamela scrunched up her nose. "Doesn't seem fair to the animal."

Mac chuckled. "When providing for your family's needs, fair doesn't come into play. A man can go out and run the countryside hunting down his dinner, or he can wait where he knows the animal will come to him. There really isn't much choice."

"But you don't hunt that way."

"No, but I follow the animals' trails and find the right place to attack."

"Why do you trap animals for their fur?"

"Because it's a job I can do in the wilderness that provides for my needs."

"What needs do you have?" Pam wasn't trying to be insulting, but she really couldn't imagine this man needing much of anything. His clothing was made from animal skins; his hat from a raccoon; his boots, leather. His rifle was manmade, but he used a bow and arrow, too.

Mac chuckled. "Not many. I tend to put the money into the family farm. Someday I'll have to settle down and take care of it. But for now, my parents manage just fine."

"Why the wilderness?"

"I don't know. I suppose it's because it's wide open and lets me be alone most of the time. I kinda like it that way."

"Oh." She'd talked too much, she supposed. She'd been told more than once by her brother to just stop talking. She'd found it especially hard on him as they traveled. When they were alone, the only person to talk with was Quinton. Now, Mac was there, and she'd started talking with him as easily as she had with her brother. "Do you suppose Jasper is still following us?"

"Haven't seen a sign of him since the night before we left the Turners'. I'm starting to think he's gone on."

Pamela breathed a sigh of relief. The constant threat of a bandit around the corner had started to weigh on her nerves. Finally she could relax.

☙

Mac scanned the skies. A large ridge of dark clouds was heading their way. "Pamela, we need to move quickly. That storm is coming in fast."

"Tell me what to do." Her eyes blazed with excitement.

"Hang on. I'm going to try to beat this storm." He slapped the reins. "Yah!"

The horses bolted forward. Mac kept a firm grasp of the reins. The rough trail, rutted from the herds of cattle using the road, made the wagon buck and bounce. He glanced at Pamela. She held on tight without complaining. Could he have misjudged her?

They were a mile out from Flatlick when the first bits of sleet hit.

"Ow!" she cried out.

"Cover your face."

The horses were breathing heavily. He slowed down the pace.

"I'm cold. How bad is this storm going to be?"

"It'll be a rough one. We'll find a place to stay, and I'll take care of the horses. They'll need a good rubdown and a treat. Got any more of those apples?" He smiled.

"For you or the horses?"

"Both." He broadened his grin.

There was little question he enjoyed traveling with a cook. Every place they stopped, Pamela would barter or pay for fresh vegetables and eggs. He'd been eating better on the road than he had been in his own cabin. He'd forgotten how much he loved vegetables with his meals. Summers on the farm, he always had healthy helpings of meat, biscuits, and vegetables to round out his meals. During winters in his cabin, however, that luxury disappeared. He kept plenty of fresh meat around. But because he needed to travel light on his way to the cabin, the extra weight of canned vegetables or even root vegetables had proved prohibitive. Perhaps he could look into planting something in the early spring that would still be there when he returned in the fall.

The wind howled.

"How. . .much. . .longer, Mac?" She shivered.

"Almost there. See that curl of smoke?"

"No, but I trust you."

Mac grinned. They were becoming more comfortable with each other as the trip wore on.

He pulled onto one of the many side trails he'd seen along the road. It amazed him how fast this area was growing each year. There were more trails to other farmers' homes. The Campbells had been in this area longer than most. They'd open their home, Mac knew, especially for a woman.

Their farmhouse came into view on the left. It was framed by a long, front pasture with fields on the left and right. A smaller plain filled the space between the back of the house and the side of the mountain.

"Whoa." He pulled the wagon to a stop. "I'll be right back."

He raised his hand to knock on the front door, but an older man in his fifties opened it first. Mac extended his hand. "Art Campbell, Nash MacKenneth. Folks call me Mac. I heard you put folks up from time to time."

"Ain't got no more room. Storm's threatening to be a bad one. There's room in the barn, if you don't mind sleeping there. It even has an old woodstove. But you be careful, now. Make sure there's nothing that can catch fire."

"Thank you." Mac pumped his hand.

"You and your missus take care, now." Art slipped back into the house and shut the door.

A few quick strides and Mac was back by the side of the wagon. "There's no room in the house, but there's room in the barn. Do you mind?"

"Do I mind? Anything is better than this." Pamela held a woolen blanket close to her chest.

"All right then, let's go make that barn our home for the night or until this storm passes." He snapped the reins. "Yah."

They entered the protection of the barn within a couple minutes. "Stay there and warm up," he directed. "I'll take care of the horses."

"No." Her teeth chattered. "I think I need to move to get my blood flowing."

"All right. Mr. Campbell said there was an old woodstove in here somewhere." Mac scanned the barn for a chimney. "Over there. Make sure there's nothing around to catch fire, and I'll get us a fire started in a minute."

She nodded, and he went to work unbuckling the horses. The stalls were filled with other peoples' horses and mules. A milk cow lowed in a rear corner. He eyed a hayloft where he'd be able to fashion a bed for them. Mac shook his head. Correction, two beds for them. He'd done well to keep his growing desires to himself. *Father, give me strength. She's a widow, and You know I'm lousy with women.*

"Mac!" Pamela screamed.

Chapter 8

Pamela dropped to her hands and knees. The end of a shotgun was not what she'd planned on seeing.

"What?" Mac came running.

The barrel slipped back out through a hole in the wall. "A barrel from a gun was pointing in at us."

"Where?" Mac frantically searched the barn.

"Through that hole." She pointed to the large knothole in the barn board.

He knelt down.

"Careful."

He waved for her to stay down, as if she were going to stand up and give someone an easy target. He looked through the crack between the wooden planks before peering out the hole. "You scared 'em off, whoever it was."

"Or they moved to another side of the barn."

"I'll go check. Do you know how to shoot?"

She shook her head no.

"Great," he mumbled. "Why didn't I try and teach you before now?"

He went to the wagon, pulled out his Kentucky long rifle, loaded, and cocked it. "Here, keep it pointed at the door. All you have to do is pull the trigger. I'll holler before I open it. Please, try not to shoot me."

She was tempted to say something coy but thought it better to hold her tongue. Mac's sense of humor wasn't the same as her own. He lined the gun up and set the barrel resting on the wagon, aimed toward the doors.

He slipped through the doors, not making a sound. *How's he do that?* she wondered. Several times over the past couple days she'd seen him walk as if he were a feather, barely leaving an impression on the ground and never making a sound.

A huge thud against the side of the barn startled Pamela. Her focus shifted away from the barn door to the wall where she heard the noise.

Realizing her error, she went back to her sentry post.

"I'm coming in, Pamela," Mac hollered. She lifted her head from the line of sight on the rifle barrel. Beside Mac stood a skinny, redheaded youngster with tattered clothing. "This here is Urias. He apparently has been sleeping in Art Campbell's barn for a while."

"And I take it Mr. Campbell is unaware."

A sly grin slid up the boy's face. He placed his hands in his pockets and shrugged his shoulders.

"Hungry?" Pamela asked. She wasn't about to tattle on the boy during the storm. After the storm might be another matter.

"I'll light the fire." Mac encouraged the boy into the room with a slight nudge forward. He uncocked his rifle and placed it back in the wagon. Lifting the canvas over the rear of the wagon, he grabbed some wood.

Pamela removed a Dutch oven, a knife, cutting board, some vegetables, water, and the biscuits she'd made earlier in the morning. "Mac, what meat would you like me to use? There's some ham, bacon, or your pemmican. I'm thinking a hearty stew would be in order tonight."

"Ham or pemmican is fine with me. Let's have the bacon and eggs in the morning. You're up for bacon and eggs, aren't you, Urias? Come and give me a hand with the horses."

Urias did as he was told but didn't speak a word. How Mac had gotten any information out of the boy before they came back to the barn was beyond her comprehension.

Pam went to work making a stew for the three of them. She also pulled a thick cotton blanket out of the wagon to use as a tablecloth to cover the dust and straw of the barn. She'd have to go into the crates to find another plate, silverware, and cup for Urias. The boy probably hadn't eaten well in a long time.

The casket of water was full. She could sponge bathe later. If she could find a private spot, she mused. Looking around the barn, she felt grateful it provided shelter, but they'd have to be well covered for the entire night. The stove was small, too small for the size of the barn. It wouldn't heat all night. But it would help some, and at least it gave them a place to cook a warm meal.

"Pam, Urias and I need to clean up. Did you warm some water on the stove?" Mac grinned. He'd never asked for warm water to clean up with before. He'd always just gone to the river. The boy was walking comfortably around Mac now.

"Yes. Dinner's ready whenever you two are," Pamela called out to them.

"Be right there."

Pamela heard some whispering. Urias was talking?

She served up the three plates of the thick stew, along with one biscuit each.

Mac paused to say a prayer. "Father, we thank Thee for this barn. We thank Thee for this warm food for our bellies, and we ask Thee for protection from the storm. In Jesus' name. Amen."

"Amen." Pamela raised her bowed head.

"Amen," Urias mumbled.

Pamela jumped up. "I almost forgot. I purchased a treat at the Cumberland Ford settlement. Mrs. Renfro was so sweet," she continued as she hiked back to the wagon. Fumbling through the small area in the rear where she kept her kitchen, she found the small jar of peach preserves. She had planned to save it for a special time, but now seemed as good a time as any.

"Peach preserves on biscuits." Mac licked his lips. "Woman, you know how to please a hungry man." Their eyes locked. Pamela shivered from the connection she felt. *How can this be?*

&

"Wonderful meal, Pamela, really hit the spot," Mac complimented. "What did you think, Urias?"

"It's good, thanks."

The boy had gobbled the food down like he hadn't eaten in a week, *which he probably hasn't,* Mac guessed.

"Is there more?" Urias held out his empty plate.

Pamela took it. "Of course there is." She went to the stove and promptly filled his plate to the brim again. "I'm afraid there aren't any more biscuits, but I'll be making some later."

"Thanks, they're wonderful. You cook good." He smacked his lips and dove his fork into the mound of food. Mac glanced over at Pamela and winked. What had happened between them earlier still warmed his heart—and terrified him.

"Urias, after you're done, you can help me set up the loft for sleeping."

"Sure," he said with his mouth full. "I usually sleep over there." He pointed to a stall now holding one of the house occupant's mules. "There's a loose board that moves enough so I can wiggle into the barn."

Mac wanted to know more of why the boy was on the run, but he needed to win his trust first. He appeared to be around fourteen, maybe a young fifteen.

"Pamela, I'll fix you a bed with sheets and blankets if you have some linens for me."

"Let me get them. How cold do you think it will get tonight?"

"It's freezing now, and the sun just set. I'd say it'll drop another ten to fifteen degrees."

"I don't have three wool blankets," she stammered. "I have another thick cotton one like the one I put down on the floor over there," she offered. "We could set the tent up and that might give us some additional warmth."

"The various blankets should do nicely. I'll even show you a trick later. You'll be warmer than you've ever been by the time I get through with you."

Pamela flushed.

"I—I mean by preparing a special bed for you." Mac's throat thickened. *How could I have implied something so forward?* He hadn't meant it the way it sounded. He knew his motives were pure. Mac groaned and headed toward the loft. He'd only planned to lay a healthy layer of hay over her once she was down for the night. How could planning to do something nice for the woman have gotten so garbled in the offering?

Urias joined him a few minutes later with bundles of blankets. "How much stuff do you have packed in that wagon?"

"You don't want to know." Mac closed his eyes at the thought. She'd pulled out something new just about once a day. She had more items stuffed in places he couldn't imagine. He'd wondered that first day why the wagon sat so low. Now he knew. She utilized every bit of space to the fullest.

"What do you need me to do?" Urias offered.

"I'm trying to make a comfortable place for Pamela. I don't want a draft to come up from under her, but I don't want the hay too hard. I'm fashioning some walls here to help hold her body heat in a closer area."

"Where'd you learn all this?"

"I grew up on a farm."

"You don't look like a farmer." Urias started molding the hay.

Mac continued working the hay, trying to catch glimpses of the boy every now and again, hoping to gain a better understanding of him. "During the winters I'm a fur trapper. What about you? What are you doing?"

"Can't find a job. Wrong time of the year."

"Where'd you get the rifle?"

"It's mine." He instantly stood, his body rigid.

"I'm not saying it isn't. I'm just asking. Where'd you come by it?" It was more than likely the one item Urias had taken from his home when he decided to run.

The boy's shoulders relaxed and he went back to work. "My pa gave it to me when I was ten."

"Not a bad rifle. Needs a good oiling. Did your pa teach you how to do that?"

"He never got the chance." Urias's eyes watered.

"I'll be happy to show you. I've got to take care of mine."

A smile as wide as the gap spread across the boy's freckled face. "Really? Thanks."

"You're more than welcome. Come on, let's go shape our bed."

"Our bed? Aren't you sleeping with your wife?"

"No. Pamela will sleep better without me." If Urias only knew. "I'm going to be up and down all night adding wood to the fire. Plus, once I put her in that hay cocoon, she won't want to get out."

"I'll have to remember that cocoon."

"Works really well, even in the wild when you only have pine needles around. You take a tarp of canvas, fold it in half, put a bed of needles under you, then pile the needles as high as you can find them around you and on top. I've often built a temporary shelter out of pine needles and branches."

"When did you start living in the wilderness?"

The boy's getting more comfortable with me. Thank You, Lord. "A few years older than you. I was eighteen."

"I'll be eighteen next year."

Mac scrutinized him, giving him the eye that said, *"I know you're not being honest with me."*

Urias looked down at his feet. "Maybe in four years."

Mac smiled. Urias did the same. "Can you teach me how to make leather clothes like you have?"

"Not in one night but maybe in the future."

Urias placed his hands in his pockets. "I don't know how to survive out here."

Mac sat down in the hay and patted it for Urias to join him. "Why are you out here, son?"

&

Pam made a batch of biscuits, prepared a loaf of bread to cook up in the morning, cleaned up, and still Mac and Urias hadn't come down. She even set some beans soaking, reasoning it might be late in the day tomorrow before they could travel on. Once, she'd gone over to listen and heard them talking about Urias living alone in the wilderness.

The wind whistled through the barn boards. Pamela stretched her back. She needed to get some sleep. "Mac," she called up at the base of the ladder to the loft.

"Sorry, Pamela, we were chewing the fat. Come on up. The bed is all ready for you."

Pamela started to climb up the flimsy ladder. "It's mighty dark up here."

"Shh, nothing to be afraid of. We won't be lighting a candle or a lamp with this much hay lying around." He winked and wrapped his arm around her waist, whispering in her ear, "Urias thinks we're married. I think it's better that way for now."

"All right." She trembled from his touch.

In full voice he said, "We have something special planned for you. Urias and I are going to sleep in this section."

"What are you planning on doing to me?" She let out a nervous laugh.

"Trust me."

"You'll like it, Mrs. Mac. I wouldn't mind if he did it to me."

Mac turned to him. "I can. Would you really like me to do it for you, Urias?"

"Yeah!" The boy's voice deepened, sounding more grown-up, less eager. Mac turned his back and held down a chuckle.

"First we get to show Pamela."

Pamela giggled. It couldn't be too bad if Urias would like it.

"Lie down here and make yourself comfortable," Mac instructed.

She lay down. "Oh Mac, this is perfect."

"Not yet. Cover up."

She obeyed. The hay was soft and comfortable. The warmth of her body soon heated up the cool air surrounding her.

Mac tossed a pile of hay on top of her.

"Hey, what are you doing?" she protested.

"Trust me. I'm creating another layer of warmth. The hay will help your body stay warmer. You're not going to feel the drop in temperature at all tonight. Except possibly on your nose."

Pamela giggled, and Urias dumped another armful of hay upon her. Soon a mound of hay a foot tall covered her. She had freedom of movement, but the weight added the feel of a very thick quilt on top of her blanket.

"Good night, Pamela."

"Night, Mac."

Urias peeked over the mound of hay. "Does it feel good, Mrs. Mac?"

"Yes, very. Good night, Urias."

"Good night. Can you do me now, Mr. Mac?"

Pamela held back another laugh. The child was living in a grown-up world but still needed to be a child. She snuggled deeper in her soft bed. Who didn't need to be pampered like a child every now and again?

Urias giggled and gave a running commentary of Mac's actions. They had bonded. *Lord, You know what Urias needs. I'm glad Mac was here to befriend the child. Perhaps he can help him find a new home. He has so many friends and acquaintances in the area, Lord. Surely someone would be willing to take him in.*

Pam closed her eyes and drifted off to sleep. The cares of this world, the storm, Jasper—they all left her. Mac was here. She was safe.

❧

Pamela's eyelids burst open. Something was wrong. But what? That's when she heard voices.

"Art Campbell said a man and a woman pulled in just around sunset last night. I figured it might be you."

"Morning, Jasper. I suspected you might be here. Ain't that your stallion?"

"Yup. So where's the wife?"

"Pamela's still sleeping. What are you doing out in this weather?"

"Got caught in the storm, same as you."

Pam turned around under the hay and tunneled out of her cocoon. Mac knew Jasper's horse was here and he hadn't warned her?

She tried to see the men below.

Jasper walked over toward the stove. "Hmm, hmm, you're wife sure can cook. She did all this last night?"

"Obviously. I can't cook like that."

"What man can? Women are good for one thing, taking care of us men."

Pamela felt her temper rise.

"She ain't like Tilly," Jasper observed.

"Nope." Mac leaned against the wagon with his arms folded across his chest.

"I don't want to wake your wife, so I'll be going now. Too bad we beat ya to the house. Mrs. Campbell keeps a mighty fine place."

"And I suspect it will stay that way," Mac countered.

Why was he saying that? Pamela shivered.

"Are you—"

"I wouldn't cross that line, Jasper. You know my reputation. I'd hate for you to experience it firsthand."

Jasper stepped back. He seemed paler. Was Jasper afraid of Mac?

"I hope the new missus doesn't fall victim to the same fate as the first." Jasper stormed out of the barn.

The first? Mac was married?

Chapter 9

Mac clenched his fist and released it. He'd hoped to get back on the road before Jasper learned they were in the barn. It had been quite a shock to discover Jasper's horse in the farthest stall last night.

The wind whistled through the boards as Mac tended to the animals. He'd have to deal with two realities today. One: More than likely they were stuck in Flatlick. Two: Jasper was heading west. He'd been staying ahead of them every step of the way.

Mac had kept the news from Pamela to give her some peace of mind. But how could he broach the subject? Jasper or one of his men would be back to check on their horses and, more than likely, to check on them.

Mac fed the horses fresh hay and water, then removed his Bible from the pack. Sitting down beside the woodstove, he closed his eyes and took in a deep breath. *Father, give me direction. I need to protect Mrs. Danner, and I'm not sure what I should do about the boy. Open Your Word to me, and open my eyes and heart to see where You're leading us.*

After his brief prayer, he opened the Bible and thumbed through the psalms.

"Whatcha doing?" Urias came up beside him and poured himself a cup of hot tea.

"Spending a little time with the Lord before we begin today."

With the mug halfway to his lips, Urias lifted his gaze and stared at Mac. "You believe all that stuff?"

"Sure do."

The young lad sat down across from Mac on the barn floor.

"How'd you sleep?" Mac asked.

"Great. Ain't been that warm for a while."

Mac grinned. "I'm glad." He scanned the pages of the Bible and turned to the Twenty-third Psalm. *"The Lord is my shepherd."* He mulled those words around. He'd read them so many times—repeatedly after Tilly's death.

Urias started wiggling his feet.

"Cold?"

"Nah, I'm fine." Urias sipped his tea.

Mac chuckled.

"What?"

"Nothing, just recalling how I had a hard time sitting still when I was your age."

Urias frowned.

Definite mistake—he'd just equated himself with the older generation. And Urias wanted very much to fit in with the adults. The boy had seen more and done more than most others his age, but he still was a child. Unfortunately, he wouldn't have the opportunity to escape adult responsibilities any longer.

Mac scanned the familiar psalm once again. *What am I missing? I trust God with my life. I trust Him with my needs. What is it I'm missing here?* He read on. *"Thou preparest a table before me in the presence of mine enemies."* Mac laughed.

"What?" Urias rose to his knees and tried to glance at the pages of the Bible.

"The verse I just read is: 'Thou preparest a table before me in the presence of mine enemies.'"

Urias flopped back down and squinted his eyes, tilting his head to one side. "You're a strange one, Mr. Mac."

Mac couldn't argue. "Tell me, do you belong in this barn, Urias?"

He looked toward the floor. "No."

"In one sense, you're Art Campbell's enemy because you haven't made friends with him and haven't obtained his permission to sleep in his barn. How would he know that you're not stealing from him? He'd see you as a thief, right?"

"I ain't stole nothin'," Urias defended himself.

Mac raised a hand. "No, son, I'm not claiming you did. I'm just saying that's what he would think if he found you in here."

"I suppose," the destitute youth mumbled.

"See, that's what makes this verse kinda funny for you. You sat down at a feast last night in the middle of your enemy's barn. God provided and took care of you and even blessed you with good, hearty food in your belly."

Urias cracked a crooked grin. "And your enemy is Jasper?"

"Yeah, you could say that."

The boy chuckled, then sobered. "Don't think Mrs. Mac finds it too funny. She's crying."

"Crying, when?"

Urias whispered, "When I came down, I heard her. I didn't say nothin' 'cause I didn't want to embarrass her."

"Smart thinkin'. I'd better go check on Pamela." Mac left the Bible open on the crate he'd been sitting on. He climbed up the ladder and found nothing but the mound of hay. "Pamela," he called. *She wouldn't have gone out in this cold, would she, Lord?*

"Pamela," he called again. He kicked off the hay from the corner of the blanket and folded it over to the left side. He found her balled in the middle of the blankets, hiding. Crying. He dropped down to his knees and reached for her. "Pam, what's the matter?"

She refused to look at him. He caressed her shoulder. "Pam," he whispered. "Is it Quinton?"

Eyes blazing of fire stared back at him. Then he knew. She'd heard the entire conversation with Jasper. She knew he'd kept a secret from her. And now she knew he kept two.

"I'm sorry," he fumbled, looking for the right words. "I didn't want to scare you. I hoped you'd get a good night's rest and we could get out first thing in the morning."

"I'm not a child," she spat back.

"I'm sorry. I was trying to protect you."

"I don't need your protection." Her words stung.

"Fine. I'll take you to Barbourville and you can hire another guide to take you the rest of the way." Mac stormed out of the loft and returned to the fire.

Urias was no longer in sight. Neither was his gun. "Great, just great." Mac dressed in his warm overcoat and slung his bow and arrows over his shoulder. *Where'd the boy run off to in this weather?*

❧

Pamela heard the barn door slam shut. Sleet and hail pelted the roof and sides of the barn. *Why would he go out in this storm, Lord? He wouldn't leave me here alone, would he?* She rolled her eyes heavenward and groaned.

She straightened up the loft, dusting off the hay from the wool blankets and folding them. Downstairs, she made a cup of tea and baked a loaf of bread. Toast, covered with peach preserves on the warmed slices, sounded wonderful.

Mac's Bible lay open on a crate. Picking it up, she closed it and moved it to the bench seat of the wagon. She noticed his pack was still there. Her shoulders relaxed. He'd be coming back. *Then where did he go?*

The boy. "Urias?" She scanned the entire area.

"It's freezin' out there," Urias said, squeezing through the loose board and wiping the sleeves of a tattered wool jacket two sizes too big for him.

"Where were you?"

"I had to. . ." He looked down at his feet. "You know."

What could he possibly have to do in this storm? "No, I don't. What is so important that you'd go out in this weather? And why did you use the loose panel?"

"You know, morning stuff," he mumbled.

Then it hit her. The very need she had herself and had been putting off as long as possible. "Oh." She felt her cheeks flush.

"Why didn't you use the door?"

" 'Cause old man Campbell could see me. And it ain't like I've been invited to use the barn."

"Oh." The child had a point. "I'm baking the bread and planning on fixing myself a couple slices of toast with peach preserves on them. You're welcome to have some. I'll fix us some bacon and eggs when I return."

"Buckle up and cover your face. The wind's blowing the ice real hard," Urias warned.

"Thanks for the tip."

"Welcome." He sat down with anticipation. She dressed and opened the door. A wave of arctic air stole her breath. Pulling her coat tight, she stuck her hands under each arm. Leaning into the wind, she struggled to make it to the outhouse.

When she returned to the barn, she discovered Urias had set a pot of water on the stove to warm and had removed the fresh loaf of bread. "Thank you, Urias."

"Welcome. Figured you'd like warm water. The barn and stove help, but it's still cold in here."

"Yes." She lifted the canvas over the back of the wagon. She prayed they had enough wood for the rest of the day and evening. They could purchase some from the Campbells, but who would want to go out and collect it? She shivered just thinking of the short trek to the outhouse.

With little effort, she had the bacon sliced, a couple of potatoes chopped and frying in the bacon fat, and eggs ready to cook after the potatoes were done.

Urias returned from taking apart his bed. "Smells great. Where d'ya suppose Mr. Mac went?"

"I don't know."

"You two fight often?"

Pam gave a quirk of a smile. "More than I'd care to admit."

"Don't be too hard on him. Us men try to protect our women."

"Oh? Just how much did you hear?"

"Enough to know that it was the best time to visit the outhouse." He leaned closer to her. "I don't know what Jasper's problem is with Mr. Mac, but I can tell the man is afraid of him."

"I noticed that, too."

"'Course, Mr. Mac's the largest man I ever seen. When I saw him come runnin' at me, I almost wet my pants."

"My reaction wasn't too different from yours." Pam smiled, removing the hash browns. Each egg sizzled as she dropped it on the hot frying pan.

"He's a good man, once ya get to know him. Don't think I'd want to be on his bad side though."

Pamela already was, and she ached to set things straight with Mac. She'd overreacted. He had a right to have a past. He should have told her about Jasper, but his past with his wife was none of her concern. After all, they weren't married as everyone thought.

The door creaked open. Mac entered, covered in ice, his long black hair laden with icicles.

"What happened to you?" She ran over to him and helped him out of his coat.

"I was looking for the boy." He shook as he stood resolute, staring at Urias.

"Me? Why?"

Pam noticed Mac's hands were blue. "Come warm up by the stove. I've fixed some breakfast. He went to the outhouse."

Mac closed his eyes.

"Sorry, Mr. Mac. You two were. . .well, it seemed like the best time to go."

Mac shook his head. Pamela picked off the ice as it started to melt from his hair and pant legs. "Sit down. I'll get you some hot tea."

Urias finished his breakfast and took his dirty dishes to the small basin used for cleaning.

Pamela whispered in Mac's ear, "I'm sorry, Mac. I do trust you. I don't know what came over me."

❧

Mac's body stung from the cold as he began to thaw out. He reached to put his arm around her waist and bring her to his chest, then caught himself. "Knowing Jasper's warm next door doesn't set well with me either." He winked.

"How long has it been since you trimmed this hair?" she asked.

"Ages."

"You don't know when your husband last trimmed his hair?" Urias asked.

Pamela's gaze locked with Mac's. She silently implored him to tell the truth.

"Pamela is not my wife. She's a recent widow. Her husband died a few days back on the trail. I came upon them right after the accident."

"But I thought. . ." Urias clamped his mouth shut.

"Most people assume like you. Even Jasper assumed, and we've been letting him hold that assumption for Mrs. Danner's protection."

"Ah." Urias looked at Mac, then glanced over to Pamela. "But ya fight like you're married."

Mac roared. "Mrs. Danner and I can get into a good row every now and again."

"Your secret's safe with me." Urias went to the woodstove and tossed a couple fresh logs in it.

Pamela cleaned up the dishes while Mac ate the semiwarm food quickly and drank two mugs of hot tea. Why hadn't he checked the outhouse before he ran off in the storm?

"By the way, the storm's just about blown its course. Down in the valley I could see the edge of the bad weather. I'd say another hour or two at the most."

"Should we get back on the road or wait until tomorrow morning?" Pamela asked.

"We'd have trouble making Barbourville before nightfall. I'm inclined to stay." Actually, Mac wanted to flee the territory and get Pamela as far from Jasper as possible. And he wasn't too comfortable about Jasper getting ahead of them. There were far too many places on the road where he and his men could jump them. "Urias, what are your plans, son?"

"Ain't got none. I guess I'll head back toward Barbourville and try and find me some work."

Mac also didn't like the idea of the boy being on his own. "I have a winter cabin east of the gap. You're welcome to come and live with me."

"Really?" The boy jumped up. "You mean it?"

"Wouldn't offer if I didn't mean it. You can go on to the cabin and wait for me to return, if you like. There's plenty of wood cut, and if you hunt around the cabin, you'll find plenty of food. An old friend of mine, Black Hawk, is staying there right now. You won't be able to see him, so you'll have to yell out a message from me. Then he'll know you're free to stay there."

"I can do that. How can I find your cabin?"

"You can't. But I'll give you directions to some folks who know how to find it." Mac ruffled the boy's fire-red curls. "I'll teach you how to hunt and live off the land."

"I'd like that." Urias smiled.

"Good. But I need a favor from you."

"Sure, what can I do?"

Mac leaned down and placed an arm around the boy's shoulders and in a low voice told Urias his plan.

As evening approached and the storm stopped, Urias went outside. Mac came up beside Pamela. "Pamela, I'm sorry I didn't tell you Jasper was here."

"Mac, I prefer to hear the bad news rather than be left in the dark."

"I understand."

Pamela reached out and took his hand. "What happened to your wife?"

He pulled his hand away. "You heard?"

"All I heard was something akin to a threat about your second wife meeting the same fate as the first. And seeing how Jasper thinks I'm the second wife, I'm kinda wondering what he might have in mind."

Mac took a step back. "Jasper had nothing to do with my wife's death." He could feel his chest rise with each intake of breath. *Calm down. Relax.* Closing his eyes, he took in a long, deep breath and let it out slowly.

Pamela reached out and placed her hand on his forearm.

"Mrs. Danner, I think it best if we don't go further with this discussion."

"Why are you afraid to talk about your wife's death?" she asked.

Mac counted to three. "Why do you avoid talking about your husband's death?"

Pamela blanched.

That should stop this dangerous discussion.

Mac stepped away just in time to hear a scuffle going on outside. He went to the door and opened it and saw Jasper holding Urias by the collar. "This thief says he's with you." Jasper kept the boy at arm's length.

Urias tried to wriggle out from his grasp.

"He's with me. You can let him go. What did he steal from you?"

"Nothing, just caught him snooping around the Campbells' house."

"I wasn't doin' nothin' wrong, Mr. Mac, I swear." Urias took a step toward Mac and ducked when Mac reached out to him.

He's been beaten more than once. Mac had seen the signs earlier, but this confirmed it.

"Heading out, Jasper?" Mac asked casually.

Urias let Mac loop his arm across his shoulders.

"Yeah, work's a-callin'. Heard some Injins left the reservation. Good bounty in catchin' 'em. Ain't no man better than me for trackin' in these mountains."

Mac held back his judgment. Jasper and his men left a trail wider than a herd of buffalo. He gnawed his inner cheek. *So, how'd I miss it?* "Good luck."

"Ain't no luck. Pure skill." Jasper barked out an order for his men to saddle up. As soon as they went inside, Mac whispered to Urias, "Did he hurt the Campbells?"

"No sir."

"Good. Go inside and protect Mrs. Danner. I'm going to make sure the Campbells are fine."

Urias slipped through the door while Mac strode toward the long front porch of the farmhouse. Art met him out front as he approached. "That kid with you?"

"Now he is. Been spending a few nights in your barn. Anything missing?"

Art grinned. "Nothing that me and the missus didn't leave for him to find."

Mac chuckled.

"We're fine. Jasper even paid two bits. Helped that more folks were staying and that you were in the barn."

Art sobered without warning. "He says you killed your wife."

Chapter 10

Pamela woke for the second morning in her cocoon of hay. This day, however, started with greater promise. Jasper was after Indians, and she and Mac were on good speaking terms. Good terms about everything except the subject of his wife's death. Her own deception added to the limitations of their honesty. But what did it matter? This was a temporary union, a business arrangement. In a couple weeks she would say good-bye and never see him again. Though, admittedly, it would be a much nicer trip if they remained cordial.

She primed the woodstove and started the bacon and the last of their eggs cooking. Normally she bartered with the folks she stayed with for additional food, but the Campbells didn't appear to be the friendly sort. Even after Jasper and his three men left, they didn't invite Mac, Urias, and herself in. *Odd,* she'd thought at the time. This morning she was even more certain of it. What had Jasper said about them to make the Campbells so nervous? It didn't matter. The barn was comfortable and, without the ice storm, actually quite warm.

Breakfast ready, she took two quarters from her purse and proceeded to the big house. As she approached, a young couple came out. "Morning," they said in unison.

"Good morning. Is Mr. or Mrs. Campbell in?"

"Missus is in the kitchen. Can't say where Mr. Campbell is," the young man, around her own twenty-three years, replied.

"Thank you."

Pamela knocked on the front door and waited. The shuffle of feet sounded behind the door before it slowly opened. "Can I help you?"

"Mrs. Campbell?"

The short, stout woman with gray hair nodded.

"I'd like to thank you for the use of your barn and give you a little something for the hay our horses ate."

"Ain't necessary." She reached out and took the money. Pamela suppressed a grin.

"Thank you again. You've been most kind."

Mrs. Campbell knitted her eyebrows together, then relaxed them. Looking to her left, then to her right, she leaned toward Pam and motioned with her forefinger for her to come closer. "You be careful, young lady. I hear your husband killed his first wife."

"What?" The question slipped out before Pamela realized she'd spoken.

"Mr. Smith, he said so."

Pamela shook her head. "Mr. Smith is not who he appears to be, ma'am. Mac actually had to keep a watch on you folks to make certain he didn't rob you. But it's one man's word over another, I guess. Good day, Mrs. Campbell, and ask folks about Nash MacKenneth, Mac, as he's known by most. I wager you'll hear a very different story."

"That's just it, dear. We have heard rumors about the crazy mountain man who killed his wife because she wanted to leave and return to the city."

Pamela felt dizzy. It couldn't be true. It just couldn't. She didn't say a word but walked straight back to the barn and sat down on the wagon's bench seat. *Was Mac the man she felt in her heart? Or was he the man who others apparently believed him to be?*

"Yea, though I walk through the valley of the shadow of death, I will fear no evil: for thou art with me; thy rod and thy staff they comfort me." Father, God, give me strength.

"Pamela, are you all right?" Mac asked.

"Fine. I just want to leave."

"All right. Urias, it's time to go."

The gangly redhead climbed down from the loft. He wore new clothes. They didn't fit quite right, but at least they weren't torn and tattered. *Where'd he get those?* she wondered. Seeing him dressed in rags had made her wish she had kept some of Quinton's clothing. Quinton. . . It seemed like an eternity had passed since last she saw him alive.

They scrunched up together on the bench seat. Mac slapped the reins. "Yah," he commanded, and off they went back to the road, heading northwest and closer to Creelsboro.

But each stride of the horses took them further from the revelation. She didn't want to believe it. She couldn't. Her life depended on the fact that it was false information. Her heart beat with a passion to know the truth. Could she ever fully trust this stranger?

No. She'd have to stay on guard, watching his every move and, most importantly, guarding her heart, for little by little, mile by mile, her heart had softened toward Mac. *Lord, I wish I'd never gone to speak with Mrs. Campbell today.*

Death was all around. The trees were bare; the ground was frozen brown. Nothing shouted life.

"Mrs. Danner. Mrs. Danner." Urias nudged her.

"Sorry, what?"

"I said it's amazing that Mr. Mac got these clothes from the Campbells."

"Yes, yes, it is. Are you staying warm?" It seemed an awkward question. The ice storm had vanished and with it the unseasonably colder weather.

"Definitely." His freckled face beamed. The child within the boy emerged once again.

"Are you all right?" Mac put his arm around her. She stiffened. He promptly removed it.

"I'm fine. Just eager to get to Creelsboro."

They meandered down the road, catching glimpses of the Cumberland River. The water seemed ice free. Little remained of the storm, though a few saplings still remained bent from the strong wind and ice. The damp ground provided another testament to the storm. Pamela prayed they would make it to Barbourville and find some dry, clean beds. Cold, damp ground and living with a growing suspicion of Mac didn't appeal to her in the slightest.

The road shifted to the left as they traveled around the foothills of a mountain. "Urias, it's time."

"Yes sir." Urias took the reins, and Mac jumped down from the wagon.

"Keep your rifle cocked." Mac waved and headed straight up and over the mountain. He moved so swiftly and quietly, Pamela shuddered at the thought of this hunter coming after and killing his own wife.

Urias turned to her. "Why don't you trust Mr. Mac?"

"I trust him."

"Not really. I've been on the run for a while now, and my home life wasn't what ya call normal. But I've learned to read people pretty well. Mr. Mac, he's a straight shooter. Liars and frauds have a way about 'em. Some can't look ya in the eye—they're the easiest to spot. Other's look you in the eye and dare ya not to believe 'em. Mr. Mac, he looks ya straight and he listens."

Pamela considered his words. He seemed too wise for a boy his age.

"Now, Mr. Campbell," Urias continued, "he's an interesting one. I'm not sure if I can trust him or not. The Campbells seem like good folks, but they were easily fooled by Jasper. Anyone with half a brain ought to be able to see that man coming a mile away. Did ya see his sidearm? Now he's a man to watch out for."

Pamela thought back on Mary Turner and how confident she'd been with her love and respect for Mac. The woman had opened her home to her, a virtual stranger, because of Mac. Perhaps it was wrong to listen to the ramblings of Mrs. Campbell. After all, Jasper had fueled her doubts and worries about Mac. And now she'd fueled them in Pam.

"Thank you, Urias."

"For what?"

"Setting me straight on a few things. Do you think this plan of Mac's will work?"

"If Jasper's plannin' what Mac thinks he is, yup. Question is, can Mr. Mac get in position first?" Urias slowed down the horses.

Pamela held the edge of the bench seat. *Please God, be with Mac.*

❧

Mac's breaths matched each of his strides. The thawing ground made the run more difficult. He prayed old man Brown was still alive and kicking. If his plan were going to work, he'd need the reinforcement. He had two hours to get ahead of Jasper and his men.

The scent of an oak fire hit him before he could make out the cabin. A sigh of relief washed over him.

"Isaiah Brown, you in there?"

"And who'd be callin' my name?"

"Mac."

"Only Mac I know has a friend I know. What be his name?"

What had Isaiah so scared? As a freed Negro, he'd always feared some-one would try to steal his papers and force him back into slavery. "Black Hawk," Mac replied.

Isaiah opened the door. The sun reflected from his nappy crown of salt-and-pepper hair, and he gave a deeply wrinkled grin to his visitor. "It's good to see you, Mac."

Mac extended his hand. "It's good to see you, too. But I need your help."

"What's the problem?"

"I suspect Jasper and his men are going to ambush me and a lady he thinks is my new wife on the western side of the bend."

Isaiah's forehead furrowed.

"I'll explain later. Can you help?"

Isaiah lowered his voice. "I's got runaways in my cabin. Don't feel right leavin' 'em."

Mac knew Isaiah would put up any slave running for his freedom, and he supposed word had gotten around as to where to find the man. "I understand. I can't stay—I need to get into position. I have a young man driving the wagon around the bend. I'm hoping to catch Jasper in the act from behind."

"Tell ya what I can do. I'll send my boy over to Johnny Fortney, and I'll join ya when I can."

Mac knew that meant squirreling away the runaways. One didn't ask questions. It was best not to know. Then you couldn't lie in court if something ever came up against Isaiah Brown.

"Thank you, my friend. Perhaps we can do some naybobbin' when I'm coming back through."

"Be nice chewin' the fat with ya." Isaiah waved.

Mac ran at full steam. He'd be pushing it to make it there on time. Hopefully, Urias had held back the horses some. Bobbing tree branches left and right, Mac forced his concentration level on where he was going rather than on what might be happening down the path.

Breathing heavily, he slowed down at the ridge, his senses alert. He didn't know if Jasper would send a man up there to watch or not. Few birds stayed in the area through winter, but enough remained in the area to help provide some indicator if people were stirring. As he suspected, no noise. In the distance he could hear the wagon. It was still moving. Cautiously, he moved in. He loaded his Kentucky long rifle, placed it over his shoulder, and positioned an arrow. Below he had a clear view of the road and the bend. The horses and wagon came into view.

His blood chilled. Jasper drove the wagon. Mac fired off the arrow as anger ignited him into a rage.

Chapter 11

Pamela twisted her tied hands. The leather straps Jasper had used bit deep. Urias lay bound and unconscious on the ground beside her. Hot tears streamed down her face. Mac's plan had sounded so wise this morning. But Jasper had outsmarted him. He'd attacked them before they hit the bend. She prayed he'd come along soon.

Pam wiggled over to Urias. *Father, please don't let Urias die because of me.* The brave young man had fought well. He'd tried to fire off his rifle, but a whip came from behind and knocked him off the wagon.

Jasper's men had pawed her as they tied her up. In wicked laughter, Jasper had warned them that Mac was still out there and it would be best if they left his wife alone. *Father, I know You don't approve of lying, and You know I've not been telling Mac the entire truth, but it paid off with regard to Mac not correcting Jasper. I'm still safe.*

She refused to think of what might have happened if Jasper knew the truth. "Urias," she called.

He moaned.

"Thank You, Lord."

How far away was Mac? Would Jasper's men ambush him? She'd seen only three of them. She scanned the ridge looking for the fourth man, but to no avail. Jasper had ridden off with her wagon very pleased with himself.

Something wasn't making sense. The Turners said no one could ever prove that Jasper and his men were at fault because he left no survivors. If that were true, why were she and Urias still alive? "Dear God in heaven, protect Mac."

Suddenly, she realized Jasper would return after he killed Mac. "Urias, wake up. We've got to get out of here."

☙

Mac slipped behind a rock after his arrow pierced Jasper's shoulder. Curses and commands passed the man's lips faster than a viper could attack. Only one man rode beside Jasper on the road. That meant two men were in the woods. But where?

He followed the ridge again. It was the logical choice for one man. A glitter of metal on the ridge proved his assumption. Mac took long and careful aim. When the dark form moved out from behind the silver gray rock, Mac fired.

He reloaded and looked for the man who had been on the horse next to Jasper. Following the left ridge, he found him slipping behind some undergrowth. Mac aimed and fired.

Two down.

Jasper broke the arrow in his shoulder and jumped down from the wagon, his gun in his right hand. "Come and get me, Mac. Your woman was mighty fine. . . ."

Mac closed his eyes and fought off the words that rushed into his mind. He breathed deeply. One man remained in the woods, unexposed. If he gave in to Jasper's taunts, he'd be killed.

"Before I killed her," Jasper taunted. "Come on, Mac. It's you and me now. Ain't it just the way you wanted it? You've been after me for a long while. Here's your chance."

Mac squeezed his eyes shut. Jasper couldn't have killed Pamela, he couldn't. *But Jasper kills all his victims. All of them. Forgive me, Lord.* Mac let out a scream and ran toward Jasper.

Jasper fired.

The bullet grazed Mac's arm. Pain fueled Mac's fury. "You're a dead man, Jasper."

Jasper's hands shook as he turned the barrel and aimed again. The shot whizzed past Mac's ear.

Jasper turned the barrel again.

Mac charged the last ten yards. His hands were around Jasper's throat before he aimed.

Jasper dropped his gun.

Mac released him.

Jasper coughed.

A shot rang out and Mac felt the bullet slam into his backside.

Jasper's lips curled in a wicked grin. "Thought you'd get the upper hand on me, huh?" He started to bend down and pick up his weapon. Mac kneed him in the chest. Reaching for the knife in his boot, he instantly had it out and at Jasper's throat.

In his anger, he'd forgotten the fourth man. He'd let himself be vulnerable. "Tell your man to back off or I kill ya."

"You're gonna kill me anyway," Jasper croaked.

"I'm not like you, Jasper. I'll turn you in to the authorities."

Jasper let out a snicker. "Yeah, like you let your first wife return home."

Mac felt his rage increase. He pressed the knife closer. "Tell him," he strained.

"We got him, Mac," a strange voice called from the woods. A young man with brown hair appeared with a rifle. Jasper's fourth man walked with his hands in the air in front of a rifle held by Isaiah Brown.

"Let him go, Mac," Isaiah said.

"He killed Pamela and Urias." Mac eased the pressure he'd been exerting on Jasper's neck with the knife.

"I'll take them to Barbourville where he can be tried and hanged," Isaiah's young friend answered.

Mac nodded.

"The sheriff will want to hear from you, Mac," the young man added.

"I'll be there."

"I ain't hangin' for killin' 'em," Jasper's man protested. "We didn't kill 'em. They're off the side of the road back about three-quarters of a mile."

"Shut up, Wilson," Jasper hissed.

"I ain't hangin', Jasper. You wanna hang, go ahead. But I ain't hangin'."

"Go," Isaiah said to Mac. "I'll watch the wagon. I'm sure young Johnny can take these two on to Barbourville." Johnny bound Jasper's hands and searched for additional weapons.

Mac ran a couple of strides down the road, then broke into a limping lope. The bullet wound in his backside burned. Blood dampened the right side of his trousers. "Pam, Urias!" he hollered.

A cold sweat covered his body. "Pamela!" he yelled louder. "Urias."

The burn in his buttocks forced him to a slower limp. *Dear God, where are they?* He examined the road. He found the place where they had been overrun. Small droplets of blood appeared on the dirt path. "Pamela!"

"Mac, over here."

Thank You, Lord. His gaze followed her voice to his right. Soon he had them unbound and informed that Jasper was on his way to the sheriff's office in Barbourville. Urias seemed dazed but was coming around.

"Mac, you're bleeding."

" 'Fraid so. A shot glanced my arm."

"Your arm, my foot. The rear of your trousers is soaked with blood. Let me look at that."

"Not on your life."

Pamela stepped back.

"There's a doctor in Barbourville. We'll let him take care of it."

"All right. I'll go get the wagon."

"I'll get it." Mac released the tree he'd been clinging to for support.

"Put your foolish male pride aside. I'll fetch the wagon. You tend to Urias. He was out for quite a while." She stomped off down the road without waiting for his response.

ॐ

"Of all the most stupid things," Pamela mumbled, working her way down the road. "The man's insufferable." A storm of emotions circled in her gut. Thankfully, Mac was alive and Jasper no longer posed a threat. He'd still have to explain how he got shot, not once but twice, and how he had time to get some other folks to come and lend a hand. She knew the man was fast on his feet, but he had had to trek up and over the ridge and back again. . . .

He won't be running for a little while. She giggled at the thought. *He won't be sitting either.*

Laughter bubbled up to the surface. Big, brave Nash MacKenneth shot in the buttocks—the irony was just too funny. She sobered a moment, considering how it must sting, then giggled again.

The sound of the wagon approaching caused her to pause. Had someone else come along and stolen it?

"Hello, miz," an older black man called from the top of the wagon. "You must be Pamela. I's Isaiah Brown, a friend of Mac's."

"Hello."

"Where is he?"

She climbed up on the wagon. "Down the road a bit. He's been shot."

"I saw it. Thought I'd bring the wagon to him rather than having him walk back."

"He won't let me take care of it, says he wants to go to the doctor in Barbourville."

"Doc France is a good doctor, does a right fine job."

"Maybe you can get him to at least put a clean cloth to the wound and apply some pressure on it." Pamela folded her arms across her chest. "Why are men such. . ."

Isaiah laughed.

"What?"

"Women and men have been asking that question ever since Adam and Eve."

After Mac and Urias were loaded into the wagon as comfortably as possible, Pamela drove the two patients to the doctor in Barbourville. Isaiah stayed with them until they reached the path to his cabin. Pamela again was struck by the kindness of Mac's true friends. Unlike the Campbells, who hadn't known him, his friends showed no fear of the man. She really needed to trust her heart.

Mac lay on top of the canvas covering the crates. Urias alternated between lying beside Mac and sitting up. The boy's constant complaints about his headache worried her. Head injuries were always such a bad omen.

With the men lying behind her, Pam thought back on Angus's words of warning. She gripped the leather reins tighter. If only she had listened. Quinton would be alive. And Mac and Urias would be safe. Even Jasper and his men wouldn't have been tempted by the contents of their wagon. If only. . .

Bile rose in the pit of her stomach. She should have been stronger. She should have convinced Quinton it was wrong to chase their parents' dream. Who cares about wide-open spaces, a profitable store? Most would care to make a profit, but accruing wealth didn't matter if it meant losing everyone. She should sell the contents of the wagon in Barbourville, then send a letter to Elijah and Elzy Creel and let them know the misfortunes that had fallen on her family. Perhaps she'd ask if he'd resell the land and business for her. She couldn't run a business, at least not one her heart wasn't in. But what would she do in Barbourville after that?

If truth be told, Jasper didn't know the half of the contents in the wagon. In one trunk the entire family fortune in cash and gold lay safely hidden. If she were wise, she wouldn't have to work. But what would she do? She couldn't stay around an empty house all day. A boardinghouse, on the other hand, might keep her busy. Pam nibbled her lower lip.

Of course, there would be the increased work of doing the linens for her visitors. Pamela looked down at her hands. Additional laundry held no appeal either.

I could teach, she reasoned. But Pamela knew she wouldn't have the patience with half a dozen youngsters clamoring for attention. No, teaching wasn't a real option.

You could marry. She grinned. The only man in whom she had been the least bit interested lay on the wagon behind her with a bullet embedded in his buttocks, and he didn't want her help. Marriage didn't seem like an option, either. Time. That was the problem. She needed time.

It hadn't been that long since Quinton died. Was she even done grieving the loss of her brother? She doubted it. There hadn't been time for anything except moving forward, avoiding the enemy—and still Jasper had almost won.

"We're nearly there," Mac murmured. She nearly jumped hearing his voice.

"How much farther?"

"A mile and a half. You'll find Dr. France's office. . . ." He rattled off the directions. Thirty minutes later, she found herself pulling the wagon up to a house. A real house. One with milled wood and glass windows. "These people are civilized," she squealed with excitement.

ða

Mac grumbled to himself. Humiliation burned deeper than the wound on his backside. If he'd only been shot in a more appropriate place—if there were an appropriate place to be wounded. Dr. France teased him, but then quietly acknowledged that of all the places one could have been shot, this one did the least damage. The muscles would heal. Mac wouldn't sit down properly for a week, but he would recover.

Urias, on the other hand, had to be watched. His head still ached, but he was holding down his food—a good sign. Mac hadn't seen Pamela for hours. She'd dropped them off and left. He'd hoped. . . . What had he hoped? That she'd be there when he came out of the doctor's office? *Must be the whiskey, Lord.* He leaned against the wall as the room blurred. He closed his eyes and opened them slowly, trying to focus.

He blinked and realized he was lying face down on. . .on a bed with clean white sheets. "Ah, glad to see you're back with us." Dr. France grinned. "You'll need to stay down for a while and drink plenty of fluids. Apparently you lost more blood than I was aware of. Your female companion returned and said she'd rented a room at a boardinghouse. I let her know that you and the boy will be spending the night here."

Mac raised his chest off the bed.

Dr. France placed a hand on his back and pushed him down. "Stay down and rest, give your body a chance to heal. Oh, the sheriff came by as well. You can visit with him in the morning. Something about giving testimony against a couple of bandits."

"Fine." Mac rolled over to his back. "Ouch!" He promptly rolled over and lay on his stomach.

Dr. France chuckled. "You'll be sleeping on your front or side for a while."

85

He pulled up a chair and sat down beside him. "What caused those scars on your back?"

Mac clenched his jaw.

"Am I correct in assuming it's a bear? I'm guessing his paw spanned eight, maybe ten inches."

"Yeah, a brown bear. It killed my wife."

"I'm sorry."

"Ain't no one's fault but my own," Mac mumbled.

Dr. France rose from the chair. "Can it ever be anyone's fault when a wild animal attacks?"

Mac punched his pillow and buried his face. *Why did everyone always feel they had the answers to your personal issues? God knows and I know I'm at fault. I should have listened to Tilly. I should have taken her back. I should have. . .*

Should have and did were two different things. How many times would he continue to go down this path of blame? When would he feel the freedom of grace and peace again? When would he be whole?

"Mac," Urias whispered.

Mac turned his head to the left. "Yeah, Urias?"

"Doc has a point about your wife."

"Don't start with me, boy."

"Sorry." Urias rolled to his side and faced the wall.

"Urias, I'm sorry. I didn't mean to bark at you."

"Ain't nothin'." Urias didn't roll back over.

"Come on, speak your piece. You've got something to say, spit it out. I'm a man, I can take it." *Most of the time,* he reminded himself.

Urias rolled back over. "I'm just guessin', but did your wife go out when ya told her not to or to a place ya told her not to?"

Mac raised his eyebrows. "How'd you know?"

"Fits. I mean, women, they don't listen."

Mac chuckled. "And how do you know this?"

"My ma. She wouldn't listen to anythin' Pa and I would say to her. Not when it came to her drinkin'. Anyway, I seen it other times, too. Men tell the women to do one thing, and they go and do another."

Not all women. At least Mac felt pretty certain they weren't all like that. "Can't judge all the women by one. Look at Mrs. Danner, she listens."

"Maybe. I don't know."

Mac rolled to his left side. His arm hurt, but it was bearable. "She's done a fair job following my instructions. Tilly, that's the name of my wife, she didn't want to live in the wilderness. We had an argument about it, and I left to go hunting for a while. I found out she really didn't love me. She loved my parents' farm. And since I'm the oldest son, she figured I'd inherit the farm. Which I will one day, but I'm not ready to settle down there yet."

"She married you for your parents' land?"

" 'Fraid so. Hurts a man's pride, ya know. Anyway, Tilly decided she'd had enough and set out on foot to return home. She never made it. I heard her screams, but I was too late. I was so angry, I fought the bear and killed it."

"But she'd still be alive if she'd listened to ya and stayed by the house."

"Possibly. Hard to say."

"Seems to me, a man who believes the Bible like you do ought to have forgiven himself. Ain't much a man can do with a strong-headed woman. I know. Pa tried. Me, I've decided to keep women at a distance. Admire their looks some and their cooking but keep them as far away from my house as possible."

Mac laughed. "Son, when love hits, there ain't a man alive who can stand up against it."

"Ain't gonna happen. I'll live in the mountains like you. I should be able to avoid most of them that way." Urias nodded for emphasis. "Ouch."

Mac snickered. Then it occurred to him. He'd secluded himself in the mountains for the very same reason. He didn't want to be affected by women again. And what happened? God put a woman on his doorstep. He flopped back to his stomach. Images of the beautiful widow played in his mind. *She's untouchable, Lord. Remove these thoughts from me.*

Chapter 12

Pamela eased out of her feather bed and stretched in the sunlit room. She'd loved every minute of the past three nights she had spent in Barbourville. The townspeople, she found, were very friendly. Mac's and Urias's injuries were minor, and a few days of rest were the doctor's orders. Many hours she'd spent alone, thinking and praying for direction. Last night, as she pored over the facts and figures in her father and brother's ledger, she'd decided to try to sell the merchandise to the Croleys' store. Today she'd take the wagon from the stable and drive it there.

She'd taken inventory at the store yesterday and decided which items would be the most marketable. These were the items she'd pitch first. The second list contained fancier items, less practical, but still useful. The third list—she wondered why they'd even brought such useless niceties along. These she would continue to use on the road as thank-you gifts to those who helped them. Something to make a woman feel special or to give the house a touch of beauty. She found wilderness women enjoyed fancy things just as much as women in the cities back East. Here, however, the women were more pragmatic. If you don't need it, don't waste the money on it. It seemed just about every item in the kitchen served more than one purpose.

Dressing for a day of business, she folded the ledger shut and made her way to the dining area.

"Good morning, Pamela, did you sleep well?" Elizabeth Engle asked, her gray hair perfectly in place. It was hard to believe the woman was seventy-five years old.

"Wonderfully, thank you, Mrs. Engle."

"Breakfast is ready. You'll have to serve yourself this morning. I'm off to the market for some fresh winter squashes. I heard the Pitzers brought some in yesterday."

Pamela smiled. She knew the older woman had her own garden but probably couldn't keep up with the amount of food her boarders consumed. Elizabeth Engle was the perfect hostess and a wonderful cook. Pamela had felt at home minutes after she first arrived.

Mac and Urias had stayed one night at the boardinghouse, then decided to take a room closer to the stables. Fancy linens, curtains, and such scared them, which Pamela found incredibly funny in comparison to the no-fear attitude they held toward Jasper and his men.

The circuit judge had come and gone. Mac had given his testimony; Jasper had denied it. Urias had given his testimony, and once again Jasper denied it. She'd been prepared to give testimony as well, but the lawyer decided "to spare a woman the harsh realities of the courtroom." She'd held back her laughter on that one. Hadn't she already lived through the actual threats associated with Jasper? Could the courtroom even compare? The prosecuting attorney also had the statement from Johnny Fortney. When Jasper's partner decided to testify against him for fear of going to hell, the judge found no reason to continue the trial. Jasper was sentenced to die by hanging on Saturday.

Resolved not to watch the man hang, Pamela needed to finish marketing her wares this day or she would not be able to avoid the center square tomorrow, hanging day. If the sales went well, there would be room to put a bed in the wagon on Saturday and continue their travels, although it would mean they'd have to leave on Sunday. Mac's inability to sit for long periods of time and the constant banging from the bench seat convinced her she needed to lighten the load. She also had decided to have the wagon framed and covered. The storm they'd traveled through a few days earlier proved there needed to be more shelter in the wagon.

The stable was more than happy to do the modifications. Mac protested but finally conceded it was her wagon and ultimately her decision. Pamela knew enough about men to understand that more than his backside had been injured. His pride had taken a substantial blow as well.

She walked down the street toward the stable. Mac walked with a slight limp toward her. "Good morning, Mac. Did you sleep well?"

"Fine."

What has him all upset this morning? she wondered.

"Look, I ain't goin' to beat a dead horse here, but are you certain you want to do this?"

"Yes, it's practical."

"But. . ."

She held up a hand to stop his protest. "Mac, I've gone over the figures. I'll still make a profit."

His eyebrows rose.

So, he doesn't believe a woman can handle simple mathematics. She untied the leather folder. "Here, look at these figures." She pointed to the column marked "purchase."

"Compare them to. . ." She slid her finger across the page. "These." She paused a minute to let him absorb the figures. "As you can see, I will still make a profit. Granted, it won't be as high as it would be if I sold the items individually, but then I would have to add in time on the shelves. Is the profit truly greater?"

"Uh. . ." He fumbled for his words. "Your husband did this before he died?"

"No." Her voice rose an octave. "I did this last night." She unfolded another piece of paper that listed the items in the three columns. "Here in column one you can see what is more likely to sell, and column two lists what might sell. The third column is hardly worth mentioning to Mr. Croley. It isn't likely he'd be interested in those items. I reckon most folks won't either. They're dust collectors on a store shelf. They look pretty, but they aren't practical for wilderness living. If a man has some extra money, he might buy a gift for his wife. But that doesn't seem all that likely to happen. I imagine I'll have most of these items five years from now still gathering dust on my shelves."

Pamela knew she'd have very little stock in the store when she arrived, but the orders Quinton had placed before they left should arrive about the time she reached Creelsboro. Her stomach tightened. *Why does this happen every time I think of this place, Lord?*

Mac removed his coonskin cap and scratched his head. "I'd say you've got a head for business."

"Probably not. I've decided to give the items in column three away to individuals as thank-you gifts along the trail."

"I need to speak with you about the trip."

"All right. Can we speak after my negotiations with Mr. Croley?"

"That will be fine. Meet me at the hillside near the ferry."

She knew he liked that view. You could see down the Cumberland River and look at the mountains toward the gap. "Fine. Where's Urias?"

"Looking for work. I must say, the boy has a good sense of needing to provide for himself."

"I think he's been doing that for a while." She leaned in closer to Mac. "I've purchased a set of clothes and a pair of boots for him. I just haven't figured out how to give them to him. Maybe you could ask him to do some things for me, and I could give them to him as payment."

Mac smiled. "I'll see what I can do. You think I'm doing the right thing, having the kid live with me?"

Pamela fought the desire to wrap herself in his arms and hug him. "I think you'll be a very good influence on him." One of the things she'd been thinking over the past couple of days was her growing attraction to Mac. She trusted him, but she still feared telling him the truth. Her fear had changed from her original concern for her safety to his uncompromising sense of right and wrong. He'd feel lied to. No, she couldn't tell him the truth, at least not yet.

ᔑ

Pamela Danner continued to surprise Mac. Not only had she endured the hard travel without one word of complaint, now he wondered if his original concerns regarding her ability to run a business were ill founded. *She obviously can work with numbers,* he acknowledged.

Mac squatted by the river and watched the current play. A small eddy formed every now and again, traveling downstream and popping back up again. Staying still and recovering, as Dr. France put it, was driving him crazy. He had to get back to doing something, anything. Inactivity would lead him to become stagnant like a lifeless river. Mac felt a bond between himself and the Cumberland. He needed the freedom to move about, to keep moving. He stood, relieving the pressure on his wound.

"Mac!" Pamela waved as she headed toward him with a bounce to her step.

"The sale went well?"

"Very. Mr. Croley purchased just about the entire stock."

"He keeps that much cash on hand?" *How much money passes through a store in the course of a couple days?* he wondered.

"Of course not. We bartered some, and he'll be making some payments."

"Payments? To where?"

She looped her arm around his. "I set up a special fund."

"Here? Are you planning on staying around?"

Pamela sighed and removed her hand. "No, but one bank is as good as another. And for the time being, this will work just fine."

"Forgive me for telling you your business, but how are you going to be aware of whether or not he makes his payments?"

"The bank will post me a message."

"And what will you do should he not pay?"

She scrunched up her nose and placed her hands on her hips. "I seem to be not understanding your logic, Mac. First you tell me the wagon is too full, and now that I've taken care of that problem and added some accommodations in the wagon, you're telling me I'm messing up again."

Mac squeezed his eyes closed and pinched the bridge of his nose. "I don't know if you realize it, but that's a lot of money you've put into a bank that you'll never be by again."

"Mr. MacKenneth, you can be the most stubborn of men that I've ever laid eyes on. And just so you understand I know more than you think I do, I realize exactly how much money is involved here. And I–I—" She clamped her mouth shut. "I've taken the appropriate steps to make certain my interests are protected."

Mac raised his hands in surrender. "I ain't goin' to argue with a woman about money. Just wouldn't seem fair."

Her face reddened. "I suppose you know exactly how much money you have in your savings, in your pocket, and in investments."

"More or less," he defended. Truth was, he wasn't certain how much money he had. He didn't count it all that often. He had some in his parents' house, in his cabin, and in the bank. In his pocket he kept some, but not much, and what he did have was nearly gone.

"Well, I can tell you down to the last penny where mine is and how much it is."

He could swear she was about to stick out her tongue at him. "Fine. I didn't ask you to come over here to argue. I wanted to ask you about moving on. I can travel some, and I don't want to hit any more bad weather."

"Fine, when do we leave?"

"In the morning."

"Wonderful. I'll see you then." She turned and marched back to the center square of the town.

He rubbed his chin, thankful he'd kept his mouth shut about her feminine attire. She'd been wearing fancy dresses every day—not that she looked bad in them. He'd wanted to ask if she'd purchased a real pair of boots to travel with, but he didn't dare. He looked down at her fleeing feet and groaned. She had to have the prettiest set of ankles he'd ever seen. *Lord, help me deliver her to Creelsboro. . .fast.*

Mac turned and looked back at the river. The Twenty-third Psalm replayed in his mind and stopped at, *"He leadeth me beside the still waters."* He blinked, focusing on the river once again. The next verse he recited more slowly. *"He restoreth my soul."* He knelt down. *Am I constantly running, Lord, so that I refuse to hear what You're trying to say?*

Listening for some sort of response, he waited a bit longer. A bird sang in the nearby trees. A gentle breeze stirred the dry leaves on the ground. The river even played its music, but not one word from God. Mac wanted answers. He demanded them. But they weren't coming, and after all these years, he wondered, should they have come?

He got up and stomped toward the stable. He'd better give them a hand and make certain that the wagon was ready to roll in the morning. *I need to keep moving, Lord.*

"Did you find Mrs. Danner, Mr. Mac?" Urias asked as he entered the stable.

"Yup. We're leaving in the morning."

Urias lifted a crate from the wagon and placed it on a nearby buckboard.

"What are you doing?"

"Mr. Croley hired me to bring over the items he bought from Mrs. Danner."

"That's great. I'm glad you found a job."

Urias grinned. "I don't think Mr. Croley knows I know Mrs. Danner, but it doesn't matter. It's a job, and it'll give me some money."

Mac knew Pamela had a hand in getting the lad the employment, but he wasn't about to tell him. "A man needs to work for his hire. Do you need a hand?"

"No thanks. I'm just about done." Urias dusted off his hands and leaned toward Mac. "Hanging is set for noon."

"We'll be long gone before then."

Urias's red hair gave a single nod. Neither of them was anxious to see a man hang.

"Is the work done on the wagon?"

"Just about. I think they're having trouble building the bed the way Mrs. Danner ordered it."

"I still can't believe she's insisting on a bed."

Urias laughed. "You two definitely look at life differently."

Mac grunted.

Urias laughed harder.

❧

Pamela let out an exasperated breath. Why did she and Mac squabble so much? She opened her drawstring purse and pulled out a small trinket.

Mr. Croley had said it was an actual Indian artifact and was supposed to bring good luck. She tossed it on the bed. It certainly didn't help her conversations with Mac. She'd been about ready to wring his neck for implying she was less than competent. Oddly enough, the more she felt attracted to him, the more his words stung.

On the other hand, she knew he'd be even more protective if he had any idea how much money she still carried in the wagon. She glanced over to her chest. The false bottom hid the family fortune. She'd worn each of her fancy dresses to keep up the illusion that she'd brought an entire wardrobe with her. Even though Jasper had been captured, tried, and convicted, she still didn't feel safe. If the residents thought Mr. Croley was paying the bank for his debt to her, they wouldn't be inclined to pursue her. One incident on the trail was more than enough.

Removing her social dress, she replaced it with a more comfortable one. Errands done, she wouldn't be going out again until morning. Tonight she would pack. Knowing Mac, he'd be here to pick her up before the sun crested the horizon.

An hour later, Pam's trunks were packed. She sat rocking in the wooden rocker Elizabeth Engle kept in the room. Pamela traced the curved line on the arm of the chair. Elizabeth had told her that her husband had carved the chair for her when she was expecting their first child. The rocking chair had been a real blessing over the years, Elizabeth said. She'd spent more hours in that chair rocking her fussy babies than she'd spent in any other chair in the house.

It still surprised Pamela how well furnished the home was. No question the late Mr. Engle produced quality furnishings. He'd made just about every piece in the house.

Pamela rocked back and closed her eyes. *Lord, I'm still in doubt about traveling on to Creelsboro, but I have no place else to go. Barbourville is tempting me to stay and make a home here. The people are friendly, but. . .*

Her mind drifted to the upcoming event in the town square. She knew justice had to be played out, but to know she was the reason a man had been hanged. . . . Pamela shook her head, hoping to clear the images from her mind's eye.

"Jasper killed many, Lord. I know that. And I'm thankful I'm still alive. I know he deserves his punishment for all those other people he's killed. I don't know; call me foolish, I guess. I just can't live where I know I played a part in the man's death."

A gentle knock on the door broke her from her prayers.

"Yes?"

"Pamela dear, it's Elizabeth. Are you needing anything else this evening?"

Pamela went to the door and opened it.

"No, thank you, I'm fine."

Elizabeth's matronly appearance of silver hair, gentle wrinkles, and warm eyes made it easy for Pam to open her heart to the older woman. "I must say, I'm sorry to see you leave so soon. You've been a most enjoyable guest."

"Thank you. I'll miss your hospitality as well. You've a beautiful home."

"Thank you. My Peter had a way with wood." The elder woman glowed.

Pamela's heart ached for that kind of a relationship. To be so close to a person that even in death you still feel a part of the other. She felt her eyes water.

"What's the matter, dear?"

"Nothing. It's wonderful to see the love you still have for your husband, God rest his soul."

Elizabeth nodded her head and smiled. "I fell in love with Peter when I first set eyes on his handsome face. But love is hard work. It takes time and patience. It used to bother me that he spent so many hours making all this furniture. Then I realized—and I must say it took quite a few outbursts on my part before I understood—that making the furniture was his way of saying, 'I love you.'"

Pamela found it hard to believe that the very items the woman cherished had been the items they, as a couple, had fought over.

"Peter also realized that I wanted more time with him and not just with the things he made. Of course, that's when the idea hit to have me work with him on the furniture. The idea of sitting down, holding hands, and just talking was completely foreign to the man. But you're right, dear. I do love him with all my heart. We had many good years together. And soon, I think, I'll be joining him."

"Are you ill?" Pamela worried.

"No, no, dear. But remember, I'm seventy-five. I can't imagine living too many more years."

"I suppose you're right," Pamela mumbled. The older woman had been so open and loving that, earlier in the week, Pamela had found herself able to unburden to Elizabeth, explaining the lie she'd been living with for days.

"Oh my, I forgot. You've lost your parents and your brother in less than a year."

Pamela took in a deep breath and let it out slowly.

"I found comfort in the Twenty-third Psalm," Elizabeth offered.

"I've been thinking on that psalm a lot. I certainly have been walking 'through the valley of the shadow of death.'"

Elizabeth placed her blue-veined hand on Pam's forearm. "Read all the verses of that psalm, not just the fourth. There's a lot more there."

"There is?"

Elizabeth winked and patted her arm. "Good night, dear. I'll see you in the morning."

"Good night." Pamela closed the door to her room, grabbed her Bible, and opened it to the Twenty-third Psalm. *What have I been missing?*

Chapter 13

Mac hoisted the last of Pamela's trunks into the wagon. She must have filled it with lead. Either that or the few days' rest had played more havoc with his muscles than he thought.

Inside he found Mrs. Engle providing a hearty breakfast for their departure. Mac ate in earnest, as did Urias. Pamela left the table early, claiming her need to arrange some items in the wagon. "Women," he muttered and forked some home fries.

"Thank you for the fine vittles, Mrs. Engle." Urias spoke with his mouth full.

"Pleasure. You take good care of Pamela Danner, you hear?" She shook her finger at Urias.

He sat up straight and responded, "Yes ma'am."

Mac chuckled. Mrs. Engle reminded him of an old schoolteacher, very strict and very poised.

"And I expect you to do the same, Mr. MacKenneth."

Mac wiped his mouth with a linen napkin. "Yes ma'am."

Urias's face went red, holding back his laughter. Mac kicked his shin under the table.

"Hey," the boy cried out.

Mac winked. Laying his napkin beside his now-empty plate, he excused himself from the table. His mother would be proud, he thought.

Urias drank another glass of milk, grabbed a couple of biscuits, and followed Mac out the front door. Mac could hear Pamela shifting things around in the wagon. She had the flaps closed. *Should I knock?*

"Hey Mrs. Danner," Urias called out.

She popped her head out through the opening. "Give me a minute."

Her golden hair draped down across her shoulders, and the blue of her eyes competed with the sky. Mac closed his eyes. "Take all the time you need."

Two minutes later, after what had seemed like an eternity, Pamela emerged through the front of the wagon dressed in her woolen traveling dress with a bonnet covering her beautiful hair.

"I'm all set, boys. Let's go."

Urias and Mac climbed on board. Mac discovered a small, long pillow covering the entire bench. "What's this?"

"Hopefully, it will help." Pamela looked straight ahead.

"Feels great," Urias piped in.

"It's nice to have you coming along, Urias, at least to Lynn Camp."

"I ain't got nothin' better to do. Besides, it's a long hike to Mac's place from here."

"You're welcome to travel the entire trip with us. I have more than enough provisions, and if we run out, I can always purchase more from the various farmers."

Mac looked over to Urias and nodded his consent. It might be nice to have the lad as a buffer between them.

A wide, toothy grin spread across the boy's face. "I would like that."

Mac slapped the reins. "Yah."

The wagon jerked forward.

"You know," Pamela said to Urias, "I'd like to talk with you about possibly working for me. I know Mr. Mac has offered for you to stay with him and learn to live off the land. And I know how exciting and important that kind of training is, but, well, I've been thinking, I could use a strong young man to help me at the store."

"Really?"

"You'd need to attend to your schooling though. If you're to grow in the job, you'd need to know how to read and write. Not to mention how to add and subtract figures." Pamela glanced over at Mac.

Ouch! If the woman had daggers in those eyes, they hit their mark. He never should have questioned her figures regarding the merchandise.

Urias's shoulders slumped. "I'll have to think on it."

"We have time. Several days if I'm not mistaken, right, Mr. Mac?" She flashed her pearly whites at him.

"Right," Mac mumbled. She probably would be a good role model for the boy, so why did it bother him? Because he had felt a bond with Urias from the moment he caught him outside the Campbells' barn.

Hours passed, and Mac found himself lying on the bed he'd protested so strongly about, while Urias led the team. Even with the fancy pillow on the bench, his backside was hurting. He scanned the rearrangement of the various trunks. The heavy midsize trunk was in the front of the wagon to the right side, opposite the bed. He looked under the bed to see that Pamela had used every bit of space for storage. The woman continued to surprise him. He noticed she'd even purchased a pair of rugged boots for the trail. He suspected they were boys' boots, but he knew better than to bring up the subject.

"Whoa!" Urias halted the team. "Right here, Mrs. Danner?"

"This is wonderful, thank you."

"Why are we stopping?" Mac rose from the bed.

Pamela pulled the flap open. "Lunch."

She came inside and shuffled through the food pantry, as she liked to call it. She pulled out a bundle. "I prepared these this morning. I figured it would save us time today."

Mac nodded and accepted the sandwich, thick slices of ham and some cheese inside a bulky whole-wheat roll. "Thank you."

"Mac, we need to talk privately. I'm going to send Urias off for a bit," Pamela whispered.

Mac swallowed.

"Urias, Mr. Mac and I need to have some private words. Would you mind eating over there?"

"Nah, I may go farther. When you two have private words, you get loud."

Pamela's face reddened, possibly matching the shade Mac felt his own face turning.

"Thank you. I'll call you when we're through."

Mac felt the wagon bounce as Urias jumped off.

Pamela placed a hand on his arm. "Mac, I have a confession to make."

Pamela nibbled her lower lip. *How do I begin, Lord?* "Mac, I did a lot of thinking while we were in Barbourville."

Mac sat upright with his legs hung over the side of the bunk.

"I wanted to speak with you without Urias hearing because I wanted to speak about him."

"Yes, you seem to have planned out his future."

His words stung. "I'm sorry. I should have spoken with you first. I have nothing compared to the excitement you can offer the child. But what about his education? Surely you would agree he needs an education."

Mac rubbed his hands on his knees. "Yes, he needs an education. But books aren't all a man needs to learn. That boy has been beaten time and again. He needs to learn others don't do that."

"I know." She sat down on the crate across from him. "I think I can give him that if he comes and works for me."

He grasped her hand and held it lightly within his. The warmth of his hands calmed her. "Pamela, I know you mean well, but the boy needs a man in his life, too. A strong man who doesn't strike out at others for no reason, who doesn't bend and hide at the first sign of trouble." His imploring gaze locked with hers. "A man needs to be treated like a man. If he came to work for you, he wouldn't know if he was loved or just hired on."

"Of course I'd love him. If I didn't, I wouldn't offer him—"

He placed his finger to her lips. "Stop. Think, please," he pleaded. "Try and consider this from a man's perspective."

She thought of her brother, her father, and how they had approached problems, how they would focus on a single objective and go after it. *How does that apply to this?* she wondered.

"It's for the boy to choose, anyway," Mac continued. "We can't go deciding his future. He needs to decide on his own." He released her hand and grabbed his sandwich. "This is very good, thank you."

He's done it again. Just like that, he's dismissed me. Pamela's temper soared to the roof of the wagon. "I wasn't through talking with you."

"I'm sorry. What else did you wish to say?" Mac placed his sandwich back down.

"I hate it when you dismiss me like that. When you think you're all-knowing. Just who do you think you are, anyway? The world's number-one expert on anything and everything? Well, you better think again, mister. Because there's one woman who sees through your pompous ways." She stormed out of the wagon.

"Pamela," he hollered.

She continued to walk away from the wagon and on past Urias. "Didn't go so well, huh?"

"That man is thicker than, thicker than. . .oh, I don't know. That rock, I suppose. I need to clear my head. Tell Mr. Rockhead I'll be back in a while." Pamela continued to walk farther away from the road. The roar of water could be heard through the trees. She headed for the sound. Deeper into the woods she went. She'd planned to confess her secret as well, but there was no talking with the man. Just as soon as she allowed herself to start having feelings for him, he stomped all over her heart.

Tears streamed down her face. "Why doesn't anyone ever listen to me, Lord?" She pushed on and found the stream. Water danced lazily over broad, smooth stones, cold and refreshing. She dampened her face.

The Bible verses she'd read the previous night came to mind. *"He leadeth me beside the still waters."*

She looked at the stream. "This water isn't very still, Lord." Looking for some quieter water, she turned upstream. Calm would be a welcome relief. She walked until she reached a small pool, the water so clear she could see down to the bottom.

Pulling the small charm she'd purchased in Barbourville out of her pocket, Pamela sat down. "This isn't working." She raised her hand to pitch it into the pool but held back. The charm was a stone carving of a wolf.

"What do you have there?"

She yelped.

"Sorry, I didn't mean to scare you." Mac leaned against a tree.

She folded it in her palm.

"Pamela, why do we argue so?" He softened his voice.

"I don't know." Tears fought to the edges of her eyes.

"I don't mean to hurt you. I know I'm no good around women, which is why I keep my distance. But it seems every time we talk, we end up arguing. Why is that?"

"I'm sorry. I don't know. I've never had this problem with anyone else. I mean arguing. I've had other men not take me seriously. Like my father and brother when I warned them about coming west. They didn't believe me, and look where it got them. They're both dead."

"When did your brother die?"

She fumbled for an answer. "Not too long ago." At least she wasn't outright lying to him. Could her deceit be a cause of their constant problems?

"I'm sorry for your losses. Look," he said, noticing the pool behind her. "Beside still waters," he whispered.

Pamela looked back at the pool and back at Mac. "Twenty-third Psalm?"

"Yup."

Lord, are You talking to me through Mac? "Mac, I'm sorry we always fight, but do you realize you've never given me credit for knowing anything?"

Mac leaned against the large boulder by the stream. "I'm sorry. I guess in some ways you remind me of Tilly, my wife. We fought a lot before she died."

"I'm sorry. But Mac, I'm not your wife, and I don't know the first thing about your problems with her. I do, however, know a little something about the problems we've been having. For example, you didn't think I was capable in business. Truthfully, I'm not so certain I'll do a great job when it comes to handling money. But I do know some things. What you don't know is that one of my chests has a fake bottom in it with more money than you've probably seen in your entire life. It's the entire Danner family inheritance."

"What? What are you doing carrying that kind of money on you?"

"There was little choice. Quinton decided it was best."

"Woman, you're crazy. Do you have any idea what would happen if word got out about that?"

"All too well." She rubbed her neck, remembering Jasper's ugly paws on it.

Mac let out an exasperated sigh and pulled her into his embrace. "I'm sorry."

She leaned against him and savored his hug. "Mac, I left the money from the sale in the Barbourville bank for that very reason. I didn't want to face another Jasper on the road, and I was certain word would get around about Mr. Croley purchasing my stock."

He leaned against the rock she had once been sitting on and continued to hold her. "I'm sorry, Pamela. I didn't realize. You're a wise woman, and you're right, I haven't given you credit."

"Thank you, Mac. That means a lot." She inhaled the deep musky scent that was all Mac. *Lord, help me, I could stay in this man's arms forever.*

A shot sounded from the direction of the wagon. Mac sprang up and ran. Pamela followed.

❧

Mac ran hard back toward the wagon. His wound protested. Urias sat backwards on one of the horses with his rifle aimed toward the covered wagon.

"What's the matter?" Mac cried.

The barrel of the rifle wobbled as Urias's hands shook. "A bear jumped into the wagon. It's a dumb one, too. He didn't leave when I shot the gun."

"Lower your rifle. I don't want you shooting me when I go in." Mac slipped to the backside of the wagon and pulled open the flaps, then moved to the front and pulled open the front flaps. A young bear stood on all fours eating either his or Pamela's sandwich. Who could tell? "Who cares?" he murmured. "Move on," he yelled at the bear, who merrily ignored him.

"You're right," Mac muttered to Urias. "It is a dumb bear."

Urias turned toward Mac and gave a full bow while keeping his perch on top of the horse.

The easiest way to handle this, Mac figured, would be to coax the critter out with some more food. Mac jumped down and went to the rear and opened the pantry. Pulling out a small ham, he unwrapped it and waved it in the air in front of the bear.

"What are you doing?" Pamela asked, catching her breath.

"A bear," Urias informed her.

She slid beside a tree.

Mac moved the ham slowly around the rear of the wagon.

"My ham?" Pamela's voice squealed.

"All for your safety, my dear." He smiled and continued to coax the bear.

The young bear licked the outer edges of his mouth, having finished the sandwiches, and sniffed the air. Catching the scent, he let out a soft growl.

Mac motioned for Pamela to work her way to the front of the wagon. The bear stumbled to the rear. "Come on, boy. Come and get it," Mac urged. Thoughts raced through his mind. *Where should I toss it? To the side? But would I get enough distance? If I feed him, how long will he follow? If I throw it down the road, I could get more distance between us and the ham. But would the distance be great enough to keep him occupied for a few minutes?*

The front paws of the bear now grasped the back edge of the rear boards. Mac leaned the meat toward the bear's snout. "That's it, Boy, come on."

Raising his snout in protest, the bear growled, then lunged.

Mac tossed the meat down the road and toward the left, hoping it would convince the animal to return to the wilds rather than pursue them. Killing an animal for no reason didn't set well.

"Run!" he shouted to Pam and Urias.

Pamela jumped up on the wagon. Urias flew off the horse and dove in. Mac ran and leapt up into the rear of the wagon. Pamela had the reins in her hands in seconds. The horses didn't need any encouragement to run and took off hard. No one spoke a word. Twenty minutes later, Mac took the reins.

Slowing the team down, he encouraged Urias, "You can put your gun down now, son."

The boy's white knuckles proved he was still concerned. "Will he come back?" Urias asked, not taking his gaze from the road behind them.

"Possibly, but his belly should be full enough to give us some distance."

Pamela slipped inside the wagon. The memory of the warmth and softness of her resting in his arms brought back the fresh clean scent of her golden hair. Mac's heart fluttered. So wonderful were those feelings, he'd started to consider thoughts of kissing her. He didn't know whether to be upset or grateful for the intrusion of their furry friend. "A blessing," he muttered.

"What?" Urias asked.

"Sorry, I was thinking how young the bear was. That's a real blessing."

"Oh. Was it a young bear who gave you the scars?"

Mac groaned.

"I ain't goin' to tell no one. But seein' that bear made me remember your story. I ain't big enough to wrestle no bear and live, like you." Urias looked down at his feet.

"Let's hope you never have to. The bear I wrestled was much older." Mac swallowed a lump thicker than the regret he'd felt a moment before when considering his growing affections toward Mrs. Danner. *I suppose I could always pay her a visit next spring when I return. Creelsboro isn't too far from Jamestown, and perhaps the young widow might be ready. . . .*

What am I thinking? Lord, help me. You know I've sworn off women.

Chapter 14

Pamela stuffed the Indian charm back into her purse. She doubted it had any effect on what just happened between Mac and the bear. But another part of her couldn't help but wonder. She also knew that Mac didn't believe in such things, and his Christian faith seemed firmly rooted. *Am I that weak, Lord? Have I been playing games with You?* She considered Angus and the others. They'd always lived in fear. Mac was the complete opposite; he faced his fears. If she had heard Urias correctly, Mac's wife had died from a bear attack. *I doubt I'd be able to face another bear, Lord.*

She straightened the supplies in the back of the wagon. The loss of the ham would change the meals she'd planned, but she knew Mac would hunt up something. She would not go hungry with him around.

The wagon bounced. She slipped and lost her footing. "Ouch."

"Y'all right?" Urias peeked his head in.

She didn't turn to look at him. "I'm fine."

Mac seemed to understand the boy. She wanted to help. Was it wrong to encourage him to get an education, to give him a job?

She reached for the canvas flaps to close the wagon's cabin. Exhaustion washed over her, and she lay down on the bed.

❧

"Hey sleepyhead, time to get up."

"Huh?" Pamela blinked. Her head felt like tangled wool just waiting to be spun.

"We're here." Urias smiled. "Mr. Mac said to wake you up. He's taken care of the horses. There's plenty of room in the tavern for us. And don't be fretting about that ham. Me and Mr. Mac will hunt us some food if we need it. But this place smells great."

Pamela sat up on the bed, adjusted her hair, and sniffed the air. Her stomach gurgled. The thought of not having to cook and to simply sit down at a fine meal pleased her immensely. "Thanks. Where are we?"

"Halfway to Lynn Camp. We should make it there tomorrow. I gotta go clean up." Urias jumped out of the wagon. "I'll see ya inside."

Her mouth dry and none too fresh, Pamela snipped a small piece of dried mint from her herb collection she'd brought along. The brittle leaf crunched, but its oils refreshed the palate.

The house had a large front porch that spanned the entire length of the building. A warm orange glow in the sky revealed tomorrow should be a very pleasant day for travel.

Pamela blinked going from the dim light outdoors to the even dimmer light indoors. A stout woman in her forties greeted her with a smile. "Welcome. Your menfolk already secured your rooms and let me know y'all be dining this evening."

"Hi. I'm Pam Danner." Pamela extended her hand.

The woman wiped hers on her apron. "I'm Bess Smith; Hyram is in the barn with your husband."

"Mac's not my husband."

"Oh, well, we don't—"

Pamela raised her hands to stop the woman. "Mac will be sharing the room with Urias. I'll be staying in the single room."

"All right." She creased her forehead.

"Mac's escorting me to Creelsboro."

"I see."

It was plain as the woman's face she didn't, but Pamela decided not to argue.

"Take a seat and I'll serve ya soon. Or you can go up to your room. It's the first room on your right when ya reach the top of the stairs."

"Thank you." Pamela decided to sit and wait for Urias and Mac.

Dinner proved very enjoyable once Mrs. Smith understood the circumstances of their traveling together. Of course, the woman now believed her guest was a recent widow. Her belly full, Pamela got up to stretch her legs before retiring for the evening.

"May I join you?" Mac asked.

"Sure. Urias, would you like to come?"

"Nah, I'm going to take in some target practice. Mac showed me a few things while you were sleeping."

"You fired a gun and I didn't wake up?" Pam knew she slept well but. . .

Mac chuckled. "No, though I'd wager you could have slept through it if we had."

"You were snoring." Urias laughed.

"I don't snore," Pamela protested, then promptly sneezed.

"Must be a cold coming on." Mac smiled.

Urias pushed himself from the table. "I'll see ya soon."

She watched him tuck his unruly red curls under his cap and exit the tavern. "He's an interesting kid."

"Yeah. I like the manners he's been showing, but I'm praying they aren't a way of trying to convince us he's something that he isn't."

"Is he old enough to be that deceitful?"

Mac helped pull her chair from the table. *What's this new behavior in Mac?* she wondered.

Pamela inhaled deeply as she stepped outside, the fresh air a welcome relief. The tavern's heat and the odors from the cooking no longer seemed quite so wonderful now that she had a full stomach.

Mac walked beside her and folded his hands behind him. "Pamela, I want to apologize. I've been far too hard on you."

"I don't know what I'm doing out here. This is my father's dream, my. . . Quinton's dream. I never wanted to leave Virginia in the first place. And it didn't help any with Angus's warnings before we left."

They continued walking along the road. The stars sparkled like finely polished silver.

"Who's Angus?"

"An old slave who worked for my parents. He's been around all my life. He said he read it in the leaves."

Mac placed his hand on her and stopped. "I thought you were a Christian."

"I am." She looked down at her feet. "Look, I know most Christians say not to believe in such stuff, but I hear them saying and doing things all the time that show they really do. Like the number thirteen. Can a number be a bad number?"

"No, I don't believe thirteen is a bad number, and personally, I don't care what others believe. But I do care about you, Pamela, and I'd hate to see you trusting in what the Bible calls the elemental spirits of this world. There's no question some of these spirits have some sort of power, but I think people give them more power than they really have. I'd love to continue this discussion, but it's getting darker and we should return. Will you stay outside and sit on the porch with me?"

"All right, but my father and Quinton argued until they were exasperated with me."

Mac roared. "Well, we know I can get that way with you, too. Come on, let me explain my thinking on the matter."

Pamela slipped her arm through the crook of Mac's elbow as he escorted her back to the house. *Lord, what's wrong with me? I love just holding on to this man.*

"I think you heard me mention Black Hawk, my Indian friend."

Pamela acknowledged his comment with a slight nod of her head.

"Well, Black Hawk had a religion that the Bible mentions as believing in the elemental spirits of this world. It's the one his ancestors taught him. His beliefs ran deep, very deep. I used to spend hours talking with him about God, the Bible, and the difference between the Great Spirit he knew and the Holy Spirit I know. To make a long story short, it took stripping the man of his heritage, forcing him to live in a place he didn't want to live, before God got through to him. I'm not saying that means what we've done in moving the Indians west is right. I'm just saying that it was what the Lord used to reach Black Hawk. My friend could relate to the Jews who were taken from their land and used as slaves.

"I don't believe all this hardship comes just so you can learn to trust God, but. . ."

Pamela pulled the charm from her purse. "I bought this in Barbourville."

"Do you know what it is?"

"They said it was an Indian charm for good luck."

Mac grabbed the charm and huffed. "No, it's a fetish. It represents a spiritual guide in the form of a wolf to lead you."

"Well, once the bear was in the wagon, I knew it wasn't working."

"Answer me honestly, Pam. Would you really want the spirit of an animal guiding you rather than the Spirit of our mighty God in heaven?"

"Of course not." She sighed. *But isn't that what I've been doing?*

"You said your friend read tea leaves. Can the leaves of tea sticking to the bottom of your cup really say anything?"

"No. Well, I don't know. It's too hard to say. So many things Angus said over the years came true."

"I can't explain how that happens, but I know I serve a God who's real. He's alive and. . ." Mac paused.

Pamela reached out and grabbed his hands. "What's the matter?"

"I just answered some of my own questions."

"You? You have questions about God? I thought you were like a preacher, you know so much."

Mac chuckled. "Far from it. And I'm not perfect, Pamela. If anyone has seen that, it's you."

"What questions were just answered for you?"

"The last verse of the Twenty-third Psalm."

"You've been reading that, too?" *Does everyone read this psalm?* she wondered.

"For years, but I just understood what the first verse, 'The Lord is my shepherd,' is saying. The last verse concludes with 'Surely goodness and mercy shall follow me all the days of my life.' I mean, I wouldn't allow myself to live in God's grace because of blaming myself for Tilly's death."

"Mac, what happened to Tilly?"

For the next few minutes Mac described his relationship with Tilly, how they courted, married, and moved to the mountains. She didn't like living in the mountains and wanted to return home. Apparently, she'd never really loved him but had married him for the family inheritance she felt would be hers one day.

"I haven't spoken about this for a couple years now, and in a few short days I've spoke on it three, no, four occasions."

"I'm sorry."

"Don't be. I'd like to be friends, Pamela. I know I haven't been the most sociable of persons, but you impress me." He fumbled with the charm in his hand. "You don't need this, Pam. You simply need to trust God, even when death encircles you."

Pam closed her eyes and bowed her head. In some far reach of her mind, she knew his words were correct, but she doubted she had faith that strong.

"I won't force you to throw this away. But I think you should." He placed it back in her hands. It felt heavy, cold, lifeless.

"Good night, Pamela. I'll see you in the morning."

She sat there for a while and let the evening's words replay in her mind. If God was her Shepherd, did she need to believe in omens and elemental spirits? Identifying the omens, the Indian charms, or fetishes as "elemental spirits" caused her to rethink the matter.

An owl screeched.

Pam jumped up and went to bed.

᠊᠊

Mac felt years younger the next morning as he harnessed the team. He'd spent his devotions praising God, at last reconciled to Tilly's death. She had known better than to leave the house. And she was responsible for her choices. Together, they should have worked things out. But he'd been so hurt by her confession that she'd only married him for the inheritance, he'd left her to fend for herself that day.

Second guessing, blaming oneself, didn't change reality.

"Good morning, Urias."

"You're in a good mood. Mrs. Smith says breakfast is ready when you are."

"Thank you. Tell her I'll be right in. Have you seen Mrs. Danner yet?"

"Nah, but the sun ain't up either."

"Yes, it is. You just don't see it because the mountain is blocking it."

Urias yawned and stretched. "If ya say so. Iffen Pamela doesn't want to sleep on the bed in the wagon, I might just sleep in."

"What kept you up so late?"

"Nothin', really."

Mac looped his arm around the boy's shoulders. "Wanna talk about it?" They headed toward the tavern's front door. "I don't know what to do. I like ya both. I want to learn to hunt and live off the land like you, but I, well, I don't know how to read so good. School ain't been held in high regard in my family. But I've seen you two reading all the time. I see Mrs. Danner working with numbers, and I know I ought to know them, too."

"You're right, a good education is important for a man. He can provide for his family wisely. And being able to live off the land can feed a family well. It's a hard choice. Perhaps you could do both."

Mac opened the door.

"How?"

"How, what?" Pamela smiled.

Mac grinned. Her golden hair, fair skin, and blue eyes set his heart pumping. *She has to feel it, too.* "Urias wants to live with you and me."

"What?" Pamela's voice squeaked.

"What I said," Urias explained as he sat down beside Pamela, "is that I want both educations."

"Ah." Pamela placed the linen napkin in her lap.

Mac sat down across from her.

"Mr. Mac says I can have both."

"How?" Pamela asked.

Urias chuckled. "That was my question."

"Easy." Mac sipped the hot tea from his cup. "The boy lives with you for a couple years. He'll get his education. Then he can come live with me. However, during the summer, I'd like him to live up on the farm in Jamestown. What do you think?"

Pamela looked at Urias. Urias looked at Pamela. Both smiled.

Mac clapped his hands. "Great! That's settled. Let's eat and get ourselves up to Lynn Camp before the sun sets."

Pamela opened her mouth to speak, then promptly closed it.

Feeling more confidence than he'd felt in a long time, Mac proposed another plan, one he favored. "Of course, there is an alternative, but I doubt it would work."

"What alternative?"

"Perhaps Urias could live with us."

Chapter 15

S hocked beyond words, Pamela finished her breakfast in silence. Hours later, sitting beside Mac on the jostling bench seat of the wagon, she continued her silence. Was Mac really suggesting they get married, or was he just teasing with his second alternative? After all, he'd said nothing about marriage. Even Urias, sleeping soundly now in the wagon, hadn't responded to Mac's second plan.

"Pam, I'm sorry. I didn't mean to be forward."

She blinked. However ridiculous his offer had been, it had met with serious interest on her part. How could she have fallen in love with a man she barely knew? It felt like ages since they had started this journey west, yet they weren't halfway to their final destination.

"I'm excited," Mac rambled on.

She continued to blink at him in amazement. Was he excited about marriage? *No! No, it can't be.* She closed her eyes and held them shut for a moment.

"At Lynn Camp there's a beautiful waterfall. When there's a full moon, a moonbow shines over the falls."

"A moonbow?" *What's a moonbow?* And how could she have confused Mac's excitement with her own wayward thoughts of marriage. *Lord, help me. How am I going to handle the rest of this trip?* she silently prayed.

"Yeah, the full moon's rays are reflected in the spray of the waterfall. It's an incredible sight. I've never heard of anything like it anywhere else."

"I would like to see it."

"Not tonight, I'm afraid. We have a new moon." Mac paused. "Pamela, I truly am sorry. I didn't mean to offend. I know you're a widow, and well, I just wasn't thinking."

How could she explain that her being a widow had nothing to do with it? Because she wasn't a widow. "Mac, I'm not—"

"Ouch!" Urias cried out.

"What's the matter?" both she and Mac asked in unison.

"I itch all over, and I've broken out with a bad rash."

Mac pulled back on the reins. Inside the covered wagon, they looked over the rash on the boy's hands and legs.

"Poison ivy," they pronounced together.

Urias raised his right eyebrow. "I itch real bad."

"I can see that," Mac said dryly. "You must have been shooting in a patch of the stuff."

"There were no leaves," he protested.

"Of course not. It's November. Strip to your underdrawers. Pamela, make some cool compresses and apply and reapply them over his skin. I'm going to hunt down some goldenseal root."

Thinking to ask him how he would recognize the plant without its leaves, she decided it would be a stupid question. "All right."

"Urias, call me once you're ready."

Relief washed over her when Mac returned. Urias had been very uncomfortable.

"Pam, do you have a—"

"Right here." She handed him the mortar and pestle she'd pulled out earlier.

"Thanks." Mac ground the mucousy roots to a relatively slimy substance. "A couple weeks back I could have gotten some jewelweed, which is much better for poison ivy, but the goldenseal root should work fairly well."

Pamela noticed he had brought more roots than he ground up. Mac applied the yellow paste. "We're going to keep pressing on, Urias. But if you get too uncomfortable again, just holler."

"Thank you." The boy's eyes seemed swollen. Pamela prayed he hadn't rubbed them with his itchy hands.

"He's very sensitive," she stated.

"I've seen worse. He should be feeling better soon. But he'll be uncomfortable for a few days. He must have been shooting in a thicket of dormant vines."

As the day wore on, Pamela found herself enjoying her conversations with Mac. He actually had a lot to say once she managed to get him talking. Periodically interrupting their conversation, Pam would crawl back to reapply the goldenseal paste to Urias.

By evening they found themselves at Lynn Camp and made their campsite not too far from the waterfall. Urias held his hands and feet in the icy water above the falls as long as his body could stand it. The goldenseal was working, but the scratches in his skin from the dried vines meant he'd be weak as his body fought off the poison oil in his blood.

With the small tent she'd purchased in Barbourville set up, dinner prepared and eaten, and cleanup finished, Pamela found herself walking with Mac toward the falls. The rushing water roared as they drew near. "It's beautiful."

Mac's gaze caught hers. "God creates some mighty fine things."

"Upstream the water doesn't appear to be moving this fast," she noticed.

"The closer you get to the falls, the more rapid the water plunges over the edge. It appears to be about 125 feet across today. I've seen it in the spring when the snow's melting. It can reach three hundred feet across."

"You've been here often?"

He quirked a grin. "A couple times a year. It's on my way back and forth."

He leaned against a large boulder overlooking the falls. He'd drawn back his long black hair, making his rugged and handsome features more pronounced. Desire to reach out and hold him, to absorb his strength, washed over her like the cascading waters beside her.

She took a tentative step toward him.

Their eyes locked.

He leaned toward her, then coughed, breaking their connection. He turned back to the waterfall. "The descent of the waterfall changes during the year. I've seen the pool so full it's only about a forty-five-foot drop. Today it's closer to sixty-five. Its length has been known to reach around seventy."

Waterfall. Feet. Who cares? Hadn't they almost kissed? *Maybe I should jump in and over the falls. Perhaps then he'd notice me.* "Interesting," she responded.

"Come on." He grabbed her hand and led her deeper into the woods.

"Where are we going?" She huffed, trying to keep pace with him. His long legs spanned three times the distance of hers.

"There's a spot up this trail that overlooks the falls. It's simply majestic."

"What about Urias?"

"He'll be fine. We won't stay too late. They say there is only one other place in the world that has a moonbow. It's this most incredible sight. I'm sorry you won't get to see it tonight."

"All right." She felt like Ruth about to say, *"Whither thou goest, I will go."* But quoting scripture, or what she remembered of scripture, with this man seemed risky at best.

He led them through a natural tunnel maybe five feet in length. Its darkness sent a wave of caution through her. "Mac, perhaps we should stay closer to the falls in case Urias needs us."

He stopped and turned before she realized it. Smack. She plowed into his chest. "Sorry." She placed her hands on his chest to push herself back.

Mac placed his hands over hers. "My mistake." He caressed the top of her hands with his.

She looked up into his deep blue eyes. She'd noticed before how they differed from her own. A darker shade. His heart beat strong and vibrant under her hands.

Mac cleared his throat. "I think you're right. We should get back."

Back? Back where? She didn't want to move. Squeezing her eyes closed, she took in a deep breath and stepped away. Perhaps it was time for her to sit in the river. How could one man make her forget all her common sense and sensibilities? *Lord, give me strength.*

❧

They walked back to the overlook in silence. Twice tonight he'd been about to kiss her. *Twice. Am I so weak, Lord?* "Pamela?"

"Hmm?" Her voice alone stirred up sweet images.

How could he ask a widow to court him in a year after she mourned the death of her husband? A year he figured would be a fair amount of time. He could manage a year. He hoped.

"If all goes well, we should get to Creelsboro in a week. We've traveled just about half the distance. If I took you there by the river, we could be there in three days. But I can't imagine trying to float this wagon down the Cumberland." Conversation was better than letting his thoughts carry on.

"I could go down to three, possibly two, trunks."

Mac smiled. "My canoe isn't that large."

"Oh."

"We can drive the wagon. There will be fewer taverns though. At this point we fork off from the Wilderness Road and head west on far less constructed trails. It'll be rough going in some spots."

"I'm sorry. I've been such a— Oh my, that's beautiful," Pamela exclaimed.

Mac turned. A large bird swooped over the waterfall.

She shivered as the crisp night air breezed past. He positioned his body to block the wind for her.

"Thank you."

"You're welcome."

He smiled. "Pamela, have you thought about our conversation regarding Indian charms, omens, and such?"

She nodded her head and looked down at her feet. "I'm not as strong as you. I know you're right, but so much has happened in the past. I don't know what to believe anymore."

"Believe in truth, God's truth, the Bible. The strength of those words is so much stronger than anything man can offer."

Her glance caught his. She turned and looked back at the falls.

"Pam." He placed his hand on her shoulder. "Death is always around us. But life is as well—abundant, radiant life. Like the moon, it's a reflection of light. It isn't the real light that comes from the sun. God loves you, Pam. He aches when you ache. He knows your losses, your hurts, and He knows your joys, your loves, and many other blessings He gives us. Trust Him, Pam, not a piece of stone or some water-soaked tea leaves. Trust real life, abundant life. Trust in Him."

She turned in his arms. Tears streamed down her cheeks. "I want to, Mac, I really do."

Gently he brushed away her tears. Her skin was so soft and velvety against his. His heart pounded in his chest. Slipping his fingers through her golden strands, he groaned and pulled her toward him.

She didn't resist. Her delicate pink lips parted slightly. Slowly his descended upon hers. They tasted like fine honey. He deepened the kiss, pulling her closer and wrapping her protectively in his arms.

She placed her hands upon his chest and pushed back slightly. "Oh Mac," she whispered, her voice shaky.

"Sor—"

She reached up and pulled his head back down. The kiss lingered. All thoughts, the sound of the rushing water, disappeared. It was just the two of them wrapped in each other's arms, savoring each other's kiss.

Then she pulled back. She trembled in his arms. "I'm sorry. I. . .we. . . shouldn't have done that."

How could she say such a thing? How could she think it? Then his clouded mind began to clear. Her husband hadn't even been gone for two weeks, and here he was kissing her senseless. "I'm sorry, Mrs. Danner. I promise it won't happen again."

"No, Mac. It's not what you're thinking."

"Pamela, I know you're vulnerable right now. I've taken advantage, and

I shouldn't have. Forgive me. I don't know what came over me."

"Forgive you? No, Mac. It isn't you. It's me."

He placed his forefinger to her tender lips. "Shh, it's not you. It's me. I'm the man, I'm older, I know better."

"What does that have to do with anything? You and I both know what just happened, and it had nothing to do with you being a man and being older. Wait a minute, I didn't mean that. It did have something to do with you being a man, of course, but. . ."

He loved it when she was riled up. He loved the fire in her eyes, the bright pink that flamed her cheeks. A miscreant smile slid up his cheek.

"I'm a widower, too. I understand these emotions right after your spouse dies. It's my fault."

She placed her hands on her hips. "If my excuse for having kissed you is because I'm missing my husband, what's your justification?"

"I don't know, a moment of weakness on my part. I assure you it won't happen again. A gentleman should never behave in such a manner."

"A gentleman? Since when are you a gentleman?"

"Don't push me, Pamela. I've apologized. Let's just leave it at that."

Mac turned and stomped back toward their campsite. He foolishly had given in to his desires, and now he'd never have an opportunity to ask her formally to court him.

❧

Pamela sat down on the rock and huddled into herself. *Why'd I have to goad the man, Lord? And what's this big deal about whose fault it was? We were both guilty. We both wanted it. I should have told him right then I wasn't married to Quinton, that he's my brother. But he got me so riled up pretending to take full responsibility. Since when is a woman not responsible for her own actions?*

Taking in deeper, more calming breaths, she closed her eyes. "He's right about one thing, Lord. I either trust You or I don't." She took the Indian fetish from her pocket and tossed it into the pool below.

"Father, give me strength. Help me tell Mac the truth." She heard a rustle in the undergrowth behind her. Pamela jumped up and returned to their campsite. Mac and Urias were both in the tent. She would sleep in the wagon. Tonight would be her first night alone under the stars since Quinton's untimely death. Knowing Mac was a shout away didn't ease her worries or concerns. Memories of the bear jumping out of the wagon didn't help either.

Once in bed, she found no rest. Images and emotions repeated over and over again in her mind. Did she truly love Mac, or was she just enamored with him? Pamela rolled to her side and moaned into her pillow. For hours she kept seeing those images, feeling those strong emotions that drew her to him. Every time she pictured herself telling him the truth, he'd storm off.

Unable to sleep, she went back to the waterfall. The water cascading over the rocky cliff drew her. She felt the cleansing work of God near the water's edge. "Father, forgive me. I've been such a fool. I've allowed men's foolish thoughts to interfere with the truth of Your Word."

Pouring her heart out to God, Pamela continued to repent for her past sins, her lack of faith, and for the foolish lies she'd been saying to keep Mac from learning the truth about her relationship with Quinton.

Tears of joy streamed down her face. For the first time in her life, she felt the peace of God. She opened her eyes and saw the heavens on fire. She blinked. Stunned, she stayed on her knees.

She screamed. "Dear Jesus, what have I done now?"

Chapter 16

The heavens blazed with fire. Stars burned as they plummeted toward the earth. *Is it Judgment Day?* Mac scrambled from the tent and ran to the wagon. He had to make things right with Pamela.

She wasn't there.

"Dear Lord, where is she?" He raced back to the waterfall. His heart pounded with excitement and nervous energy. So many stars fell from the heavens it appeared to be day. But he knew it couldn't be. The sky itself remained black.

Pamela was on her knees overlooking the waterfall.

"Thank You, Lord," Mac whispered.

"Pam," he shouted.

There was no response. She couldn't hear him over the rushing waters. He came a bit closer, moving more slowly. He heard her crying. She appeared to be weaving back and forth.

"Pamela," he called again.

She turned, jumped up, and ran to him. "Oh Mac. I am so sorry. I was wrong, so very wrong. And now the end of the world has come and you'll never know."

He opened his arms, and she collapsed into them. "It's not the end of the world." He glanced back up at the sky. "Perhaps it is. But nothing can be that bad."

"I lied, Mac. I lied to you. I'm not who you think I am."

"What? You're not Pamela Danner?"

"No, I mean, yes, I am but. . .oh Mac, I'm so scared. I was praying to God, asking for forgiveness for my life, for lying to you, for everything I've ever done wrong. And when I opened my eyes, the heavens were on fire. I'm such a wretched person. I've insulted God."

"Shh, please slow down and tell me what this is all about." Mac cradled her protectively in his embrace.

He watched as thousands of stars burned long white trails across the sky and continued to fall at an incredible rate. Objectively, he knew she couldn't have sinned so much that her mere confession would set the heavens ablaze, but he couldn't help wondering what she had done to believe she had.

Yet if this was the sign of the return of Christ, how much time on earth did he have left? And why should anyone's sins against him matter? Thankful he'd spent some time with the Lord the previous morning, he knew he had little to repent for. Little, except for the kiss he'd shared with Pamela a few hours ago. Mac fired off another prayer, asking for the Lord's forgiveness.

"Come on," he said gently to Pamela, "let's check on Urias. If one of those fireballs hits, I don't want him to be caught unaware."

She followed in silence. He wondered if she were going into some kind of shock. Not that he wasn't on the border of it himself. Never had he seen anything like this before. The scent of sulfur hung in the air. Was this the hellfire and brimstone some preachers spoke of?

At the campsite Pamela again fell to her knees and continued her silent pleading with God. What had this woman done? And what did she mean by she wasn't who he thought her to be?

The money. He eyed her cautiously. Was she a bank robber? Or worse? Had she caused the wagon to roll and kill her husband? No, that wasn't it. She wasn't that kind of person. She had too much compassion and too much fear to be that brutal. What could she possibly have done that kept her on her knees crying before God?

Father, am I so full of pride that I can't see my own sins? Should I be on my knees repenting? He searched his heart and knew he was free of the guilt of Tilly's death. Daily repentance kept him right before God. Pamela, on the other hand, did have mixed-up views of God. And her beliefs in omens and superstitions were definitely not healthy. *Lord, I know I'm not perfect, but I am content in my relationship with You. I have peace; I'm not afraid.*

Reaching the tent, Mac entered and nudged the boy's shoulder. "Urias, wake up."

"Huh?" A lump of red curls rose from the bedroll.

"The heavens are on fire. You best get right with God Son. I think it might just be the end of the world."

"What?" Urias stuck a finger in his ear and wiggled it.

"Look." Mac flung aside the tent flap and exposed the brilliant view. "The sky is on fire."

Mac grinned. "That is my point. Come on; join Pamela and me. I'm afraid one of these fireballs might hit the wagon or tent."

Urias scrambled for his pants and hiked them up as he stumbled out of the tent. "I swear, I didn't do nothin'."

"Look, I'm not one to force my religion on anyone, but the Bible says in Mark 13:25 that when Jesus comes again, 'the stars of heaven shall fall, and the powers that are in heaven shall be shaken.' The choice is yours."

Urias's eyes widened. "What can I do?"

"Pray, pray like you never have. If this is the end of the world, time is short."

Urias knelt down near Pam and silently pleaded with God.

Mac knelt beside him and praised God. *Father, forgive me for forcing the boy. If this isn't right, help me love him into the Kingdom. I just don't want to see him go to hell.*

After prayers, they all gathered together and sat in silence, watching the heavens burn. Mac kept wondering why he was still here. If this was the end of the world, why hadn't anything happened? Where was God, and why were they still sitting on earth?

"Mac." Pamela's voice cracked.

They'd been watching for hours.

"I'm not a widow. Quinton was my brother."

"What?"

"Quinton was my brother. We weren't married."

Anger welled up within him. She'd lied. She did say she had a brother, but. . . He'd felt so guilty for kissing a recently widowed woman, only to discover now that she wasn't a widow. "But you said—"

"I never said he was my husband. You said it. I simply didn't correct the mistake. I didn't know you. I feared for my safety. A man was more than likely going to give a woman more sympathy for being a widow than a—a. . ."

Mac took in a deep breath. She'd deceived him for her own selfish reasons, and he'd fallen into her trap. Just as he had for Tilly. *What kind of fool am I?*

"Fine," he said, cutting her off. "You repented. It's between you and God, not me."

"I'm sorry." She left Mac and Urias and returned to the wagon as the last of the fiery missiles streaked across the blackness.

❧

Pamela snuggled under the covers. Fear over the past couple hours had exhausted her. Finally, Mac knew the truth. But the pain she'd seen in his eyes—Tilly had deceived him, and he'd married her. She knew he felt the same sting from her own omission.

&

The next few days went by in silence. Urias wasn't too sure about his forced prayer to give himself to God. Mac barely spoke a word. And Pamela listened to other travelers speaking about the night it rained fire. Many, like Urias, had confessed their sins and accepted salvation due to fear. If she was grateful for anything, it was that she'd confessed her sins before the stars burned.

They reached Jamestown in five days. Mac's parents willingly opened their home to Pamela and Urias. She wondered if she could travel the next two days to Creelsboro on her own. Or possibly hook up with another group of travelers heading down there. Of course, Mac wouldn't hear of such a thing. He still took his oath to Quinton seriously, and no matter what his feelings might be about her, he'd fulfill his promise. Pam knew that in the depths of her heart. She ached for Mac. She wasn't like Tilly, at least she hadn't meant to be. The closer she came to Creelsboro, the more she didn't want to go. Her father's dream had become her nightmare. Where would she ever find peace?

Pam worked her way toward the woods behind the farmhouse. She needed time to think. The dry, empty fields ready for planting next spring reminded her of how empty her own heart was. She'd fallen in love with a man who could never love her because she'd deceived him. There had been peace, comfort, a sense of belonging when she was wrapped in Mac's arms. Now, she'd never know that peace again, unless. . .

She eyed the large farmhouse. She thought about her experiences on the trail the past five days. They'd been long and hard. When Mac had said the road wouldn't be as nice as the Wilderness Road, he hadn't been fooling. Mac had taken to running again. He had let Urias and herself ride the wagon. He claimed he needed to keep his muscles in shape or he wouldn't be able to get back to his winter cabin before the severe storms hit.

The image of the rugged mountain man dressed in his leathers, running ahead of them or beside them, sent chills down her spine. His long black hair danced on his shoulders as he stepped with a perfect beat. "God, what can I do to show him I'm not like Tilly?"

"Hello," a gentle feminine voice called from behind Pam.

She closed her eyes, took in a deep breath, and turned to face Mac's mother. "Mrs. MacKenneth. I'm sorry, I didn't hear you come up." Had

Mac learned that trait from his mother?

"When I'm lost in thought, I often don't hear so well. Nash has told me about your losses. I'm sorry."

Nash? Oh, right, Mac's first name. He seemed more like a Mac than a Nash. "Thank you."

"He's also been telling me about this young boy you two rescued on the road. He says you've offered him a job at your store."

"Ah, yes. Mac also invited Urias to come and live with him," Pamela replied.

"Forgive me for being forward, dear, but why would you want to take on the responsibility?"

Pamela didn't know anymore. "I like the boy, and I thought I could help him receive an education. He isn't able to read, you know. He thinks he's hidden it from us, but I've seen the signs before."

"I taught my children at home."

Pamela smiled. She'd wondered where Mac had received his education. "You were a good teacher."

"Nash always had a way with books and learning. Betsy, well, she couldn't be bothered with it. Lisa loved to read, but numbers. . .she just never got the hang of them." Mac's mother motioned to the space on the bench beside Pamela. "May I?"

Pamela slid over. "Of course."

"My dear, if I'm being nosy, just tell me, but what happened between you and Nash?"

Pamela kneaded her hands in her lap. "Nothing, we just sort of grated against each other from the start."

Mrs. MacKenneth looked down her pencil-straight nose and raised her eyebrows.

"It didn't help that I lied to him," Pam added.

"Ah, about your being married."

She nodded. "I never really said I was married to Quinton. Mac assumed it, and I just felt I was safer if he believed I was a widow. Is that so wrong? A woman alone in the wilderness with nothing more than a tall mountain man looming over me?"

Mrs. MacKenneth chuckled. "I see your point. But once you knew you could trust him, shouldn't you have told him the truth?"

"I tried, but every time something came up or we'd argue about something else. Begging your pardon, Mrs. MacKenneth, but your son can be a pretty obstinate man."

The older woman patted Pamela's knee. "Oh, I seem to know a little about that. Tilly didn't understand that, and she pushed and pushed Nash. He's never talked much about what happened between the two of them, but something happened on his trip here with you. He's finally released the guilt he's carried for so long."

A loud clanging noise echoed in Pamela's ear. Mrs. MacKenneth jumped up and ran toward the house. "Emergency," she hollered.

❧

Mac laid his father on his bed. "I'll get the doctor."

"What's wrong?" His mother's voice shook as she glanced through her bedroom doorway.

"Dad's hurt. I think he might have broken a hip. I'm going to get the doctor. I'll be back as soon as I can." He slipped on his coonskin cap and within two strides was out the front door.

"What's the matter?" Pamela asked, huffing. Catching her wind, she braced herself against the porch railing.

"Father's had an accident. I'm getting the doctor. Help my mother." Mac jumped off the porch. "Please."

He ran toward the center of town. Finding the doctor at his home had been an answer to prayer. Within seconds they were in the doctor's carriage and speeding back to the farmhouse.

Hours later, Mac had some memory of telling the doctor all he knew about the accident, but when he found himself pacing the front porch, he had no true memory of the event. Had he dreamed it? Was it real? Had the accident even happened?

The front door opened with a creak. "Doc, how is he?" Mac asked. Everyone gathered around the doctor.

"His hip is broken. You called it right. Hopefully it will mend well. He'll need to stay off it for weeks."

Mac nodded. He would make certain his father stayed down. "Thank you."

"You're welcome. Sorry I couldn't give you better news. I've set the bones in place as best I could, but it's up to the good Lord to bring healing in a joint like that."

Mac swallowed the lump in his throat. He couldn't picture his father an invalid. The man hadn't been sick a day in his life except for a sniffle now and again. "I'll take care of him."

"You do that, son. I'd best get going. The missus baked me an apple pie, and all that good cooking in your kitchen got my stomach a-churning. Good night, Mac."

"Night, Doc."

Urias stood beside him. "Does this mean we won't be going to your cabin in the gap?"

"Afraid so."

"What about bringing Mrs., I mean, Miss Danner to Creelsboro?"

The point of Pamela not being Mrs. Danner still stuck in the pit of his stomach. "Tell the folks I'll be back shortly."

"But, what about—"

"Later." Mac ran off again, this time to the neighbor's farm. If anyone could be trusted to take Pamela Danner to Creelsboro, it was Tanner James, his childhood friend and neighbor.

Thirty minutes later he stood on Tanner's front porch, explaining the situation. After a quick handshake, the men parted. Tanner would take Pamela Danner to Creelsboro in the morning. Urias would join them, and the boy would then decide where he wanted to live.

Mac reached the farm about dusk. The dim light from the oil lamps glowed, welcoming him home.

"Nash, your father's been asking to see you." His mother wrapped her soft, cuddly arms around him.

"How is he?"

"In a lot of pain, but the medication the doctor gave him has been helping."

Pain medication. His father would never take the stuff unless he was in agony. Mac released his mother and went to his parents' room. His father lay motionless on the bed. This once-vibrant man appeared weak. Mac's stomach tightened. Beside the bed, a lone chair stood. He knew his mother had kept it warm since the accident. He sat down and prayed.

"Nash," his father croaked. "I'm glad you're here, son. I'll need you to take care of the farm."

"You know I will. I've asked Tanner to take Miss Danner to Creelsboro."

His father gripped his hand and gave it a gentle squeeze. "Thank you. God brought home at the right time, son."

Mac smiled. "Yeah, I believe He did. Rest, Father. I'll see you in the morning."

His father nodded his sparsely covered head, then closed his eyes.

Mac got up to leave the room and found Pamela in the doorway with a tray of food. No doubt she'd overheard the news that he wouldn't be taking her to Creelsboro.

"I thought you might like to have something to eat while you visited with your father," she said.

He reached for the tray. "Thank you. I'll eat in the kitchen."

She nibbled her lower lip. "I take it I leave in the morning?"

"Yes. I've asked Tanner James to escort you to Creelsboro. He's a good man. I've known him since I was five. You can trust him. And he knows you're not a widow."

She pursed her lips.

Mac sighed. "Sorry, that was uncalled for. I'm tired, and I have a lot on my mind."

"I'll go pack." Pamela retreated down the hallway, the hem of her skirt fluttering out behind her.

Tomorrow couldn't come soon enough. Every time he saw her, he wanted to wrap her in his arms. But he'd been a fool once, and he wasn't about to be a fool again. Tilly had taken every ounce of trust he had in the opposite sex and thrown it away. Pamela was no different. She was a liar, too. He had to keep reminding himself of that. It was the only sane thing to do.

He set the tray on the kitchen table and removed the pie tin she'd placed over his plate. The aroma made his stomach gurgle. Unlike Tilly, the woman could cook. Bowing his head, he said a prayer of thanks and asked the Lord to give Pamela safe passage to Creelsboro.

The next morning he found himself up early milking the cows, tending the chickens, feeding the livestock. Tanner and his wife, Elsa, drove over in their wagon. After brief introductions, he waved Tanner, Pamela, and Urias on their way to Creelsboro. Elsa returned to her farm.

Later Mac found himself in the barn. He noticed lots of little things that were out of place, partially finished. His father was slowing down. Perhaps the time had come for him to stay in Jamestown and take over the farm.

Chapter 17

Creelsboro was a small town full of people. More people traveled through the area than actually lived there, Pamela had observed over the past two months. She had finally decided to put the store up for sale and hoped to return home to Virginia in the spring.

If she'd learned anything over the past several weeks, it had been that she didn't belong in Creelsboro, never had. Quinton would have thrived here. But Pam knew she could never enjoy it. Marriage proposals came daily from men heading west. The other merchants didn't take her seriously until they needed some of her stock.

She'd set up a system of regular shipments of supplies that kept her store well stocked. The prices she could charge for items were practically criminal. But there was no joy in turning a profit. Her mind continued to replay the events of November thirteenth, the night it rained fire. The night she fell in love and lost him.

People still spoke of that night. Some folks had started attending church services after their hurried confessions. At recent Sunday services, however, she'd noticed the congregation thinning. Thankfully, her confession had not brought down the heavens. But the fear of that moment still struck deep in her heart as a reminder to stay right with the Lord and not fall into the silly notions she had been so easily swayed by.

News was spreading of a scientist, Denison Olmsted, and his findings about the meteor shower. He claimed folks from Boston to Ohio had seen the incredible display. He also said it would be seen again—that the meteors were from a cloud in space. Pamela wouldn't argue the man's findings; they seemed logical. She only knew that God had used that night to set her on the right track with Him. That she didn't need to live in fear of the elemental spirits of this world, as Mac had pointed out.

The thought of moving back home to Virginia where she had friends and neighbors was her only refuge. Living alone in a settlement full of men brought an even greater sense of loneliness. She knew she could never love another man as deeply as she loved Mac.

The bell above the door jangled. Pam glanced over. "Urias." She smiled.

"Hi, Miss Danner. How are you?"

"Fine, fine. Tell me, what brought you down to Creelsboro? You look like you've grown a couple inches. What are they feeding you on that farm?"

Urias grinned and stuffed his thumbs behind his suspenders. "Lots. But it's hard work, and Mrs. MacKenneth insists on my schoolin'. She taught Mac, ya know."

"I know." Pam opened her arms. "Come here; give me a hug. I've missed you."

Urias bounced over the counter and gave her a bear hug.

"How's Mr. MacKenneth? Mac's dad," she qualified. She didn't want Urias to think she was asking about Mac. Not that she didn't want to know, longed to know, how he was doing.

The boy hoisted himself up on the counter. "Doing good. He's gettin' around with a couple canes now."

"That's wonderful. I've prayed for him often."

Urias smiled.

"What did you say brought you down here?"

"Supplies." Urias crossed his arms and looked around. "Not bad. You own all this?"

"For a little while. I'm selling it and moving back East."

"Why? I mean, after all it took to get here."

"It's a long story really, but I never wanted to move here. It was my father's dream and my brother's."

Urias nodded his head and nibbled his inner cheek.

"Do you have a list for the supplies you need?"

"Oh, sorry. Nope. Mac's gettin' 'em."

"Oh." Obviously Mac didn't want to see her. It didn't matter that she ached to see him.

The bell on the doorjamb jingled. A blast of cold air filled the room.

"Parson Kincaid, what can I do for you?"

He removed his black hat and folded it in his hands. The thin, middle-aged man was dressed in black from head to toe except for the backward collar of white. "Miss Danner, there is a reason for you to come to the church."

Pamela placed her hand on the counter, bracing herself. What could she have done wrong? "What's the matter?"

"Truthfully, I've never heard of such a thing. But the gentleman insists."

"Parson, is everything all right?"

"Honestly, I'm not sure. In all my years, I've never seen it done this way."

Curiosity was definitely getting the best of her. "All right. Let me gather my coat."

Parson Kincaid nodded his head and placed his hat back upon it. Pamela slipped to the back room and retrieved her wool coat.

Urias stood by the parson. "Would you like me to come?" His freckled face didn't hold the same joy it had moments before.

Perhaps it was wise to have him with her. Not that she couldn't trust Parson Kincaid. He and his wife, Martha, had shown her great kindness over the past couple months. He'd helped her understand that repentance freed her from God's judgment, that she didn't have to live in fear.

"Sure." She slipped the key from the folds of her apron, locking the door after they all exited.

They walked in silence across the hard, rutted street. Winter frost lined the tops of the ruts. When they entered the church, she found it warm and comfortable. "Go to the altar," the parson instructed. "There's a message for you there."

She opened her mouth to speak. He smiled and placed a hand on Urias's shoulder. "You'll need a few minutes. I'll keep the boy with me. Holler if you need me."

Pamela's insides quivered like a new fawn trying to stand on its legs for the first time. Working her way down the center aisle, she approached the small oak table with white painted sides and a dark stained top. Carved on the front panel were the words REMEMBER ME. She closed her eyes, knowing the words were Christ's regarding communion. On top of the table a small oval of white lace accented a small circle of gold. A rolled-up piece of paper rested within the band.

Her hands trembled.

She reached for the band and pulled out the paper. Unfurling the note, she read the words, *"Forgive me."*

❧

Mac stood in the shadowed room off to the side of the altar. Pamela dropped the note and braced herself, holding the edges of the table. With her head bent, she asked, "Where are you, Mac?"

Closing the distance between them, he silently stood behind her. "Right here," he whispered. A whiff of her delicate perfume tickled his nostrils. "I've missed you."

"I don't understand." Her profiled body held fast, not turning around to face him. Her knuckles whitened.

Father, help me say the right words here. "I'm sorry for not giving you a chance to speak. Mother's made it abundantly clear that I was rather hardheaded."

A gentle smirk rose on her pink lips.

"Please, forgive me, Pamela. I held against you what Tilly had done to me. It wasn't right, and it wasn't fair. I can't blame you for being afraid in a wilderness area with no one to trust. And most importantly, with Jasper hot on your trail. I assumed you were Quinton's widow. Your decision to simply let me continue with that misimpression was no different from my choice to let Jasper think we were married."

Her body trembled.

He ached to close the distance between them but didn't dare.

She squeezed her eyes tighter. "I loved you," she confessed. "You hurt me."

He took the final step that remained between them. He could feel the heat from her body. Still she remained resolute, not wavering.

"I'm sorry." He dropped to his knees and placed a hand over hers.

"Why didn't you come to the store? Why haven't you tried to contact me? A letter, a message, something. . .I don't understand. You couldn't get rid of me fast enough." She turned and looked down at him.

"I wanted to. I really did. But I didn't know how. I've been praying and waiting. Honey, the waiting has been the hardest part. I wanted to come before now. But Father needed me. The farm couldn't be left unattended for that long a period. I even thought of sending Urias. But God said no. He said to wait. I love you, Pamela. I know it seems rather late to say that, but I do with all my heart. I never thought I could love another woman. I put myself in an area where few women lived. And the ones who were nearby were married. I tried, I really tried to avoid women. But God had other plans. I know that now. But I fought Him every step of the way."

Tears fell down her face.

Mac stood and pulled her close. "I'm so sorry. I love you. I want us to be together. I've even arranged for us to be married."

She placed her hands on his chest and pushed out of his embrace. "You what? This ring is for today?"

He looked down and scuffed the floor with his right foot. "Uh, yeah."

"You are really something, Mac. You come into my life and expect me to just drop everything and go running off with you." She placed her hands on her hips. "I have responsibilities, you know. I guess you expected me to just marry you and ride off into the sunset, forgetting any responsibilities I might have."

That had been the plan. It had sounded good before he heard it from her lips. Now he wasn't too sure. "Yeah."

A whistle went streaming through her teeth. "Have you heard of courting?"

"Yes, but. . ." How could he word this without losing her?

"Mac, there's a lot we have to know about each other before we talk marriage."

"Like what?" He sat down on the front pew. She came up beside him and sat down.

"I don't know. But we don't know each other all that well."

"We traveled together for almost three weeks, isn't that enough?" His voice rose.

"Shh," Pam admonished and placed her hand upon his.

This is not going the way I had planned. He sighed.

"Mac, I. . ."

He turned, embracing her, and captured her lips.

She moaned. *Or was that him?*

Pulling away, she gasped, "Mac, stop."

"I love you, Pam. I want you."

"I love you, too, but. . ."

Joy filled him. He placed his finger on her lips. "Don't, not just yet. Let me enjoy what you just said."

Pamela shook her head from side to side and laughed. "It wouldn't be boring."

"What?"

"Marriage to you."

"Please, Pamela. Please marry me. I brought Mother and Urias as witnesses. I even convinced Parson Kincaid that you'd agree."

"No, Mac. Not here, not now. Not like this."

"I don't understand." He slumped back into the pew.

"Let me try to explain. I have a business. Are you planning on staying in Creelsboro?"

"No, I thought you'd come back to the farm with me. I know you didn't want the business."

"You're right. I don't, and I've put it on the market."

"See." He felt like a little boy.

"See what? That I should be irresponsible and just lock up the business and not sell it first?"

"It'll sell."

"Yes, it will. But if I simply closed the store, I'd lose money on the sale. I'm certain you are aware that an active, successful business is worth far more than a closed one."

"I don't care about money."

Pamela chuckled. "I know. And I'm not as concerned as you think. But I do believe the Bible tells us to be good stewards of what we have. And I don't believe it's being a good steward to simply walk away from one's obligations. In the same way that you couldn't walk away from your father's need for you on the farm."

"Very well, you've made your point. But I still want to get married."

Pamela chuckled. Seeing Mac pout sent an image of a young boy, their son, and how he would behave in years to come. "I do, too," she confessed.

"You mean it?"

"Yes." She smiled.

"Yahoo!" he shouted.

"But not today."

"When?"

"In time. A woman needs to plan her wedding, make her dress, prepare, you know?"

"Honey, I don't understand women all that well. You, for one, know that. But if you need time, I can wait."

"Mac, where will we live? On the farm? In the wilderness? Where?"

"The farm. Dad will never be able to run it again. He'll get around and all, but he won't have the strength. However, we'll need to take a trip back to my cabin in the gap. There are some items I'd like to keep." He leaned up beside her. "I thought we could make it a romantic getaway for just the two of us."

"Oh Mac." She threw herself into his arms and kissed him. "I'd love that. There is one thing you should know." She whispered into his ear.

"You traveled with that much?" His eyes bulged.

"Yes. Can you handle the dowry?"

"I guess. What are we going to do with that kind of money?"

"Building our own private house might be nice."

Mac laughed. "Anything you'd like. Just promise me you'll marry me?"

"I promise." His sweet lips were upon hers before she could say another thing. *Thank You, Lord, for the night it rained fire.*

Hogtied

Dedication

I'd like to dedicate this book to my granddaughter, Hannah Elizabeth.
Having four older brothers will present some challenges
in your life as well as great blessings. All my love Hannah,
and Grandma loves your beautiful smile.

Chapter 1

U rias, please reconsider."

"Mom, I've prayed. I've got to go."

Dad came up beside her and massaged her shoulders. "You go, son. Do what you have to do; but remember, we'll need you in time for the spring planting."

"Yes sir. You two mean the world to me. I promise I'll be back." Mom and Dad MacKenneth had opened their home to him seven years ago. They'd become his family, and he now looked differently on life.

Pamela MacKenneth stepped toward him and wrapped her arms around him. Urias embraced her tenderly. "I promise, if I can't find her this year, I'll leave her in the Lord's hands and trust that she's all right."

"I understand. I'll miss you terribly. Don't forget to say good-bye to Grandma and Grandpa," she encouraged.

"You think I'd be able sit again if I didn't say good-bye to them?" His adopted parents laughed. *Well, that helped lighten the mood a little*, Urias mused.

"Did you pack all the items we went over, son?" his father asked.

"Yeah. Thanks for all the help."

"You know I would love to be hiking up those mountains with you."

He knew all too well. His father loved the mountains, but he loved his family more. When Urias had first met up with Pam and Nash "Mac" MacKenneth, they'd been working their way through the Cumberland Gap area along the Wilderness Road. Somehow it seemed far more than seven years ago. Grandpa Mac had an accident, and Urias's adopted father took over the care of the family farm. Of course, he and Mom weren't married at that time, and it took a bit before Dad came to his senses and asked her to marry him. But he finally had, and now they were a family of six—including Urias.

But Urias needed to find his first family now. He'd heard rumors that his younger sister was living in the Hazel Green area around Mount Sterling. He'd gone last year and hadn't found her. In 1837, Urias and his family had attended an Association at Hardshell Baptist Church. That's when he heard someone mention they once knew an O'Leary—and she had red hair just like him. Of course, red hair and Irish names seemed to go hand in glove. But he'd been searching for Katherine every fall right after the harvest ever since. This year he'd stay through the winter and give it one final look. It didn't matter that he'd given every merchant he met his name and a message as to how he could be reached in Jamestown.

Unfortunately, Jamestown was several days' travel from the Hazel Green area.

Sucking in a deep breath, Urias broke the merriment. "I gotta go. Pray for me."

"You know we will, Urias." Pam wiped the tears from her eyes.

Urias choked back his own. These two people loved him so much. He never felt anything less than a part of their family.

"Urias," Nash Jr. called out from behind him. Urias turned toward the young boy's voice.

"Hey buddy, what ya got there?"

"A present." Urias remembered the first time he held Nash when he was only a few hours old. It didn't seem possible that people could start out that small.

"Is it for me?" Setting his Kentucky long rifle against the wall, Urias knelt on one knee to put himself at a more equal footing with the boy.

"Uh-huh." Nash handed it to him with a smile that lit up the small child's face. It was wrapped in a scrap of cloth he recognized Mom had been working on a few days before.

"Thank you." Urias opened the cloth and found an old arrowhead. "This is wonderful, Nash. Thank you."

"If your powder gets wet, you can use it to fight off a bear." Personally, Urias hoped he wouldn't have to fight off any bear, ever. The scars on Mac's back were enough of a warning to stay clear of those critters as much as humanly possible.

He reached out and ruffled the boy's thick black hair. It was so much like his father's. "I'll remember that."

Dad winked.

Mom held back a chuckle at the boy's naiveté.

When the MacKenneths and Urias first met, he had a minor run-in with a bear. Thankfully, it was more interested in their ham than in them.

"Urias," his sisters said in unison. Molly, the older of the two, smiled. Her first two adult teeth were just beginning to show in the empty space. Sarah was two years younger than Molly, but she kept trying to wiggle her front teeth, hoping they'd come out soon like her big sister's had. Molly had long, dark, curly hair like her father. Sarah had straight brown hair like her mother.

Molly held a hand-wrapped package with a bow around it. "We made these for you."

"They're your favorite," Sarah added.

"Thank you, ladies. They smell wonderful," he said as he took the bundle of cookies and placed it in his pack.

He hugged and kissed each of his siblings, said his good-byes, and headed to his grandparents' house. He and Mac had built it after Grandpa Mac's accident—a single story, with ramps to go in and out of the place. Grandpa had been in a wheelchair for seven years, and Grandma tended to his every need. She also attended to Urias's education. After a brief but cheery good-bye, he headed out on horseback toward the mountains. "Lord, please let me find Katherine this time."

❧

"Kate," Prudence called as she entered the darkened barn. She'd seen her retreat there once before. "Kate," she called once again.

"Pru?"

"Yes, it's me. Where are you?" Prudence blinked as her eyes adjusted to the lack of sunlight.

"Up here in the loft," Kate whispered.

Prudence climbed up the rustic ladder and saw Kate sitting there with her knees up to her chest. "Are you all right?"

Kate closed her eyes and her gorgeous red curls—which Prudence had envied more than once—bobbed as she nodded.

Prudence knelt in front of Kate and pushed those lovely locks from her friend's face, exposing the most beautiful green eyes one could wish for. But something overshadowed the beauty she'd seen in this servant gal. "You've been crying. What's the matter?"

"Nothing. I'm sorry." Kate wiped the tears from her face with the hem of her gray cotton dress. "What do you need?"

"I don't need a thing. I was looking for you. Now tell me why you've been crying."

Father had purchased Kate from a traveling salesman a couple of years prior. Kate never talked of her past, and Prudence wasn't sure she wanted to hear about it either. Servants weren't always treated well, and slaves were treated worse. Kate wasn't a slave, but Father paid her no wages, and she had no freedom to up and leave. Father called her a bond servant, saying that once she worked off the price of her bond, she would be free to go. But he'd never said what that debt was—not that he ever had a mind to discuss private financial matters with the women in the family. Mother preferred it that way. Prudence, on the other hand, wanted to know. She'd listen in the shadows, overhearing Father's business deals. Many times he'd make a profit. But Prudence knew her interest was foolishness. No woman was allowed a place in business, no matter how quickly she could calculate the figures.

She'd snuck into her father's office more than once to try to find the papers regarding Kate, but she never came up with any. If only there was something she could do for this poor woman.

"No, Miss Prudence. Pay me no never mind."

Prudence reached out and held her friend. "Please tell me."

"Your father is thinking of selling my bond."

"No. You'll never pay off your bond if he sells you."

"I know, but I don't care. I've nothing to live for. I'm useless to anyone but to fix their meals and clean their house. I'll never be free to marry. I've been beaten since I was ten and my brother ran away. Mother used to beat him. Once he was gone, she started on me. Then one day she came home and said she'd sold me to a man, and I was to keep my mouth shut and do what the man asked and not say a word about it."

"I'm so sorry." Prudence didn't have to ask what Kate would have been forced to do.

"Ain't your fault. This be the best house I've been in, in six years."

"I've got to do something. Father can't sell your bond to another. Perhaps he'll let me pay for it."

Kate's freckled face looked straight at her. "You have money?"

"No, but I know where I can get some. I'd have to disguise myself as a man, but I think I could pull it off. I know how men deal with business."

"Miss Prudence, that be too dangerous, and your pa wouldn't permit it."

It was true. He wouldn't. But she'd have to do something. *God, help me to help Kate. She needs to know she has value. It isn't her fault she's been thrown into a life of servitude.*

"Trust me, Kate. God will help me and help you."

"God doesn't like someone like me."

"Oh, fiddlesticks. He likes you just fine. You're a good woman, Kate. You've been my friend and confidant for two years. I'm indebted to you. I promise with all that I am, I'll do whatever it takes to release you from this bondage."

Prudence wrapped the frail woman in her arms. Kate ate little and she slept even less. Her pale skin seemed a tinge gray in recent days. If God didn't do something soon, she'd probably spend her whole life in bondage—and that wasn't a way for anyone to live or die. "I love you, Kate."

Fresh sobs raked over the worn and weak body of her friend. Kate was only seventeen years old, but she looked closer to thirty. Prudence shuddered to think what had happened to her before coming to live here. Kate would flinch at the slightest movement back then, nearly jumping a couple inches off the floor when anyone spoke to her. She'd clearly been abused by someone who'd owned her bond.

"You said you have a brother?" Perhaps she could try to find him.

Kate nodded and smiled. "He's four years older than me. He left home a year after Pa died. Ma beat him bad. . .broke his arm and jaw one night. After he healed, he ran. He told me I'd be fine because Ma liked me and had never struck me. But he didn't know I'd be the closest target."

"I'm sorry. What's his name? Perhaps I could find him."

"Urias. But I think he's dead." Kate turned and held her knees to her chest once again.

Prudence's hopes for finding Kate's brother were quickly dashed. It was up to her. Kate had no one else in this world. *Father God, how can I help?* she prayed.

Five days later, Urias rode into Hardshell, Kentucky, and up to the only church in thirty miles. It was the same church where he and his family had attended the Association gathering three years before when he'd heard Katherine's name. The church was a log building covered with boards. He stepped inside onto the puncheon floor, the split logs smooth from use. At the moment, only the parson occupied the rectangular space where fence rails substituted for seats. It wasn't much compared to the church he and his family attended back in Jamestown, but it would stand the test of time, Urias reasoned.

"Parson Duff." Urias extended his hand.

The older man reached out his beefy hands, grasped Urias by his upper arms, and held them as though Urias were an old friend. "And how do I know you, son?"

"My family and I came to the Association back in '37. I don't reckon you would remember me. My name's Urias O'Leary. My parents are Mr. and Mrs. Nash MacKenneth from Jamestown," he said as Parson Duff released Urias's arms, then took his right hand.

The parson stood a couple inches shorter than Urias, but his presence seemed larger. A far-off look gathered in the man's eye, and a smile spread across his broad lips. "There were several folk out to the Association. Grand time, grand time. The Lord be praised." Parson Duff released Urias's hand and looked him straight in the eye. "What is it I can do for you, son?"

"I'm looking for my sister. I've spent the past three years searching these hills, with no luck."

"And who might your sister be?"

"Her name is Katherine. Katherine O'Leary, unless she married. She's only seventeen, but in the hills—"

"The girls can be married at thirteen." Parson Duff finished his sentence.

Urias nodded. If Katherine was happily married, he'd stop worrying. But the growing sense of urgency to find her this year had made him wonder if she might actually be in danger.

"Come with me outside, son." Parson Duff led him out the front door of the church. "Can you describe her for me?"

"Apart from her having hair the same color as mine, we share the same green eyes. I don't know what she looks like beyond that. I left home seven years ago when I was fourteen. She was ten at the time."

The parson walked him over to his horse. "Fine animal."

"Thank you."

"Urias, there's a family over toward that there hollow whose son came for a good, long visit. Fine young man by the name of Shelton Greene. His father is a bit concerned about him. Now it ain't my place to say what Shelton is sufferin' from, but he did mention a gal named Kate with red hair and green eyes. I reckon if you go and see him, he could tell you if this Kate is your sister."

Urias's heart leapt for joy. Could it be this easy? Could he have found her on his first day? Every time in the past when he'd come to the church, the parson had not been around. "Thank you. Thank you so much." Urias jumped up on his horse and grasped the reins. He stopped for a moment. "Where can I find this man?"

Parson Duff chuckled and gave him simple directions. An hour later, he'd met up with Shelton Greene.

"You say you're Kate's brother?" Shelton asked.

"I don't know. But I'd like to meet her. Is she here?"

The young man—all of sixteen he'd guess—looked down at his feet. "No. Kate is a bond servant to my father."

"A bond servant?"

"My father bought her two years ago. She has to work for him until her debt is paid in full."

"And how much does she owe your father?" Urias couldn't believe his sister had become a bond servant.

"Don't know. Father keeps his business dealings close to his chest. If you don't mind me asking, can you afford to buy her bond?"

No matter what the price, if it was his sister, he'd pay it. How could this have happened? Poor Katherine. He should have tried harder to find her years ago. Dad would have helped him. "I'll find a way."

Shelton gave him directions to Hazel Green and the Greene plantation. "Thank you. I'm much obliged."

Urias mounted his horse. *Had Mother been worse on Katherine? Dear God, please let this woman be her. And enable me to negotiate with her owner.*

He could spend the winter trapping. Perhaps that would bring in enough. Urias gave the horse a gentle prod with his heels. "Yah!" he ordered.

The winter would mean more months his sister would have to remain in another person's possession. Urias shuddered at the thought. No man should own another. Urias set his jaw. His nostrils flared. He couldn't get to Hazel Green fast enough. "Yah!" He snapped his whip above the horse's head.

Chapter 2

Prudence spent the better part of the night working on possible ways to purchase Kate's bond. The greater problem would be to convince Father to let her buy it. His way of thinking, that women do not belong in business, was totally without merit in Prudence's opinion. But alas, the entire world seemed to feel that way. Prudence had never fit. Today was no exception.

She tapped on the oak door to his office. "Father," she called.

"Prudence." He beamed as he opened the door.

That's a good sign. Prudence took a step into the inner sanctum of his domain. "I wish to speak with you on a matter of importance, if you can spare a moment."

"For you, my darling, anything."

Her heart beat wildly. "I'd like to speak with you on a business matter."

Hiram Greene instantly sobered. "Daughter, when are you going to accept the fact that business is not a matter to worry your precious little head over?"

"This is precious to me. It regards Kate. I wish to purchase her bond."

"Nonsense. She works for us presently. There is no need for you to purchase her."

"But Father, I want to give Kate her freedom."

"Child, she'll have her freedom when she pays off her bond."

"When will that be?"

He looked down at his desk and started to fiddle with some papers. "These matters are hard to understand. Trust me; I shall deal fairly with her debt."

"Is selling her, when her debt is nearly paid off, fair to her?" Prudence challenged.

Her father's face brightened with a shade of red she'd rarely seen. "I will not have you questioning my decisions. You must stop this meddling in men's affairs. I'll never find an appropriate suitor for you if you keep this up. Now, go discuss this with your mother. Perhaps she can put some common sense into you."

Prudence stomped out of her father's office, balling her hands into fists. If she didn't hold her tongue, Kate's debt could be worsened. She probably should have talked with her mother to begin with. Mother could persuade Father to do some things. Precious few, Prudence admitted. "Mother," she called.

"In my sewing room, Pru," she answered.

Their thirty-minute conversation proved fruitless as well. Why couldn't she get her parents to see reason in this matter? And how could Kate know when her debt was paid if she didn't know how much it was? Father had been less than honest in some of his business deals. Prudence had seen the paperwork. But challenging him on this had been a huge mistake.

She left her mother's sewing room and sat on the front porch. The deep golds, yellows, and reds of the autumn leaves painted a gay feeling—unlike her own frustration.

A rider came up the road to the house. He sat tall in his saddle. Without getting off of his horse, he stopped and asked, "Would this be Hiram Greene's home?"

"Yes sir. May I help you?"

"I need to speak with him on a business matter."

The tall stranger dismounted. Prudence got her first glimpse of the man. He had red hair, freckles. . . "May I say who's calling?"

Kate was walking toward the front porch, her head down.

"Urias O'Leary."

"Urias?" Kate squealed and Prudence questioned.

Urias turned to the voice behind him. "Katherine?" He ran to her and swept her into his arms. "It is you." A lump the size of the Kentucky hills stuck in his throat. Tears filled Katherine's green eyes. He held her close, hugging her tightly. "I've been looking for you for years. I'm so sorry. How are you? Are you all right? Where have you been?"

Katherine pushed herself from his arms and looked down at the ground. "I'm a servant of Mr. Greene's."

"I've come to get you, Katherine. I won't take no for an answer." He could feel the heat of his temper begin to rise. He slowly counted his blessings. *One, I've found Katherine. Thank You, Lord. Two, she's alive and safe. Thank You, Lord. Three. . .* "I can't believe I've found you."

"Nor I," Katherine replied through a halfhearted smile.

He thought she'd be more excited to see him. He turned back to the lady of the house. "May I speak with Mr. Greene?" he asked.

"I'll let him know you are here."

The brown-haired, petite lady scurried into the house. Urias turned his attention back to his sister and asked, "Did Mother sell you?"

She nodded yes.

"Katherine." He lifted her chin with his forefinger. "I'm sorry I took so long. I went back the following year, but you and Mother had moved. I've been looking for you ever since. What happened?"

"My daughter says you are Kate's brother." Hiram Greene stood all of five feet five inches, if Urias was any judge of a man's height. At six feet, he would easily tower over the older gentleman, but Mr. Greene stood on the top step and Urias remained on the ground with a half dozen steps between them.

"Yes sir. May I take her home with me?"

"Now, Mister...?"

"O'Leary," Urias supplied.

"Mr. O'Leary, I'm a businessman, and I can't be letting my help run off with any man that comes along. How can you prove to me she is your sister?"

Is the man blind? We both have the same hair and eye color and obviously have similar features. "You have my word."

Hiram Greene chuckled. "Come into my office, son. Let's see what we can work out."

Urias gave a parting glance to his sister, then followed the man into his two-story mansion. The front room opened into an entryway larger than the living room in his parents' spacious farmhouse. Urias wondered how long he'd have to work before he could earn enough to purchase his sister's freedom. It was apparent, without Hiram Greene saying a word, he would not simply hand her over. And he would be far less likely to release her with nothing more than Urias's promise to pay off her debt. But Urias determined to plead his case.

"Mr. Greene," Urias began upon entering the gentleman's office.

"Mr. O'Leary," Hiram Greene interrupted. "Please take a seat. May I call you Urias?"

Urias nodded.

"Fine, fine. Urias, I'm not above selling Kate's bond."

"Sir, if I may be so bold, I have little funds with me. But I can give you my word I will return to my home and come back with the appropriate funds. How much is my sister's bond?"

"Now, now, before we talk figures, I would need to calculate how much it is. As to the matter of your leaving and returning, that will be fine. But your sister will remain with us until the debt is paid."

Urias thought for a moment. If she'd been with the family for two years, what would be the problem?

"However, I must tell you, I've had another offer to purchase Kate's bond."

"What? You can't sell her. She's my sister." Urias knew he should keep his anger in check, but there were some things a man just couldn't stomach, and ever since hearing of his sister being sold into servitude, it had been souring something terrible.

"I'm a reasonable man, Mr. O'Leary, but the hour is late, and I'd need something more than your word of your return to consider your offer over that of another."

Urias suspected the man was just trying to up his price. "How much?"

⁂

Prudence leaned closer to the back wall of the coat closet. Sequestered in her hiding place, she could hear just about everything that went on in her father's business negotiations. Urias O'Leary was not pleased to see his sister in such a condition and, for that matter, neither was Prudence. Something had changed over the past couple of months with Kate—she seemed more despondent. At this time last year, she had sported a healthy tan. Now Kate's coloring was pasty, at best.

"Five hundred dollars," her father replied to Urias's third request to know just exactly how much would be needed to meet his sister's bond.

"Five hundred dollars?" Urias reached into his pocket. "I have twenty."

Her father let out a wicked laugh.

"A hundred and a fine steed. Would you take it and let me return with the rest?" Urias pushed.

She could just see her father rubbing his chin as he always did, sitting back in his chair behind the desk. "If I take your horse, how long would it take you to return?"

"It was five days on horseback, so possibly a month."

"Fine, a month and five hundred dollars, and you'll be able to purchase your sister's indebtedness. The horse stays here as collateral. The sun is setting, Urias. Have dinner with us, and you may spend the night in the barn."

"Thank you, but I won't impose."

Prudence leaned against the back wall. *Five hundred dollars! No wonder*

Father wouldn't let me pay the debt.

"May I visit with my sister?"

"After her chores are finished, which will be after our dinner is served and she's cleaned up the dishes. You're welcome to have dinner with us."

"No, thank you."

Prudence couldn't blame him for not wanting to create more work for his sister. Little did he know that Kate was only one of three in the kitchen.

"The barn is yours for the night, if you wish," her father once again extended his offer.

Words were mumbled, and Prudence couldn't make them out.

She had some money in her room, she knew, but not that much. *Think, Pru, think.* Then it hit her—Thomas Hagins was selling some hogs. If Urias herded them down to the Cumberland Gap, he could turn a profit. The question was: Would Mr. Hagins take Urias's word, unlike her father? And would Urias want to herd hogs? A mental flash of Urias following a herd of large hogs through the winding foothills to the Cumberland went through her mind.

She slithered out of the coat closet and waited in the front room for Urias to leave her father's office. She had to help him. Kate needed to be free. She needed to live once again. Prudence thought back on what Kate had spoken of yesterday about her life as a bond servant, about her mother, and even her brother. The abuse had to end. If Pru couldn't convince her father to give her Kate's bond, then she'd do what it would take to help Urias purchase it.

Urias stomped out of her father's office but refrained from slamming the door. His temper showed by the redness of his face.

"Mr. O'Leary," Prudence whispered as he passed by. "Meet me in the barn. I have an idea to help free your sister."

"What? Who are you?"

"Prudence Greene. Your sister is my best friend. I want to help."

He set his hat upon his head. "A friend doesn't. . ." He stopped short of completing his comment.

Prudence figured she knew what the man was going to say, but now was not the time or the place to be discussing such matters. Her father would have her head if he found her discussing business one more time. Mother had already threatened to send her east to some high society fashion school for ladies. Thankfully, Father had talked her out of that for the time being.

"The barn, Mr. O'Leary." She hurried up the stairs, praying her father hadn't heard her brief discussion with Urias. At the top of the stairs, she turned down the hall and down the back stairs, sneaking out the back door to the barn. It was the long way to go, but the best way when you didn't want to be intercepted. The barn door creaked as she opened it. The smell of fresh hay and oats wafted past her nose. "Urias?" she called. "Are you in here?"

The door creaked open again, letting in some golden light from the sunset. Prudence ducked behind the tack wall. The tall, thin frame of Urias O'Leary was highlighted in a dark silhouette. He led his horse by the reins into the barn. "Come on, boy, you'll have a comfortable home for a while."

Urias O'Leary was a handsome man, and he seemed to have a peace about him in the way he handled himself.

He stroked the horse's head. "I'll be back for you as soon as I can, boy."

"Urias," Prudence called.

Urias spun in the air and pointed his rifle straight at her.

"It's me. Prudence."

He lowered his weapon.

"Tell me what you must, woman. I need to be on my way."

"I have an idea," Prudence said.

⁊⁊

Urias sat on a rail and listened. She had an interesting plan, he had to admit, and he certainly knew the Cumberland Gap area. From here down to the Wilderness Road would be a trick though. He'd have to get some detailed directions. The big question was whether he would be able to purchase five hundred hogs with only some of the money down. Would this Thomas Hagins trust him more than Hiram Greene did?

"Your plan has merit, but. . ."

"I know. But would Thomas extend the note to be paid upon your return."

"Precisely."

"I could give Thomas my word."

The petite woman did not appear frail; she seemed like she could take on the world, given the right incentive. "Would he believe you?"

"I don't rightly know. Men don't like women talking business."

He wouldn't argue the point, but he'd long since learned from his adopted mom that women could have as much of a head for numbers as a man and quite possibly a better head from time to time. Urias didn't have five hundred dollars for Katherine's bond, and while his parents might have enough, the question still remained how he'd manage to pay them back. He could spend the winter furring, but that would only bring in some of it. But it would be worth it—anything to get Katherine out of a life of servitude. On the other hand, Prudence's idea would bring a quicker income in less than a month's time.

"Urias, I do love your sister. She's become like a sister to me. But we must act quickly. I found Kate crying in the barn yesterday. Apparently the subject of her being sold again had come up. I tried to purchase her bond from Father myself, but he wouldn't listen to me. He knew I would simply forgive her the debt, and it just reinforced his thought that a woman had no sense of business. Perhaps he's right. I can't see the logic in one man owning another or, in your sister's case, owing a debt that seems never to be paid up."

"My mother never would have sold Katherine for five hundred dollars." He jumped off the rail. "Don't get me wrong. She would have sold Katherine, but she would have sold her cheap. I don't understand how the bill could be so high."

Prudence sighed. "I don't know the nature of your sister's debt to my father. But I do know he would charge her for her food and clothing."

"But he doesn't pay her a wage."

"Precisely. That would keep her forever in his debt."

Urias kicked up some hay from the barn's floor. *Lord, I'm upset here. Calm me down so I don't do or say something foolish,* he prayed.

"Urias." Prudence placed her hand on his shoulder. He turned to her. He could see the tears in her eyes. She truly did care for Katherine and her well-being. His heart softened.

"I'm not angry with you. Truthfully, I'm more upset with myself. I never should have left without bringing Katherine with me."

"You were merely a boy at the time. How could you have cared for her?"

"I would have found a way. And I know Mom and Dad would have taken her in just as they took me in, if she were with me at the time."

"One can't look back and change things. We have to decide what to do now. I'm worried about her. Kate's not looking well. I think she's lost the will to live." Prudence began to cry. "We must help her."

Urias wrapped the woman in a compassionate embrace. "God will help us."

"Amen." She sniffled.

"Get your hands off my daughter!" Hiram Greene bellowed.

Chapter 3

U rias released Prudence and jumped back.

"How dare you!" Hiram Greene's eyes bulged. His entire face resembled that of a setting sun.

"Father, it isn't what you think!" Prudence cried.

"Get into the house!" Hiram ordered.

"But Father, Urias. . ."

"Urias, is it?" The older man fumed. "Get to the house, now, before I take a switch to you."

Urias's hackles went up. "Nothing improper happened."

Hiram faced Urias. "Don't you be telling me what is what, boy. I have a mind to send you packing."

"Daddy!" Prudence cried.

"Get!" He pointed to the open barn door.

Urias chastised himself for not having shut the door when he entered. He knew Prudence had planned on meeting him in the barn. And he knew it was not socially correct for a man and woman to meet privately. He hadn't thought about that. He'd only been thinking about his sister and how hard it was going to be to get her out of this servant lifestyle.

"Sir, if I could explain."

"I don't think there is a thing you can say that will placate me in this situation." Hiram scrutinized Urias's horse. He relaxed his shoulders and asked, "Is he fast?"

Urias nodded. He didn't know what to say at the abrupt change in Hiram's demeanor. He'd never met a man who behaved quite like this before.

"Does he have papers?"

"No. I bred him from one of my father's mares and a wild horse I captured."

"Hmm." Hiram went over to the horse. "He has good lines."

"Yes sir." What else could Urias say? How could this man be so belligerent one moment, then congenial the next?

"You'll spend the night in the barn. If you leave, I'll call the law on you. I need to speak with my wife on the matter of your inappropriate actions with my daughter."

"Nothing—"

Hiram held up his hand. "I'm not interested in what you have to say, son. You're a stranger to me and so is your kin. Your word means nothing. Have I made myself clear?"

"Yes sir."

"Good. Supper will be in thirty minutes. I'll send Kate out with a plate for you."

"Yes sir." Urias stepped up to his horse and loosened the saddle.

Hiram Greene marched out of the barn, then turned back around at the doorway. "Fine-looking horseflesh. Mighty fine."

Urias knew horses, and he knew Bullet could run like the wind. He'd been offered a fair dollar a time or two for the steed. But he'd always held back from selling him. He'd been considering purchasing his own place to raise horses. Horse racing was beginning to be big business in Kentucky, and a man could do well breeding prime stock for the competition.

Hiram Greene, on the other hand, had the wealth of high society, while his business negotiations seemed more like wrestling a pig out of the mud. Urias felt certain he was paying more than his sister's bond. But what did it matter? He'd buy her freedom.

Urias finished removing the horse's tack and put him in an empty stall with some fresh oats. He groomed the animal; it had been days since he'd had a good brushing. He'd just finished cleaning up when his sister came in with a plate of food.

"What did you do, Urias? The house is in an uproar."

"Nothing," he grumbled.

"I don't think I've ever seen Mr. Greene this angry before. Prudence is in tears. The missus is beside herself." Katherine sat down beside him. "You be a bit of a handful, Urias. Seems little has changed."

She had grown into a fine-looking woman—no longer the thin little girl with huge front teeth and pigtails. "My life is good, Katherine. I'm going to get you out of here. I promise."

"Where have you been?" she asked, handing him his plate.

"For the first six months, I ran from spot to spot. I barely had much to eat, except for the food I could catch. My hunting skills back then left a wee bit to be desired. I found a barn I could hide in, and I was staying in there when I met Mom and Dad."

"Mom and Dad? Father's been dead for nearly nine years."

"I'm sorry. Mac and Pam MacKenneth took me in and made me a part of their family."

Katherine looked down at the floor.

"Katherine, we've searched for years. When we returned the following fall, no one knew where you and Mom went off to."

"Mom sold me by then. I don't know where she is. She took the money and run, I guess."

His mother was a horrid woman, but never in his wildest dreams would he have suspected she would sell her child for profit. "How could she sell you?"

"I don't want to talk about it."

"I'm sorry."

"I wish ya'd found me sooner," she whispered.

The lump of potatoes stuck in his throat. He forced it down. "I tried, Katherine. I've been looking for you for six years. Unfortunately, we only had a short period of time in which to do our searching. So every fall we'd return to the area and ask people questions. Three years ago, at a revival down in Hardshell, we heard there was a gal fitting your general description who was a servant in someone's house. So I've been concentrating up here. I met up with Shelton Greene in Hardshell, and he told me where you were and how I could find you."

"Are you able to buy my bond?"

"I will. I have to go home and borrow the money from my parents, but somehow I will buy it, Katherine. I promise you won't have to stay here too long."

"It hasn't been a bad place to work," she mumbled.

Urias reached over and placed his hand on her arm. "Katherine, I'm sorry you've gone through all of this. I should have taken you with me."

Tears welled in his sister's green eyes. Urias could feel the same happening in his own.

"I'll pack my bags." She stood to leave.

"Katherine, I can't take you with me. Mr. Greene does not trust me. My word means nothing to him."

Katherine nodded. "Very well," she droned, her words reaching down to the pit of his stomach. Urias doubted he had ever seen a person this depressed before. He couldn't leave his sister here much longer. She needed rescuing, and, thank God, he'd been sent to rescue her.

"I love you, Katherine. You've never stopped being in my prayers."

"Prayers?" Her eyes flickered like fire and her face flushed. "Prayers are worthless."

&

Prudence couldn't believe her ears. Her parents had been arguing for the better part of an hour. Not a morsel of food had been touched on either of their plates. Father insisted she had disgraced the family and must be married immediately. Mother felt marriage was a bit extreme. Finishing school was Mother's answer, and had been for the better part of a year.

Urias O'Leary might also feel marriage a bit extreme, Prudence guessed. What had she done by meeting with him? *Dear Lord, please intervene.*

Prudence left the table and dining room as quietly as possible. Her parents weren't talking with her—just about her and around her. She felt fairly certain Mother could talk Father out of a forced wedding, which she had no interest in participating in. But should she warn Urias? The only way would be to go out to the barn. Kate hadn't come back in from her visit with her brother. Prudence pondered for a moment, hesitating in the hallway. If she went out to the barn, Father would be furious enough that no matter what reasoning power Mother had, it would be useless. She chose the stairs and the solitude of her bedroom.

In her room, Prudence prayed. She opened her money box and removed what little savings she had. Eighteen years old and not yet pledged in marriage—it had been a source of contention in her home since her sixteenth birthday. Women in the hills of Kentucky were married at thirteen or fourteen, and Prudence was rapidly approaching her spinster years. But marriage should be more than an arrangement between her father and some business partner's son. At least, she'd always hoped and prayed it would be. She wanted love. Someone who loved her more than her father's money.

Oddly enough, when Father began spouting off her need to marry Urias, the possibility hadn't seemed completely intolerable. He was a handsome man, and a girl could get lost looking into those marvelous green eyes. Prudence shook off the thought. She wouldn't be forced into marrying for simply talking with a man. They'd done nothing wrong. Fortunately, she had found a brief moment to explain to her mother what had transpired before her father came into the house, ranting and raving.

But something wasn't right about the price of Kate's bond. Father would never pay that kind of money even on a good horse, much less for a servant. But why would he overcharge Katherine's brother? He'd always been a fair man in business. But recently he'd been making some strange decisions—from what little she had heard in the closet beside his office. *I really must stop eavesdropping,* she reminded herself for the hundredth time.

She really didn't care about knowing the personal details of other people's lives. She merely wanted to understand the workings of finance. For some reason, it had always piqued her interest, even as a small child.

Wrapping her small savings into a handkerchief, she set it aside to have Kate take out to Urias. Sitting down at her writing desk, she penned a brief note to him, letting him know the monies were to purchase additional hogs. She blew the ink gently to finish off the drying, folded it neatly, and placed it inside the folds of the handkerchief, then scurried down the hallway to the rear of the house to the servants' quarters.

"Kate," she whispered, tapping the door.

No answer. She turned the crystal knob and pushed the door open. Kate wasn't in her room. Prudence worked her way down the back stairway to the kitchen. Again, no Kate. Where could she be?

Prudence heard her parents still discussing their problem of what to do with their daughter. Sometimes Prudence wondered if she'd been born into the wrong family. Kate had to be in the barn with Urias.

Taking in a deep breath, she hurried out to the barn and prayed she wouldn't get caught. She didn't enter but stepped in the doorway and called out to Kate.

"She's not here," Urias answered.

"Do you know where I might find her?" Prudence asked. "Urias, I have something for you. I'm leaving it wrapped in a white handkerchief by the door. I can't come in or Father would be beside himself. You should be warned; he's planning on us getting married."

"What?" Urias popped out of the dark shadows of the barn. "I'll not stand for it."

The sharp response hurt, even though she knew Urias was right. The idea was ridiculous. "Mother is trying to convince him to send me off to finishing school. Please take this. It's a little more to help you buy more hogs."

"Prudence, I have not decided whether or not to purchase the hogs."

"But?" Prudence stepped closer to the door and to Urias.

"I cherish my parents' counsel, and I've been praying and thinking I should speak with them. But if I leave my horse to insure my return, that will take weeks. I simply don't know what to do. Katherine doesn't trust me. I don't know if I can blame her. She didn't say anything but. . ."

"Oh Urias." She stepped forward and placed her hand on his forearm. "You have to give her time. She's had a rough life, and you seem to have had a good one."

He squeezed his eyes shut. "I should never have left her with our mother."

"You were a boy. Don't be—"

"So hard on myself? That's the problem. I was only thinking of myself. I never thought what my mother would have done. She was a drunk and she beat me. Of course she'd beat Katherine once I was gone. I never looked beyond myself. This is all my fault."

"No. I can't believe that. I don't know you, but a child can't be responsible for an adult's actions. You weren't responsible for your mother beating you any more than you're responsible for your mother beating Kate." *How can I get through to this man?* "Stop thinking on the past, Urias. Kate needs you now. You're here now. Take this." She handed him the handkerchief. "It's all I have at the moment."

His fingers brushed hers as he reached for the proffered gift. A flash of heat shot through her like a bolt of lightning.

"That settles it!" her father shouted from the back stairs of the house.

"Settles what?" Urias whispered.

"Our marriage." Prudence blushed.

Dear God in heaven, help me, Urias prayed.

"Prudence Greene, get in this house this moment!" Hiram Greene shouted for all to hear.

The barn began to spin. Urias grabbed the rail to stabilize himself. This couldn't be happening. No one would force someone to marry for simply speaking with another. It wasn't legal, was it?

Urias stuffed the handkerchief in his pocket as he watched Prudence walk toward her father. Her shoulders drooped farther with each step closer. The man was a tyrant, or so it would seem. *If he treats his own daughter this way, how does he treat Katherine?* Urias closed his eyes and tried to keep his mind from thinking the worst.

"Mr. O'Leary, come to my office," Hiram ordered.

If ever a man needed divine inspiration and wisdom, it was now. *Lord, I am up against a post here. Prudence says her father is going to insist on us getting married. I can't do that. I need Your help and guidance.*

Urias dusted off his pants and walked toward the front door. He couldn't leave this plantation soon enough. But first he had to get something in writing concerning Katherine's bond and the agreement he had with her owner. Then he'd shake the dust from his heels faster than any disciple leaving an unholy city.

He walked into the house and straight into Hiram Greene's office. There he waited, counting time by the construction of a small spider web in the upper right-hand corner of the brick fireplace. The sun had set, and a bracing coolness filled the house. *Perhaps it isn't only the weather,* he mused. Should he light a fire? Would it be considered neighborly or imposing?

Finally, he sat down in a fancy, hand-carved oak chair. He quieted his heart and prayed.

"Mr. O'Leary." Urias startled as Hiram Greene marched into his office. "I've called for the preacher, and you shall marry my daughter this evening."

Urias held down his temper. "With all due respect, Mr. Greene, I will not marry your daughter. We did nothing improper."

"You will marry my daughter, or I will not sell you your sister's bond. This is not negotiable, Mr. O'Leary." Hiram Greene sauntered across his office and sat down behind the desk as if he didn't have a care in the world.

"You can't do this. You can't force your daughter to marry me or me to marry your daughter. We had an agreement for my sister's bond."

"Yes, but that was before you dishonored me and my house by your indecent behavior with my daughter."

"I did no such thing!" Urias defended.

"I beg to differ, sir, and since I am the head of this household and I make the decisions here, that is my final decision. You will marry my daughter when the preacher arrives, or I'll have you thrown in jail." He leaned forward. "This is within my power and my right as a father."

Not only had he threatened to not sell Urias his sister's bond, now he threatened a jail sentence. If the circuit judge came around these parts as often as he did in Jamestown, Urias could be sitting behind bars for quite a while.

Urias heard a team of horses and a carriage coming up toward the house. "Preacher is here, son. What's it going to be?"

Chapter 4

Prudence cried throughout the entire ceremony. The things her father had said to her were so hurtful, she didn't even want to think about them. He also told her that if she didn't go through with the wedding, he would sell Kate to someone else and put Urias in jail until the circuit judge came by—which, in Prudence's estimation, would be next spring. She had little choice but to stand beside Urias and repeat the vows the preacher performed.

Once the ceremony was over, Urias placed his hat upon his head and exited the house. Who could blame him? She certainly couldn't.

She ran up to her room and cried as she packed her bag.

"Prudence," her mother called from behind the door. "May I come in?"

Prudence didn't bother to answer. Since when did it matter to her parents what she wanted? Her mother entered the room. "Darling, look at the bright side—you have a husband."

Prudence narrowed her gaze on her mother.

"All right, maybe that was the wrong thing to say. But you're not getting any younger."

What little dignity Prudence had left flew out the window. Even her own mother thought the only way Prudence could get a husband was to be forced into a marriage. "This is not a marriage, Mother; it's a jail sentence."

"Maybe he isn't a bad sort."

What little she knew of Urias, he wasn't a bad sort at all. He cared deeply for his sister, enough to persistently search for her for years.

Prudence opened her closet door and pulled out her carpetbag.

"What are you doing?"

"Packing. I'm married now. Don't I have to live with my husband?"

"But I thought you and he would live here."

Was her mother that oblivious? "Mom, he has a family, a job of his own."

"But your father said—"

"I don't know what Daddy said, but I know one thing; he cannot control Urias O'Leary. If he hadn't threatened Urias with the loss of his sister's freedom and jail time, I doubt he would have married me."

"Oh my dear, I don't want you to leave. I'd hoped he'd move in with you."

"No, Mother, he has his own life. Somehow, I have to figure out a way to share it." *But not for long. There has to be a way to have the marriage annulled.*

There was a knock at her open door. Prudence glanced over. Kate stood there, shaking. "Urias told me to tell you he'll be leaving in the morning and return as soon as he can with the money for your father."

"Thank you." Prudence sighed.

"See? He is a reasonable man. You can stop packing now." Her mother exited the room.

Prudence dumped the contents of her carpetbag out and began repacking. This time she packed for a wilderness journey. Her mother might be pleased with her staying, but Prudence needed to leave this house, and she needed to help earn Kate's freedom. Somehow, she and Urias would figure a way out of this foolish marriage. Then hopefully Prudence would find a place for herself in this world apart from her family—a place where people would accept and appreciate all of her hidden talents.

"Prudence," Kate whispered, "I'm sorry."

"Hush. This isn't your fault. It's my own. I shouldn't have gone to the barn a second time. I should have waited to find you to deliver the. . . What does it matter? It's over, it's done with, and now your brother is paying for my foolishness. I'm the one who is sorry."

"Can I help?" Kate asked.

"Thank you." Prudence grabbed the carpetbag and set it right side up on the bed once again. The handle came off in her hands. Fresh tears filled her eyes.

❧

Urias woke at the sound of the rooster's first crow. He rubbed the back of his stiff neck and moaned, then stood up and stretched. He doubted he'd ever had such a fitful night's sleep. Every hour he seemed to wake with the nightmare of the evening before. Married at the end of a pointed sword. Granted, there had been no blades present, but it certainly had felt like it.

All night he kept having this nagging feeling that something besides Hiram Greene's daughter's honor was at stake in this forced marriage. To threaten Katherine's freedom and jail time meant the man didn't play fair in business. That realization only solidified Urias's original thought that the bond he'd agreed to pay was much higher than the debt his sister owed.

He reached for his saddle and proceeded to hitch Bullet up. Urias had decided somewhere around the middle of the night that since he'd been forced to marry Prudence, the original agreement for the purchase of his sister's bond was null and void. With Bullet, he could possibly make it back to Jamestown in three days. Time was of the essence now. Hiram Greene was not a man to be trusted. If he would force his daughter to marry a stranger with no respect for her feelings, would he honor the agreement of selling off Katherine's bond? And now that Urias had found her, he wasn't about to lose her.

The barn door creaked open. Urias chastised himself again for not having closed it last evening when he rendezvoused with Prudence.

Prudence stood there with a hastily mended carpetbag in one hand and dressed for travel. Her brown hair was pulled back under a white cotton bonnet. She was a beautiful woman; he'd give her that. But no man should be forced to marry her. What was Hiram Greene's problem?

"Good morning," she said in a timid voice.

"Morning. Going somewhere?"

"With you," she replied and walked over to him.

"No, no. I agreed to marry you, but I'm not taking you with me," Urias stammered. "I mean, I'm not taking you with me to my parents' house." That didn't sound right either.

She squared her shoulders and replied, "I'm your wife now."

"I'm well aware of that fact."

"What I mean to say is, I'm free to go with you and I want to help. With my help, we can herd the hogs to the Cumberland Gap in less time."

He had forgotten about her ingenious plan regarding raising the money himself. "I was planning on speaking with my parents and borrowing the money."

"How long would that take?" she asked.

"Eight days—ten at the most. The problem would be how fast we could get the funds."

She nodded. Urias knew—he wasn't sure how he knew—but he could tell she was conjuring up a scheme of some kind. "I'm not of a mind to tell you what to do, but for the same amount of time, we could probably herd some hogs down to the Cumberland Gap and back again."

The idea of not owing his parents five hundred dollars for his sister's bond was appealing. With the profit, he'd be able to buy his own property and start breeding horses.

"Even if we don't raise enough capital," she continued, "I'm certain we'd raise enough for Father to release Kate. Especially since we are married now."

Urias sunk his hands into his pockets and felt the folded handkerchief she'd given him the night before. He pulled it out and opened it. Inside he found some money and a note. Reading it, he realized once again how deeply this woman cared for his sister.

She reached over and placed her hand on his forearm. "Urias, please. Can we at least talk with Thomas Hagins and see if we can barter with him?"

"Have you ever lived on the road?" he asked. He continued to ready the horse for travel.

"No," she admitted. "I promise not to complain. Maybe it is my pride, but I resent what Father did last night. Besides, I need to leave this house, and our marriage gives me the opportunity to put distance between myself and my father."

He couldn't blame her there. If he'd been that man's child, he'd be livid, too. *Perhaps that's why Prudence's brother is staying with their uncle in Hardshell,* Urias mused. "All right. You can come. And, yes, we'll talk with Thomas Hagins. But if he won't work a deal, you return home, and I'll go to Jamestown to get the money needed. Agreed?"

"Thank you."

He glanced down at her ladies' heeled boots. "Do you have a more rugged pair of shoes?"

"No."

"Is there a place nearby where we can purchase you a pair?"

"There's a general store not too far from Thomas Hagins's place."

"Good." He reached for her bag to fasten it to the horse's saddle. "You'll ride; I'll walk. We'll get farther that way."

She nodded her agreement. Urias didn't know if this was the makings of a contrite spirit or whether the wealthy young woman had always expected such favors. It didn't matter; with those boots, they wouldn't get far.

He hoisted her into the saddle. A bolt of awareness shot through him. For the first time, he realized this beautiful woman was his wife, and there wasn't a thing he could do about it, one way or the other.

&

Prudence sat mesmerized in the saddle. Urias's touch had been so gentle and yet so full of power when he helped her up on the horse. If Father hadn't forced them to get married, would something have developed between them? She contemplated that the entire five-hour journey to Thomas Hagins's place. They talked little on the trip. For the most part, she just gave him directions. She didn't know what to think of Urias. One minute he seemed warm and compassionate; the next he was distant—almost cold. They had to find a way to annul the marriage. No one should be forced to live like this.

Of course, that was what Kate's life must have been like these many years—forced to live for the wishes of others. Forced to do things that were. . . Prudence stopped the thoughts. Kate had never said outright that she'd been abused by some of those who'd owned her bond. But something had happened to her—something that clearly made her feel unworthy to be considered equal with others.

Kate was why she was on this horse. Kate was the reason she'd stand up and give up her own life and her own happiness to save another from a life of servitude.

They walked up to the white-trimmed house of Thomas Hagins and knocked on the door.

"Miss Greene, what a pleasure to see you." Thomas Hagins extended his hand.

Prudence accepted it. "It's good to see you, Mr. Hagins. May I introduce my husband, Urias O'Leary?" Thomas Hagins's eyebrows shot up as his eyes widened. Did everyone think she was unfit to be a wife? "Urias, Mr. Hagins."

"Husband? My dear, it has been too long." Thomas shook Urias's hand.

"We've come to do business, sir. My wife and I would like to purchase some hogs to take them to the Cumberland Gap. Prudence seems to believe there is a good profit there for a man."

"She's a right smart one. 'Tis true, I've made a dollar or two myself. Unfortunately, I no longer have the legs for the journey. Price is $1.25 per hundred pounds of hogs. How many do you want?"

"I've got a hundred on me, and I can leave my steed as a deposit. I was hoping you might be willing to let me purchase five hundred hogs and bring the money back to you after I return from the Gap."

"I don't know. That's asking an awful lot."

Prudence couldn't help herself. "Mr. Hagins, I realize you don't know my husband, but he is an honorable man." *After all, he married me.* "If my father thinks enough of Urias to give my hand in marriage to him, that should speak for something."

Thomas rubbed the day's growth on his chin.

"Let me look at the horse."

Urias looked up and winked. Prudence smiled. For the first time in her life, a man hadn't put her down for speaking her mind.

"Fine-looking steed. I'd be interested in buying him for the purchase of the hogs."

"He's yours if I fail to return with the money. But I need him. If I could trouble you for a mule to help carry our packs, that would be mighty fine of you. I'd be willing to pay for the animal," Urias offered.

"The horseflesh alone is worth more than the hogs. You've got yourself a deal, son." Thomas and Urias shook on it.

The men worked out the details while Prudence worked out some food supplies for the road with Mrs. Hagins. Urias had given her back the money she'd given to him yesterday. The Haginses put them up for the evening. Urias slept on the floor and gave the bed to Prudence. Neither one of them was ready to make the marriage complete, but it still stung to realize she was not wanted by her own husband. Prudence silently cried herself to sleep for the second night in a row.

Chapter 5

Urias and Prudence woke early the next morning and ate the hot breakfast Mrs. Hagins had fixed for them. By six, they began herding the hogs toward the Cumberland Gap. Urias had spent the better part of the evening speaking with Thomas about hogs and how to best herd them. Before going to bed last night, he had fashioned a couple of willow switches to snap and prod the hogs forward.

By noon, they had covered only a couple of miles. At this rate, they wouldn't make the gap before snowfall. Frustrated, he sat down to the meal Prudence had prepared. "Thank you," he said, taking the offered dish from her hands.

"You're welcome. I purchased a few things from Mrs. Hagins last night to make our travels more comfortable."

"How are your feet?"

"I find the shoes quite comfortable. The two pairs of woolen socks seem a bit much, but I'm sure you're right about blisters from new shoes if I don't wear them."

"You may still get them. You can sit on the burro if you need to."

"Thank you. I'm all right." She looked down at her plate. His heart tightened once again, knowing what this marriage was doing to her.

"Urias, we're not moving fast enough, are we?"

"No, but I figure it will take a day or two to learn how to move the hogs forward."

Her face brightened.

"Once we've got them on the path and moving at a good pace, we should make up for some of the lost time."

"How long before we hit the Wilderness Road?"

"Three days—possibly four." Urias finished off his meal. "Thank you." He handed her the empty plate. "I'll get the hogs moving while you clean up. They can feed along the way. There's a fresh water stream that should help the hogs recover from the journey. They won't eat much, but we don't want them to lose too many pounds before we get there.

"I'll keep my eye out for quail for dinner tonight. Do you like quail?" Urias asked.

"Yes. That would be nice. You'll have to teach me some about cooking on an open fire. I know a little, but precious little, I'm afraid."

Urias nodded. He couldn't fault her for her upbringing, and he knew there were some folks who lived in cities who didn't understand how to live off the land. But still, a woman should know how to cook. He thought back on his warm meal of beans with chunks of ham thrown in. *She knows how to cook some things,* he amended.

Urias picked up his long switch and started snapping it in the air above the hogs' heads. Instantly, they started to move. Down and around the curvy mountain trail they traveled until, five hours later, they arrived at the clearing Thomas Hagins had recommended.

As he settled the hogs in for the evening, he noticed Prudence silently making a campfire. *The quail.* He'd forgotten all about them. He'd been too focused on the swine and getting them to the field. He finished counting them and took off for the woods. With any luck, he'd find a couple quail before too long.

He examined the ground, looking for telltale signs of the bird. Generally, they nested on the ground. He looked for overturned leaves and scratching in the dirt. What he didn't expect to see was the large set of tracks to his left.

He glanced back at the camp. They were vulnerable. He'd have to stay awake the night to be on guard.

ða

"Bear?"

" 'Fraid so," Urias answered.

She couldn't believe her ears. He'd found bear tracks on the edge of the forest. "Won't hogs be mighty tempting for them?" she asked.

" 'Fraid so," he repeated. "I'll stay up most of the night and guard the herd."

She should have been offended that he wasn't thinking about guarding her, but she had to keep reminding herself this wasn't a real marriage. He wasn't a man who loved her. He loved his sister and had done whatever it took to get her free. "I'll keep watch, too."

"One of us should sleep."

"I'll watch the first shift, then wake you. You can watch the second half of the night."

"How is your aim?" he asked.

"Fair. But the shot should be loud enough to hopefully send the bear running."

"Or wake me. I'll load the gun for you, then set up the tent for the night. Are you all set for dinner?"

"Yes. I'll have the quail ready in an hour—possibly a little more."

Urias nodded and left her to her own devices. She knew how to cook, but an open flame scared her. She'd been working overtime, trying not to complain or give Urias cause to send her back home. The truth was, her body ached in places she didn't know she had. She'd always thought of herself as having good stamina, but this walking was pulling muscles in her legs, feet, and back. What she wouldn't give for a warm bath.

She finished plucking the quail and set them on a stick she had braced over the fire, then removed her new shoes. Her feet needed to soak in the stream. Prudence yelped, not realizing just how cold the water had become.

"You all right?" Urias hollered from the edge of the woods.

"Fine," she replied. The stream soothed her aching feet. At first, it felt like needles pricking her, but then her feet were numb to the cold. She stepped out and dried off her feet. What she wouldn't give for a pair of satin slippers. Instead, she put on a pair of wool socks and walked back to the fire. She turned the quail and continued to make the area ready for a meal.

Urias returned with an armful of wood. "This should help keep the bears away. Would you like to practice with my rifle?" he asked. The Kentucky long rifle stood about as tall as Urias.

"If it wouldn't be a bother."

"Be happy to show you. The trick is in the balance of the barrel."

She'd observed Urias for the better part of two days now, and she still couldn't figure out the kind of man he was. He seemed kind but also easily riled. He spoke few words, but when he did, he tried to make pleasant conversation with her. What intrigued her most was his bringing her in on the discussions referring to the purchase of the hogs. No man had ever recognized any points she made regarding finances before.

After dinner, Urias spent a few moments helping her hold and aim the rifle. He showed her how to load and reload it. He even let her do it in front of him, without saying a word. By the time he settled in for the night, she decided he was, overall, a patient man. In her small world, that was a rare treasure.

The various sounds of the night critters kept Prudence awake. At midnight, she woke up Urias, then crawled into the still warm bed-roll. His scent was on the blankets, and Prudence found herself inhaling the teasing fragrance. Sleep came quickly, and Prudence slipped into a deep rest.

The next morning, she and Urias worked better as a team. They each tended to their own chores and found themselves and the five hundred hogs on the road by six. At the end of four days, the rhythm of working together and moving the hogs became smooth. They found themselves at the end of another long day, sitting back and enjoying the stars.

"Prudence, forgive me for asking, but why do you think your father forced us to marry?"

Prudence let out a deep sigh. She'd been expecting this conversation for days. They'd been talking with each other, getting to know one another, but never saying anything deeply personal. "He sees me as an old maid who will never marry."

"Why? You're an attractive woman. You're pleasant company. It doesn't make sense." Urias tossed the remains of his coffee from his cup.

"It's me. I'm the real problem. I like talking finances, and most men feel a woman has no place in business nor the mind to discuss such things. Unfortunately, I've spoken a time or two when I shouldn't have, embarrassing a few men by showing them their errors in calculations."

Urias chuckled. It was the first time she'd heard him laugh. She decided she liked the sound of his laughter and would like to hear more of it.

"My mother—my adopted mother," he corrected, "is very good with figures. In a way, you remind me of her."

Prudence smiled. He'd spoken often about his parents, and the respect he held for them was obvious to anyone who had an ear to hear.

"My folks will help us figure a way out of this marriage."

Shocked, Prudence blinked. She'd foolishly allowed herself to start falling in love with Urias. "We can have it annulled," she said.

"How's that work?"

"I'm not really sure, but I think we simply explain to a judge how we were forced to marry, that we never"—she felt the heat rise on her cheeks—"never had a true marriage, and the judge writes a letter of annulment."

"Would that mean we were never really married?"

"I think so. But I'm not a lawyer, and I've never known anyone who has done it. A few years back, I heard about a marriage the parents had annulled after the kids ran off and married. They were both thirteen at the time. They lied about their ages, so the parents were able to dissolve the marriage."

Something she'd been wrestling with was whether God considered them married. And if He did, were they free to have the marriage annulled? That would be something to discuss with the preacher one day.

"Truthfully, I don't know what is right or wrong here. My folks will help us, I'm sure. But if we got this annulment, what would you do?"

"I'll find a job or something. I couldn't return home. Father would be mortified."

Urias reached over and placed his hand upon hers. "I'll make certain you're cared for."

Prudence changed the subject. "You best get some sleep. Morning is going to come quickly." In her heart, she longed to be cherished and cared for. But the man she would like to love her would never get past how they had been forced to be married. "Good night." Prudence walked over to the herd of swine and made herself as comfortable as possible for the first watch. *Lord, I'm so confused.*

❧

Urias's mind was filled with the possibility of an annulment. The four days on the road together had been pleasant enough, but they were not husband and wife. They didn't love one another like his parents—or even his grandparents—loved each other. They weren't even like his biological parents, who'd bickered all the time. *We just. . .are. The only thing holding us together is the mission of procuring Katherine's freedom.*

He had to admit, though, Prudence had not complained once. She worked hard, followed his instructions, and provided security for the much needed rest. He looked out of the tent. Prudence sat, bent over, rubbing her feet, a silhouette painted by a slivered moon. It made no sense to him why any man wouldn't want a wife like Prudence. Any man except him, that is. It was strange. . .in so many ways, she represented the kind of woman he would like to find in a wife. But the reality of how they married could never be blotted out of his mind or hers, he presumed. Why would she want to be bound to a man she'd been forced to marry? It was clear she'd been thinking about an annulment. He hadn't given that idea any thought.

Prudence stood there shaking. Something was wrong. Urias bolted out of the tent. "What's the matter?"

"Nothing," she sniffled.

He lit the lantern and could see she'd been crying. "Prudence, what's the matter?" He trailed the light down her body. Her feet were cracked and bleeding. "You should have said something."

Urias scrambled back to his pack and pulled out some horsetail, then ground the grassy herb into a poultice. He fetched some water from the stream and set the pot on the fire to warm it. "You're riding all day—possibly the next couple of days—on the mule. It's those new boots. I should have known better than insisting on new boots for a journey such as this."

He cradled her feet into his lap and gently washed them. He applied a warm cloth and gently dried them.

"What are you doing?"

"Obviously, I'm washing your feet. Next I'll apply the horsetail poultice and wrap them with clean linen."

As he worked, he felt Prudence relax her muscles and let him apply the healing balm and wrap her feet in a clean, dry cloth. Once done, he took her in his arms and carried her to the tent. "You're going to rest tonight. All night," he insisted. "I'll take care of breakfast. It won't be as tasty as yours, but it'll fill our bellies."

"I'll be all right," she protested.

"Prudence, let me take care of you. It's the least I can do after all you've done. We'll be in Flatlick tomorrow. I have some friends there. I'll treat you to a warm bath. And Mrs. Campbell is a fine cook."

"Campbell? Aren't they the folks who let you hide out in their barn? Isn't that the same place you met your parents?"

Urias smiled. "Good memory. Yes, they are. I was just a naive kid and didn't realize they knew I was sleeping in their barn. Dad pointed out the obvious to me and let me know how it was that I just so happened to find some food around the place." He chuckled at the memory.

"We're through the hollows," he continued. "And tomorrow we'll be traveling on a much larger road." Urias had admired the beauty of the hills, but his appreciation dissipated a little each day with the strenuous march and concentration on the animals. He'd had to help more than one hog out of the briars.

"I should be fine by morning," she argued again.

"Let me take care of you, Prudence. If I have to, I'll simply order you, and you, being my wife. . ."

"Men," she huffed.

"Women," he huffed right back at her. "Look, I appreciate your willingness to help and all the hard work you've done, but your feet are injured. They need to heal, and we have many more days on the road. If we don't take care of them now, they'll get infected and you'll get sick. We can't afford the time for that. I'm merely being practical."

"I see," she acknowledged, her voice strained.

He held the lantern up to get a clear view of her face. "Prudence, I didn't mean to offend you." Urias felt certain this had to be one of those times when men say one thing and women think another. He'd experienced it a time or two watching his parents. They would be trying to explain themselves to one another while neither understood what the other was saying. Eventually they'd work it out, but Mom would tend to get weepy during the process and Dad a bit touchy.

"I'm fine, Urias. I'm just tired and my feet hurt."

"All right." He lowered the flame in the lantern. "Call me if you need anything. I'll make some bandages for your feet in the morning, if they need it."

"You've done enough."

"For being a rich girl, you sure don't like being pampered, do you?"

"Nope. But you're not a poor boy, are you?"

Urias let out a nervous chuckle. "No, I guess not. The MacKenneths own quite a spread, and Dad taught me how to hunt. Before Grandpa hurt himself, Dad used to spend the winter trapping. But the real money came from Mom. I don't know exactly how much it was, but her inheritance seemed substantial. Mom has a real mind for business, quite like yourself, as I mentioned a few days ago. Anyway, she and Dad work out their business affairs together. She's been encouraging me to get into horse breeding, mainly because I like working with horses. But she also sees it as the means for me to make my own way in the world."

"I can't imagine it. My mother doesn't even know what she spends on household expenses. I think Father prefers it that way."

"The MacKenneths are good people."

"They sound it. Kate will like living with them."

"I hope so. Of course, I'll want to build our own house so Katherine has a place of her own as soon as possible."

"She deserves it."

"You best get some rest and let your feet heal. Good night, Prudence."

"Good night, Urias."

She lay down and pulled the blanket over herself. Urias thought back to the image of her cracked and bleeding feet. He should have noticed sooner. *What kind of a husband am I?*

I'm not, he reminded himself.

It would be too easy to forget what happened to force them to marry. How could they possibly make a marriage out of something so wrong?

Urias took up his sentry post. The hogs slept quietly beneath the black sky filled with more stars than a man could count. The moon gave a sliver of a smile. They were getting close. Soon he'd be able to sell the livestock and return to Hazel Green, rescue Katherine, and put an end to this bizarre marriage.

He inhaled the crisp night air and walked closer to the fire. A twig snapped from behind the tent.

Chapter 6

Prudence savored the memory of Urias's touch. He'd been so gentle, so loving, and yet she meant nothing to him. What would it be like to feel his touch if he truly loved her? She shivered just thinking about it.

"Prudence," Urias whispered. "Stay down; we have some company."

"Who goes there?" Urias bellowed into the darkness.

Prudence stayed in the tent.

"Just passing through." A strange male voice came from the edge of the woods behind the tent. "Saw the fire, wondered if you wanted company tonight!"

"You're welcome to warm yourself by the fire," Urias offered. "Where you from?"

"Hazard. How about yourself?"

"Jamestown," Urias answered.

"Hauling hogs, eh?"

"Yup. What about you?"

"Just making my way over to the ford."

"I have some friends who live around Hazard. Do you happen to know the Fugates?"

"The blue people?"

Blue people? Prudence didn't understand the conversation these men were having.

"Yes," Urias answered.

"Can't say that I know them. Know about 'em, but I don't know them myself. Ain't never had no reason to bother them. How'd you know 'em?"

"My father and I were doing some hunting one year and stumbled into their hollow."

"Folks don't pay them much mind. They stay to themselves."

Prudence's curiosity was up now. But she was under orders to stay put. Yet she wanted to know about these blue people. The test of will began. It had always been hard for her to sit and not speak when she wanted to know something.

"They're good folk. Takes a bit to get used to their color, but after a while you don't seem to notice it."

"Ain't never had an interest. Folks say they're cursed. Personally, I stay away. I'm not saying they're cursed or nothing, but it ain't natural for a man to be blue skinned."

Blue skin? This was too much. She had to know. She opened her mouth, then abruptly closed it. She placed one hand over her mouth to keep from speaking. She thought of all the possible reasons Urias would want her to stay hidden. The stranger might kill her. *That's a good reason.* She removed her hand from her mouth.

Prudence heard the click of a gun.

"Tell your man to step back from the tent," Urias ordered.

Prudence watched the man by the fire raise his hands into the air.

"Tell him," Urias ordered a bit firmer.

"Come on over, Oren."

"With your hands in the air, Oren," Urias added.

Prudence watched with fascination as her husband handled the strangers. *Perhaps they're robbers,* Prudence wondered. She'd never seen a real criminal before.

"Hope you men don't mind sleeping side by side." He ordered the men to lay down beside the fire and tied their hands and feet to one another.

"Sorry to put you through this, boys, but I need to protect my wife."

Prudence's heart fluttered.

"How'd you know he was out there?" the first stranger asked.

"There were two of you when I first called out. But besides that, I could smell ya. Ever heard of soap?"

"We didn't mean anything."

"Let's just say I'm an overprotective husband who can see in the dark."

❧

Urias let the guys loose in the morning. Once he exposed their plan, they probably wouldn't have robbed him, but he wasn't taking any chances. He'd leave Prudence with the Campbells and finish hauling the hogs over to the Cumberland Gap without her. With those two out there, he needed to protect her. Mac had trained him well on how to listen and watch the signs of being tracked. All morning, he'd watched to see whether the men had doubled back or continued their way north. Thankfully, they'd continued north.

He'd set Prudence on the mule this morning. She seemed nervous.

They didn't talk about what happened last night until they stopped for lunch. Urias heated up some beans and a couple hunks of bacon. "Sorry." He offered her the poor substitute for a meal.

"I should be able to make our dinner this evening." She glanced down at her plate and back up to him. "Urias, who were those men last night?"

"Two lazy men looking for a quick way to earn a dollar."

"Bandits?"

"Not yet. Hopefully, they've learned to stay away from folks traveling on the road."

"How'd you know the other man was in the woods?"

"There were two distinct movements when I called out, but only one man came forward. Which meant the other would circle around and try to sneak up on me. First, they wanted to see how many were in our camp."

"I was terrified."

"I'm sorry about that. We should be traveling with two rifles, one for you as well. I'm a fair shot, though not as good as my father. He's taught me a lot about traveling in the wilderness. Most of the time you're safe, but the closer you get to the towns, the more you tend to run into bandits."

She took a small bite of her beans.

"It will be all right, Prudence." He laid a reassuring hand on her shoulder. "I'll make certain nothing happens to you."

"You said something strange last night, and the stranger seemed to know what you were talking about. What are blue people?"

Urias chuckled. *If you've never heard about them, it's hard to believe at first,* he reminded himself. "There's a family—the Fugates—in the hills around Hazard. Anyone who lives there knows about them, even if they don't know them. Their skin has a blue tinge to it. Some folks are afraid of them, and the Fugates keep pretty secluded up in their hills. If you're ever in the area, don't mention someone being blue in referring to depression. They'll fear you're cursing them."

"How strange."

"I'll admit it took a bit to get used to seeing them, but they're really fine folks. Nothing different except the skin color. Have you ever been in cold water too long and your lips turn purple?"

"Of course."

"Well, it's something like that. We all have blue in us. If you look at your arms and look at your veins, you see it. For some reason, their skin's just blue."

"Very peculiar."

Urias finished off his beans. "We best get a move on if we're going to make it to the Campbells' by nightfall."

"What about the hogs? Do they have room for all them?"

"Since it's past harvesting time, I don't think there will be a problem with the hogs sleeping in one of the fields."

"A real bed would be nice," Prudence sighed.

He couldn't fault the woman. She'd never lived on the road like this. She'd been treated with a life of luxury. Yet, she never complained. His admiration for her and her strong will increased each day. *She'd make a man a fine wife one day.* Urias shook off the thought. *No need to go thinkin' like that,* he chided himself, then went straight to work. With everything set to go, he went over to Prudence to carry her over to the mule.

"I feel so useless. Can't I walk?"

"Indulge me. Let's get those feet healed." Urias lifted her. Prudence's unique scent overwhelmed him. "You've got pretty eyes," he blurted out.

Her eyes widened and searched his own. A gentle smile rose on her face. "You and your sister have the same eyes. Not quite the same, actually. Yours seem to have little flecks of gold around them."

He began walking slowly, fearing he would be unsteady on his feet. *How is it that she affects me so?*

Prudence chuckled. "Your ears get red when you're embarrassed. Hasn't anyone told you how beautiful your eyes are?"

"My mom has told me on more than one occasion that my wife. . ." He wouldn't finish that statement. Not to Prudence. This situation was getting awkward, to say the least. He placed her on the mule, forcing himself not to drop her out of sheer embarrassment.

&.

Prudence kept replaying in her mind Urias's touch, his words, his kindness, and his embarrassment. Truthfully, she found herself thinking about him most of the day. She watched how he worked with the animals—how he watched the trail, always alert. He was a true mountain man, or rather one very comfortable in the mountains. There was little more than a path most of this trip down to the Wilderness Road. He took his time herding the pigs through some of the narrow spots.

But mostly her mind kept drifting back to his words: *"You've got pretty eyes."* A girl could go a week with no food on that compliment. At least this girl could. No one had ever paid her much attention. Father claimed it was because of her constant blabbering about finances. No man would be interested in a woman who spoke on such matters.

But not Urias. He didn't mind. He actually appreciated her business sense. Her heart sank. By forcing this marriage, Father had ruined any chance of her and Urias ever getting to know one another. Urias would never be content to love her. He'd do his duty, but the freedom to love had been stripped away. And, truthfully, she'd never know if he was just doing his duty or truly loved her. More than anything in this world, Prudence wanted to be loved. Her parents loved her in their own way, but they were always trying to force her to be something she wasn't, never appreciating her for what skills came naturally. *Will I ever have my own life?*

"Watch out!" Urias yelled.

Prudence startled from her musings. She jerked the reins. Slippery rocks covered with morning dew sprawled out just down the path.

Urias ran over to her. "Are you all right?"

"Fine. Sorry. I wasn't paying close attention."

"Prudence, I was going to tell you this later, but you're going to have to stay with the Campbells while I finish bringing the hogs."

"I don't want to stay with the Campbells. I want to finish going with you."

"You're not able. By the time I come back, you'll be able to walk again."

"I can walk now," she protested. She didn't mind taking it easy for a day, and her feet were in bad shape, but she could still walk. Painfully, but she still could do it.

"No. Your feet are a mess. I won't be responsible for you injuring yourself. Katherine is my sister and my responsibility," he argued.

"I love your sister and I want to help."

Urias closed his eyes and waited a moment before he spoke. She felt certain he was collecting his thoughts. "Prudence, I know you care for Katherine, and I appreciate all you've done. But, honey, your feet are in serious need of healing."

"Then wait for me. Perhaps we can take a day or two, feed the hogs at the Campbells' farm, then continue on."

"Look, you'll do as I say. You're my wife, and if I say it's going to be this way, then that's it."

Prudence clamped her mouth shut. All the warm feelings she had for Urias had just rolled down the hollow. She would get the annulment and earn her freedom. She would not live under another tyrant.

Chapter 7

U rias glanced back at Prudence. By the set of her jaw, he knew she was still angry with him. Ordering Prudence to do anything was not the right course of action. He knew better, but he didn't know what else to say. She was too stubborn for her own good.

The sun was low on the horizon by the time they came up to the Campbells' farm. He ran ahead and knocked on the old farmhouse door. Mrs. Campbell opened it.

"Urias?"

"Yes ma'am."

"Well, come on in. It's been ages. How are you?"

"Fine, fine. I need a favor. I'm herding some hogs down to the Cumberland Gap, and I was wondering if my wife and I could spend the night."

"Wife? When did you get married?"

Urias felt the heat rise on his cheeks. "Fairly recently."

"Of course you can stay."

"My wife has injured her feet—from her new boots. I'll bring her in, then take care of the hogs, if that's all right with you."

"Of course. Bring the poor child in. I'll warm some water and get out the salts so she can soak 'em real good."

"Thank you." Urias turned and ran back to Prudence and the hogs. He explained what was going to happen as he led the mule toward the house.

Prudence simply nodded. Apparently she still wasn't ready to speak with him. He lifted her off the mule and carried her to the front door. Mrs. Campbell had him set her on an overstuffed chair in the living room, and, after a brief introduction, he left the two women and rounded up the hogs. He set them in the fenced-in area to the right of the barn and noticed something was wrong. There was little feed for the winter, and the wood supply wasn't fully stocked. It then occurred to him he hadn't seen Mr. Campbell. He walked behind the barn and found a grave and tombstone. Urias choked down a sob.

He stood there for a moment, then went into the house. "I'm sorry. I didn't know about Mr. Campbell."

Mrs. Campbell's eyes filled with tears. "He died just after planting the west field."

Urias stepped up to Mrs. Campbell and wrapped his arms around her. "I'm so sorry. I'd like to do some chores for you while I'm here."

Mrs. Campbell stepped back and wiped her eyes with her white apron. "I'd appreciate that. I'm going to sell the place and move in with my daughter. She and her husband live in Barbourville. The farm is too much for me, and the boys aren't interested in the place."

In all the years he'd known the Campbells, he'd never seen her sons. He'd heard them talk about their daughter on several occasions. "I'll set you up with enough wood for the winter. It's the least I can do."

"Thank you. Neighbors came around and harvested what there was of the corn. I've gotten rid of most of the livestock, except for a cow, a horse, and the chickens. I can handle chickens just fine."

"Write a list of things you need done. I'll go to the Mercers' place and purchase some grain for the hogs." He turned to Prudence. "If you don't mind, I'd like to stay here for a couple of days and help Mrs. Campbell out."

Prudence's face brightened. "I don't mind."

Didn't think ya would. "Great. I'll be back later. May I borrow your horse, Mrs. Campbell?"

"Of course, son. Do what you need to do."

He wanted to lean over and give Prudence a kiss. Where that thought came from he didn't want to know. He set his hat upon his head and said, "I'll be back."

Urias headed for the front door. With his hand to the knob, Prudence called, "Urias, aren't you forgetting something?"

She wants a good-bye kiss? He glanced back at Mrs. Campbell. She didn't know their marriage was a sham. "What?"

She held up the brown leather purse that held her money.

"Thanks." He winked. He'd completely forgotten about money. He just knew what needed to be done and had only a very short time to do it.

He left the house, readied the horse, and headed for the Mercers' place in less than ten minutes. Mentally, he went through a quick list of what he could do to help Mrs. Campbell out in a day—possibly two. He didn't want to take the time, but Prudence needed it for her feet, and Mrs.

Campbell obviously needed some help.

Frank Mercer was more than happy to sell off some feed. He also agreed to send his boys over in the morning to give Urias a hand. "They'd been meaning to come by and help Mrs. Campbell anyway," he said apologetically.

Back at the farm, Urias fed the pigs, blending the grain with some water and various edible greens he'd found along the road. After that he went to the woodpile, stacked the split logs, then proceeded to split those already cut. Tomorrow, he'd have to go into the woods and down the standing deadwood.

The clang of the iron triangle that hung on the front porch rang. Urias brushed the sweat off his brow, extinguished the lantern, and headed for the house.

"Wash barrel is over there now," Mrs. Campbell directed, pointing to the right rear corner of the house.

"Thank you."

"Don't take too much time. Dinner's getting cold. We've been waiting on you."

"Sorry." Urias snickered as he headed to the barrel. "Women."

☙

Mrs. Campbell's treatment for Prudence's feet had her feeling much better. They weren't as raw as when Urias treated them the night before. Mrs. Campbell also lent her a pair of fur-lined slippers that felt absolutely wonderful. Urias didn't know it yet, but she'd been up walking around and helping Mrs. Campbell prepare dinner.

Urias also didn't know that the room Mrs. Campbell had put them in only had one bed and very little space for Urias to sleep on the floor. Somehow Prudence knew she would have to convince Urias to sleep on the bed. He'd been up the entire night before, worked the hogs hard to come here before nightfall, and he'd been working hard all evening. The man was going to collapse if he didn't get some rest.

She wanted to prepare a hot bath for him but didn't feel she had the right to ask Mrs. Campbell for such a sacrifice. One thing was certain: She'd be leaving with Urias when he left. Prudence didn't want to be glad that Mr. Campbell had passed away, but his passing had allowed her the time she needed to heal and continue with Urias.

The front door opened, and Prudence watched Urias remove his boots before entering. "Evening," he said and smiled.

"Good evening. We've made dinner for you," Prudence offered.

"Come on in and set a spell, son, before you drop. A man can't work that hard and not stop for a rest. Even the Good Book tells us we need to rest."

"Yes ma'am." Urias stepped into the front room.

"I've set you two up in the upstairs front bedroom. The other rooms are not fit for guests, I'm sorry to say. I've been rummaging through our belongings and deciding what to keep, what to get rid of, what to pass on to others. . . ." Mrs. Campbell sniffed. "It's not an easy task. I hope the two of you never have to go through it."

Prudence didn't know what to say. The woman truly loved her husband and missed him, but she wasn't pining away for him. She was getting on with her life, near as Prudence could tell.

"That'll be fine, thanks. What smells so delicious?"

Mrs. Campbell beamed. "Just something we cooked up."

"We?"

"Your wife helped. She's handy in the kitchen."

"I know but. . ." Urias looked down at her feet.

"They're feeling much better, and with these, it's easy to walk around." Prudence lifted her skirt slightly to give Urias a peek of the slippers.

"They look warm." He scrunched his eyebrows together. "They look familiar." He turned to Mrs. Campbell.

"Good eye, son." Mrs. Campbell led them to the dining room. "They're the pair your father made me several years back."

"Your father made these?"

"Dad is quite handy with animal hides." Urias sat down in the designated chair.

Prudence sat down beside him.

"Shame on you, son. You're as good as your pa. You mustn't keep those hidden talents away from your wife."

Crimson washed over Urias's face.

"Come now. Say the blessing before this dinner is stone cold."

"Yes'm." Urias led them through a brief but meaningful prayer, asking the Lord's blessing on Mrs. Campbell.

"The Mercer boys will be coming over in the morning to help me with the wood. Between the three of us, I'm sure we'll have enough for the winter by the end of the day."

"I can't thank you enough." Mrs. Campbell reached for the casserole dish and offered it to Urias first. He took out a huge helping and passed the dish on to Prudence, who spooned out a much smaller portion.

"You don't each much, child." Mrs. Campbell received the dish from Prudence.

"My stomach hasn't been feeling too well."

"Are you with child?" Mrs. Campbell asked.

Prudence could feel the heat on her face rage as bright as what had appeared on Urias's. "No, I don't believe so."

Urias stared at her and blinked.

Oh no, Lord, I've given Urias the wrong impression. "We haven't been married that long," Prudence amended, trying to motion with her eyebrows that she was saying that for Mrs. Campbell's sake.

&

The stew and biscuits stuck in Urias's throat. Had he been forced to marry Prudence because she was with child? Had Hiram Greene seen him as a dupe? Urias's temper rose a notch. He forced the morsel down his throat, closed his eyes, and prayed for grace. If Prudence was with child, that would present another problem. How could he abandon her while she's expecting? And what happened to the father?

He took another forkful of the stew and examined his wife a bit more closely.

"Don't take long," Mrs. Campbell answered.

Prudence's face was beet red now.

Now things were beginning to make sense. Someone had gotten Prudence pregnant and run out before Hiram Greene knew of his daughter's sin. Which is why he was so upset at their meeting privately in the barn. Would Prudence have tried to seduce him to convince him the child she was carrying was his?

Dear Lord, give me wisdom.

"Forgive me. My daughter and son-in-law are expecting again. It's their fifth. My mind just wanders over to the subject of babies."

Prudence cleared her throat. "It would be nice to have a child one day."

Urias balled a fist under the table, then opened and closed it again and again.

"They are wonderful, but they are a handful," Mrs. Campbell went on.

Had Prudence offered to come on this trip hoping he'd share the bedroll with her? The more he thought of it, the angrier he became.

Urias forced down his meal as fast as he could. He needed to get out of here, away from Prudence, and away from the trap that was squeezing the life out of him. He'd married her for Katherine's sake. She'd married him for herself. All the noble things he'd begun to think and feel about

Prudence were all based on lies. She wasn't sacrificing for a friend. She was trying to con him and have him be the father of her child.

Mrs. Campbell finished her ramblings. Urias didn't know what she had said, nor was he in the frame of mind to care. His plate nearly cleaned, he pushed it away. "Wonderful meal, ladies. If you'll forgive me, I have a few more things to do in the barn." He turned to Prudence. "Go on to bed without me."

The chair scraped the floor as he stood up. "Thank you again for your hospitality, Mrs. Campbell."

"Urias, can't it wait until morning?"

Prudence got up and walked over to him. She placed her hand on his forearm and whispered, "It's not what you're thinking."

He wanted to believe her; he really did. But so much had happened in the past week, how could he know for sure? *Time,* he answered himself. Time would certainly reveal if Prudence was with child.

"Urias," Prudence said in full voice, "you haven't slept. You need your rest."

Urias felt the throbbing headache he'd been ignoring for hours. Prudence was right. He needed to sleep.

"Very well. If you'll excuse me, I'll retire for the evening."

Mrs. Campbell smiled. "You two go ahead. I'll take care of the dinner dishes."

Prudence's eyes watered with tears.

Doesn't the woman know how to turn them off?

"I'll show you our room," Prudence said, her words soft and kind, so contrary to the thoughts he'd been thinking about her for the past few minutes.

Silently, he followed her up the stairs. When they entered the room, she turned and shut the door. "You're sleeping on the bed. I won't hear of anything else. I'll sleep on the floor." She wagged her finger at him. "If you say one word of objection, I'll scream, and you'll have some serious explaining to do to Mrs. Campbell."

"What's to explain? You're my wife. My pregnant wife, I might add."

"I am not. Don't you go believing Mrs. Campbell's speculations, Urias O'Leary. I've not"—she pointed to the bed—"with a man, ever, and I'm not about to start tonight. So get your mind out of the pig slop and get to bed before I really say what's on my mind. I'm going downstairs to help Mrs. Campbell with the dishes. I best find you sound asleep when I return."

Urias let out a strangled chuckle.

"What?"

"You're beautiful when you're angry."

"Ugh." She pushed him backward, and he landed on the bed. She stomped out of the room and down the stairs.

Urias sat up, unbuttoned his shirt, undressed, washed from the basin near the bed, and put on the clean nightshirt Mrs. Campbell provided. He laid back on the bed and thought over the dinner conversation, then the few moments alone with Prudence. *A real marriage with her wouldn't be boring.*

Thump. Glass shattered. A scream bolted Urias out of the bed.

Chapter 8

Pain seared her skin. Prudence held her hand over the wound.

"Urias," Mrs. Campbell called out, "come quick!"

"I'm here." Urias stood in the doorway of the kitchen in an oversized nightshirt and bare feet.

"What happened?"

Tears threatened to fall. She wouldn't give in to them. Urias already felt she was slowing him down and wanted to leave her here.

"I don't know."

"It was the strangest thing. We were drying the dishes, and the glass in her hand just shattered," Mrs. Campbell offered.

"Let me see." Urias carefully stepped around the bits of broken glass scattered on the floor.

Prudence looked up at Urias. "I'm sure it's nothing."

"Show me anyway, please."

Mrs. Campbell took a broom from the closet. "Watch your step." She swept the glass from behind Prudence. "Lift her up and carry her out of here," Mrs. Campbell ordered.

He lifted her in his arms. His touch was loving—unlike his words earlier.

"This is getting to be a habit."

"I haven't cut myself before."

"No, I meant the carrying you part."

"Oh." Prudence could feel her face flush.

"I'm sorry," he whispered. "I shouldn't have said those things."

Prudence trembled in his arms. He set her in the same overstuffed chair in the living room. "Let me get a lantern to look at that cut."

Prudence looked down at her arm. Her fingers were lined with blood. *How deep is it?* She fought off the desire to check and kept the pressure on the wound. Her hand was starting to throb from the lack of circulation by her applied pressure. Prudence closed her eyes. The sight of blood didn't help her already uneasy stomach. She always had a fairly weak stomach when it came to certain things.

Urias came in with his hands full. In one hand he had a lantern, in the other, clean cloths and a roll of thin cotton fabric, perfect for dressing wounds. He also carried a bowl with water in the crook of his arm. He placed the lantern on a table and sat down on a stool beside her. "Let me see."

Prudence lifted her hand and looked at the wound for the first time. Her stomach flipped, and a cold sweat swept over her body. The gash was at least three inches long, and she could see bits of fat and muscle. Her stomach rolled again.

"Look away before you pass out on me," Urias ordered. "Please," he said, softening his tone.

She obeyed and looked out the window to the night sky.

"I need to flush the wound before I can bandage it. It should be stitched up. I'll do what I can."

Mrs. Campbell came in. "How is it?"

"Deep, but not too bad. About three inches long."

"I'll get my sewing kit." Mrs. Campbell marched out of the living room.

"I don't have anything to numb the wound. When she starts sewing, it will hurt. I'll hold your arm still for her. Are you all right?"

Prudence bit her lower lip and nodded.

Urias held a clean cloth down on the wound. "You'll do fine. If you can walk on those feet of yours, you should be able to put up with Mrs. Campbell sewing you up."

"Is that supposed to encourage me?" Prudence asked.

"Pay him no never mind. It will hurt like a possum with its tail on fire, but it will heal faster."

Urias got up from the stool and offered it to Mrs. Campbell. He stood between her and Mrs. Campbell and got ready to hold Prudence's arm tight.

Mrs. Campbell positioned both of them, then warned Prudence, "Hold your husband's thigh real tight. When the needle hurts, simply tighten your grasp on Urias's thigh. If he can put up with the pain you're giving him, then you're doing fine."

Prudence wasn't too sure how that would be the case, but she did as she was ordered and reached around Urias's thigh. It was firm and muscular, much the way she imagined it would be. Embarrassed by her own wayward thoughts, she felt grateful that neither Mrs. Campbell nor Urias could see her face.

"I'm going to begin now," Mrs. Campbell said and pushed the needle into Prudence's arm. She bored her fingertips into Urias's leg.

"How many stitches do you think it will take?" Urias asked, his voice strained.

"Far more than I'll put in."

Prudence lessened her grip on Urias. He didn't flinch once the entire time Mrs. Campbell stitched up her wound.

"I'll wrap it up," Urias offered.

"Give it a lot of padding. There will be some more bleeding through the night. Change it first thing in the morning, then you can tighten it a bit more."

"Yes ma'am. Thank you." Urias resumed his position on the stool.

"Thank you, Mrs. Campbell. I'm sorry about the glass."

"Fiddlesticks, dear. I'm sorry you were injured."

"Mrs. Campbell, if it's all right with you, I'll sleep in another room tonight. Prudence will need the full bed to stretch out her arm."

Mrs. Campbell nodded. "In the middle room, there's a small path to the bed through the crates. Just watch your step."

"Thank you." Urias wrapped the cotton strips around Prudence's arm.

Once Mrs. Campbell was in the kitchen, Prudence spoke up. "At least neither of us will be on the floor tonight. Thank you."

"Go to bed, Prudence. I'll see you in the morning." Urias walked over to the door, put on his boots, and stepped out.

What have I done now?

&

Urias's leg throbbed. He had to get some cold water on it right away. And well water would be the coldest. Ice would be best, but there was none to be found. Even if there was, he wouldn't use it on a wound. *How long are that woman's fingernails, Lord?* He'd almost given in to screaming but noticed Mrs. Campbell was on her last stitch. Outside, he limped to the well. He didn't think she'd broken the skin, but it sure felt like hot pokers stabbing him now. With his luck, he'd be black and blue in the morning.

Urias pumped until a cool stream of water poured into the small bucket at the end of the spigot. He placed the wad of cotton linen he'd brought out with him into the water, then placed it on his throbbing leg.

Before the torture, Prudence's hands had sent a feeling through him that seemed foreign and yet familiar. The contact, for a moment, seemed to almost make him feel. . .feel what? What was the feeling he had experienced? Completeness? But how could there be oneness with a forced marriage? It wasn't a sanctioned marriage. It couldn't be. God wouldn't honor a marriage of this sort.

The Bible story of Esther came to mind. God honored Esther and her marriage to the king, even though he wasn't Jewish. The circumstances of her training to be his wife and of the pagan rituals involved did not honor God, yet God honored Esther and her marriage to the king.

Urias removed the warming cloth and placed it back in the bucket of cool water.

God may have honored that marriage because He had a greater purpose—the salvation of the Jews from their treatment in that country. Urias's marriage was for a noble purpose—the saving of his sister from her bondage, but. . .could God honor their marriage?

Urias shook the thought off as he placed the cold cloth back on his thigh. When it warmed again, he cooled it again and placed it on his forehead rather than his thigh. His head throbbed from the lack of sleep. He needed to get to bed and recover from the trip, emotional fatigue, and the tremendous burden he'd accepted for the sake of his sister. "Lord, be with Katherine. Keep her safe."

He scanned the heavens. The stars shone in all their glory. "Add Prudence to that request, Lord. The woman tries hard, but she's got to be in pain with those feet and now this wound on her arm. I don't know what to do with her, Father. I do want a wife and children one day, but I'd like to be able to choose who that woman would be. I don't feel right sending her back home to her parents. They don't seem to appreciate her. On the other hand, I don't know what I could do for her. I don't have my own farm to hire her on, but she doesn't seem the sort to work with her hands, anyway."

The past few days' journey floated through his mind. Not once had Prudence complained about the work, the trail, or her injuries. "She deserves a husband who loves and appreciates her for the way You've gifted her. Father, send her a husband quickly. She needs a husband."

What's she going to do once our marriage is dissolved? he wondered. He removed the cloth from his forehead and combed his hair back from his face with his fingers. He shook off the thought and headed back to the house. He needed rest, and thinking about Prudence would prevent him from sleeping.

&

Urias woke the next morning and went to the barn before the sun rose over the horizon. He milked the cow, fed the chickens, and took care of a few other odd chores to help Mrs. Campbell. Her moving in with her daughter seemed the most logical thing to do. The small farm was too much for a single person, not to mention an older woman.

The smell and sound of bacon frying in the griddle greeted him when he walked into the house. Mrs. Campbell stood at the stove. "Thank you, Urias. It felt wonderful to sleep in this morning."

"You're welcome."

"How'd you sleep?"

"Fine." Urias placed the bucket of fresh milk next to the sink.

She smiled. "How's the leg?"

For an old gal, she doesn't miss much. "Sore. . .and shaded with some interesting colors of purple and blue."

"Sorry. I thought of giving her some whiskey but—"

"Happy to help. The leg will heal."

"Urias, it's none of my business but. . ." She paused to set a plate of eggs, bacon, and fried potatoes on the table, then motioned for him to sit down. "How well do you know this girl?"

His back went stiff. Had she noticed they weren't acting much like a husband and wife? Or had she seen or heard something from Prudence that concerned her? Urias let out a long, slow breath. "We're still learning about each other," he replied.

❧

Prudence stood on the bottom stair, eavesdropping on Urias and Mrs. Campbell's discussion.

"She doesn't know the first thing about canning and preparing foods for the winter. How's she supposed to handle being a farmer's wife?"

"Guess she'll have to rely on folks like yourself to teach her."

Prudence smiled. Could he be expecting her to become his real wife? Did she want that? Admittedly, the attraction between them was growing. Perhaps that's why it hurt so much to have him thinking she was with child.

Mrs. Campbell chuckled. "You're only going to be here a day or two."

"She's a quick learner. I've been impressed with her on the trail. She's picking up things very quickly."

Mrs. Campbell let out a hearty laugh. "You're doing like your parents, eh?"

Urias chuckled. "Appears that way."

Doing what like his parents? The major problem with eavesdropping was you didn't have the freedom to ask questions when points of interest came up. Prudence stepped down the final step to the floor and walked into the kitchen. "Good morning," she said.

"Morning. How's the arm?" Urias sat at the table with a plate full of eggs, bacon, potatoes, and corn bread. There was enough on his plate to feed two. He sank his fork into his eggs and continued to eat his meal.

"Sore. I haven't looked under the bandage yet."

Mrs. Campbell turned from the stove and placed another plate with a smaller portion at the place setting next to Urias. "Come, sit down. There's more if you would like some."

"Thank you." Prudence sat down. "This is more than sufficient."

"Would you like me to take care of the bandage?" Urias offered, holding a forkful of eggs halfway between his mouth and the plate.

"If you wouldn't mind. I think I could manage, but it would be awkward."

"Be my pleasure."

Mrs. Campbell set a plate for herself on the table and sat down with them. "Keep it clean and it should heal well."

"I'm concerned about taking you out on the trail for that very reason."

Prudence's heart landed in the pit of her stomach. The fear that had plagued her most of the night had come true. He planned on leaving her with Mrs. Campbell while he finished the trip to the Cumberland Gap.

"Honey, I don't want an infection to set in."

Honey? That's the second time he called me that. Does he actually care for me? Or is this to put up a front for Mrs. Campbell? Urias didn't seem the kind of man that would deliberately deceive folks.

"He's giving good counsel, Prudence. A gal can't stay all that clean on the road. I ain't never hauled no pigs, but when my husband and I were much younger, we made the trip east a few times, taking sheep and cattle to Virginia. It was an excellent way to earn good money. But the road was dusty."

Prudence sighed. "I suppose you both are right."

Urias reached over and placed his hand upon hers. "I'll stay through tomorrow and set out at dawn."

"Can one man handle all those hogs?" Mrs. Campbell asked.

Urias leaned back in his chair. "I suppose I should hire someone to come along with me."

"But that will cut the profit." Prudence covered her mouth. The words just slipped out.

Urias smiled. "Right. Why don't we wait and see how your wound is tomorrow night? Then I'll see if one of the Mercer boys can lend a hand."

Prudence lifted her gaze and zeroed in on her husband. Her husband—could her father's arrogance have been a blessing in disguise?

Chapter 9

Urias worked hard until sundown. Frank Jr. and Samuel stayed the better part of the day. And Frank mentioned he'd be willing to lend a hand with the hogs if Prudence wasn't ready for travel. Urias knew Prudence didn't want to be left behind, yet what choice did he have? On the other hand, a few days with Mrs. Campbell could be helpful for Prudence to learn more about being a farmer's wife. Not that he was hoping she'd be his "real" wife one day.

As he stacked the wood beside the house that had been split earlier, giving Mrs. Campbell an easier distance to travel in the winter months, the biblical story of Esther popped into his mind once again. Was God trying to say something to him?

The clang of the iron triangle in the front of the house meant it was time for supper. He set the logs on the pile and brushed his clothes down. He needed a good scrubbing, not to mention the state of his clothing.

Scraping his feet on the porch before entering the house, he found Prudence standing at the door waiting for him. "Hi. How was your day?"

"Fine." She held her hands behind her back and had a smile as wide as Cumberland Falls on her face.

"What?" he asked.

"I made you something."

"Oh?" He pulled his boots off and left them by the door.

"Mrs. Campbell would like you to wash up before dinner."

Urias chuckled.

"She put a clean set of clothes for you on the bed. I'm to bring your dirty clothes down for a good scrubbing."

"They can use it."

"Uh-huh."

Urias fought off the urge to smell his armpits and headed up the stairs, taking them two at a time. He halted halfway up and turned to see Prudence stepping on the bottom step. "What did you make for me?"

"You'll see." She grinned once again.

Urias continued up the stairs and went to the front bedroom. Folded in a neat pile were a clean shirt and a pair of pants.

Prudence leaned on the doorjamb with her hands still behind her back. "You've got my curiosity up. What are you hiding?"

"You'll see after you give me your dirty clothes."

"Am I to undress in front of you?"

Prudence blushed. "Sorry." She stepped away from the door and waited in the hallway.

Urias closed the door, slipped off his clothes, then reopened it enough to pass them through a small opening. Prudence hesitated, then grabbed the soiled clothes with one hand while keeping her injured arm behind her.

"As much as I want to see my surprise, I think I should wash up and dress first."

Prudence's face beamed hot-coal red. Without saying a word, she hurried down the hallway and descended the stairs.

Urias let out a light chuckle, then went to the basin to wash. He looked at the bruises on his leg. They were a deep purple, and the soreness had continued throughout the day. Clean and dried off, he put on undergarments and the shirt, then sat on the bed and wrapped a warm damp towel around the bruised thigh.

"Urias. . ." Prudence opened the door.

He jumped off the bed. The towel slipped to the floor.

"Oh!" Prudence gasped. "Did I do that to you?"

Prudence stared at the bruises on Urias's thigh. "Can I do anything for you? Get you anything?"

Urias cleared his throat. In a whisper, he said, "Prudence, I'm not dressed."

"Oh right. Sorry." Prudence stumbled out of the bedroom. She assumed he'd be dressed by now. *Why did I come upstairs, anyway?* she wondered.

The bruises on his thigh were the size of silver dollars. The door opened slowly once Urias was dressed. "Come on in."

"I'm so sorry," she apologized.

"It's all right."

"Do they hurt?"

"Huh?"

She pointed to his thigh. "The bruises."

"Not too bad. Now can I see my surprise?"

He was worse than a child at a birthday celebration. "It's not that special, but I had some free time today, and Mrs. Campbell had the yarn so. . ." She handed him the gift.

"A scarf. You made this?"

She didn't know whether to be upset with him for his assumptions about her upbringing again or to take it as the compliment it appeared to be. She decided on the latter. "Yes, I learned to knit from my grandmother."

"It's beautiful." Urias wrapped the scarf around his neck. "And warm, too."

"Thank you. I'm glad you like it."

Prudence then felt that awkward silence that often fell between them when they were alone. Not knowing what to say, she stepped back.

"This is really sweet. Thank you, Prudence. I spoke with Frank Jr. today, and he's willing to lend me a hand with the hogs if you're not up for travel. Speaking of which, how's the arm coming?"

"It's still sensitive, and it's bled a bit, too."

"Would you like me to change the dressing?"

"If you wouldn't mind, I'd appreciate it."

"Sit on the bed and I'll get the supplies," Urias ordered.

Prudence realized she didn't mind his orders—he didn't bark them out like her father. She watched him as he went to the dresser that held the cotton strips of cloth. His red curls seemed masculine on him, quite unlike his sister's, which enhanced her femininity. He turned around.

"What?" he asked.

"It's frivolous really, but you and your sister have the same hair, and yet the curls look feminine on her and not on you."

Urias chuckled. "I'm glad I don't look like a girl."

Prudence blushed. "I didn't mean that."

"No. I know what you mean. I grew my hair out once. Dad wears his rather long. I had to be careful how I brushed mine. If I didn't, you could do me up in a dress and not be sure if I was a boy or a girl. Short hair made more sense. It's easier to care for, and I don't have to worry about it." He approached, carrying the cotton strips for the fresh bandage, and sat down on the bed beside her. "Once I let my little sisters Molly and Sarah play with my hair. They had it all teased up like a beehive. If you set a bonnet on my head, I would have looked quite cute."

Prudence giggled. "I'd like to see that."

"Not on your life. Little sisters playing is one thing but. . .well, a man must maintain some level of self-respect."

Without thinking, Prudence reached out and touched his hair. "I don't think you could pass for a woman now."

"Thank you. I tried to grow a mustache, but it's not thick enough yet, and it looked funny—like a fuzzy red worm lying across my lip."

Prudence let out a full laugh now.

"Give me your arm, please."

She reached over to him, and his hands set a flicker of awareness so bold up her arm that she almost pulled it away from his touch. He cut off the knot that held the bandage in place and proceeded to unwind it. With each revolution, her arm tingled as the blood surged through to the wound.

When he reached the pads on top of the cut, he lifted them slowly. In a couple of places, the pad stuck to the wound. "Ouch!" Prudence cried out.

"Sorry. I'll need to dampen those spots. These are probably places Mrs. Campbell could have placed another stitch."

Once all of the bandage was off, she got a good look at the wound. "It's going to be a nasty scar, isn't it?"

"Probably. Depends on how you heal. I scar easily. My dad, not so easily but. . ." His words trailed off.

"But what?"

"Well, Dad's back has these huge scars from when he tried to save his first wife from a bear attack. He was too late."

"I'm so sorry."

"It happened long before I met him."

"You and your family have lived such interesting lives." At the moment, Prudence felt she would love to be a part of Urias's family. He was a kind man, a gentle man, yet she still couldn't figure him out.

"We've traveled a bit more than most farmers. What about you? Did your family ever travel?"

"When I was younger. I remember trips into the city. But for many years now, we've stayed close to home. Father goes off, but he doesn't take the family with him. He says it's business, but I have my doubts." Prudence cut herself off from saying anything further that could incriminate her father.

"Prudence, I know I'm paying more for Katherine's bond than I should. Is your father in financial trouble? Is that why he insisted we marry?"

"No, not that I'm aware." Prudence looked down at her lap and played with the material of her dress. "He forced you to marry me because he doesn't believe any man would want me."

"That's nonsense. You're a beautiful woman."

"Who speaks her thoughts when women should keep silent."

"Look," he said as he lifted her chin with his forefinger, "I know what your father says about women and money, but he doesn't speak for all men. Some of us appreciate a woman with a good head on her shoulders."

Her heart started pounding. She took quick, short breaths. She searched his eyes, those wonderful green eyes. She wanted him to kiss her. Moving ever so slowly, she leaned toward him. And he leaned toward her. He slipped his gaze down to her lips and back to her eyes.

"Prudence, Urias, dinner is ready," Mrs. Campbell hollered from downstairs.

"Be right there," Urias answered. He finished replacing the bandage and took up the soiled strips.

Prudence sat like a boulder on the bed. What had just happened? Were they falling in love? No. . .she'd already fallen. But could Urias feel the same way? *Oh dear Lord, help us understand what's happening.*

ॐ

Urias kept his distance after dinner. Out in the barn, he looked for any possible odd job that would keep the separation between him and Prudence. He hoped he could sleep in the spare bed again tonight. Sharing the same room with her right now could prove to be dangerous. What was he thinking earlier?

Fess up, boy. You know you wanted to kiss her and taste those sweet lips. Urias picked up the pitchfork and headed over to the stall.

And that's what bothered him so much. He wanted to kiss her. But what he feared most was that the want would become a need. It was borderline, at best, at the moment. Leaving Prudence with Mrs. Campbell while he finished the trip would probably be best for both of them. They were spending far too much time with one another. He found her to be an attractive and smart lady.

Why had Hiram Greene forced a marriage on both of them? To Urias, it seemed to be more than Hiram Greene's fear that he couldn't marry his daughter off. And this whole business with Katherine's bond being so high after her having worked for two years. . . Well, something wasn't adding up. Urias needed more facts to understand the matter, but he doubted Prudence knew what was going on. She seemed as upset with her father for the forced marriage as he was.

Married to a woman he couldn't touch. It didn't seem right. Everything about this marriage was false. Yet there was something about Prudence that he was drawn to. He recalled her giggle when he'd talked about what his sisters had done to his hair. They were only three and five at the time. It was a fun memory.

Urias pitched the hay from the stall to the wheelbarrow.

"Urias," Mrs. Campbell called from the opened barn door.

"What can I do for you?"

"You can stop taking care of my chores and spend some time with that pretty little wife of yours."

Urias turned away and pitched some more hay. "I will. Prudence understands."

"Does she? I sure don't."

He couldn't explain to Mrs. Campbell. It was bad enough that she knew that he was married before his parents knew.

Urias placed the pitchfork against the stall. "I'll come in."

"Good. I started some water boiling for a hot bath. I know your wife needs a good soak. She'll need your help washing her hair."

"I can't."

"Why not?"

Urias pulled in a deep draft of air. "Mrs. Campbell, I need to tell you something. When I was a boy, I ran away from my mother because she'd beat me when she was drunk. Apparently, after I left home, my mother started beating my sister, Katherine, in my place. From what Katherine says, Mother sold her into bondage six years ago. She's been working as a servant ever since. It took me five years to find her."

"I'm so sorry, Urias. But what's all this got to do with you not being able to wash Prudence's hair?"

"Prudence's father owns Katherine's bond. Prudence was talking with me about how I could earn some money selling hogs to pay Katherine's debt when her father caught us. And, well, he forced us to get married. He said either that, or I'd go to jail and he'd sell Katherine's bond to someone else."

"What? Is this man a fool?"

"I couldn't wager a guess on that. He's overcharging me for Katherine's bond—of that I'm certain. Even Prudence agrees with me on that. Prudence is my legal wife, but we've not. . ."

"Oh, I see. I'll help Prudence bathe." Mrs. Campbell turned toward the house. "You're welcome to stay in the other room if you wish."

"Thank you. I don't know what this marriage means. Prudence says we can get an annulment, but I want to speak with my parents on the matter first."

"You have my prayers, son."

"Thank you. Prudence is a sweet woman. She's got a good head on her shoulders, and her parents don't seem to appreciate her."

Mrs. Campbell smiled. "Perhaps the good Lord can take something horrible from this situation and make something beautiful."

Could He? Urias wondered as she left the barn. *Would He?*

Thoughts of Prudence danced through his mind once again—the feel of her soft skin, the gentle fragrance that was her scent. . .a scent so intoxicating it drove him to want to kiss her.

"Argh!" Urias lifted the pitchfork once again.

The sound of a horse's hooves pounding over packed dirt interrupted him in midstride. He turned to see a horse come running up between the house and the barn, its rider hollering, "Is there a Urias O'Leary here?"

Chapter 10

Prudence heard the stranger holler and bolted through the front door of Mrs. Campbell's farmhouse.

"How can I help you, sir?" Urias said. It was hard to see him in the moonlight.

"Are you Urias O'Leary?"

"I am. What do you want?"

"I've been trailing you for a few days. Hiram Greene over in Hazel Green said to give you a message."

"What's that?"

Prudence hurried down the steps of the front porch.

"He says you owe him a dowry for his daughter."

"Dowry?" Prudence and Urias said in unison.

"Yup. Says you up and run off with his daughter after you were wed, and since you're taking her from the house, you have to pay him for her."

Prudence could see Urias clearly as he balled his gloved hand into a fist.

"Where are you headed?" Urias asked the stranger.

"Back to Mount Sterling in the morning. Does the owner rent rooms?" he asked, gesturing toward the farmhouse.

Mrs. Campbell placed her hands on Prudence's shoulders. "Don't have any available indoors at the moment. You can spend the night in the barn if you need a roof over your head."

The stranger lifted his hat. "Thank ya, ma'am. I'd appreciate it. The wind's blowin' enough for a storm to come through later this evenin'."

"Very well. That will be two dollars for the night, and I'll have a warm meal for you in ten minutes."

"I appreciate it."

"Urias, would you show the man where he can bunk down for the night?"

"Yes ma'am."

Mrs. Campbell trailed a hand down Prudence's good arm and tugged.

"Come on. We've got another plate to fix." Prudence and Mrs. Campbell headed back into the house to retrieve clean dishes they'd already put away from their dinner.

Who is this stranger? And why would Father say Urias now owes him a dowry?

"Your father must be a strange one," Mrs. Campbell muttered on the way to the kitchen. "Urias just told me about your marriage. Why is he wanting a dowry now?"

"I don't know. I do know some of Father's business dealings in recent days haven't gone so well, but I've never known him to cheat a man. At least not like this. Up a price maybe, but never do something like this. I can't believe it. Mother mentioned something about Urias moving into the house and living there. Can you imagine?"

"No, not at all. Your father has Urias over a barrel, and he knows it. How much were you expecting to earn from the hogs?" Mrs. Campbell questioned.

"With what we owe Thomas Hagins for the hogs, we might have a hundred left after paying the five hundred to Father for Kate's bond."

Mrs. Campbell let out a slow whistle.

Urias came in and stomped his feet at the door. "What is your father trying to pull this time?" he bellowed.

"I don't know."

"Did you and he plan this? How'd that man know where we were?" Urias paced back and forth in the large kitchen. "Your father didn't even know we were selling the hogs. For all he knows, we're heading to Jamestown to fetch the money from my parents."

Holding down her anger, Prudence said, "I won't even attempt to answer your absurd first question. As for how Father might know where we are, Thomas Hagins could have paid him a visit. He was certainly surprised to find out I was married."

Urias stopped and looked out the rear window. The sun had completely set now, and he stood facing a black canvas.

"Excuse me for interrupting," Mrs. Campbell began, "but I'd say that man in the barn is someone for hire. Perhaps he'd be willing to help you take the hogs down to the gap. And during your trip, you might find out more about. . .Mr. Greene, is it?"

Prudence nodded.

Urias turned around and faced the women once again. "That idea might have merit, Mrs. Campbell. What do you think, Prudence?"

All the anger she held for Urias instantly dissolved. He was outright asking her opinion. "As much as I don't want to let you go on without me, it might be the best thing. I wonder how much Father paid him to deliver the message."

"Enough to make it worth my while." The stranger stood at the kitchen doorway. He'd come in unannounced and without making a sound.

"Who are you?" Urias asked.

"Sherman Hatfield. I was just passing through town when I heard how Hiram Greene was angrier than a hornet and wanting compensation for you just running off and leaving town with his daughter."

"What about Katherine?" Urias prayed nothing had happened to her since he left.

"Who's Katherine?" Sherman motioned to the table. "May I?"

"Certainly. Have a seat. The food's just about heated up." Mrs. Campbell stirred the meat in the frying pan.

"Thank ya. It's mighty kind of ya, Mrs. Campbell."

"No problem at all. Now, what about Urias's sister, Katherine?"

"Don't know the woman. Can't say."

"She's a bond servant in my father's house. She has long red hair— same color as Urias's," Prudence informed him.

"Oh, I recall seeing her. Frightened little thing. Practically hid in the shadows. Only spoke when spoken to." Sherman locked his gaze on Urias. "She's your sister?"

"Yes." Urias sat down across from him at the table. "Did she appear beaten?"

"No. . . Hey, wait. Are you telling me he beats her?"

"No," Prudence interjected defensively. "My father may be a lot of things, but I've never known him to lift a hand against another."

Sherman gave a nod. "Didn't ya give the man a couple of goats for your wife? Even the poorest of us in the hills pay the wife's family off with something."

"He never asked me to pay a dowry." Urias wasn't about to explain the coerced nature of the wedding.

Mrs. Campbell placed a plate of ham, fried potatoes, and glazed carrots in front of the stranger.

"Thank ya. Smells great."

"You're welcome." Mrs. Campbell sat down at the table. "Set a spell, Prudence."

Sherman Hatfield glanced at each person around the table. "I'm just the messenger. I ain't got nothin' to do with Hiram Greene's personal business."

That might be true, but it was mighty peculiar for a man to travel this far just to deliver a message. "How long have you been on the road?"

"Three days. You moved those hogs right quick. The trail was easy to follow."

"I wasn't trying to hide out."

"I reckoned that be the case. Still, seems odd for you to run off with the man's daughter and not pay the dowry."

"He never stated he wanted one," Urias repeated, defending his actions.

"Urias, I don't think Daddy can charge you a dowry after we're married."

"That is probably true, but you're forgetting he simply won't release Katherine's bond. And he'd have me arrested for running off with his property if I don't pay your dowry." Urias leaned back in his chair. How was the Lord at work in this? He should have gone home straightaway and spoken with his parents. They would have known what to do. At least he hoped they would have. At the moment, he was clueless.

Urias sat straight up and leaned forward toward Sherman. "How'd you happen by Hiram Greene's place?"

"I met up with him in the city. We had some unfinished business. I stopped by to help finish the matter."

"Can you be more specific?" Urias pushed. Something wasn't adding up. No one would travel three or four days out of their way just to give a message that could have been conveyed when Urias arrived to pick up his sister. The more he knew of Hiram Greene's business dealings, the more certain he became that Katherine did not owe Mr. Greene the money he claimed she did.

Sherman scooped the last of his potatoes onto his fork. "Mighty fine meal, Mrs. Campbell. Thank you."

He placed two dollars in small change on the table.

&

Prudence hadn't slept a wink. First she learned that Urias had told Mrs. Campbell their arrangements concerning their wedding. Then the stranger came, giving them a message from Father demanding a dowry. Could life get much worse? *Just when Urias and I are beginning to know one another, this happens.*

Rolling over onto her side, she looked out the window. A light frost had come during the night. Urias needed to get those hogs to the Cumberland Gap. He couldn't wait for her arm to heal, and they couldn't afford any more expenses. How was he going to pay for her dowry? Father had to have some plan or reason to change the debt for Urias, but what? And if he didn't pay, would Father release Kate?

She replayed the same questions over and over again in her mind. Pushing the covers off, she slipped on the bathrobe Mrs. Campbell had lent her and went to Urias's room.

"Urias," she whispered, tapping the door lightly. "Are you awake?"

Hearing no answer, she placed her hand on the brass doorknob and turned it to the right. Prudence stepped into the room and found the narrow pathway to the bed. "Urias," she called again.

As she moved toward the bed, she discovered he wasn't there. "Where is he?" *The barn*, she remembered. *He wakes up before the sun.*

She ran down the stairs and out the front door. "Urias?"

He leaned his red head out the door and smiled. "What woke you up so early this morning?"

She walked to the end of the front porch. She felt the chill of the air on her toes first. "I didn't sleep."

Urias came over to her. "What Sherman said?"

Prudence nodded.

Urias hopped the porch rail and took her in his arms. "I'm sorry. We'll work this out. Somehow, we'll work this out. I need to take the hogs today. The sooner I deliver them sold, the sooner we can deal with your father."

She shivered in his arms.

He looked down at her feet. "Where are your slippers?"

"I left them in the house. I thought you were in your room."

Urias scooped her off her feet into his arms. "Come on. Let's get you inside."

Prudence wrapped her arms around his neck. Her heart ached over what her father was doing to this sweet man. *He'd make the perfect husband, but he'll never be free to love me, all because of Father.* She buried her head into his shoulder.

"Shh. It's going to be all right. I don't know how, but I know God will see us through. I might have to go home by myself and tell my parents about the situation I got myself into, but I'll be back for you. You can't live with a man like that. There's no telling what he'd do."

"Father's never behaved like this before. I noticed some problems in his financial sheets, but nothing that would warrant cheating a man."

Urias brushed the hair from her face, his touch so gentle, his gaze so consuming.

"You've got beautiful eyes, Prudence."

She felt the blush rise on her cheeks.

"And I love that shade on you."

Prudence gave him a loving swat. She was still in his embrace as he entered the house and carried her up the stairs. *Is he going to. . .* Her eyes widened at the thought.

In her bedroom, he placed her on the bed. He knelt down in front of her and brushed off her feet. "They've healed well. How's the arm?"

"Still hurts." Had she misread the signals? Was he just being the kind man that he was? Her face brightened another shade.

"Would you like me to change the dressing before I leave?"

"No, thanks. Mrs. Campbell will help me change it."

"All right. Lay down, Prudence." Urias reached out and touched her cheek. "You need to rest, honey. I'll be back as soon as I can."

He tucked her in, then held her hands. "Pray with me, Prudence. Together we'll hear from the Lord about what He wants us to do."

Another jolt of excitement ran through her. This was no longer physical; it was much deeper than that. Urias respected her, believed in her, and wanted to pray with her. He sought her counsel and trusted her enough to pray with him for the answers to their problems.

Tears streamed down her face as she listened to Urias pray, then added her own prayers. He stood up. With his thumb, he gently rubbed away her tears. "God has the answer for us, Prudence. We have to trust Him, because nothing else is making much sense."

"You're right," she admitted.

He kissed the top of her head and slipped out of the room. A peace washed over her. Within minutes, she heard Urias call the hogs and heard them squealing as they exited the fenced-in yard.

Prudence closed her eyes and started to fall asleep.

A loud bang reverberated through the air. Prudence sat straight up.

Chapter 11

U rias aimed his rifle at the two men who jumped out of the bushes. "You don't want to see how fast I can reload this rifle, do you?"

The two men he and Prudence had met on the trail a couple of days earlier walked out with their hands in the air. "We don't mean no harm."

Urias reloaded the Kentucky long rifle, keeping his gaze fixed on the two men. Perhaps it was time to buy a new firearm that held more than a single shot. "You two didn't learn the first time, huh?"

"We didn't realize it was you," the thinner of the two men mumbled.

"Ain't no never mind to me. I'm still going to take you in to the sheriff." Urias had the rifle reloaded and ready. "Unless you want to prove to me you can be of more use to society than stealing from it."

"Whatcha got in mind?" the younger man with porcupinelike hair asked.

"If you two help me haul these hogs to the Cumberland Gap, with no stopping to camp—just to let the hogs rest for a spell—I won't press charges. If, however, you try anything, I'll run you in to the closest sheriff faster than you can spit yer tobacca."

They looked at each other and shrugged their shoulders. "Sounds fair."

"Good. Get your packs and let's get a move on." Urias cracked the whip above the hogs' heads to encourage them forward. The two men would test his skills, but they could be a huge blessing. With two additional men pushing at the rear, he could make better time.

"What do we do?" one hollered.

"Cut yourself a willow twig and snap it above their heads and keep walking forward. They'll move."

Urias kept an eye on the road and an eye on his back. He'd made sure the men were not armed. He wasn't letting his guard down for a moment. As they passed the Mercer farm, Frank Jr. met him on the road with a full pack.

"Frank, ask your dad to check on the Campbell farm, and tell him everything's all right."

"Sure." Frank ran up the hill toward his house. Urias caught a glance of the men behind him. "Don't be getting any funny ideas. Frank's dad is a deputy."

Urias heard the men grumble.

Frank Jr. came running back. "Where do you need me?"

"In the rear. Show those two what to do. Watch 'em closely, then send them toward the middle. I'll feel better with you taking up the rear."

"Gotcha." Frank ran to the rear of the herd. He was a couple years younger than Urias. As children, they used to play together.

They kept a steady pace for four hours, took a break for an hour, and pressed on again. The two would-be robbers actually demonstrated themselves to be quite good with the hogs. In crossing the New River at English Ferry, they swam the hogs across to avoid the ferryboat fee. They continued on that way through the night, and by noon the following day, they had made it to Cumberland County, where Urias sold the swine at $3.50 per hundred pounds, net.

Having more than enough to purchase Katherine's bond and pay Prudence's dowry, Urias gave each man ten dollars with his thanks. Urias learned his two hired hands were brothers, who'd decided that making an honest wage was far more profitable than robbing folks on the road. Frank and Urias spent the night at an inn to let some distance develop between them and the brothers.

The next day, Urias sold the mule and purchased a horse. He and Frank rode the horse back to Flatlick with no evidence of the brothers following behind. They arrived at the Campbell farm, surprised to find more uninvited guests.

"Urias?" Prudence cried and ran to meet him on the road.

"Who's here?" he asked as he slid off the saddle.

"Mrs. Campbell's daughter. We've been packing up her belongings. You bought a horse?"

"Yup. Got a good deal for him. He's no racing horse, but he'll get us through the hollows in more comfort than the mule."

"Didn't Thomas say a mule was better to travel the hollows with?"

"Yes, and I probably should have kept the mule but—it's a long story. I'll tell you after I get to the house."

"All right. It's good to see you. I've missed you. Why'd you shoot your rifle when you left?"

"Again, it has to do with that long story. Have you got a hot meal for a hungry man?"

"Not ready. But I can have one fixed up in no time." Her smile capti- vated his heart. The push to get the hogs sold left little time to think of Prudence and their growing attraction. But the ride home with Frank had given him plenty of time to think. Too much time to think. He had the money. He could pay her dowry. But what would happen after that?

"Urias?"

"Huh?" He emerged from his dazed state.

"I really missed you."

Urias nodded. He couldn't speak. His deceitful heart would betray him. A man ought to know better than to give in to a woman who'd been nothing but trouble since the day he'd set eyes on her.

But was it her fault? No, at least not entirely her fault. But if she hadn't come into the barn that second time...

And if he hadn't wrapped her in his arms.

"Urias?"

"Huh?"

"I asked how you made out with the sale."

"I got enough to buy Katherine's bond and your dowry. Unless your father upped the price again, I'm going to negotiate low for you."

Prudence's smile faded.

"I didn't mean that the way it sounded. I don't want your father to know how much I earned selling the hogs. He'll ask for more money. I'll offer him three hundred for your dowry, and we'll work from there. How's that sound?"

Prudence cleared her throat.

He'd hurt her again.

"Very wise," she croaked out.

"Prudence, I didn't mean to say you weren't worth more."

"I know."

You have a funny way of showing it, Urias mused. And he found him- self constantly feeling hogtied, not knowing what to say or do around this woman. He'd been forced to marry her. He was now attracted to her. But as much as he wanted to, he couldn't trust her, not completely. He wanted to—she'd done nothing to show she was less than trustworthy. Yet still he had his doubts. And those doubts would keep him from tak- ing her into his arms and kissing her. Even though that's exactly what he'd wanted to do when she'd run up to greet him.

❧

Prudence found herself wanting to walk rather than riding double with Urias. Instead, he'd gotten down and led the horse through the narrow spots on the trail. It was well blazed by the hogs. No wonder Sherman Hatfield had found them so easily.

Her time with Mrs. Campbell had been quite an education. She'd learned little things about farming, canning, and planning out the food for the winter. She'd even been taught how to smoke a ham. When Mrs. Campbell's daughter arrived, they spent the entire time making the house ready for Mrs. Campbell's departure and packing up her most precious belongings. Prudence knew she would probably never see Mrs. Campbell again, but the woman had left a mark on her life that would never be erased.

They made camp near a small brook, and Urias set up a privacy area for her to wash. Tonight, she realized, they'd be sharing the tent. There were no more hogs to guard, and, from Urias's tales of the rest of the journey, the would-be robbers were well on their way to making their own legitimate fortune.

The awkward moment came when it was time for them to go to bed for the night. "You can sleep in the tent."

"Urias, that's foolish. We're two grown adults and married. I trust you."

He opened his mouth to speak, then closed it. He didn't trust her. That was their problem. One of their problems.

"You don't trust me, do you?"

He turned away from her.

She walked over to him and placed her hand on his shoulder. "Urias."

He turned, took her in his arms, and captured her lips. Prudence found herself caught up in the emotion and returned the kiss with equal fervor. She wrapped her arms around his neck, and he pulled her closer. Finally, he broke it off.

They stood there for a moment staring at one another. He was breathing hard. Prudence wasn't sure she was breathing at all. She could hear her heart pounding in her ears.

"I'm sorry. That shouldn't have happened. Go to bed, Prudence. Now." Urias walked off to the stream.

She watched for a moment until she saw him pull his shirt off, then turned and ran into the tent. Urias was right. They couldn't spend the night beside one another.

*

Prudence woke the next morning, shaking. It was cold, but she doubted the shakes had anything to do with the weather. They'd have to get the annulment as soon as possible. She didn't know how long she could live with this man and be pushed aside time after time.

It was painfully obvious he didn't want to have feelings for her.

"Time to get up," Urias called out. His words were crisp and to the point.

"I'll be right out." She changed into her traveling dress and added another layer of a light wool coat. "It's freezing out here," she said, crawling out of the tent. She stood up and straightened her skirts.

"Warm yourself by the fire while I take down the tent."

"Don't you think we ought to talk about last night?"

"Nope. It was a mistake. It won't happen again."

"Ah." Prudence warmed her back by the fire, holding her palms toward the flames. All night she'd wondered what he would say regarding their passionate kiss. While she could understand him wanting to say it was a mistake, the fact still remained that they were attracted to one another. And with each passing day, she wanted to be Mrs. Urias O'Leary. Yet as they got closer to Hazel Green and her parents' home, she knew Urias wanted nothing more than to rescue his sister and get as far away from her father as possible. She couldn't blame him. Prudence's own contempt for her father grew daily. She had never seen him treat another in business in such a way.

The big question in her mind finally erupted into the open as she hollered, "Urias, when are we going to get the annulment?"

He stopped dead in his tracks and turned around. "We can't until after Katherine is far away from your father. I also will need it in writing that she is sold to me. I won't have that man come after me again for more money."

He was visibly upset.

"Where does that leave me?"

He relaxed his shoulders. "I told you before. I'll take care of you until you can find a husband or a job to support yourself. I've given my word, Prudence. I won't go back on it. I'm not like your father."

She wanted to argue with him about the kiss they had shared. But if Urias was set on his plans to dissolve the marriage and marry her off to the next available man, then she would have to fight her growing attraction to him. Prudence lifted the hem of her skirt and said, "I'll walk first this morning," then proceeded to stomp past him and the horse. *He can load the beast. I'll just continue north.*

❧

Thomas Hagins's farm came into view. *Thank You, Lord, we're almost there.* Prudence and he had barely said a word to each other since last night's kiss. He'd been arguing with himself all night and all day for giving in to such a foolish temptation. He felt a responsibility to her, but what that was, he wasn't sure.

"Mr. O'Leary, Prudence, welcome back. How was your trip?" Thomas Hagins greeted them as they dismounted the horse. "Where's my mule?"

"I sold him and bought this horse. It was better for traveling with the two of us."

"Them roads through the hollows must be wider than I remember 'em." Thomas scratched his chin.

"Not really—except for the trail the hogs left behind. But that will grow back by next summer." Urias pulled out the money he owed Mr. Hagins, not showing him the rest of his earnings. This trip had made him leery of just about everyone. Generally, he was a trusting soul, but that trust had gotten him in a lot of trouble this trip. First, he ended up with a wife. Second, he had to pay an overpriced bond for his sister. Third, he now had to pay for a wife he hadn't wanted to begin with. He just couldn't risk Mr. Hagins asking for an additional fee, too.

Thomas took the proffered cash. "Was almost hoping you wouldn't return. I could sell that horse of yours for more than what you owed me on those hogs. Ever consider selling him?"

"Nope. He's my stud."

"Fine stock in that one. He's in the barn. I just took him in for the evening."

"Thank you."

"Can I get you anything else? Do you two need a place to stay this evening?" Mr. Hagins offered.

Prudence remained uncommonly quiet.

"No," Urias answered. "Prudence is eager to see her parents." *And I'm eager to get my sister.* The sooner his business in Hazel Green was done, the better Urias would feel. The knot in his stomach had been tightening for the past couple hours on the trail.

"Of course. Well, it's been a pleasure doing business with ya, son." Thomas pumped Urias's hand. "Anytime, anytime."

"I appreciate your trust in me. Thank you."

They said their salutations, and Urias went to the barn to retrieve Bullet. "Hey boy, how you doing?"

The horse whinnied and nuzzled his muzzle in Urias's chest.

"I missed you, too, boy." Urias saddled the horse and checked his shoes before leaving the barn.

Prudence still sat on the old horse, her back straight and the reins in her hands.

"Ready to go home, Prudence?" he asked.

She nodded her head and nudged the horse forward. Urias trotted Bullet up beside her. He missed their pleasant conversation. The day had been excruciatingly long because of the silence.

"Tonight I'll sleep in your parents' barn."

She turned to him. "Do you think that's wise? Won't my father be expecting us to behave like man and wife?"

"I honestly don't care what your father thinks, one way or the other. He forced this marriage. He didn't have your best interest in mind. He's up to something. I don't know what it is, but I want to be alert and careful."

"My father isn't a criminal," she defended.

"There are a variety of ways for a man to rob another. Your father's way is more genteel, but it still amounts to cheating a man. And you and I both know he is cheating me."

"Urias, I know things look really bad, but Father's never behaved like this before. I really don't understand why he's doing this."

The sun was setting quickly, and Urias wanted to reach the Greenes' home before dark.

"Prudence, I don't want to argue with you about him. Since he is your father, I'll keep my peace, but I will not relax my guard. I need statements in his writing and to have them witnessed by another. Which of your parents' hired servants would stand by their word that they signed a paper as a witness and won't lie about it later if your father should try something foolish again?"

"You mean which ones can read and write?"

"That, too."

"I can sign. A judge can't say I'm biased, since I'm married to you and he's my father."

"Let me think on that."

"What's there to think on? You can trust me. You know I'm not pleased with Father's actions. . . ."

Urias held up his hand. "It's not that I don't trust you. I don't want to put you in that kind of a position, in opposition to your father. Your relationship with him is strained enough as it is. What are you going to do when you're married and have children? Aren't you going to want your children to know their grandparents?"

"Fine," she huffed.

What did I do this time? Urias wondered.

Twenty minutes later, they arrived at her parents' home. Something seemed odd and out of place. Urias scanned the area. No one moved. Nothing moved. There wasn't even a flicker of light coming from the house.

Prudence jumped off the horse and ran inside, calling for her parents.

Scanning the yard, Urias approached the barn, still on the horse. The family wagon was gone, along with Mr. Greene's horses. Anger burned up Urias's spine. Hiram Greene had run off with his sister.

"Urias!" Prudence screamed.

Chapter 12

Prudence worked at the tight ropes binding her parents. "Urias!" she screamed once again.

"Mother, Daddy, wake up!" How long had they been tied up together?

"Where are you?" Urias called.

"Father's office," she answered. Frantically, she tried to undo the hemp rope knots. They were too tight. "Help!"

Urias ran in. "What happened?" He bent down beside her. "Let me."

With his sharp knife, he cut the handkerchiefs from their mouths first, then proceeded to cut the ropes binding their hands and feet. "Get a couple cool, damp cloths and some water."

"Are they. . . ?" She couldn't bring herself to ask.

"They're alive, but they've been tied up for a while. Hurry."

Prudence ran to the kitchen and dampened a cloth and poured out a glass of water. She ran back to the den and found Urias carrying her mother to the sofa. "Dampen her forehead and face, then start massaging her arms and legs. The blood needs to start pumping."

Prudence did as instructed and watched Urias do the same with her father.

Her mother's eyelids flickered.

"Mom. Mama, can you hear me?"

"Mr. Greene." Urias tried to rouse her father by lightly slapping his face.

Prudence did the same to her mother. "Mama, please."

"They're coming around." Urias shortened the distance and placed a loving hand on her shoulder. "Father," he began to pray, "please bring the Greenes back in good health."

He removed his hand. Her shoulder felt the separation.

"Their wagon and horses are gone from the barn. I'm going to search for Katherine."

Prudence had completely forgotten about Kate and the other servants.

"Please do. I'll take care of my parents."

"I'll return as soon as I can. Where do you suggest I look first?"

"Her room. It's at the end of the hall upstairs."

He ran out of the room. She couldn't blame him. *Where is Kate? And the other servants?* She continued to rub her mother's hands and feet, alternating every few minutes and doing the same to her father. *What happened here? Robbers?* She'd never heard of such a thing in the area. But someone had taken her parents' wagon and horses. And someone had left them tied together to aid in their escape. But who? And why?

Prudence pondered the many questions in her mind over and over again. Her father wasn't in the kind of business that brought unsavory characters into the area. What had happened?

She'd been working on her parents for what seemed to be an eternity, yet only three minutes had passed. Urias hadn't returned. She didn't like not having him beside her. He brought comfort and peace into her life just by being there. *Oh Daddy, how could you have ruined my only real chance of happiness by forcing Urias and me to marry?* Her unspoken thoughts had plagued her constantly each day she spent as Urias's wife.

Her father moaned.

Thank You, Lord! "Urias! Father is coming to," she called out. She wasn't sure if he could hear her, but if he was within earshot, he would want to know. Wouldn't he?

"Prudence, get another cloth for Katherine." Urias carried his sister in. "There are a couple of others in the same shape. I'll bring them in here." He placed Katherine on the floor and scurried out of the room.

Prudence placed the cloth from her mother's forehead onto Kate's, then ran to the kitchen, pulled a couple of towels out of the cabinet, and pumped a bowl and pitcher full of water. Father always had a few glasses in his office.

Back in her father's den, she found Urias had deposited Franni, the cook, and Henry, who'd been working for her parents for as long as she could remember, on the floor near Kate.

"Prudence," her father's hoarse voice called out.

❧

Urias sat in amazement listening to Hiram Greene tell his tale of what happened. Something wasn't adding up, and, by the look on old Henry's face, he knew it, too. When the hour grew late and the women had settled in for the night, Urias stopped Hiram in midstream. "The women are gone. Tell the truth, Mr. Greene. This wasn't your average robbery," Urias challenged.

"The boy ain't so dumb, is he?" Henry spoke up for the first time.

"Hold your tongue, Henry," Hiram barked.

"Look, as best I can tell, you owe someone a large amount of money. You've asked for more money than my sister's bond is really worth." Urias held up his hand to stop Hiram Greene from defending himself. "I'm going to pay you what you asked for, but don't take me for a fool. You also sent word that you wanted a dowry for your daughter. Now, that says plain and simple you need money and you need it fast. Am I correct?"

Hiram fell back into his chair.

"I'll be leaving now. Thank ya again for savin' us, Mr. O'Leary. Don't knows how I could ever repay it." Henry extended his ashen hand, and Urias shook it.

Hiram Greene kept his head bent down. Urias leaned on the desk, hovering toward Hiram Greene. "Now, are you going to be straight with me?"

Hiram looked up with bloodshot eyes. "It's just a temporary setback. I gambled on the horse races and lost a lot of money to a man who apparently takes his gambling wagers seriously."

"How much do you owe?" Urias pushed away from the desk and sat down across from his father-in-law. It seemed impossible to believe that he was now related to this man. But family is family, and even if it was only on a temporary basis, there were ways a man should treat another even if the other didn't treat you the same.

"Fifteen hundred—if Sawyer Bishop doesn't deduct the value of the items he removed from the house."

"And where can I find him?" Urias stood up and grabbed his coat.

"What are you planning to do?"

"I'll offer him a compromise on your debt. I can't pay it all, but I can come pretty close. That should appease him long enough for you to raise the additional $250."

"I don't know when I can pay you back."

Urias placed his hands on his hips. "Let me make one thing perfectly clear. I'm not giving you a loan, nor am I paying a dowry for your daughter. You did not ask for one when we were forced to be married, thus it is not required of me to pay you one. However, with that being said, you are family, and I will help you this one time. I will not expect to hear from you again concerning any financial arrangements between us. I will pay what is due for my sister's debt. The additional funds are a gift."

All sorts of admonitions and exhortations begged to come out of Urias, but he held his peace. Only God could convict a man like Hiram

Greene. No amount of human reasoning would get through to him. He looked at life through the narrow focus of his own needs and didn't notice anyone or anything around him unless it served his own personal gain.

"Before I leave, I want my sister's release from your bondage."

Hiram dipped a pen into a small jar of ink, tapped it on the rim, then wrote a simple note. He blew it dry and handed it to Urias.

"Thank you."

"You can find Sawyer Bishop a couple towns over in Salyersville."

"I'll return tomorrow evening." Urias slipped out of the office with the paper in his pocket.

Prudence met him in the hallway with tears in her eyes. "You don't need to do this."

"For your parents' sake, I must. Now, you and Katherine get ready for our trip to Jamestown. We'll leave day after next at first light."

"What about the annulment?"

Urias's back stiffened. They had agreed on an annulment. But that kiss still blazed in his memory. She was right. An annulment was best. "We'll take care of that in Jamestown, after I get you out of harm's way."

He turned to leave.

"Urias."

She stood there shaking. He wanted to take her in his arms and chase away her worries and fears. "It'll be all right, Prudence. Pray for safe travel."

"I already began."

He chuckled. "Your father doesn't know about that closet?"

Prudence smiled.

"What closet?" Hiram Greene asked.

இ

If it hadn't been for her father's contrite spirit after coming so close to death, Prudence was certain she'd be unable to sit for a week once he'd heard how she'd eavesdropped on his business meetings.

The next evening, she and Kate were packing their bags in Prudence's room. For the first time, Kate hadn't had to work to serve the family. Prudence wanted to treat her as an equal. Admittedly, she had treated her as a servant even though she'd been a close friend. "Kate, the weather is getting colder. Wear two dresses. That will give us another layer and an additional dress for when we arrive in Jamestown. Without a wagon, we can't bring much."

"Tell me. What's my brother like?" Kate pleaded.

"He's a kindhearted man. And I've never met anyone so aware of what's happening around him. The night we ran into a couple of robbers—"

"Robbers?"

"Yes. Oh Kate, I was never so scared. But Urias stayed in complete control. I felt so calm and peaceful around him. I've never felt that before, even with my own father." Prudence stopped herself from revealing her heart. She and Urias would be filing for an annulment as soon as possible. No need for Kate to know the truth. "You'll be proud he's your brother."

"It's all so strange. I know he's my brother, but my brother was this small, gangly boy that left home years ago."

Prudence held off the images floating in her mind of just how handsome and rugged Urias was. Her heart actually quickened its pace when she saw him. "It must be. But he's a caring man. He stayed an extra day in Flatlick just to help a widowed friend."

"Is he a good husband?"

How do I answer that one? Truthfully, she decided. "Given the right situation, I think he'll make someone an excellent husband." Prudence lowered her voice. "Urias and I will get an annulment as soon as possible. I can't trap him in a marriage that isn't a real marriage. He deserves a wife that will love him for the man he is."

Kate stopped packing and put her hands on her hips. "I don't understand. Why would he be paying your father's debt?"

"Neither do I. He's a man of honor and principles; that's for certain. But I don't begin to understand what goes on in his mind."

"He sounds a bit like our father, from what I can remember about him. Pa knew our mother was drinking too much. And he tried to keep her away from the drink. Once he died, she had no one to stop her, and she got bad. Real bad. She never beat me as badly as she beat Urias though."

Prudence took in a deep breath. "Father hasn't been the best man to live around, but he's never laid a hand on either myself or my brother. I can't imagine what it was like for you or Urias."

"You don't want to." Kate placed her dress in the carpetbag. "What about these?" She held up the silver hairbrush and mirror that had been handed down from Prudence's grandmother.

"I'll wrap the mirror in one of my dresses. I can't take many personal items, but that's small enough and important enough to take with me. Perhaps in time I can return and pack some more of my things."

"Did Urias speak of his home? What's it like?"

"He lives with his adopted parents. He said it was a large farmhouse. He didn't go into details of how many rooms and such. But he mentioned he was going to build his own house soon." Prudence wondered if there truly would be room for her and Kate in the house. She also prayed for the hundredth time for Urias's safety.

"When do you expect him back from his errand?"

"I don't know. He seemed to think he'd be back in time for us to depart as soon as the sun rose over the horizon tomorrow. I hope he arrives soon."

Kate cocked her head to the right and scrutinized Prudence. "You love him, don't you?"

Feeling the blush rise in her cheeks, she turned back to her packing. "I'm simply concerned for him, is all."

Kate chuckled. "You can try to deceive me if you wish, but I see that light in your eyes every time you speak of him."

"I don't know if I love him. I do care. But love takes time for a man and woman to discover. How can someone love a woman he was forced to marry? It doesn't seem right."

"I guess you're right." Kate went back to her packing. "I ain't never been in love. Ain't likely to happen either."

"You can't say that, Kate. You never know."

"Perhaps."

Prudence saw that far-off look in Kate's green eyes. Prudence vowed never to push Kate to tell her about her past. The bits and pieces she had shared were enough to know it had been a horrible time since she was sold into bondage by her mother. Mrs. Campbell had shared with her some of the things that could happen to servants and slaves by their owners. She prayed Kate could move beyond her past and feel the peace Prudence felt around Urias.

"God may just surprise you yet."

"You know I don't give no never mind to Him. He ain't helped me a day in my life." The bitterness of the past tinged Kate's voice.

Prudence reached over and lovingly placed her hand on Kate's. "I know you have a hard time believing in God, but He's real. And isn't it likely that Urias finally finding you before you were sold again was God's answer to Urias's prayers?"

Kate softened. "Maybe. But I ain't giving God credit. Urias found me."

Prudence knew Urias to be a godly man. How would he deal with his sister's unbelief? Would the MacKenneths accept Kate in their home, knowing she didn't believe in God?

Prudence resolved that if the MacKenneths wouldn't allow her to live there, she'd have Kate live with her. Together they would be able to provide for themselves. She hoped.

Prudence heard the sounds of approaching hooves. She glanced out the window. A solitary rider approached the house. *Urias.* Her heart skipped a beat. Kate was right. She did love this man.

Chapter 13

Urias drove the wagon back to Hiram Greene's estate. He'd been battling with the Lord and his anger the entire trip. He never would have guessed the cost would be so great. It was one thing to give a man money—quite another to give him your future. *And for what? A man who hogtied me into marrying his daughter?*

"Yah." He snapped the reins and encouraged the horses forward. Bullet had been his future, his farm—his stock. Now he'd have to wait another season or two to get another stud like Bullet. Thankfully, he still had the mare and stallion back on the farm. But you never knew if you'd end up with a male or female or one with lines as excellent as Bullet's.

"Lord, I can't begin to understand why I had to sacrifice the horse for Hiram Greene. But Sawyer Bishop wouldn't hear of any other arrangement once he caught sight of Bullet. I still have a substantial amount of money after exchanging Bullet for part of the debt, but it's a cold compromise." Urias took in a deep breath and watched the white vapor rise from his mouth. "I'm sorry, Lord. I'm just having a hard time accepting how much this is costing me. First, I get tied down with a wife I don't want. Then, I get involved with another man's troubles. When is it going to end?"

The stars flickered in the black velvet sky. There was little Urias could do. He could have left Hiram Greene to the repercussions of his own making, living out his own bad decisions. But that wouldn't be fair to Prudence. Not that she would have known. Well, besides the fact that he and Prudence had come upon her parents near death's door. How long would they have survived in those chairs?

The memory of Kate's pale face and bluish hands still made him tremble. To do business with a man who could do that to others seemed wrong, terribly wrong. And yet there had been little choice. If he were to live with himself, he had only one option and that was to give up Bullet and his future. He was beginning to wonder if he'd be tied down to Prudence the rest of his life, as well.

He'd never know the kind of love his parents knew. He was destined to live out a life of servitude for the sake of others. "How unfair is that, Lord?" he called out to the heavens.

A single rider passed him on the road to Hiram Greene's estate. "Nice night," the stranger called out.

"Bit chilly," Urias replied.

"Grows hair on the chest." The stranger chuckled and headed off.

Five minutes later, Urias found himself in Hiram Greene's barn, unfastening the horses and settling them in with some fresh water and oats.

"Urias?" Prudence called as she ran into the barn. "You got Father's carriage and horses back."

"Yup," he mumbled.

"Are you all right?"

"Fine. Fine."

"I saved some dinner for you. Come back to the kitchen and I'll heat it up." She flitted out of the barn as swiftly as she came in.

He wasn't in the mood to play husband and wife. She could try all she wanted, but she really wasn't his wife.

If she didn't care, would she have bothered with your dinner? he challenged his own wayward thoughts.

"Urias," another feminine voice gently called. Katherine came into the barn a bit more timid than the last time he'd seen her.

"Katherine, you're looking better."

"Thanks to you and Prudence. She says you are going to build your own house when you return to your family's farm. Is this true?"

I'd been planning on it. "Not until spring. More than likely it will take me a year or two."

"If you don't mind me asking, where will I be staying?"

"I'll set you up in my room. I'll make a spot for myself in the barn. You and Prudence can share my room. It's a busy household. I'll enjoy the peace."

"What do you mean?"

"Don't get me wrong, I love my younger brother and sisters, but they can be a handful. Little Nash gave me this for the trip." Urias reached in and handed Katherine the arrowhead. "It's in case I run out of bullets and run into a bear. Of course, the poor boy doesn't know I wouldn't have time to fashion a bow and arrow first, but it's the thought that matters. You'll like him, Katherine."

Katherine hunched her shoulders. "I'm nervous about going there,

Urias. I won't fit in."

"You'll fit in just fine. Remember, these folks have been praying for you and your safety for years."

Katherine opened her mouth to speak, but closed it instead. *How peculiar,* Urias thought. It's the second time he'd referred to God and had a negative response from her. Urias pinched the bridge of his nose. His sister had been through a lot. She didn't say anything about it, but she didn't have to. The way she walked, the way she held her shoulders, her head—everything pointed to a life of abuse and little encouragement. "It'll be all right, Katherine. Trust me."

"I'll help Prudence warm up your dinner." And that was that. She was gone as quietly as she arrived. Only this time, Urias knew what she was thinking. Trust.

&

Prudence placed the cast-iron frying pan on the woodstove in the kitchen. She took off the kettle of hot water and poured it over some ground coffee beans.

Kate stepped into the kitchen and removed her shawl. "Did you see Urias's horse in the barn?"

Prudence thought for a bit. "No, I don't think I saw Bullet. You don't suppose. . ." Her words trailed off.

"I don't know horses, but the way your father was carrying on about Urias's horse, I figure he was worth something."

"Yes, he was. Urias was planning on using that horse to start his farm for breeding horses."

Kate went to the cupboard and pulled down a plate for Urias. "Do you think he had to trade his horse for your father's debt?"

The back door creaked open.

"Yes, but we won't speak another word on the matter, is that clear?" Urias said as he scrutinized Kate and Prudence.

Prudence nodded and turned away. *Father not only cost Urias and me the chance of ever having a real relationship, he's now cost Urias his future.* Prudence took the wooden spoon and stirred the beef and gravy stew.

"Smells great." Urias gave a mock smile when she looked up.

Kate put her hands to her hips and said, "If we be of a mind to question you, you ought to be of a mind to tell us. What happened?"

Urias pushed up his sleeves and dipped his hands into the washbowl by the back door.

"Let's just say there was little negotiating with Mr. Bishop. I had to pay in full. He wouldn't accept a partial payment, no matter how large it was. Now, I don't wish to discuss the matter again. I did what needed to be done, and that is all."

Her stomach quivered, and Prudence fought the shakes at hearing the great sacrifices Urias continued to make for her and her family. He didn't need to. He just did. She'd never met a man like him. But she also felt terribly guilty for the actions of her father, for the condition of his financial affairs, and for the abuse Urias had taken out of concern for his sister. Her disappointment in her father rose once again. "You should tell Father. Perhaps he'll pay you back."

"As I said, ladies, I will not discuss this further."

Prudence's back stiffened at Urias's firm tone. He'd seldom been that sharp with her on the trail. She glanced over to Kate and noticed her shoulders squared.

"Forgive me." Urias sat down at the kitchen table. "It's been a long day, and I've had little sleep. If you'll be so kind as to serve me up a plate of that wonderful stew, I'll be more fit for company."

Prudence filled the plate. Kate cut him a thick slice of bread and placed it in front of him.

"Thank you, ladies. This is a fine meal, indeed. How is the packing coming?"

"We're just about ready," Prudence offered. "Without Bullet, perhaps we should consider bringing less."

Urias scooped a forkful of his supper, then put his fork back down on his plate. "Please sit down and join me." He reached out both of his hands. "Pray with me."

They joined hands, and Urias led them through a brief prayer, thanking the Lord for His many blessings and asking for safety on the trip home.

"How long will the journey last?" Kate asked.

"By horseback, three days—possibly a piece of a fourth. Walking it will take several days more. However, I have a mind to speak with Thomas Hagins again and see if I might be able to purchase another horse and a small wagon. Because Bullet was so valuable, I still have some money."

Prudence looked over to her husband. What was he thinking? Obviously, he was upset to lose Bullet, but how could he be upset one minute and calm the next? She looked over to Kate, who seemed just as puzzled about Urias's behavior.

"What's all the tongue wagging going on in here?"

Prudence watched her father walk into the room.

"Mr. O'Leary, you've returned."

Urias wiped his mouth on the cloth napkin. "Yes sir. Your debt is paid in full."

Prudence watched the silent communication that flowed between Urias and her father. Something else, or some greater sum of money, was owed. Her father's face brightened to a deep crimson shade. His shoulders slumped, and he looked down at the floor. "Thank you. I'll pay you back."

"That won't be necessary." Urias sopped up the last of his stew from his plate with the remaining corner of his bread. "We'll be leaving in the morning." Urias stood up from the table. "Thank you for the dinner, Prudence, Katherine. I'll see you in the morning." He placed his hat upon his head and slipped out the back door.

Prudence turned and looked to her father for a possible answer to Urias's bizarre behavior. Her father's face reflected a similar guarded expression. He excused himself and silently departed the room.

Kate looked at Prudence. "What is going on?"

Chapter 14

Hiram Greene had a lot to answer for, but Urias felt convinced he wasn't the man to address him on the matter. It was all the years of listening to Dad telling him to respect his elders, Urias figured. It didn't make much sense with a man like Hiram Greene—he'd been fooling his family and neighbors for years. Urias now knew his secret and, he prayed, Hiram's shame might keep him from making the same mistake twice. One thing was certain: Urias had never been put in such an awkward position before. Hiram's life and the lives of his family would have been in jeopardy if Urias hadn't paid off Mr. Greene's gambling debts.

Gambling was one of the hesitations Urias had about raising horses. Horse racing was becoming a statewide interest for folks in Kentucky. And folks were willing to pay well for good horse stock. Urias enjoyed horses, and Bullet had been his pride and joy. He'd bred him to be a fast horse with strong lines, and he was. Now someone else would be earning the money from breeding Bullet.

Farmers had need of a horse that could pull the plows and work hard to earn their keep. They didn't have to be fast, but they did have to be strong and steady. Unfortunately, the average farmer was unable to pay higher prices for a good racehorse. Urias had heard that the army was always on the lookout for good, strong stock. But profit would be slower in coming, and it would take more time to earn the funds needed to build his own house. That was something he'd been dreaming of for a long time, but something even more pressing, now that he'd found Katherine.

Bullet would have been the stud he would rely on to develop his horse farm. But Bullet was gone, and so were the dreams and plans he had for the future. *How am I going to provide for Katherine and Prudence, Lord?*

"Urias?" Prudence called from the barn door. He'd slept in the barn last night. Hiram Greene hadn't even offered him a bed.

"Unbelievable," Urias muttered, then said aloud, "I have our horse just about ready. Are you and Katherine all set?"

"Yes, but breakfast is ready. We've been cooking for an hour. Mother had us make some provisions for the road."

Prudence stepped closer to him. "Urias?"

"Hmm?" he mumbled while cinching the saddle.

"Mother wants to know why you didn't spend the night with me."

Urias couldn't believe Prudence could be so open with him. She truly deserved better parents. "What did you say?"

"I told her we don't see ourselves as truly married."

"What did she say?" Urias asked, then turned to face Prudence. Her beauty made him question more than once why they hadn't acted on being man and wife.

"She suggested I stay home and let you go your way with your sister."

He didn't expect to hear that. Then again, Prudence and her family were full of constant surprises. Urias cleared his throat. "Is that what you would like?"

"I don't know." Prudence sat down on a sawhorse. "I've been wanting out of my parents' home for a very long time, yet we aren't truly man and wife. I can't live like this either. But you've given so much to my family. I can't begin to understand why you needed to give Mr. Bishop Bullet for my father's debt, but I trust your word on it."

"Prudence, you and I both know this marriage is a sham. We married to secure Katherine's freedom. If you would like to stay in your parents' home, I will not stop you. I'll sign whatever papers you wish to dissolve our marriage."

Tears welled in her eyes. Urias wanted to reach out and hold her. He kept his hands in place.

"I want a real husband, Urias. But I need a man who can respect me and what I think on matters. All the men in this area, the marrying ones, are not interested in a woman like me. Are there others like you and your family in Jamestown?"

Urias felt his gut wrench. The idea—the thought of another man holding Prudence. . . He shook the thought away. She didn't belong to him. He had no rights to this woman. "I suppose there are some. I never gave it much thought."

Prudence sighed. "My family has been enough of a burden to you, Urias. I'll stay."

The tears that had threatened to fall now ran silvery tracks down her cheeks. She stood up and headed back out the door. "Come in and have a warm breakfast before you and Kate leave," she called over her shoulder.

Stunned, Urias stood there gazing at the open door with the sun rising over the mountain. Then it hit him. He'd been afraid all along that she, as well as her parents, had cooked up this marriage. Now he was certain. They had all used him. They used him to pay off their personal debts. *Well, she might think she's free. . . .*

Urias stomped out of the barn and toward the kitchen.

❧

Urias marched to the table and sat down without washing up first. Prudence thought to suggest it, but there was something in his rigid movements that she recognized. He was upset. *Does that mean he wants me, Lord?* She fought off the foolish thought and asked, "How would you like your eggs?"

"Fried." He placed his napkin in his lap. "Prudence, I've given the matter some thought. You'll come with me and work off your father's debt."

"What?" Anger burned in her heart. Hot tears formed in her eyes. "Fine. Anything you say."

"You can be my bond servant," he said.

Prudence took quick, short breaths. She was to be her husband's slave? The man she loved wanted to treat her like property? Her hands shook as she dropped the eggs into the frying pan. They sizzled against the hot iron. "Fine. But if you don't mind, please don't tell my parents."

Urias coughed, then gave a slight nod.

Prudence finished cooking his eggs and placed them on the plate in front of him. She discarded the pan and left him to his meal. After all, a servant wasn't allowed to eat with the family. In her wildest dreams, she never would have thought Urias to be so cruel. If being a servant was what it would take to help her parents, then she'd be the best servant she could. Truthfully, she'd have to rely on Kate instructing her in how to do most of the tasks.

She ran up the stairs and collapsed on her bed. A couple minutes ago, he'd been so reasonable. Not that she didn't want to be with Urias—she ached to be a real wife to him. But now she couldn't imagine it. Perhaps it was a good thing they weren't really husband and wife.

"Prudence?" Kate called. "What's the matter?"

"Nothing." Prudence wiped her eyes. "Urias is eating. We'll be leaving soon."

"I'm all ready. I'm scared," Kate confessed.

Me, too. "It'll be all right. He loves you." *Unlike me.* Prudence knew self-pity would get her nowhere. She would settle up with Urias just how much she owed and how long it would take for her to work off her bondage. She would not allow him to treat her like others had treated his sister. *Did he forget that I gave up my life for Kate, too, Lord?*

Prudence followed Kate down the hall and down the stairway to the kitchen. It struck her odd knowing that Kate was once her servant, following orders, and now she would be Kate's servant. *Father, give me strength. Help me to not displease Urias,* Prudence silently prayed.

&

The eggs and sausage sat in the pit of Urias's stomach. He'd gone too far with Prudence. He never should have insisted that she be his bond servant. Her working off her father's debt would have been far more than enough of a sacrifice. But he'd been angry, and when he was angry, he could get himself into a heap of trouble.

Scouting ahead, he checked the trail before the women passed. Being alert would take all of his concentration. Sleep had eluded him last night, and after the two days of hard travel, he should not have insisted they be on the road so early this morning.

Hiram Greene had fumbled over his words of thanks when Urias and the ladies departed. Urias even thought he saw a tear in the man's eye when he gave his daughter a hug and a kiss good-bye, confirming Urias's darkest thoughts of the plot the parents and Prudence must have put together. It was Prudence who sought him out and suggested they run the hogs to the Cumberland Gap. It was Prudence whose bold presence in the barn caused Hiram to be angry and force a marriage upon them.

It took effort to lift his feet off the ground and place them in front of him. If walking was this difficult, how was he ever going to get these women to Jamestown? He glanced back at the women. They seemed to be talking about him. The way Katherine kept looking at him, the way Prudence kept avoiding looking at him. . . She must have told Katherine he'd made her his bond servant. Urias groaned. This would be the longest trip he'd ever been on.

He scanned the area in front of him and pushed himself to keep walking. Running might be better. Even his parents would not be happy to hear what he'd done to Prudence. Admittedly, he wasn't too proud of himself either. On the other hand, everything seemed to add up that Hiram and Prudence had conspired against him. He was an easy mark. Hiram held Katherine's bond and realized Urias would have done anything to gain his sister's freedom, including paying higher than normal fees and taking those hogs to the Cumberland Gap. A smile swept across his face.

He had enjoyed that trip with Prudence. She'd been more than just a good traveling companion. The memory of the kiss they shared stabbed his conscience. She felt so wonderful in his arms. The kiss, so warm and inviting.

Urias shook off the memory. *The devil comes in all forms,* he reminded himself.

The only real question was: How soon could he have this marriage annulled?

&

"I'm scared, Pru. If he can do to you what others did to me... I'll be surprised if he doesn't treat me like a servant, too."

"Something happened when he went to pay Father's debt." Prudence gnawed her lower lip. "I could have had the marriage annulled immediately, and he was free to leave with you."

"Why is he making you work for your father's debt?" Kate tossed her head from side to side.

"I don't know." *Why did Father make Urias pay for Kate's debt?* Maybe she truly didn't understand business matters. As her father suggested time and time again, it's a man's world.

Prudence was afraid to speak her fears. How was it that the man she started to understand on the trail was not the same man on this new trail? It didn't make sense. But then again, nothing had made sense since Urias O'Leary came into her world. And sharing her fears with Kate, who seemed to live in constant fear, didn't seem fair to her.

"Kate, we'll have to trust the Lord for our protection."

"Humph." Kate snickered. "Ain't been much good in the past. Don't know why it be much good in the future."

"Kate, I know things have happened to you, but I doubt those same things will happen with Urias. He seems to be a man of honor. Remember what I said to you about Mrs. Campbell and how he took care of her needs?"

Kate nodded.

"That same man is still in there. Whatever happened for him to lose Bullet has to be a deep wound. Those take time to heal."

"You're defending him?" Kate gasped.

"I suppose I am. I came to know Urias on the trail. He is not the same man we talked with last night or this morning. Whatever it is, we need to give him some time to work it all out."

"I know he's my kin, but I don't know him and I don't trust any man. I can't."

"Then let me do the trusting for the both of us. Things will work out." Prudence fired another prayer toward heaven. *Please, Lord, make everything work out. Don't let Kate suffer too much longer. She needs to know people care about her and love her. I know Urias does, even if he has a funny way of showing it to folks. I can't begin to understand why he wants me to be his bond servant, but if that is what I must do for Kate, then I'll do it.*

"You're praying, ain't ya?" Kate asked from behind her on the horse.

"Yes," Prudence admitted.

They continued on in silence, three people bound together by love and family, yet separated by the very same things. Prudence wanted to cry. Her heart ached. She didn't know what she'd done to bring about Urias's wrath or why he would hold her to her father's debts, but she'd done something to trigger his behavior. At least, it gave that appearance.

They traveled this way for days, barely talking one with the other. This time the journey was uneventful, unlike the last trip and the numerous events they'd endured while taking the hogs down to the Cumberland Gap. When they arrived on the tenth day at Jamestown, Prudence couldn't believe her eyes. The house was large and well cared for. There was a smaller single-story house also set on the property, which she assumed was Urias's adoptive grandparents' home that he'd told her about building with his father.

"Urias," cried a small, black-haired boy, who ran out to greet them.

Urias caught the child in his arms and swung him up in the air. "Good to see you, Nash."

A small group of people gathered on the front porch.

Urias carried the youngster to the porch. "Mom, Dad, it's good to see you." Urias went up to the couple and gave them each a hug and a kiss.

Prudence looked over at Kate, who also appeared to feel out of place.

"You found her!" Mrs. MacKenneth stepped off the porch and went right over to Kate. "Welcome to our home, Katherine. We've been waiting and praying for you for a long time."

"Where's Bullet, son?" Mr. MacKenneth asked.

Urias glanced over at Prudence, then back to his father. "It's a long story. I'll tell ya later."

"And who might you be?" Mrs. MacKenneth asked in a gentle voice.

Kate stood rigidly in place as their attention turned to Prudence.

"I'm—"

"She's my wife," Urias said, cutting her off. "In name only. It has to do with Bullet."

Mrs. MacKenneth paused for a moment, then opened her arms and embraced Prudence. "Welcome to the family."

Unable to respond, Prudence stood there just like Kate had done a few moments prior.

"Mom, the ladies would probably like to freshen up and get off their feet. They've been walking for miles. We pushed to get here before nightfall."

"Oh, certainly, do come in. Where are my manners?" Mrs. MacKenneth asked no one in particular.

Mac, as Urias had referred to him on more than one occasion, cleared his throat. "You ladies go freshen up a bit. Urias and I can take care of the horse and baggage."

Kate and Prudence glanced at each other, following Mrs. MacKenneth into the house. It was decorated with nice furnishings—nothing from a fancy cabinetmaker, but all looking extremely homey and functional.

"Come. Follow me. I'll set you up a pitcher of warm water to clean with and some fresh towels. Would you like to change your dresses as well?"

"Thank you. That would be wonderful, Mrs. MacKenneth." Prudence spoke up first.

"Please call me Pam. And my husband goes by Mac."

"Thank you. . .Pam. I can prepare the water," Kate offered.

"Nonsense. Tonight you're guests. Tomorrow you'll be family and given your own lot of chores to be done. Urias's room is at the top of the stairs, second door on the right. Make yourselves at home, and I'll bring up some warm water."

Prudence took the lead. Kate seemed too unsure of herself. Prudence took Kate by the hand and led her up the stairs. "Come on. I can't wait to get this dress off."

Kate giggled.

They found the second room on the right and opened the door. Inside they found a room filled with books and hand drawings of horses. Prudence could smell Urias's compelling scent in the air. "This is his room," she blurted out.

"How do you know?"

Prudence pointed to a framed sketch on top of the dresser. "That's a picture of Bullet. Can't you tell?"

"If you say so. A horse is a horse, and they all look the same to me."

Pam came into the room carrying a pitcher of water and a kettle. "I brought up a second pitcher. I figured with two of you, you'll be needing more. I know when I come off the road, one pitcher is barely enough to hold me over before I can take a bath. I'll have Mac and Urias set up the tub for a hot bath tonight."

"I wouldn't want to impose." Prudence hoped Pam wouldn't take back her offer. A hot bath would be perfect.

"Nonsense. It's no trouble. Besides, Urias will need one as well. He'll get the tub after you two." Pam winked.

Kate giggled again.

Prudence smiled. Pam was everything Urias said she would be and more.

"Now, which one of you is going to tell me how it is that you married my son?"

Chapter 15

"All right, son, out with it. What happened?" Mac asked.

"It's a long story. Our mother sold Katherine as a bond servant. Her latest owner was Hiram Greene, Prudence's father. Hiram wanted me to pay her bond before he'd release Katherine. Prudence told me of a way to earn the money without having to come home and ask you for it. While she was explaining her idea to me in the barn, her father came out. He insisted that we marry after we were caught speaking to one another again later that night. He said I had dishonored his daughter."

Mac leaned back against the rail of the horse's pen. "And you agreed to this?"

"I was forced. He said he wouldn't sell Katherine's bond to me unless I married his daughter."

"You should have come home and talked with us. I would have paid Hiram Greene a visit."

Urias chuckled. His father was larger than life in most men's eyes. There was little doubt Mac would have put some fear into Hiram Greene.

"Prudence said we could get the marriage annulled since we haven't been as man and wife."

His father crossed his arms in front of his chest.

"So, you sold Bullet to pay for your sister's bond?"

"Not exactly. Prudence and I bought some hogs and ran them down to the Cumberland Gap. Oh, by the way, you should know that Mr. Campbell passed away. I helped Mrs. Campbell for a couple days, but her daughter came and fetched her by the time I returned from selling the hogs."

"I'm sorry to hear of Mrs. Campbell's loss, but you can tell me more on that matter later. Tell me how it is that you had to sell Bullet."

Urias pulled in a deep breath and let it out slowly. "Hiram Greene has a gambling problem. While we were at Mrs. Campbell's farm, a rider came up and delivered a message to me from Mr. Greene saying I now owed him the price of a dowry for Prudence. Truthfully, the money I made from selling the hogs covered both Katherine's bond and Prudence's dowry, but when we arrived back at Hazel Green, we found Mr. and Mrs. Greene tied and bound to a chair and unconscious. Their servants were scattered throughout the house in the same state."

Mac combed his hands through his long hair.

"Mr. Greene confessed that he owed a man the money I was to pay him, plus a bit more for a gambling debt. Since I'm married to his daughter, even though in name only, I felt an obligation to pay the man's debt. When I got to the house of the person to whom Mr. Greene owed the debt, I discovered the debt was much higher and that he would not take a partial payment. He wanted it paid in full or not at all. We came to an understanding, and I gave him Bullet. Since the debt came from gambling on horse racing, I figured Bullet would be an acceptable bartering tool. He was."

"That was an honorable thing to do, son. And a hard sacrifice. But what are you going to do about your wife?"

"I don't know. I don't want her to live in that house with Mr. Greene. They've not appreciated her. And to force their daughter to marry a stranger. . .well, it just seemed wrong to me. But I've done something foolish. At least, I hope it was foolish."

His father let out a half chuckle. "You mean more than what you've told me so far?"

"Guilty. I should have come home and sought your counsel, but Prudence's idea made so much sense. And I wanted to be a man and take care of my sister."

"I understand, son. Go on. Tell me what else is wrong."

"After I came back from paying off Mr. Greene's debt, Prudence offered to get an annulment right away. I suspected, and still do, that she and her father conspired together. Was this their plan all along?"

Mac rubbed the back of his neck. "You know, son, I couldn't say. I don't know these people. I'm afraid this is something you're going to have to come to terms with." He studied Urias a moment, then added, "There's more, isn't there?"

"Yes." Urias felt heat rush to his cheeks. "I told Prudence she was to be my bond servant to pay for her father's debt."

"You're going to have to work harder on tempering your impulsiveness, son. I don't want you owning anyone, slave or bond servant. You can tell the woman she's not in debt to you and take it from there."

"Yes sir. I've been trying to tell her for the past ten days on the trail home. But there's never been the right moment. We've talked little since we left Hazel Green. Even my own sister doesn't talk with me. Prudence says Katherine wasn't treated well by some of her previous bond owners."

Mac laid his hand upon Urias's shoulder. "I'm sorry, son. I'll fill your mother in after we're down for the night. I expect she'll want to move Sarah into Molly's room tonight to make room for Katherine until you build your new home next spring."

"You can put Katherine and Prudence in my room. I'll bunk in the barn or on the sofa on really cold nights."

Mac gazed into Urias's eyes. "That will be fine. I'll want to hear more about this, but for now, what you've said is sufficient. We can chop down some trees for your house, and we'll spend more time on this matter, alone and away from everyone. I'm sure you have your reasons for suspecting Prudence, and you may be right. But if that were the case, why would she come here willingly?"

❦

Prudence tried not to toss and turn too much in the bed. Everywhere she placed her head, she could smell Urias. She could see him in his artwork, in the items scattered throughout his room, and the books on the shelves. The titles alone were enough to tell about him.

The worst thing of all was that he had asked her to speak with him privately in the morning, to join him in the barn where he'd be milking the cows.

Pam had tried to break the tension in the air when Urias and Mac came in from the barn. It seemed hopeless. The children were the only cure. They talked and talked, asking question after question. Thankfully, they were mostly aimed at Urias.

There was little doubt in her mind that Urias had told Mac about the circumstances that led to her becoming Urias's wife. Prudence felt certain her version to Pam was far shorter than Urias's to his father. Neither parent seemed happy about her presence in the house, and Kate was no help. She was so afraid these people would treat her as a servant, she hardly said a word.

Urias answered all of his younger siblings' questions and even entertained them with a tale of swimming the hogs across the Cumberland River. Prudence could picture it clearly. She hadn't been with him at that point of the trip, but every time he mentioned it, she wished she had been. Staying with Mrs. Campbell had been a blessing, yet it had begun the separation between Urias and herself. Prior to that, they had begun to trust one another.

The memory of their kiss bored a hole in the pit of her stomach. The friendliness, or even a mild effort of being communicative, vanished after Urias sold Bullet. More than anything, Prudence wished she could have gone with Urias to meet with Sawyer Bishop. Had he taken advantage of Urias? Or was there more to her father's debt than a simple gambling wager? No one would leave people tied to chairs for a simple debt, would they? Wouldn't it be easier to have taken Father to court and sued him for the monies owed? Did money owed in a gambling debt constitute no debt at all in a court of law?

Prudence tossed again.

"Will you stay still!" Kate whispered.

"Sorry."

Prudence shared the bed with Kate. There was ample room for the two of them, and even if she could sleep, she'd still be bothered by Kate's tossing and turning.

"I be up all night with this here strange bed. I ain't never slept on anything like it before," Kate whispered.

Prudence hadn't thought about the bed, its size, or the firmness of the mattress. It was firmer than most she'd slept on before, but if Urias could sleep on the ground with no worries, perhaps a firm mattress was more to his liking. Personally, she enjoyed a medium state of firmness. Not too soft and not too hard. "It's better than the ground."

"Aye, that it is." There was a moment of silence, then Kate started chatting on about the house and the strangers in it. "And Urias is so at home with these people."

"Yes, he seems quite content. Those children really love him."

"Aye. Babes they are. Every one of them. But they love Urias and treat him like a big brother."

"Yes." Prudence had often wondered what it would be like to have an older brother. "Kate, did you like having an older brother?"

"Ain't never thought about it. I suppose it be so. Urias was always there, looking out for me." Kate rolled on her side and faced Prudence. "Pru, how long do you think you'll be Urias's bond servant? Can a man do that to his legal wife?"

❧

Urias spent most of the evening making the loft habitable, eventually building a bed out of fresh hay and covering it with some canvas, then a sheet. Perhaps he should ask his grandparents if he could sleep on their sofa by the woodstove. Winter hadn't settled in yet, and already the wind howled through the barn.

Who was he kidding? It wasn't his bed or the place he was sleeping that kept him awake, but rather the possible scenarios of how to deal with Prudence. Should he take her to Creelsboro, where she could find a job and they could find an attorney to annul their marriage? Or should he have her work off some of her father's debt? Not as a servant but. . .but what? Urias couldn't afford to pay her and have a portion of her salary go toward the debt—which, his conscience reminded him, he'd told Hiram Greene was a gift. *That was before I knew what it would cost me.* He didn't have an income of his own, and without Bullet, it would be awhile longer before he could begin breeding horses as a profitable business.

Urias glanced down at the pair of horses he had bred, of which Bullet was their product. They were a fine pair. The wild stallion didn't care to be penned in. He seldom stayed still in the stall. Most of the time, Urias kept him out in the corral, but he wanted the stallion to get used to being in the barn before winter. The mare was expecting once again, but it would be a couple years before he could ride that horse. He glanced to the right, where a yearling stood. Its lines were similar to Bullet's but not quite as powerful. She would be a good breeder like her mother.

Closing his eyes, he tried to go to sleep. He continued to ignore the nagging feeling that wanted to bring up the anger he felt toward Hiram Greene and Prudence and how they'd tricked him into paying their debts. He knew it was wrong to be angry, that he needed to forgive, but neither had asked for forgiveness.

Prudence apologized for her father, he mused, then shook off the memory. He would not be fooled by the beauty of Prudence Greene, by the gentle way she spoke, or her so-called love for his sister. She was like her father, he reminded himself over and over again.

◈

Morning came early, along with the body aches from lack of sleep. Urias stretched and milked the cow.

"Morning, son." His father walked in. "Good to have your helping hands around here. Now, tell me about these hogs."

Urias went into a detailed description of his and Prudence's trip with the hogs and about their stay with Mrs. Campbell.

"You've had quite the adventure. Did you really need to swim the hogs across the river?"

"Only to save money. By that point Mr. Greene had passed along his demand for a dowry payment."

His father leaned against the stall's planks. "Seems to me if Prudence was aware of her father's debt, she wouldn't have put herself out and traveled with you."

"That's what doesn't make sense. I've asked her to come speak with me this morning. I have a mind to absolve her from the debt, but the matter of our marriage is still an issue."

"Son, I'm not going to presume to know what the answer is on this one. Seems to me a man really is married if he marries a woman, even if he marries her in name only. It also seems to me that the good Lord doesn't take to marriage as being a conveyance. If you vowed to God to marry this woman, you are married."

"It wasn't a real wedding—just some rushed-together service in her father's office."

"I see. And doesn't the Bible speak about obeying the laws of the land?"

"But. . ." Urias's shoulders slumped under the pressure.

His father came up beside him and laid a hand on his shoulder. "I understand your not wanting to take her as your wife. But if you gave your word, you might just have to live with it."

Urias swallowed hard. He had fully intended to make Prudence his wife when he said his vows. He didn't even think or know about an annulment until Prudence mentioned it. He'd given his word. Like it or not, Prudence was his wife.

"Pray on the matter, son. This afternoon, let's go fell some trees for your house."

If he worked quickly, Urias knew he could get the foundation done before the frost set in for the winter. "Yes, I imagine we won't be able to build until spring."

"Depends on the winter. But we'll do what we can before the weather turns bitter."

He finished milking the cow and handed the bucket to his father. "I'm going to spend some time with the Lord before I speak with Prudence."

Mac squeezed his shoulder. "I know you'll do the right thing."

But do I want to do the right thing? Urias wondered. *Is it right for a man to be bound to another person who doesn't really love him? Who used him?*

Falling on his knees, he pleaded with the Lord for some understanding of what to do. After an hour, he heard Prudence call, "Urias? Where are you?"

He got up and went to the edge of the loft. "Up here."

"Should I come up?" she asked.

He glanced back at his hay bed. Apart from that, there was nothing to sit down on. "I'll be right down."

He climbed down and prayed once again. As he walked toward her, he could see her fear. "I want to apologize for insisting that you become my bond servant. I was angry, and I took it out on you."

Prudence nibbled her lower lip and looked down at her feet, giving a slight nod.

"I am not going to require you to pay back your father's debt."

She looked up at him with her big brown eyes. Urias swallowed. "I've decided to honor our marriage and keep you as my wife."

Her eyes widened. "All right," she stammered.

Chapter 16

Prudence didn't know what to say to Urias when he said he intended to honor their marriage. Now, three months later, she still didn't understand what that meant. She worked night and day helping out with the children, the house, and even working with Urias on his new house. The exterior walls were up, but they hadn't been able to do any work on it for the past six weeks. The winter winds made it too cold.

But what did it mean to be husband and wife when you were nothing more than strangers? They still hadn't spent any time alone with one another, and she still stayed with Kate. Kate, on the other hand, was no longer afraid. She felt comfortable with the MacKenneths. It was a blessing to see her free. But Kate's freedom only magnified Prudence's entrapment. The marriage had been to help Kate, but still they had no real life together. She loved Urias and how he treated others, but he constantly avoided her.

Today things would be different. Today she would confront him and suggest they annul the marriage. She couldn't live like this. Even life in her parents' home was not like the loneliness she felt living in Urias's home.

Prudence marched up to Urias's house. She had seen him leave to take advantage of the break in the weather. "Urias?" she called.

"In the back room," he answered.

It wasn't that he was unfriendly, but they never had time alone. They did not behave as married people. "Urias, there's something we should talk about."

"Sure." He brushed the sawdust off his handmade leather pants.

Her stomach flipped at the sight of him.

"What would you like to talk about?"

"Us."

His face reddened. "What about us?"

"Urias, I can't go on like this. I feel I don't belong here. I feel I don't belong anywhere."

"I see."

"No, I don't believe you do."

Urias looked down at what he'd been working on. Prudence followed his line of vision. *A bed.*

"Prudence, I know I'm not much of a husband, but I can't escape how we got married. I was forced to marry you."

"I'm fully aware."

He closed the distance between them. "No, you don't understand. I promised I'd take care of you, but I can't get past the manipulation. Did you or did you not work with your father to have me pay off his debts?"

"What?" She stepped back from him. "Is that what this has been all about? You think I knew of my father's gambling debts? You think I set you up to pay him off? Are you forgetting something?"

"Your helping me with the hogs. I know," he finished her thoughts.

"Exactly. Why would I do that if I were working with my father?"

"For the dowry," he said in blunt response.

Dowry. She'd forgotten her father's additional request. "I see. Well, in that case, I wish for you to make me your bond servant again so I can pay off my father's debt, and once that's paid off, I'll be free to leave."

"Is that what you want?"

No, she wanted to scream. She wanted her husband, a real marriage. She wanted to be able to love Urias and feel the comfort of his embrace once again.

"Prudence, I don't want you to owe me anything." He looked back at the bed frame he was working on. "You're free to leave. I will not hold you here."

"What about our marriage?" she asked.

"Do what you would like on the matter. I'll sign any papers you would have me sign." He brushed past her. "Excuse me." He left her standing there alone in the room. On the floor was the headboard for a bed. A bed for two.

❧

Prudence's words still burned in his ears. He went out to the back woods. There was nothing like chopping down a tree to work off your anger. He'd been making their bed. How could he have been so foolish? Of course, she didn't want to be married to him—not for real.

With each passing day, he'd watched her. He'd watched the way she played with the children and helped around the house. He had to admit he'd been keeping her at a distance, unsure of what to do and how to go about it. He thought if he put together their bedroom, he'd have an opportunity to explain that he really did want to make this a real marriage, not in name only, as it had been for the past four months.

Now she was going. She didn't really care for him, did she?

For the past month, his father and mother had been giving him lectures on how he treated Prudence unfairly. They were right. He'd been treating her more like a visitor to his home—a temporary visitor who had overstayed her welcome. But Prudence hadn't overstayed, had she? He'd told her what to do and when to do it since they'd first met.

Life had been different on the trail, where they talked as equals, working together to take the hogs to the Cumberland Gap. When it had been just the two of them. If they had stayed on the trail for a day or two longer, he would have made her his wife in all the ways that a husband and wife become one. But that hadn't happened. Instead, they came upon her parents, tied and gagged. He'd met with Sawyer Bishop and paid off Hiram Greene's debt. He thought back on the conversation with Bishop that caused Urias to start wondering about Prudence's true intentions. Had he misjudged her?

Urias planted the ax in the tree and walked back to the cabin. "Prudence?" he called out.

He ran into the house, but she was gone.

He ran to the large farmhouse. "Mom, have you seen Prudence?"

"No. She left awhile ago, looking for you."

"She found me. If you see her again, would you tell her that I'm looking for her?"

"Yes. Is everything all right?"

"No, but it will be."

Urias ran out to the barn. His mare was missing. "Where did she go?" He mounted the stallion and tracked her heading to Creelsboro. Before long, he caught up to her, riding the mare without a thought in the world.

"Prudence," he called.

She turned around. "Urias?"

"Stop," he ordered. "Please." He softened his tone.

She halted the horse.

"Prudence, I don't want you to leave."

"Why?" Tears began to fall from her already red and swollen eyes.

Urias's gut tightened. "Because I want our marriage to work."

"Why?"

Urias closed his eyes. Why did he want their marriage to work? "Because I want us to get back to the trail. I want us to try to be the people we were on the trail."

"I haven't changed."

Urias looked down at the reins in his hands, then looked up at her. "Prudence, Sawyer Bishop told me that your father had tried to pay him off once before."

"Oh?"

"He said your father offered to give you to Sawyer as his mistress to pay off the debt."

"He did *what?*" Prudence's face reddened with anger. "So this is why you believed I was in on some scheme with my father?"

"Yes, I'm ashamed to say. Can you forgive me?"

"Forgive you? I want to—"

"I'm sorry, Prudence."

"The more I learn of his business dealings, the more ashamed I am of my father. He tried to sell me?"

"That's what Sawyer said, although I don't know that his word is any more trustworthy than your father's." Urias dismounted and reached up to Prudence, encouraging her to come down from the saddle. "Let's sit down over here." He pointed to a browned grassy hill.

Prudence started to cry all over again. He held her in his arms, taking in the sweet fragrance that was her unique scent. He'd missed that. After a few moments, he lifted her face and pushed back a few strands of hair. "Can we start over?"

"Why would you want to?" she sniffled.

Urias smiled. There was hope. "Because I'd like to get to know my wife, the real woman, not the image I've concocted in my mind based on what others have said and done."

A slight smile edged up the corners of her mouth. "I'd like that."

Unable to let the moment slip through his hands, he pulled her close and kissed her. As with their first kiss, their passions ignited. Urias pulled back first. "Honey, I. . .I mean, we can't."

She knitted her eyebrows, and a delicate wrinkle formed in the center of her forehead.

"What I'm trying to say—and doing a miserable job of it—is that if we are to be man and wife, I don't want it to be because of our marriage at your parents' house. I want us to be married in my church, with God's blessing."

A smile lit up her face. "I'd like that, too."

"So would I. But first, let's wait a bit and make certain this is what we both want."

"Urias? Can I be perfectly honest with you?"

His heart thundered in his chest. "Yes."

"I've been in love with you since we were on the trail."

"Really?" Urias beamed.

"Yes. It must be those green eyes."

Urias wiggled his eyebrows. "Mom always said my wife would fall in love with them. When you're a teen with my coloring, you're made fun of—a lot."

"I think you're rather handsome." Prudence blushed.

Urias leaned forward. Prudence blocked his lips with her fingers. Why she was stopping the kiss made no real sense, even to her, except that they both had said they wanted to wait and have a real wedding.

Urias leaned back. "You're right. We'll need to take this slowly."

"Urias, if we're to be husband and wife, am I to strictly follow your orders, or do I have a say in matters?"

Urias chuckled, then picked up a small twig. "I want to hear your opinions. I valued your advice and insight on the trail. I just couldn't get past my anger."

"You had a right to be angry. But wouldn't it have been wiser to speak with me about it?"

"Perhaps. But under the circumstances, I doubt I would have trusted your word any more than that of any other stranger," he said.

"Ouch."

"I'm sorry, but we need to be honest. I don't want there to be any further secrets between us."

"Agreed." Prudence sat back, balancing herself on her elbows. She looked up at the sky. "Do you think winter will end soon?"

"I hope so. I want to get our house done."

"Will Kate be moving in with us?" Prudence could feel the heat rise on her cheeks.

"I'll have to speak with my parents. If they're agreeable to let her keep my old room, then I don't see why she would need to stay with us. At least not at first. I'm torn, Prudence. I want Katherine to feel like the place is hers but. . ."

"Will she ever feel that way about any place?"

"Exactly. She and I have talked some. She's still pretty angry with God, but she's coming around. I can't say that I blame her for feeling bitter, considering some of the things she's gone through."

"I know. She said that it's hard to believe in a loving and compassionate God when she's seen so little evidence of that in her own life. Part of what attracted me to you in the beginning, Urias, was watching you live out your faith. However, I was beginning to question your faith in the past couple of months."

"Ouch." Urias chuckled.

"You said, be honest."

"That I did. And I can't say I blame you for wondering. It bothered me to sell Bullet, but that was minor compared to what I thought you had been a part of."

"Do you really think my father would have sold me?"

"I honestly don't know. He certainly was a desperate man."

"He was getting more and more upset with my not producing a suitor, and all the men I discussed finances with seemed to think I had two heads. But you never did. That's another thing that attracted me to you, I might add."

"I love how you sacrificed yourself for a friend. When I saw your feet all marred up on the trail and your not complaining about it, I thought to myself, 'she's an amazing woman.' "

Prudence smiled. "Where do we go from here?"

Chapter 17

Shaking off the dust and pieces of dried grass was easy compared to the shakes in his legs. He'd just committed to Prudence, even asking her to remarry him. If only he could get his stomach to relax. He opened his hand and offered it to Prudence. She slipped her delicate fingers into his rough, open palm. Again he fought down a surge of trembling born of emotions that threatened to overwhelm him whenever they were close. She loved him. She'd loved him for a while, and he'd never known it.

He scrutinized the fine lines of her face. Was she shaky as well? "Nervous?"

"Terrified. Are you sure?"

He nodded, not trusting himself to speak.

"That sure, huh?"

He swallowed the lump in his throat and spoke. "Honey, I'm unsure what to say, how to act around you."

"Be yourself, Urias. That's the man I fell in love with."

"I can do that." But could he tell her that he loved her? Did he love her? Or was there a part of him just trying to make do with a situation that he'd gotten himself into without thinking, just reacting?

He helped her up on her horse. She felt wonderful in his hands. There was a connection between them, but would it last?

"I think you're right about waiting awhile, Urias. Let's make sure we're doing the right thing this time."

"Yes. How long do you want to wait?" he asked and mounted his horse.

"For spring? Summer?" she suggested.

"I should have most of the house ready by spring. We can aim for that."

"What about your parents? What will they think about all this?"

That I should have done this a long time ago. "They like you, Prudence. They'll be fine with our choice. It's a sensible one, don't you think?"

"Yes, but. . ."

He lifted his reins and waited for her to continue. She went no further.

Should he pry? There was the matter of not keeping secrets one from the other, but did that include all of their innermost thoughts? "But?"

"Nothing, really."

"Do you have doubts about our getting married—I mean a real marriage?"

She looked away from him and up the hill at an outcropping of granite protruding at an odd angle from the steep slope. He'd never noticed that before.

"Yes, there's a part of me that would like to be married. Then there's a part of me that has wrestled with our marriage having been the most regrettable decision I've ever made."

Ouch. She's really being honest. "I've wrestled with the same, but, given the same circumstances, I'm not sure I would have done it differently."

"Kate needed our help."

"Agreed. But our marriage, if there is to be a real marriage, can't be based on what anyone else needs or wants."

"That's my point. If we are to truly have a real marriage, we ought to at least start by courting. I mean. . .I realize we've been living in the same house and have spent numerous days on the trail together but. . ."

Urias hadn't thought about courting. They were married already. The church wedding wasn't even required, legally, although he felt in his heart it was necessary. But courting—does a man really have to go through all those fancy steps? *She's already said she loves me,* he argued with himself.

"If you're thinkin' what I think you're thinkin', that's exactly why we need to court."

"Huh?" Urias scratched the back of his neck. "I don't get it. We're already married. Why would I need to. . ." He caught himself before he set a waterfall in motion. He was missing something here, he knew. She knew it, too, and it wasn't likely she'd tell him. He'd have to figure this out on his own somehow.

"I don't think we should make any marriage plans."

Urias shook his head, blinked, and kept himself from sticking his finger in his ear to see if he truly had heard what he thought he heard. "But I thought we just settled that we'd aim to get married in the spring."

She wasn't going to give him a hint of what was on her mind, he realized, and at the moment, he wanted to be upset with her for not telling him. Instead, he found himself wondering what he didn't understand and why it was so important to her to be courted.

"Urias." She reached over and placed her hand upon his. "I'll go back to the house with you, where we can think about this for a few days. Is that fair?"

He nodded, not sure what he had done to cause this change in plans. Hadn't she just confessed her love for him? Didn't they just share a tender and passionate kiss? What more is there? *I even told her I wanted to get the marriage right and marry in front of You, Lord. Please help me out here.*

The world was silent. A cardinal—male, judging by its brightly colored feathers—perched on a tree and sang out loud and shrill. Was he laughing at Urias not understanding or simply trying to tell him what the answer was? In either case, Urias didn't know, so he waited for Prudence to turn her horse around before he turned his. They headed back to the farm together, but even more distant than they had been for the past three months.

What have I done now?

đa

Prudence fought down her anger. She wouldn't tell Urias what she longed to hear him say. She wanted him to treat her as if she had worth to him. She wanted to be cherished, at least just a little bit. She knew it would take years before Urias would ever confess his love for her, but he could show some respect. *I guess that's why I want him to court me, Lord. Am I wrong? Am I expecting too much from a man, from Urias? Shouldn't a wife be treasured? At least in a little way?* she prayed.

"Prudence," Urias called out as his horse trotted up to her. "What's wrong? Forgive me for being ignorant, but I honestly don't know what I've done this time."

Prudence gently pulled back on the reins. She scanned his wonderful green eyes, pleading for her understanding. "A woman," she stammered, looking for the right words. "Me—I really don't want a marriage just for the sake of a marriage. I want to know that my husband cares for me."

"I care," he defended.

"Urias, look at your parents. They love one another. They show it in the little things they say and do for one another. I'm not saying I'm expecting you to love me like that. I know that our marriage will always have the blackened past of how we began as husband and wife. But. . ."

Urias climbed down off his horse and came up beside her, reaching up for her. "Come on." He held up his arms. "We have more to talk about."

She wanted to fall into his embrace but stayed firmly planted in her saddle. "Wouldn't it be best to give us a couple days to think about this?"

"No, I think we need to talk more. I've upset you. I've apparently said some things wrong. We need to clarify everything in order to be able to think for a while. If'n you need some time to think after we have a clear understanding of our future, that would be fine."

Prudence released the reins and slid into his proffered embrace.

"That's better. Now, the Good Book says we ought not to let the sun go down on our anger."

"The Good Book also says husbands are to love their wives. Should we be married if you don't?"

"I do love you. I mean," he stammered, "I think this love can grow, but it'll need time."

He loves me. Prudence held back a smile. "What kind of love do you have for me?"

He sat on the ground and waited for her to join him. "Most of the time, it's love one shows another person. I don't want to see anything bad happen to you. I feel a sense of duty to protect you. Not really duty—I don't know if I can explain it. It's kinda like my father's protective love for his family, but I know it isn't as strong as that. However, if anyone tried to hurt you, I would fight for you. I will protect you."

Prudence took in a deep breath. *It's a start.*

"You say you love me, Prudence, but how do you know it's the love a wife should have for a husband? How do you know it isn't just physical attraction? We both have to admit, there is a powerful attraction between us."

The heat of a deep blush spread across her cheeks and down her neck. "I don't know why or how I love you. I know it doesn't make much sense. It's little things, really. . . . How you care for Kate. . . How you sacrificed for her. How you treated Mrs. Campbell and others on the trail. There's a million little things you've done that make me think I love you. I guess that's why it's so hard to stay living here, knowing you don't care for me in the same way."

Urias chuckled. "There's a ton of little things that I love and admire about you, too. It's the way you are with the children, the way you sacrificed for Katherine, and the way you help others and give of yourself. Even the way your mind works with numbers—to name a few."

She held back the tears.

Urias leaned over and faced her, their noses less than an inch apart. "You need to hear these things, don't you?"

She nodded.

"You're a beautiful woman, Prudence, inside and out. I'll admit I don't know if the passion I feel is the basis for the deep love a man and wife should share, but I believe God will honor us if we honor Him. I'm willing to work on being a good husband if you're willing to work on being a good wife."

"What do you want in a wife?" she asked, silently praying it was more than her father wanted from his wife yet less than some of the things he'd grown to expect from her mother over the years.

"That's a hard one. I want your help in financial matters, and I think together we can build a good farm for breeding horses. But I want you to be willing to make me talk when I want to be alone. Sometimes I'll need to be alone, but somehow I need my wife to be able to figure out when those times are. I'm like my dad in that respect. I can spend weeks at a time away from anyone and be very happy. Mom will be able to help you understand how to keep me from my shell of solitude. Oh, and my wife needs to cook." He wiggled his eyebrows.

"I think I can do that."

"I know you can." Urias reached over and traced his thumb across her jawline. "Daily kisses from my wife would be another good thing."

She swatted his hand. "You've had your daily limit."

Urias let out a guttural laugh. "I didn't say a single kiss, my dear. I said kisses."

❧

Urias planed down the rough wood to put the finishing touches on his and Prudence's bed. It would be his wedding present to her. Unfortunately, she'd seen it the day he proposed to her. Courting Prudence turned out to be a good thing, he decided. They were learning more and more about one another, and the desire to be married to Prudence grew steadily each day. The wedding had been planned for one month from now, and he had precious little time to finish the house. Katherine had decided to stay in the big farmhouse and help Pam with the children. Mom was expecting another child and was having a difficult time getting around. Katherine saw she was truly needed and appreciated being asked to help out.

If the Lord blesses, Urias pondered, *hopefully Katherine will someday help Prudence in the same situation.*

"Urias," Prudence called out.

"Stay put," he ordered and covered the bed frame with a piece of canvas. He went out and found her in the newly finished kitchen.

"Hi." She looked down at her feet. A sure sign he was in for a special treat.

"Hi." He closed the gap between them. "Did I tell you how beautiful you look this morning?"

Prudence blushed.

An ever-deepening sense of love, honor, and how unique Prudence Greene O'Leary truly was swept over him anew. Daily he was learning to appreciate her sacrificial love, no longer just for Katherine, but for himself and others as well. She was a gift from the Lord. Colossians 3:19, a verse his father challenged him on—*"Husbands, love your wives, and be not bitter against them"*—rang through his mind one more time. Was there any bitterness left in him regarding Prudence and her father's deception? He'd long ago realized Prudence had no part in the deceptions of her father. And he even had some grace to extend to Hiram Greene, knowing how hard it would be to admit to his wife and family that he'd made a terrible mistake.

"What's the matter?" she asked.

"Nothing."

She placed her hands on her hips. "You're not being honest with me. I thought we agreed no more secrets," she challenged.

"I'm sorry. But must a man tell his wife everything he is thinking?"

"Perhaps not everything. The reason I came over was to try to persuade you to join me on a picnic."

"Picnic?" Urias looked for a basket of food. Prudence's cooking continued to whet his appetite. She'd been taking lessons from his mother and grandmother, as well as Kate. "It's not that warm out—unless you were thinking of eating in here."

"No, I had another place in mind."

"Oh?" Clearly, she'd been planning something special. Desire wanted him to say yes. Reality won the day. "I do have a lot of work to do." He paused, then added, "If I'm to have this house done by the time we're married."

Her shoulders slumped. She put on a fake smile. "I understand. What can I do to help?" She scanned the kitchen. The cabinets were done. The counter and wood sink were in place.

Urias had ordered a couple cast-iron stoves, which were expected to be in later this week. The stone floor was a safety feature he'd learned about from his father that would limit household fires from indoor cooking. The empty space where the stove belonged was a reminder of work still not done.

"Honey, I'd really like to take off the afternoon and spend it with you, but we have to keep our focus if this place is to be ready by the time we're to be married."

"I know you're right. It's just that. . ." She let her words trail off as she glanced into the main living room of the house. Her posture changed, and she locked her gaze on his. "I've been thinking about the horse breeding and wanted to discuss it with you."

Since their hog expedition, there hadn't been much in the discussion of finances. In part, Urias felt it was due to the business with her father's debt. "What do you have on your mind?"

"I was trying to calculate how much hay one needs to store up for the winter in order to feed a horse. Which got me to thinking about how much space we'd need in a barn, especially once you have several expecting mares. How much land will we need for this grain? And is the land you've been given large enough for the plans you have?"

Urias rolled back on his heels. "You've been thinkin', all right. First, we don't have enough land to feed a lot of horses, yet. I've set my sights on a spread a few hours from here. I won't have the funds for an additional year with the loss of Bullet. I don't know if the land will still be available by then. If not, we can't go that large scale that quickly. We'll have to start off slow, build up some revenue, then make some purchase arrangements with various area farmers."

"What about the barn?"

"In my mind, I have a plan to build a series of stalls, making it a long, narrow barn with storage room in the loft."

"Where are you planning on building the barn, and when?"

Urias chuckled. "Next year. But it will be built in sections. It will grow as our needs grow."

She smiled.

I must have said something right, he reflected as he suppressed a grin.

Chapter 18

U rias sat with a sheet of paper, laying out all that he and Prudence had discussed earlier in the day, on his lap. The house was quiet. He turned up the wick of the kerosene lamp for a better view. He held up the paper. "This is amazing, Prudence. You've put everything down in writing."

It had taken courage to make such a bold overture in their relationship, but after their many discussions, she felt it was time to brave it and see if her husband would truly want her opinion about business matters.

"What's this here?" He pointed to an income column.

"Those are stud fees. I thought we might be able to make use of Bullet's father's service for others looking for a horse with good lines. He's a bit wild, but I think that fire will be helpful in pitching his worth."

"Hard to say. Some folks worry about their mares being beaten up by a wild male."

She nodded. She didn't know that could be a problem but instantly saw the point Urias was making.

"But it's a good idea for raising more capital." He scrutinized the paper a bit more. "What's this?"

Prudence giggled. "That's an idea for after the harvest. I was thinking. . ." How could she put this? "I was thinking, since the foal isn't due for some time, perhaps we could take another trip through the Cumberland Gap."

"Another trip?"

"Yes. I was thinking we did so well with the price of the hogs last time that it might be. . ."

Urias laughed out loud, then caught himself. "Honey, I have no interest in hauling hogs over the trail ever again. If I have to, I will, but. . ."

She'd had doubts about putting that suggestion down on paper, but the thousand dollars they earned the last time seemed like good pay for a couple weeks' work.

"Honey, I want to raise horses, not hogs," Urias finished.

"I suppose it wasn't that great of a suggestion."

"No, I'm not saying that." He reached out his hand and lifted her chin with his first finger.

"If we left from here, we could take a wagon," she pressed. It wasn't that she really wanted to be on the trail with the hogs again.

"This isn't about the pigs or making money, is it?" he asked.

"No," she confessed.

"Time alone?" he asked.

She nodded.

He put the paperwork aside. "Pru, I had in mind to take you away for a couple weeks after we got married. Just you and me. The problem is, it'll be the height of spring planting, and I'm needed here."

"I know. I understand."

He reached out to her. She kept her eyes fixed on his and took the final step that separated them. "What if we ran off to the minister now?" she whispered in his ear.

"What about the house?" He wrapped his arms around her.

She leaned in and placed her arms on his shoulders. She didn't care about the house, a fancy bed, or anything. She only wanted to be with Urias. They'd been husband and wife for five months, and she didn't want to wait any longer to be his wife in every way. "I love you, Urias. I—"

He placed his warm fingertip to her lips. "What about the plans everyone has made on our behalf? Hasn't Mom been working on a gown with you?"

She pushed back from his arms and nodded. "You're right," she admitted.

He pulled her back and held her tightly. His warm breath tickled her ear. "I love you, too, and I'd like nothing more than to be married tonight. But one of the things the Lord's been showing me is we're both impulsive by nature. We both jump, then look where we've fallen. As much as I hate to admit it, I think we were right in setting the wedding date for when we did."

She wanted to kiss him. She was afraid to kiss him. They were married, but they both agreed they wanted a marriage where God was placed at the center, not themselves. She laid her head on his shoulder. "I think the Lord's been telling me the same thing during my quiet time," she admitted.

"Tell you what we can do." He paused. "We can do our devotionals together. Perhaps not in the morning." He chuckled. She still struggled getting up as early as the rest of the household did. "But in the evening after dinner, we could spend some time in the Bible and prayer. What do you think?"

"I'd like that." Although if she was being perfectly honest, it wasn't what she had in mind for being alone with Urias.

"I think it will be a grand adventure. In some ways, we look at various issues in very different ways, but ultimately we still come to the same conclusions. We could have very spirited discussions from time to time, I would think." He winked.

"More than likely," she agreed. "Should we go over those figures some more?"

&

"Urias," Katherine called as the kitchen door slammed shut behind her.

"Katherine? What's the matter?"

"Nothing. Pam told Prudence you didn't want her to come to the house, so she sent me."

"How is she?"

"She's fine. If you call nervous fine. How are you?"

"Good."

"You've been working night and day." Katherine scanned the bedroom. "This is beautiful. She'll love it."

A smile rose on his face. He hoped Prudence would like it. If anyone would know her tastes, it would be Katherine. "I'm glad. I wanted to make the room special for her."

"You really like her, don't you?"

"She's a remarkable woman."

Katherine nodded, then sat down on the bed. "Pru asked me to check on you and to make sure you weren't too tired. She's worried about you."

"I'm fine. Tell her I'm anxiously awaiting the next two days."

Katherine smiled, then looked down at her lap. She laced her fingers together and released them a couple of times. Urias had learned long ago not to push Katherine—to let her have the time needed to collect her thoughts. He placed a loving hand on her shoulder. She didn't flinch. He silently praised the Lord.

She glanced up at him, her green eyes pooled with fresh tears. "I'm happy for Prudence. I'm glad you two are going to make a real marriage out of this horrible mess."

Urias sat down beside his sister. "Katherine, I love Prudence, and I want to be the best possible husband to her. I'm also here for you. I'll do anything I can to help you. Prudence and I both will."

"Do you really think God cares for me?"

"Yes. I know you've been through a horrible ordeal. I can only imagine what you went through. But God does love you, and He was always there. I know it doesn't make sense sometimes. We feel so lost and alone, like God has deserted us. And I can't begin to explain why God lets bad things happen to people. I remember from the Bible about Job and all he went through. I sometimes think about my situations and how horrific they seem at the time. Then I compare it with Job and what he went through and realize I haven't got it so bad."

"How could Mother sell me like that?"

"I don't know. She wasn't a well woman. We both know the drinking caused her to change. She must have been desperate for money and driven by the need for alcohol. That doesn't excuse her actions, just explains them. At least that's how I've come to look at it. I was mighty angry at Mother for what she did to you."

"You were?"

"Yup. I think I took it out on Prudence, which she didn't deserve."

"I don't recall you ever being real angry. I mean, I saw you upset, but you weren't punching or hitting anything. You never yelled."

"Katherine, I've learned to control my anger. I saw what it did with Mother. And I've seen what Mom and Dad have worked through when they were angry. The Bible says 'be ye angry, and sin not.' It took awhile, and I'm still working on it, but we can get angry and not sin."

"I want to believe like you, Prudence, and the MacKenneths, but I can't forgive God for letting it happen to me."

Urias's stomach tightened. He knew Katherine still didn't recognize that she had her own sins to seek God's forgiveness for—that it wasn't God who needed to be forgiven. This was not the time or place to press the point. "I understand. You were a child, an innocent child. Bad things should not happen to innocent children. But you weren't killed. There are many worse things that could have happened to you that didn't."

"I feel so dirty—so worthless," she confessed.

Urias took in a deep breath. "You were sinned against. God loves you, and He wants you to be free from the bondage of those who sinned against you."

"I want to be free, Urias. I truly do, but the memories come back to haunt me night after night."

He gently explained how to ask the Lord into her heart and how to rebuke evil thoughts when they came in. But he saw she wasn't ready to take that final step. He would continue to pray for Katherine's freedom from the past, as he knew he'd have to pray to be rid of the renewed anger within himself for the men who had abused his sister—as well as their mother for selling her into bondage.

"I love you, Katherine. I'm sorry those things happened to you."

"It's not your fault. I used to think it was. If you'd never left, nothing would have happened to me. But I don't know. She could have sold both of us, couldn't she?"

"I never thought about it, but you're right, she could have." Urias silently thanked the Lord for His salvation and for His grace in allowing him to run into the MacKenneths on the trail.

"I'll think about what you said. Maybe someday I'll be able to forgive God and accept His grace."

"I'm always here for you," he offered. "And so is He."

She gave a slight nod and left him sitting in the bedroom. Taking a moment to pray, he handed over his renewed anger and his sister, Katherine, to the Lord. Urias didn't have the answers for her. He couldn't explain why such awful things had happened to her. He knew precious little of what exactly transpired, but her demeanor and the few comments she'd let slip were enough to know that someone, at least one of the men who had owned her bond, had taken advantage of her. He was ever so grateful that Hiram Greene had purchased her. Urias caught himself at that thought. Yes, he was grateful to Hiram Greene. "Lord, You're amazing." Urias jumped to his feet and headed to his parents' house.

&

Two more days, Prudence reminded herself. She and Urias would be married, with God's blessing, in two more days. She couldn't wait. His news about being thankful for her father struck a chord. She hadn't forgiven him for how he'd handled Kate's bondage. Business or not, it wasn't right. Urias was right. Her father needed to be forgiven. *But how do I forgive my own father, who was willing to use his own flesh and blood for his own personal gain?*

She walked behind the house and up the small hill. She'd found the secluded place quite by accident one day and ever since had used it as a place to pray and gather her thoughts. The MacKenneth home was a large farmhouse, but with so many people, a place for solitude seemed very needed.

She sat down on a log that provided a perfect place for a moment's rest, closed her eyes, and began to pray. She never heard the approaching footsteps.

"Hello." Grandma MacKenneth smiled as she took her seat on the log beside Prudence. "Forgive me for intruding."

"It's all right," Prudence politely answered.

"I've seen you come a time or two and thought you might like a listening ear. If not, I'll be on my way once I catch my breath. How do you like this little spot?"

"It's wonderful." She realized she mustn't have been the only person who thought it was the ideal place for solitude.

"I've tried to keep it as natural as possible, but every now and again I'd have Timmon come up and pull some small bushes or trees that insisted on growing in the circle. That was before his accident of course."

"Do you come up here often?"

"No, not too much anymore. Caring for Timmon requires a lot of my time."

"I understand."

"I'm getting on in years, so I'll just be frank. Do you love Urias?"

"Yes. But he isn't the reason I came up here."

"What seems to be troubling you?"

"My father. I'm sure you've heard."

She placed her hand lovingly on Prudence's knee. "A little. But why don't you tell me."

"You know the circumstances of how Urias and I were forced to marry and about Urias paying off my father's gambling debt."

"Yes. Go on."

"Well, the man he paid told Urias that my father had once offered me in exchange for his gambling losses. Had he accepted my father's offer, I would have become his mistress."

Prudence saw the compassion in the woman's eyes.

"I'm sorry. One doesn't like to learn that a parent or parents didn't cherish them. I may be wrong, but I think your father is sin sick. He's lost in the sin of his gambling. I would guess, due to the great expense Urias had to pay, that your father had been gambling for a long time. The thing about sin is, it blinds us. We don't really see straight. We do things we wouldn't normally do because we have lost our judgment—our ability to understand right from wrong correctly. We justify to ourselves our sinful acts and go on as if the rest of the world is ignorant, or worse."

Prudence thought for a moment. "Father can be rather arrogant," she admitted.

"I imagine your parents love you, and, if you think about it for a bit, you'll remember times of love and joy in your house."

"Yes, there were plenty of those moments when I was younger. It's only been the past two years that they decided I should be married and that my open concern about business matters was not healthy."

Grandma Mac laughed. "Well, forgive the man for those years. You don't want to be starting your marriage with Urias being angry with your parents. Give it to God and leave the nonsense of sin behind you. Your father will one day come to terms with what he's done and is doing.

"Now, enough talk about your father. How are you feeling about getting married in two days?"

"I can't wait," Prudence bubbled out with the answer.

"Wonderful. You've got a good man in Urias. He'll make a good husband."

"He already has been."

"I keep forgetting you're already married."

"In name only. But he's treated me like a wife. Oh, there was a time when he didn't appreciate me because he believed I had conspired with Father. But even during that time, he never said anything or did anything to dishonor me. I know he's a wonderful man. I just hope I can be a good wife to him."

"You will, dear. Just relax and be yourself. That's the person he's fallen in love with." She tapped Prudence on the knee once again and pushed herself up off the log. "I'll leave you be for a spell so you can work out the details with the good Lord about your father. Just remember, God thought him worthy enough to die on the cross for, especially for his shortcomings and sinful nature." Grandma Mac winked.

Prudence watched the old woman take tentative steps down the path toward the smaller house. Prudence thought back on Grandma MacKenneth's parting words. *Was she right? Was it as simple as putting Father's sin in perspective as to how God views sin and the sacrifice of the cross?*

Chapter 19

Urias polished the tops of his boots with the back of his trouser legs for the tenth time in as many minutes. He stopped long enough to pace the back room off the sanctuary. Pastor Cloyse had spoken to Urias about ten minutes ago, assuring him that Prudence would be arriving shortly. The last time he peeked, the church was filled with friends. Of course, weddings were a major social event for the small town of Jamestown. Everyone knew everyone else, and all came out.

He'd stayed up half the night, putting some finishing touches on the house, then tossed the rest of the night in anticipation of today. He knew he was making the right decision, yet he still fought the doubts of the past. Thoughts of questioning Prudence's involvement in her father's decisions had poked their ugly heads every fifteen minutes. He countered them with the facts: who Prudence was, how she acted, and how hurt she'd been to learn the truth of her father's ways. Urias knew in his heart she was innocent. He also knew he'd grown to love her and appreciate her.

"Father, bless our marriage," he prayed.

"It's time." Mac poked his head through the doorway. "Ready, son?"

Urias nodded, unsure of his voice.

His father chuckled and gave him a slap on the back. "The butterflies won't last long. Once you see your bride coming down the aisle, every doubt will fly away."

"Thanks."

"You're welcome. I remember it all too well. Seems to me there was a young lad who helped set me straight about how much I loved Pam and that I was a fool if I let her get away."

Urias chuckled. "Prudence is a good woman."

"Yes, she is. She'll make you a mighty fine wife."

"Thanks, Dad."

"Pleasure."

The piano music began. Urias took the lead and walked across the front of the sanctuary, taking his position to the left of the pastor and watching for Prudence to come down the aisle. First came Katherine, dressed in a light pink linen dress. She was beautiful with her red curls and green eyes. His heart cried out a silent prayer for his sister. She needed healing, and Urias knew he couldn't heal her. He could only love her and support her in any way possible.

The tempo of the music changed. Urias looked up, and Prudence, in a white dress with a flowing skirt, stood at the entrance of the church sanctuary. Her long brown hair was spun with lace, and the veil covered her face with the slightest of shadows.

His heart skipped a beat. His palms instantly dampened. He started to brush the tops of his boots once again and caught himself just in time.

A smile brimmed from ear to ear. She was beautiful, and she was a gift from the Lord.

Slowly, Prudence made her way down the aisle.

The people in the church seemed to disappear. The only person he saw was Prudence. His gift from God.

"Dearly beloved. . ." The minister began the service. Urias kept his gaze fixed on Prudence. She seemed as nervous as he had been a few moments earlier. He held her hand in his. They faced the pastor and said their vows, dedicating themselves to one another and the Lord.

"You may kiss the bride," the pastor concluded.

Urias lifted the veil and took in her beauty for a moment before closing the gap between them. The kiss was sweet as honey. He pulled back slightly and whispered, "I love you."

"I love you, too," Prudence replied.

They were finally one before God and man. Urias looped his arm and waited for Prudence to place her hand in the crook of his elbow, her touch so intimate, so tender, and so natural. They belonged together. Urias was never more certain of anything in his entire life.

જ

Prudence's cheeks ached from smiling.

"Ready?" Urias whispered.

"Yes," she replied. The desire to leave the reception and begin her life as Mrs. Urias O'Leary had peaked an hour ago. The reception was nice, with lots of folks wishing them well. Everyone had brought in food, and Pam and Grandma Mac had even made a three-layered wedding cake.

Prudence couldn't ask for a better reception. Apart from wishing her family was here, it was perfect.

Urias flashed his intoxicating green eyes at her and winked. "We'll say our good-byes now."

He took her by the hand and pronounced their departure. A few folks shook their hands, but most just waved them off. The small carriage waited outside the church. A flutter of excitement climbed up her spine as Urias's strong hands went around her waist and helped her step up into the carriage, its narrow bench the perfect setting for an intimate conversation between a man and wife.

Without saying a word, Urias hurried around to the other side and climbed aboard. Taking the leather reins in hand, he snapped them. "Yah."

The carriage lurched forward.

"How are you?"

"Fine."

He placed the reins in one hand, then wrapped her in a loving embrace with his free hand. "I love you, Prudence."

"I love you, too."

He let out a pensive breath.

Prudence leaned her head on his shoulder. "Can you tell me my surprise now?" She'd been wanting to know for weeks what he had been doing in their bedroom.

The lilt of Urias's laughter warmed her. He smiled down at her. "I hope you're not disappointed."

"How could I be? I don't know what it is."

"Sure you do. It's just our bedroom and the bed I made."

"I know that. But why the big secret?"

He kissed the top of her head. "I don't have much to give you, honey. I had enough to purchase the gold ring, but between building our house and trying to recover from the loss of Bullet, I honestly don't have much money."

"There's always another trip with some hogs."

Urias groaned. "I know. But while I don't have much money, I do have a little talent with wood. Our bedroom and a few of the other final touches on the house are my wedding gift to you."

She sat up straight. "Urias, you've worked so hard. You didn't have to. I would have been content with anything."

"I know that. But it was something I could do. Besides, you're worth it.

You're a precious jewel, Prudence, and I wish to honor you with the smaller gifts in the house."

What could she say? She had no gift to give. She had no money, and she had little talent or skills in much of anything. Growing up with servants left one a bit unprepared for the world outside of one's own environment.

He turned to look at her. "What's wrong?"

She hesitated for a moment. "I don't have a gift for you."

"You're my gift, honey." He kissed her gently on the cheek.

She cuddled back into his embrace. Could life be better than this? She was in love, and the man she was in love with loved her.

They rounded the bend to the entrance of their new home. It was small, but plenty for the two of them.

"Prudence, there's something we haven't talked about."

A fear of concern tingled up her back. "What's that?"

"Children. I would like to have children. Did you mean it when you told Mrs. Campbell you'd like to have children one day?"

The fear melted. Warmth filled her chest. "Yes, I would like to have children."

"Depending on how the good Lord blesses, I'd like a pack of 'em."

"Pack? Like in wolves?"

"No. Well, a lot of kids, just not wild ones."

Prudence chuckled.

"We're home." He pulled back the reins, then stood to his feet.

He helped her down. Prudence savored the warmth of his hands upon her waist. Then he spun her around in his arms and stepped toward the front door. "May I carry you over the threshold, Mrs. O'Leary?"

O'Leary. It felt right, even though she wasn't from an Irish or Scottish background. She wrapped her arms around his neck and gave a brief nod.

"What would you like to see first?"

"The bedroom." She felt the heat rise on her face. "You've been the most secretive about that room."

"The bedroom it is." Urias carried her through the front door and straight back to the bedroom. "Close your eyes."

"Come on. I've waited this long."

"Shh. Bear with me for a moment longer."

She complied and closed her eyes. She could feel him turning his body to carry her through the doorway. Inside the room, she heard the door close. He set her down. "Keep them closed just a little longer."

Her body shook in anticipation. She could smell a fresh flame burning.

"All right. Open your eyes."

Slowly, she opened them and scanned the room. "Oh Urias." Her gaze landed on the hand-carved bed. "You did all this?"

"Yes. Do you like it?"

"I love it." She stepped forward, reached out, and touched the smooth surface of the wooden roses carved across the top of the headboard. "It's absolutely beautiful."

"I stained it to simulate a rose color. It's been waxed with five layers."

On the wall were sconces with small mirrors behind the candles. "How could you afford all this?"

"I found an old mirror and cut it up to fit. I used the bits of mirror around the house to enhance the lights. You'll see when you see the rest of the house."

The bed was dressed with a lovely wedding ring quilt. "Who made this?" She fingered the corner.

"Grandma."

Overwhelmed by the old woman's generosity, tears welled in her eyes.

He came up behind her and placed his hands on her shoulders. His breath whispered on her ear. Love flooded around her heart.

"What's the matter?"

"Nothing. I don't deserve this."

"Prudence, you must learn to accept your value in my eyes. Come here." He led her to the bed and sat down beside her. His thumb lightly brushed away the tear on her cheek. "You are a wonderful person. What happened between your father and myself is in the past. We're married properly now; nothing can change that. I love you and you love me. Nothing else matters."

"I do love you," she confessed. "I think I fell in love with you the moment I met you. At least—the very least—with your green eyes."

Urias chuckled. "Mom was right. She said my wife would adore my eyes."

"You have a wise mother."

"Yes, but I have an equally wise wife. I love you, Prudence. I love who you are, how wise you are with numbers and understanding business. I'm looking forward to our life together. This"—he slowly fanned his hand around the room—"is a small token of the love and appreciation I have for you."

How could a woman ask for more? Prudence leapt into his embrace. She and Urias were beginning their lives as one in God's design. Their lips touched, and completeness filled her. *Thank You, Lord.*

A Place of Her Own

Dedication

I'd like to dedicate this book to my agent, Tamela Hancock Murray, for her faith in me and in the Lord. Thank you. May the Lord continue to bless you as you work for Him and for your authors.

Chapter 1

Jamestown, Kentucky, 1845

A untie Katherine!" The bedroom door rattled in its hinges. "Daddy says you hafta cook breakfast," her four-year-old nephew, Tucker, cried out.

Katherine O'Leary pulled the covers up over her head.

Last night, little Elizabeth Katherine, her newborn niece, had kept the whole household awake, crying. Unfortunately, it wasn't the first time. Oh, to have solitude. If only God would grant such a gift. But how?

Elizabeth's colic wasn't the only thing that had interrupted Katherine's sleep. The tragic events of the past still marred her dreams. Occasionally she'd wake from a nightmare. Prudence, her sister-in-law, and Pamela, Katherine's adoptive mother of sorts, encouraged her to not accept those thoughts, to allow God's grace to wipe them clean. And she believed He was able to do that. But the fear remained.

How could the MacKenneth family love her and her brother, Urias, as their own? Oh, it made sense with Urias, she supposed. But why her?

"Auntie Katherine!" The door rattled again.

She took in a deep breath, tossed the pillow aside, and pushed her body up to a sitting position on the edge of the bed. Urias had spared no expense in making her the four-poster bed and bedroom set. "I still wish I had my own place," she grumbled, slipping her slippers on her feet and sliding into a robe. But how could she earn the money to even buy the materials required to build her own house? Let alone actually build one.

If I were married. . . The developing knot in her stomach tightened another notch.

In the kitchen, Katherine found the morning basket of eggs, fresh from the hen house, sitting on the table. She sliced some bacon and tossed it into a large cast-iron frying pan. The tantalizing smell as it browned made her stomach wake up. She chopped a few potatoes and fried them in the bacon drippings, adding a touch of onion and some salt and pepper. After removing the potatoes, she cracked some of the eggs into the pan.

"Smells wonderful," Urias remarked as he stepped into the kitchen. Her older brother had the same red hair and green eyes she did. He pulled out a chair and sat down.

"How's Elizabeth and Prudence?" she asked, scooping the potatoes out of the frying pan and onto the breakfast plates. She placed Urias's in front of him.

"Sleeping finally. I didn't want to wake either of them. That's why I sent Tucker in to get you up. Have the boys come in from their chores yet?"

Chores were a part of farm life. Everyone pitched in from the time they could walk. "I'm assuming Vern fetched the eggs. But I haven't seen Tucker in from milking the cow yet."

Her brother put his fork down and leaned back in the chair. "You look tired. Did Elizabeth keep you up, too?"

"Yes. But it also took me a long time to get to sleep last night."

Urias narrowed his gaze. "What aren't you telling me?"

Katherine placed the hot frying pan on the counter and sat at the table, bringing a basket of biscuits with her. "I'm just tired, that's all. Been thinking foolish thoughts, like wanting my own place."

"Ah, all in good time, Katherine. You know you're welcome here for as long as you want to stay."

"I know. Thank you." How could she make him understand the deep desire for her own home? Most women went straight from living with their parents to living with a husband. Since she had no expectation of having a husband, the dream of having her own place burned within her.

"Truthfully, I considered sleeping in the barn last night." Urias chuckled.

"I hadn't thought of that." Sleeping on a bed of hay would have been better than not sleeping at all. She'd have to remember that the next time Elizabeth couldn't sleep.

Urias winked and picked up a biscuit. "Thanks for all you do."

Katherine cleaned off the remaining breakfast from the table. Did she truly want to be alone? Would she even bother to make a meal if she were by herself? She took the kettle off the stove and poured the heated water into the sink.

"Aunt Katherine!" Tucker came running, red-faced, into the room. "Vern's in the pigpen. And he's stuck."

❧

"Father, I've taken care of all your business deals as best I'm able." Shelton held a tight rein on his emotions. They'd been arguing for the better part of an hour. "I had to sell every bit of livestock just to keep a small piece of land for you and Mother to have a roof over your heads. You've not only put yourself in a terrible standing with your friends, but you've ruined our family's reputation in the area. The only way the bankers would extend credit to me was if your name was no longer on the property."

Hiram Greene slumped in his chair and put his hands over his face. "I know, I know. Moving is our only option. Your mother can't live with my shame."

"Urias claims there are many business opportunities in his area. Perhaps I'll be able to purchase some land over there. I honestly don't know. We have so little left."

"What about buying some hogs here and selling them in Virginia, like Urias did?" Hiram asked.

I'm not a farmer, like my brother-in-law, Shelton thought. *I have no idea how to herd a bunch of pigs several hundred miles.* "I have thought about that," he said. "And I might have to do it—and anything else I can to help this family."

Shelton scanned the old den. The faint smell of old leather and dried books lingered in the air. But few of the lavish furnishings remained. Everything of value had been sold to pay off debts.

"Your life won't be like it was before," he told his father. "I've managed to maintain one servant, but apart from that, you'll have to do everything around the house yourself while I'm away."

Tears welled in Hiram's eyes. "Your mother will never forgive me for what I've done."

Shelton placed his hand on his father's shoulder. "We'll get through this somehow."

Hiram nodded.

Shelton hated to see his father in this position. It just didn't seem right that a man who was so skilled in business could ruin himself gambling on a few horses. After the bank auditors went over his father's books with Shelton, it became painfully obvious that Hiram Greene had been juggling the finances for years to cover his debts. Every penny Shelton had brought into the family had gone to pay the people his father had kept at bay for so long.

If it hadn't been for the dire straights the family was facing, Shelton wouldn't leave his father alone right now. But he had two reasons for going to Jamestown, Kentucky. One was to find a place where his parents could resettle without the stigma of the loss in their social standing. The other was to find out if the love he still held in his heart for Kate was real. For years he'd been praying for her and begging God to rid him of these foolish boyhood fantasies. Instead, his attraction to her had deepened. It didn't make sense. He hadn't seen her in five years. Prudence barely mentioned her when she visited. Of course, Shelton had kept his questions to himself, not wanting to appear overly curious.

Only once had he mentioned his love for Kate, and his father had reacted vehemently. Shelton received a long and loud lecture on their family's precious standing in society, and how one couldn't lessen himself by marrying someone of a lower social class.

His father had sent him away for several months to visit with cousins. During that time Kate's brother, Urias, had found her, purchased her bond to set her free, and married Shelton's sister, Prudence.

Prudence seemed content in her simple life with Urias and the children. She had found a man who loved her for who she was and how God had knitted her together, not how society felt a woman should behave. Shelton longed for that same acceptance.

"Son," his father said, breaking into Shelton's thoughts. Hiram gazed at his son as if he could read his thoughts. "I've shamed the family enough. Don't you shame us further by getting involved with that. . .servant girl."

Shelton's back went ramrod straight. "I don't believe you have the right to speak on the matter, Father. If God works out a relationship with me and any woman, no matter what her standing in society, I would be honored to take her, if she would have me. After all, you've ruined any chance of my ever having a wife who could fit your social standard."

A deep sigh escaped his father's lips. "You're right. I'm sorry."

Shelton worried about the downcast mood his father seemed to be in lately. He acquiesced far too easily during arguments and discussions. That wasn't like him at all. But ever since Hiram's world came crashing down three months back, he'd lost all his zest for life. Even the salt wells and the businesses he'd invested in no longer held any interest for him.

"Are you certain you and Mother don't want to come with me?" Shelton asked. "Prudence must have had her third child by now."

"I wouldn't want to crowd Prudence and Urias's home, especially with a new baby. Just send a message when you've found appropriate housing and we'll come as soon as possible."

Shelton tried to ignore the "appropriate housing" reference. He wondered how his father would survive the ridicule of not being the man he had so painstakingly built himself up to be. The reality was, his father was not the man he appeared to be. His business savvy had ended years ago when he started gambling. All of his financial dealings from that point on seemed to be based on whether or not he could hedge his bets on the horses.

Shelton fought down a wave of anger. For years he'd been the only one bringing in the family income, and he never knew it. If it hadn't been for his hard work, his father's business would have gone under long ago. And his father had been less than generous in his compliments.

Shelton's only prayer these days regarded his father's humility and his own need to extend grace. Grace to a man who'd done precious little to do anything constructive for himself. Thankfully, the bank examiners saw Shelton's financial prowess long before his father acknowledged it.

For the past four years, Shelton's primary duties had revolved around the earning potential of his stud horses. He'd had to sell most of his stallions to cover his father's debts. But he still had one stud horse, plus one mare that would bring a foal in a couple of months. Between the two, he hoped he could earn enough income to keep his family fed through the winter. He didn't know what else he could do.

All he did know was that someone had to protect his mother from his father's foolishness, and he was the only son. He hoped that by going farther west his family could find a place to call home.

He'd heard folks talk about large herds of wild horses roaming the plains out west. Catching a few more mares would be the only way to build a breeding farm again.

Since horses represented his father's vanity and self-destruction, Shelton wondered if developing a different skill might be more advantageous. Digging a salt well had produced some income, but salt wells were little challenge. And he had an eye for horse breeding, no question. Besides, he needed to find his own way in this world. And he wanted a fresh start. The idea of moving to Jamestown, or even farther west, excited him.

"I expect to arrive in Jamestown in a couple of days," he told his father. "I've heard a man can sell anything in Creelsboro. Perhaps I can find some work there."

"Perhaps." Hiram stood and faced Shelton. "I'm sorry, son." He extended his hand.

Shelton pulled his father into an embrace. "It's going to work out. I promise."

Hiram nodded and walked away.

Shelton followed his father's slow movements. *Lord God, bring peace back to my father.*

Taking in a deep breath, Shelton stared at the far wall of the den, behind which he had squirreled away one prized family heirloom. He hated keeping it a secret from his father, but if Hiram knew about it, Shelton was certain he would give in and sell it.

He set his hat on his head and flung his leather saddlebags across his shoulder. If he wanted to get a jump on his journey, he had to leave now.

Kate's lively green eyes and head full of red curls flitted across his memory. Shelton closed his eyes, trying to hold on to the vision a little longer. *Lord, I love her, and she doesn't even know it. Show me if I'm just carrying on like a lovesick puppy or if what I feel for her is real.*

A knock at the front door interrupted Katherine's dishwashing. She grabbed a towel and dried her hands as she headed toward the door. Between Elizabeth's crying all night and Vern getting his head stuck between the slats of the pigs' feeding trough, it had already been quite a day. Wondering what new catastrophe might be just around the corner, she opened the front door. "Can I help you?"

In front of her stood a rather handsome young man with broad but slight shoulders. He stood about four inches taller than her. "Kate?"

She gripped the doorknob tighter and nodded.

"You don't recognize me, do you?"

Tucker ran in from the sitting room. "Uncle Shelton!" he screamed in excitement.

"Shelton Greene?" Katherine squeaked.

His hair had darkened to a rich brown hue, like a fine walnut stain on a piece of oak. His eyes, which reflected the deep blue color of the sky just after sunset, drew her. The doorknob slipped through her fingers.

He knelt down and captured his nephew into his arms. "Tucker! How's your mommy and daddy?"

"Fine. Daddy is in the fields. Mommy is upstairs with 'Lizabeth."

A deep smile spread across his face. "You have a new sister?"

"Uh-huh."

Realizing she was keeping the man standing outside, Katherine stepped back. "Come on in. I'll get Prudence."

"Thank you. It's nice to see you again, Kate."

The rich tones of his voice sent a shiver across Katherine's belly. Shelton Greene did not look anything like the boy she'd known when she left his home. Now he was a man, and a rather handsome one at that. Not that she had the right to notice, she scolded herself.

"Uncle!" Vern sang out, running up to Shelton and vying with his brother for the newcomer's attention.

By the time Katherine reached the top of the stairs, she found Prudence already on her way down, with Elizabeth in her arms.

"Is Shelton really here?" she asked. Her eyes lit up with excitement.

"Yes, although I didn't recognize him."

Prudence looked puzzled, then smiled. "Oh, that's right. You didn't make the trip to Hazel Green with us, so you haven't seen the changes in him. I was pretty shocked myself. He's matured into a rather distinguished young man."

Katherine blushed.

Prudence giggled. "It's all right, Katherine. Your secret is safe with me."

Secret? What secret? That I find the woman's brother attractive? The heat in her face intensified.

"Excuse me while I go find out what's brought him all this way."

Katherine stood at the top of the stairs. She wanted to know the answer to that question, too, but it was none of her concern. She slipped into her room to give the family some time to be with one another. But she couldn't get the image of the handsome visitor out of her head.

Unlike his father, Shelton had never treated her like a servant—well, except for that one day when he. . . Katherine stopped herself from recalling that memory. No one knew about that, and it was better left in the past.

Chapter 2

S helton stood by the mantel over the fireplace. An array of finely crafted, hand-carved animals decorated the thick shelf. "Who made these?"

"Grandpa Mac and my dad," Urias answered, escorting Prudence to the sofa. "Now that the children are down for their naps, we can finally talk. So, what brought you here?"

Shelton explained the family woes as he scanned the downstairs open area for Kate. After assuring himself that she could not hear their conversation, he leaned close to his brother-in-law and spoke in a lowered voice. "Urias, I discovered you paid my father three times the prescribed debt for your sister's bond."

Urias smiled. "Prudence and I know my mother would never have sold Katherine for such a high price. But it doesn't matter; I would have paid anything to get my sister out of servitude."

Prudence caressed her husband's arm. "How's Mother handling their situation?"

"Not well, I'm afraid. And Father isn't dealing with it either. I swear I could see him plotting another way to get money before I even left for Jamestown. I honestly don't know how to help them. I sold off the salt mines and almost all of the property to a coal mining company. That covered most of Father's gambling debts. The bankers will take the house if I don't come up with a viable plan to repay the remainder of the loan Father took out."

"Even if you do pay off Hiram's loan, do you think he could keep himself from gambling again?" Urias asked.

"There's no guarantee. He admitted that he is to blame for the family's situation, but I sensed he wasn't completely repentant. With me gone, however, I suspect he and Mother will find it pretty uncomfortable living in the town where he lost everything."

"That might be good enough motivation for your father."

"I agree."

Urias nodded gravely. He had the same green eyes as Kate's, yet different in a way Shelton couldn't put his finger on. "How can I help?"

"Getting a job is my top priority at this point, one that will pay me enough to cover my own expenses and Father's."

"There might be work on some of the farms in the area. Crockett's paper mill may be hiring. You might even find some work on the docks in Creelsboro."

Prudence stood. "I'm going upstairs to write a letter to Mother. You two can go over all the details."

Shelton watched his sister's slow gait toward the stairs. "Is she all right?" he asked Urias.

"Elizabeth's birth took a bit more out of her than the boys, but she's doing well." Urias motioned for Shelton to take a seat, which he did. "Now, let's go over your options."

"As you know, my income from breeding horses has held off the creditors for the past year. I'm hoping I can earn a little with Kehoe and Kate." He and Urias both shared a love for breeding powerful horseflesh with sleek lines.

"We can let folks in the area know about your stud horse. Introducing new bloodlines into the local stock might be a benefit the farmers would want to take advantage of. But I don't see how it will solve the immediate problems your parents are facing."

Shelton rubbed the back of his neck. "If I sell the house and remaining land, there should be enough to buy something in this area."

"Do you have the authority to do that?"

"Yes. The bank wouldn't extend any more credit to my father until he relinquished title of the property over to me."

"I'll get the word out. We'll find some work for you. In the meantime, I can hire you on to do some of the chores on my farm. Mac and Pamela might be able to use your help, too, and since their place is right next door—"

"I couldn't do that." Shelton rose to his feet. "You're family."

Urias stood beside him and placed a hand on Shelton's shoulder. "We'll talk about it tomorrow. Tonight you can sleep on the sofa."

"The barn is fine."

"Nonsense. Like you said, you're family." Urias nodded. "I'll get some sheets and a blanket from Katherine. I suspect she's already put a kettle of hot water on for you to bathe from your journey."

"Thank you."

Urias gave him a hearty pat on the back. "We'll pray and see what the Lord says. You're welcome to stay as long as you need to. Tomorrow, if you like, we can set up a little room for you in the barn."

"I'd be most grateful."

Katherine scurried into the room, carrying a bundle of sheets, blankets, and what appeared to be a feather pillow. Shelton swooped up the bundle from her hands. Stunned, she stood there frozen, her vivid green eyes wide with some emotion he couldn't quite identify. Was it shock?

"I'm sorry. I didn't mean to startle you."

She lowered her head and looked at the floor.

"Kate, you're not my servant."

She scurried out of the family living area. A moment later he heard a door close and latch. She was afraid of him! Why?

Shelton recalled the last moments he'd spent with Kate five years ago. He'd tried then to tell her how he felt. His tongue had felt like cotton. When he attempted to kiss her, she'd started to run away. He had ordered her to stay.

Dread suddenly filled him. He had been only sixteen—and a fool.

He plopped the linens on the sofa. Driven to clear the matter up, he marched toward Kate's room.

❧

A charge of lightning had coursed through Katherine's body when Shelton's fingers brushed up against hers. Behind the closed door of her room she felt safe. Her body leaned hard against the wall. Her mind flew back to five years ago, two weeks before Urias had come to rescue her.

Katherine hid her face in her hands. The shame, the fears. . . Her knees weakened. She fell into the bed and buried her face in the pillow. Tears soaked the quilt Grandma Mac had made for her when she first arrived.

A gentle tap on her door caused her to cling to the quilt.

"Kate, it's me," Shelton whispered. "Please open up. I wish to speak with you."

She couldn't face him. She couldn't allow him to ever be near her again.

Shelton gave another tap on the door. "Kate, I'm sorry. I just realized what you must have been thinking all these years about me. I never meant to hurt you."

Fresh tears poured down her cheeks.

"Forgive me, Kate. Please."

Katherine refused to speak. She couldn't even if she wanted to. A lump the size of an apple stuck in her throat. She slid off the bed, pulling the quilt with her and wrapping it around her. Sitting Indian style, she rocked back and forth as the demons of the past surfaced.

Memories of the beatings from her drunken mother switched to the peddler who had once owned her bond. He was a gambler, and she hadn't stayed with him long. She washed his clothes, fixed his meals, and thanked God daily that she was alive. She prayed her mother would rescue her. But Mother never came. Soon the ugly truth of what her mother had done to her became clear.

As Kate grew older she became the property of other men. No one knew the horror of the favors she'd had to endure.

"Oh God, please don't let these memories come back," she cried into the quilt.

She had lost her faith and her identity when Wiley owned her. How Michael Pike ever purchased her bond from that ugly man, she didn't know, but she'd been grateful to be owned by someone who didn't beat her.

Hiram Greene purchased her a year after that. She'd lived with the Greenes since the age of fourteen. They had never abused her the way the others had. But watching Prudence, who was about the same age as she was, enjoying the normal pleasures a young girl would have, was difficult. And living in the Greene house, seeing all their wealth and luxury, made her life even harder. But Prudence Greene proved to be a true friend. The love she showed her allowed her to once again step out in faith and trust God. She'd asked God to forgive her for her anger, for her lack of faith, and for the sinful life she'd been forced to live.

But in moments like these, when her mind traveled over the darkness of the past, she found it hard to believe God had truly forgiven her. She knew it in her head. She knew it from His Holy Word. And there were moments when she knew it in her heart. But this was not one of those times.

"Kate?" Shelton called softly.

"Please," she moaned. "Just go away."

After several moments, she heard muffled footsteps fading away down the hall.

Katherine curled into a fetal position on the floor, not having the strength to climb back into her bed, and cried herself to exhaustion.

੧੦

During his first two weeks in Jamestown, Shelton performed many odd jobs at the various farms in the area, but still hadn't found full-time employment. Urias had helped in every way he could, including setting up a temporary room for him in the barn. But it seemed Shelton's best bet was to move to Creelsboro to try to work for one of the companies helping folks go west, or to work for Crockett's paper mill.

The tension between him and Kate had been constant. He wanted to get to know her as a woman, but she avoided him. She spoke in his presence only when others were around, and she hid in her room most of the time. One thing seemed certain: He couldn't be the right man for her when she was terrified of him. He had his answer.

He gathered his sparse belongings and began to pack his saddlebags. A move to Creelsboro would give Kate back the freedom to move around in her own house.

The barn door creaked. Shelton blinked at the sudden stream of light. Kate's silhouette paused, then she walked into the barn. After glancing over her shoulder, she closed the door behind her. She sneaked over to the farthest horse pen and pushed the hay from the wall, exposing the floorboards.

Again she paused and looked around. Shelton knew he should make a noise and let her know he was there, but he held his breath instead. What could she be doing?

Kate lifted a floorboard and pulled something out. He couldn't see from his angle what it was. Obviously she was hiding something, but what? And why?

She returned the item and secured the board and hay back in place.

He slipped out of the shadows. "Kate."

A startled yelp escaped her lips. Her eyes widened with fear.

He grabbed her arms. "I'm not going to hurt you."

She trembled from his touch.

He released his grip. "I'm sorry. I only wanted to speak with you, to apologize for the time at my father's house. I acted foolishly. I was sixteen and so in love with you I couldn't think straight. I should never have forced you to kiss me. That was wrong."

She nodded but kept her eyes averted.

"Kate, please speak to me. I'm leaving today."

Her gaze shot up to his. "Leaving?"

"Yes. I can't stay here and have you afraid all the time. It isn't right. This is your home. You should not live in fear of me."

Kate seemed to lose her footing and stumbled to the left. Instinctively, he reached out and caught her by the elbow. She stared at her feet once again.

"Please stop looking down. You're not a servant, and I don't like seeing you behave like this."

"Why?"

Indeed, why did it bother him so much? Oh, he knew in part it was because of his feelings for her in the past. But it went beyond that. A horrible injustice had happened to her. "I want to be your friend, Kate."

"Katherine," she corrected.

"Katherine," he repeated. "It suits you better."

"Kate's my bondage name." She squared her shoulders and stared straight at him.

"Then I'll try to never call you that again."

A slight smile crept up her cheek for the briefest of moments, then was gone as quickly as it had appeared. She gazed at the floor. "You shouldn't leave because of me."

"I just want us to be friends." With every ounce of willpower he could muster, Shelton held his hands at his side rather than lift her delicate chin. "I saw you put something under the floorboards."

She raised her head.

"What are you hiding? If you don't mind telling me."

"I do." She marched to the spot where she had been, opened her secret hiding place, and removed a small wooden box. "Now I'll have to put it somewhere else."

Shelton saw fire in this woman, despite her past. A fierce determination. His desire to get to know her grew. "You don't have to. I promise I won't touch it."

She eyed him for a long moment. "It's not really a secret. Urias made the box for me."

So why bury it? he wanted to ask, but refrained from doing so.

She traced some sort of carving on the top of the box with her finger. "I could keep this in my room, I suppose, but the boys get into everything."

Shelton chuckled. "That they do. I was always into something when I was a boy. Prudence squealed on me more times than I can remember."

She placed the box back under the floorboard. Then she stood and took a step closer to him, but kept herself at least eight feet away and did not make eye contact. "Why are you here?"

Two reasons—and one of them is you, he yearned to say. "Father lost a lot of money gambling. I thought breeding horses here might provide enough income to support my folks and myself. I have to do what I can to help them."

She snatched a quick glimpse of him, but quickly averted her gaze again. "Why? Shouldn't your father pay for what he's done?" Her voice quavered.

"Perhaps. But Mother is innocent. Even though I'm not proud of Father's gambling, I won't let my mother suffer if I can help it."

I don't know how I can provide for her, but I'm going to do it, somehow, with God's grace. He fought down his anger by picking up his horse brush and running it down Kehoe's neck.

"You always did like spending time with the horses."

The realization that she had noticed something personal about him brought a sweet pleasure that strengthened his resolve. "Kehoe is good stock and should sire quite a few champion horses if he's bred with the right mare. I can't wait until. . ." He hesitated, not wanting to reveal that he'd named his horse Kate. ". . .until my mare delivers." He leaned back on his heels. "Katherine, I—"

A bloodcurdling scream came from the house.

Chapter 3

Katherine raced toward the house. Shelton passed her and leapt to the top of the porch without touching the three stairs. The front door banged against the wall as he rushed inside. The blood pounded in her ears as she lifted her skirts higher to run faster.

Inside the house she found the family in the living room. Prudence pressed little Elizabeth close to her chest. Shelton had a small blanket wrapped around his right hand. On the floor stood a wild raccoon on its hind legs, clawing at Shelton.

"Get everyone out of the house," he ordered. "Go to Mac and Pamela's."

Katherine glanced at the gun rack over the fireplace mantel. The rack was empty. She sighed. Urias and Mac were out hunting for venison. Katherine scanned the room for the boys, then remembered they had gone to Grandma Mac's an hour earlier.

Shelton grabbed the fireplace broom and blocked the critter's path to Prudence. "Get out of here," he ordered through clenched teeth.

The two women slowly backed up the few paces to the open doorway, then ran toward the MacKenneths' farmhouse.

Tears streamed down Prudence's face.

"Are you all right?" Katherine asked, not slowing her pace. "Is Elizabeth okay?"

Prudence sniffled. "We're fine. Just terrified."

Katherine knew she should be frightened as well. Men couldn't come within a couple of feet of her before fear washed over her. A crazed animal in the house should cause a far worse panic. Instead, she wanted to fight the small beast, take charge, and rid the house of the problem.

She stopped. "I'm going back. Shelton must have a rifle in the barn."

Prudence stopped and faced Katherine. "You take Elizabeth. I'll go help Shelton."

"No. Your baby needs you. I could never live with myself if something happened to you. I'm certain the animal has rabies."

"I've handled a rifle. Urias taught me to shoot."

A memory from the past floated through Katherine's mind, of a time before Urias left home, a time when they were a family. "Poppa taught me to shoot, too."

Prudence took in a deep breath and released it slowly. "All right. But take careful aim. I'd like my brother to grow old and gray."

Katherine ran past the house and straight into the barn. She rummaged through Shelton's belongings and found his rifle. Lifting it, she discovered it was much heavier than the one her father had shown her so many years before. It also had two barrels. Could she shoot this and not hit Shelton? Fear slithered through her body. Her breathing became more ragged. She closed her eyes and slowly inhaled. She couldn't let fear control her now, as it had so often in her life.

She reached for the lead bullets and powder, loaded the two barrels, and marched toward the house. The sheer weight of the gun forced her to carry it with both hands. How could she possibly fire it?

The angry growls of the sick creature cut through the air.

Katherine quickened her pace and lifted the rifle as she crossed the open threshold.

Shelton pivoted around to see who had entered the house. The wild animal lashed out and bit him on the leg.

She aimed the rifle but did not have a clear shot of the raccoon. Shelton kicked, forcing the animal to let go, but it bit down again. He whacked the broom handle across the raccoon's head.

Dazed, the creature fell to the floor. Katherine aimed and pulled the trigger. A clean shot perforated the raccoon with lead balls.

Shelton cried out in pain and leaned against the wall.

"Take your pants off," Katherine ordered. "We must clean that wound."

❧

Shelton reached for his belt buckle but thought better of it. "Give me that knife." He pointed to the large carving knife hanging on the side of the kitchen cabinet.

Kate placed the gun on the table and hurried to the cabinet.

Shelton gritted his teeth against the excruciating pain.

"The animal looks rabid," Katherine said as she handed him the knife.

He glanced at the heap of fur and fangs. Foam dripped from the creature's jowls, leaving no doubt as to its condition. The question was, could he survive this attack? "Boil some water," he ordered.

Kate's back stiffened. He'd done it again, made her feel like a servant. "Please," he amended.

Kate nodded and did as he'd requested.

Setting the tip of the blade against the outer seam of his pants, he ripped the material from the knee down. Blood poured out of a deep wound. One of his arteries must have been punctured.

He watched Katherine fill the lower front part of the step-up cast-iron stove with kindling. He opened his mouth to tell her to add more for a quicker blaze, but promptly closed it. Kate would know her way around a stove.

Shelton didn't like seeing this side of himself. Had he always been this insensitive to others? Had he looked down on people stationed in a lower social class than his own? Was he as guilty as his father of treating Kate like a servant?

A fresh wave of pain coursed through his body. He let out an audible groan.

Katherine turned and ran toward him.

Shelton blinked. The room began to spin. He slowly closed and opened his eyes, trying to focus.

"Sit down," Kate ordered. Authority oozed from her command. He'd never seen her like this. He followed her order.

"Place your injured leg on this chair." Kate pulled his flapping pant leg away from his skin. She leaned closer to the wound. "It's deep and nasty. You might need some stitches. That coon must have twisted back and forth once he got his teeth into you."

"It felt like it."

"I'm going to get some cloths to wash the wound." She started to leave.

"Don't touch it, Katherine. I don't want you getting sick."

A slight turn of her delicate pink lips made him aware that she was pleased about his concern for her. *Perhaps there is a chance for us to develop a relationship after all.* Then again, how many days did he have left? The mortality rate from rabies didn't give a man a lot of hope. *Please, God, if we're to be together. . .* Wasn't that the real question? Were they meant to be together? Apart from this momentary act of kindness, Kate was still terrified of him.

"I'll be right back. Don't move."

He gripped the chair tighter in her absence. He couldn't let her see how much his leg hurt. The large knife lay on the table. Shelton picked it up and tried to get a good angle to lance the wound.

"What are you doing?" Katherine stood before him, her hands on her hips.

"I have to get out the poison."

"This isn't a snakebite."

"I know, but—"

"We need to wash it first."

"Katherine, are you in there?" Pamela MacKenneth called out from the porch.

"In the kitchen. Shelton's been bit."

"Ain't that bad," he lied.

Pamela flew into the room and examined his leg. Shelton felt like a lame horse lying on the ground with a gang of people looking over him trying to decide if they should shoot him and put him out of his misery.

"Pour water over the wound, Katherine. Flush it out several times. Then we'll pour hot water over it—as hot as he can take it—to try to kill off any infection before it starts."

Katherine pumped a pitcher of water and poured it over his leg.

"You're losing a lot of blood," Pamela said, washing her hands in the sink, then wiping them on a dishtowel. "We're going to have to stitch up the wound. Katherine, where does Prudence keep the whiskey?"

"Upper right-hand cupboard. I'll get a needle and thread. And some towels to clean up that mess on the floor."

"Thanks."

Shelton's eyelids drifted shut. He forced them to open. They complied only halfway. He had to fight.

Then again, why? *Heaven is a wonderful place*, his mind sluggishly told him.

Mother needs me, he inwardly debated. He forced his eyes to open farther. They slid right back down.

"He's losing a lot of blood," Kate said.

"Take off his belt and make a tourniquet."

After a moment's hesitation, Katherine unhooked his belt and pulled it off of his hips.

Pamela held a glass of golden-brown liquid to his lips. "Drink this."

He sipped. It burned a path down to his stomach.

The pressure Kate applied as she wrapped the belt around his leg made him want to kick her away. He bore down on the back of the chair and groaned.

"Finish the whiskey, Shelton."

The warmth of the liquid nectar started to calm his body. *No wonder a man can get addicted to this stuff.*

The pain began to subside. His mind grew more fuzzy. A smile developed on his lips. Images of Katherine wrapped in his arms swam around in his head. "Oh my sweet, sweet Kate."

❧

"We can start now," Pamela said. "He's rambling about his horse."

"His horse?" *Or me?* Katherine loosened the tourniquet. Blood poured instantly from the wound. She tightened it again.

Pamela pulled the thread through the needle and began to repair the wound while Katherine held the injured leg still.

Fifteen minutes later, Pamela had sewn the last stitch and Shelton started snoring. "We're going to have to move him, and I'm afraid the only open bed is in your room. We can't have him exposed to the children."

"I understand."

"I'll help you get him to bed. Then go scrub yourself till you're pink. I left room between the stitches so the blood can escape as the artery bleeds. You'll need to stay the night with him, opening and closing that tourniquet every fifteen minutes. Can you do that?"

"I'll try."

Pamela nodded. "I know it'll be hard staying awake all night. Then again, I hear Elizabeth doesn't allow for much sleeping anyway."

Katherine chuckled. "True."

Together they lifted Shelton by the shoulders and dragged him onto her bed. "Keep the wound moist for a long as possible. Moisture helps the rabies bleed out of the body."

A shiver of fear slithered down Katherine's spine at the thought of spending so much time alone with a man.

"Are you all right?" Pamela asked.

"Fine. He just weighs more than he seems to."

Pamela chuckled. "Be glad he's only five-seven. Try heaving Mac into bed. Worst patient I ever had. Thankfully, he is rarely ill."

Mac MacKenneth was a huge man, but he didn't scare Katherine. Not like Shelton did. Of course, she'd only known Mac as a happily married man, a good Christian man.

"Guess I'd better go burn that raccoon," Pamela said.

"I'll clean up."

"Open the tourniquet again first. Then go clean."

Katherine nodded. *Lord, help me be a good nurse to this man, even though I am terrified of him.*

For hours, she sat by his bed, doing her best to follow Pamela's instructions and to understand her own emotions. Shelton was an attractive man. And he seemed so kind, so brave. Why did she fear him?

She noticed sweat beading all over his bronzed skin. A fever was rising.

Chapter 4

Shelton ached from head to toe. His leg felt like it was on fire. Kate's gentle ministrations had eased the pain somewhat. He licked his parched lips and opened his eyes. She sat curled up in a chair next to the bed. Her golden red hair cascaded over her shoulders as she slept.

He blinked and refocused. He'd never seen her with her hair down. His mind must be playing tricks on him. Kate's hair always sat on her head, with no more than a few wisps falling down the sides.

Shelton's leg ached. He reached down to release the pressure on the tourniquet, but it wasn't there. He leaned back again. The slight movement made him groan.

Kate jumped upright. "I'm sorry. I fell asleep. What's wrong?"

"Where's the tourniquet?"

"Mac came by and examined the wound, as well as his wife's handiwork. He said to take off the tourniquet. Slight bleeding will help the healing."

"Does he think. . ." Shelton knew rabies could be fatal. But he couldn't form the words in his mouth.

"Mac said only time will tell."

Shelton closed his eyes. *Father God, please keep me alive to help my family.*

Katherine placed a cool, damp cloth on his forehead. "Shelton, why did you send us away? If I had stayed. . ."

"Prudence and Elizabeth were in danger." He focused on her deep green eyes. "And so were you."

"I. . ." She clamped her mouth shut.

What was she going to say? They hadn't spent much time together since his arrival two weeks ago, but several times, he'd seen her stop herself from saying what was on her mind.

"Speak," he ordered.

She narrowed her eyes. "I am not your servant. I will not be ordered about like a. . ."

A twitch of pleasure pulled at his lips as he tried to suppress a smile.

"What?" Her nostrils flared.

"Kate. . .I mean, Katherine. . .I didn't mean—" A surge of pain raced up his leg. "Please, go back to your room. I'm fine."

Katherine stepped back and blinked. In a soft whisper, she said, "This is my room."

Shelton appraised his surroundings. The furniture was well made, hand crafted by Urias, no doubt, but it lacked the feminine look and smells he remembered of Prudence's room. He lifted the covers to slip out of bed. "I'm sorry. I'll go to the barn."

"You'll do no such thing." Katherine stomped her foot for emphasis. "You're to stay off that leg for at least two days. And I'll not be facing Pru's wrath for the rest of my life by being responsible for your death."

He leaned back against the headboard. "Katherine, you're not responsible."

"Yes, I am." Her face flushed. "If I hadn't come into the house when I did, you wouldn't have been bitten. This is all my fault."

He reached out to her.

She stepped farther into the shadows. "Go back to sleep. It's late. You need your rest."

Not wanting to move his leg again, he closed his eyes. The room darkened. The door creaked. Katherine had left him. If only he could let her slip out of his heart as easily.

❧

Katherine pulled the quilt higher over her shoulder as she shifted on the living room sofa. She hadn't gone back into her bedroom since Shelton had woken up. How could she have thought that she could spend the night in there with him and care for him?

A gentle hand shook her shoulder. "Your room is free now," Urias said. "I helped Shelton move back to the barn. And Prudence changed your sheets."

"How is he?"

"He's fine. Mac says the wound is healing well. You did a good job. Now, go to bed and get some sleep."

Katherine lifted her head from the sofa and stared through her bedroom doorway. Why had Urias taken Shelton out to the barn? Did it bother Shelton to be in her room?

"You could have left him in there."

"Shh. He's fine. Mac and I will take good care of him. You just rest."

She couldn't argue. It seemed like ages since she had a good night's sleep.

Katherine woke to the smell of fresh meat roasting. How long had she been asleep? She dressed and headed into the kitchen.

Prudence looked up from basting the meat that sat in the large pan. She beamed. "Good morning, sleepyhead."

"What time is it?"

"Going on near five," she said as she slid the roast back into the oven. "Dinner is just about ready."

"I slept the day away?"

"Your body seemed to require it." Prudence closed the oven door, then stood and stretched her back. "Tell me, did the old nightmares return?"

Katherine drew herself up straight. "Why do you ask?"

"You cried out during the night."

The tiny muscles around her spine seemed to tighten even more.

"You should tell Urias about the abuse you've suffered. Your brother is not a foolish man. He knows what goes on in the hearts of evil men."

"I don't want to. Besides, he's better off not knowing."

Prudence floured her hands and began to shape the biscuit dough. "The only way to rid yourself of these demons is to share them with the right person. You've told me a few things, but I know you haven't revealed all that happened to you. Perhaps your own flesh and blood. . ."

Katherine stared at the floor. "I'll think on it."

Prudence wiped her hands on a clean towel. "Promise?"

"Aye."

"I love the Irish brogue you slip into from time to time. Urias does it, too. You two are so much alike."

Katherine could not see the comparison. They were brother and sister, so they shared similar physical features, but Urias lived such a contented life. Even after opening her heart to God last year, she didn't feel much different. She still felt damaged. *A sinner will always be a sinner.* Katherine sighed. She would never be truly free from the tyrants who once owned her.

Prudence pulled her into a hug. "Remember, Katherine, you are free in Christ. You're not in bondage to past sins. Jesus has forgiven you."

"I know." *But I still feel bound to the past. What's wrong with me?* She knew she wasn't trusting in the Lord as she should.

Katherine forced a smile. "What can I do to help?"

"Finish setting the table while I put the food into the serving dishes."

As Katherine arranged the plates on the table, a deep-seated fear washed over her. Should she tell Urias about her past? Or keep her problems to herself?

Throughout the meal, Katherine kept a barrage of questions flowing toward the children. She didn't want to think about last night's nightmare. She didn't even remember having one.

After the children were put to bed, Urias joined her in the sitting room. "You should get some sleep, too, Katherine. I'm going to Creelsboro in the morning for Shelton. While I'm gone, his bandages will need tending. And Prudence could use a hand with the children."

A contorted smile rose on her lips. If she arranged things well, perhaps she could go to Creelsboro, too. It was time to start moving on with her life.

⁊&

Shelton leaned on the makeshift cane and hobbled about the barn. He'd been up since the crack of dawn, waiting on Urias. He knew his leg wasn't up to a horse ride, but with a little luck he might persuade Urias to take the buggy instead. They could tie Kehoe to the rear. Anyone who knew good horseflesh would spot Kehoe's qualities a mile away.

"Shelton?" Katherine whispered as she poked her head into the barn.

"Over here."

She turned toward his voice, squinting in the diffused light of the barn. "Urias said he was going into Creelsboro for you. Why?"

"He agreed to try to find some breeders there who might take a look at Kehoe. If we can catch some settlers going west, I'd offer them a discounted rate for quick cash."

She glanced behind her shoulder. Shelton guessed she didn't want anyone to see her in the barn alone with him. "When is the season for breeding horses?"

"All year, but mainly spring till fall." He leaned hard on his cane. "I was hoping to convince Urias to take the wagon this morning and let me come along."

"Perhaps I could go with you instead. I've been meaning to take a trip to Creelsboro."

"Are you sure?" Shelton brushed her hand with his. "We'd be sitting side by side."

I'll do whatever's necessary. "I have to go into town."

"You're safe with me, Katherine," he assured her.

A single nod. No words, no eye contact. *What has happened to her?*

"You're bleeding." She pointed to his trousers. "Perhaps we'd better go another time. Right now, you should concentrate on getting well."

"I'm fine." He held the cane tighter as a wave of dizziness washed over him.

Katherine placed her hands on her hips. "You're being awfully pig-headed."

Shelton wanted to spar with her but decided not to push this new willingness to spend a little time with him. "Wait over there," he said, pointing toward the large barn door, "while I change my trousers."

She raised her right eyebrow as if to question him, then lowered it and went out the door.

He removed his boots and pants, then wrapped a blanket around his waist. "You can come in now."

Urias appeared in the doorway. "Katherine says you had a foolish idea of running into Creelsboro today."

"I thought with the wagon—"

Urias wagged his head. "You obviously weren't thinking." He scanned the bleeding wound. "Katherine will clean that up. But you're getting back in that bed."

"Urias—"

"And if you get out again before I say you're ready, I'll personally set a hundred-pound keg on your chest to hold you down." Urias glared at him until Shelton sat on the bed, then he stomped out of the barn.

Katherine entered moments later with a fresh basin of water and a clean cloth. Merriment danced in her eyes.

"You think this is funny? Your brother is ordering me about like a child."

"He is a very protective man."

Pain shot up Shelton's leg, like a knife cutting deep into his skin. He moaned.

Katherine came to his side. "Lay your head down. I'll take care of this."

He wanted to resist, but the dizziness he'd experienced earlier hadn't entirely left and he felt the room spinning. The soft pillow encircled his head. Katherine placed her delicate fingers on his forehead. "You have a high fever. You should stay down and let your body heal."

"Yeah," he mumbled. He'd lie there forever if she'd stay by his side.

She placed a cool cloth on his forehead. Then he felt her heavenly touch on his leg.

"It's still a little red, but the blood is drying to a dark brown scab. That's good. It means there be no sign of infection. You should be up and around in no time."

Shelton chuckled. "I like your Irish brogue. You don't use it much."

"No, I don't."

"Why not?"

Katherine applied some pressure on the wound. Shelton grimaced. "Sorry. I'll try to be more gentle."

"You're fine. It's just sensitive. Thank you for all your help."

She acknowledged with a simple nod of her head.

Shelton wished she would open up and confide in him. "Katherine, what's your biggest desire in life?"

"A place of my own," she blurted out. Her hand stilled. "I'm sorry, I didn't mean to say that."

Shelton sat up, adjusting the blanket to maintain modesty. "Your secrets are safe with me." He winked, remembering the day he'd discovered her secret hiding place in the barn. He'd kept his word and never looked to see what she had hidden in that small box. Perhaps it was a tidy sum of money she'd saved in the hope of being able to someday afford a place for herself.

"Why did you want to go to Creelsboro?"

"I'm hoping to find some work, as a seamstress perhaps. I'm not smart enough to be a teacher, although Grandma Mac has been giving me lessons. My mom didn't care much for book learning. But I've learned a lot since I moved here."

"I think you're a very smart woman." He could see her in a schoolhouse, teaching the children and living in a private room off the back. Unfortunately, there didn't seem to be a place for him in that picture. "Seamstress, huh?"

"Yes." She smiled.

"I may have a small job for you. Perhaps you could repair the trousers I had on the day of the raccoon attack?"

"Of course."

"I'd be happy to pay you."

"There's no charge for family."

"I'm not your family, Katherine." *But I want to be.*

"Close enough. You're my brother's brother-in-law." Katherine chuckled. "Besides, I thought you were going to Creelsboro in order to earn some money."

"I told you you're a smart woman."

She wrapped the clean linen around the wound and secured it. "All done. I'll leave you now and send Vern in with lunch later. Get some rest. You're looking pale."

"Thank you, Katherine."

He watched her leave, then took in a deep pull of air. He leaned back against the headboard of the old bed. Perhaps he still had a chance with Katherine after all.

Shelton reached over to the small table, which held a glass of water and some herbs that Mac had brought in. His head started swimming and he felt like he could fall out of bed without even moving. He'd deal with Katherine another day. Today he had to concentrate on recovering and living.

With time, he might just be able to win her heart. *But only if she gives it to me freely*, he reminded himself. He would not force her. He would not demand. He would wait patiently, treating her like a skittish mare.

That's it! He smiled and knitted his fingers together behind his head. Katherine was like a wild mare; a firm but gentle hand was in order for her to trust him.

Chapter 5

Katherine pumped water into the barrel to wash clothes. Urias had built an outdoor shelter for a laundry room of sorts for spring and fall cleaning. It was the time to get all the quilts, blankets, and sheets ready for winter.

As she agitated the water, she thought back on the past couple of days and caring for Shelton. It seemed odd but good to be near a man and not be frightened. They talked more and more, and for the first time in her life she felt like she had a male friend.

On the other hand, she noticed things about him that seemed totally inappropriate. Like how handsome he was, and how strong his hands were. She wondered what it would be like to be held in his arms. She shook off the images and went back to cleaning the dirty clothes.

"Katherine?" Shelton's voice spun around her spine, giving her strength, not fear. *Thank You, Lord.* "Would you like to travel to Creelsboro with me tomorrow?"

She dropped the agitator in the barrel and dried off her hands on the long apron that protected her dress. "Do you think you're well enough?"

"I believe so. I wouldn't want to stress my leg too much, but the buggy would allow me to put it up some."

Katherine thought about the wagon. It had a panel in front, and they could both place their feet up there. "Has the fever returned?"

"No, thank the Lord. Mac says that I'll have to wait another week before we know for certain if I'm infected. But the prognosis looks good."

Katherine fired off another prayer for Shelton. She didn't want to lose her friend.

"Are you still hoping to obtain employment in town?" he asked.

A slight heat rose on her cheeks. She'd wanted to go the other day to find a job. She'd also entertained the hope of finding a man heading west who might want a wife. After a couple of days of prayer, however, she knew that wasn't the answer. If she were ever to be given the gift of a spouse, it would have to be for more than convenience or escape. Oddly, the person she'd wanted to escape from was the one she now wanted to be near.

"Katherine?"

She snapped from her musings. "Forgive me, me mind was rambling."

"If you'd rather I not know your personal dealings, I understand." Shelton leaned against the rail.

"I have some items I've sewn that I'm hoping to sell to the merchants."

"Speaking of sewing, thank you for mending my trousers."

"You're welcome." She reached for the agitator.

"Well, I'll leave you to your task. I didn't mean to interrupt."

"Shelton." She paused. She'd just about confessed to him that he wasn't an interruption. "Why did you name your horse Kehoe?"

"It's a derivative of the Irish word for horse."

"Really?"

He looked at his feet.

"Why would you choose that name, then? You're family isn't Irish, is it?"

"No." A deep crimson color ran up his neck. He cleared his throat. "It just. . .seemed like the right name at the time."

Am I the reason? Katherine dropped the wooden handle. *Lord, it doesn't make sense. I was just his servant.*

"Katherine." He reached out to her. "I've always cared a great deal for you."

She resisted the temptation to place her hand within his. Physical contact with a man, apart from tending to his wounds, was something she didn't want to venture into. A violent flash from the past cut off her vision. Instinctively she rubbed her right wrist. She squeezed her eyes shut against the pain, the horror.

"Katherine?" Shelton's voice soothed her. His hands landed ever so slightly on her shoulders.

Her heart raced. Cold sweat beaded across her forehead and upper lip, then total darkness.

❧

Shelton caught Katherine's body before her head smashed on the ground. *What's wrong with this woman? One moment she's fine, the next she faints.* Hoisting her delicate frame in his arms, he carried her to the house. "Prudence," he hollered, kicking the closed door with his foot.

His sister opened the door. "What happened?"

"I don't know. We were just talking and the vapors overtook her."

"Place her on her bed. I'll get a cool compress."

Shelton thought back on their conversation just before she passed out. He hadn't said anything upsetting to her. He'd just been embarrassed. How could he explain that he'd loved her so much he named his horse after her?

Shelton laid her across her bed. The same bed he had lain in right after the raccoon attack. He groaned.

"She's not that heavy. You must be losing your strength, little brother." Prudence placed a cool cloth on Katherine's forehead.

She moaned.

Praise You, Lord, she's all right. "Why would she just faint like that?"

"Women do that from time to time."

"Oh." The idea of it being a female issue disconcerted him so much he fumbled his way out the door and left his sister to tend to Katherine. *Thank You, God, that I was born a man!*

He heard voices and knew Prudence and Katherine were speaking. He set his hat more firmly on his head and marched outside. Every fiber of his body urged him to do something, anything. A ride, he decided. Taking Kehoe for a hard jaunt sounded wonderful.

In the barn, he saddled his horse and headed south toward Creelsboro.

Thirty minutes later, Shelton pushed Kehoe to a fast gallop. He couldn't remember the last time he'd taken the animal out for a decent run. A good workout would be healthy for Kehoe, not to mention how much it would benefit his owner.

A small stream of sweat rolled down Shelton's spine. He eased up on the reins and patted Kehoe's neck. "Feel good, boy?"

Shelton stopped at Jobbes Fork and let the horse drink. Kehoe enjoyed the speed. Shelton did, too.

The gentle run of the river soothed Shelton's rankled nerves. Perhaps Prudence was right and Katherine was just having some kind of female problem. But from the way her eyes went distant a couple of times during their conversation, he didn't think so. *She's like a timid mare, Lord. Only worse. More like a battered horse.*

"No, Lord," he prayed. Surely nothing that serious had happened to Katherine. But a few days back he'd had a similar thought.

Shelton hoisted himself off Kehoe. The leather creaked as he steadied his feet on the ground.

Did he really want to know about her past? His mind imagined the worst thing that could be done to a female child. It made his stomach churn.

Lifting a twig, he pierced the packed sand of the riverbank. He jammed the stick in farther. "I'm madder than a snake, Lord. I know I shouldn't be, but I am. Men like that should be hung." He walked along the edge of the river, reminding himself not to assume something he didn't know for sure was true.

The wind stirred the top of the pine trees across the river. Water cascaded over a fallen tree trunk. "Lord, take this anger from me. I don't like being this way."

Working at the mill was beginning to sound better all the time. It would be steady work, and the more Shelton felt anger building up in him the more he needed to do some physical exercise. Unfortunately, being a part of the higher social circles, he'd never learned to do much of anything other than take care of his horses.

With determined steps he limped back to his horse and headed toward Crockett's paper mill. It was time for him to get a job. If he was hired, he'd save all his money and buy some land. Perhaps in a year he'd have a place built for his parents. Then he could think about becoming involved with Katherine. Maybe by that time he could handle his mixed emotions.

❧

"Are you feeling better?"

Katherine smiled at Prudence, who was adjusting the cool compress against her forehead. "I'm fine. I don't know what came over me."

"When did you eat last?"

Katherine thought for a moment. At breakfast she'd nibbled at the counter, but didn't sit down to eat with the family. "I had a piece of bacon this morning."

"That's not enough," she chided. "Now, tell me what happened out back."

Leaning her head into the pillow, she closed her eyes. "A dark memory overcame me." She'd leave it at that. Prudence wouldn't pry.

"That's been happening a lot lately, hasn't it?"

Katherine nodded.

"Is it because my brother is here?"

"I thought so at first, but now I'm not sure. Maybe this will be the last time."

Prudence gave her a slight smile. "Stay in bed and rest for a while. I'll send Tucker in with something for you to eat."

"Thank you." Normally she would have objected at having someone wait on her, but today she didn't have the strength to fight. "Prudence?"

"Yes?" Her sister-in-law turned in the doorway.

"I think it's time for me to move to Creelsboro, find a place of my own. I can supply some of the merchants with articles of clothing to sell."

Prudence shook her head. "Please don't make any plans right now. If you can stay a little longer, you might not want to move to Creelsboro."

Katherine sat up on the bed. "What are you talking about?"

"I can't say right now. I'll speak to Urias and tell him your plans." Prudence turned to leave.

"Pru?"

"Talk to Urias," she said as she left.

"Where is he?" Katherine called out, but no one answered.

Urias and Mac had been gone a lot lately and they seemed to bring little home from their expeditions. That was quite unlike them. Mac could track anything, anywhere. He wasn't Indian, but he'd spent a lot of time with some before marrying Pamela.

Katherine picked up her sewing kit and the shirt she'd been making for Shelton. If she were to move out on her own, she'd have to sell it to help pay the rent.

She enjoyed the special friendship she shared with Prudence. But the desire to move away from the house was stronger now than it had ever been. Shelton was the cause of that.

No, she admitted, it wasn't Shelton's fault. Katherine closed her eyes. "Lord, it's my own sinful desires. How can I even entertain the thought of wanting to be in a man's arms after what I've been through? I can't ruin Shelton's life. I'm not fit for marriage. And he talks daily about providing for his parents. I know I could never be comfortable around Hiram Greene. Please, Lord, help me. I can't be a burden to my brother any longer."

She wiped her eyes at the gentle knock on her bedroom door.

"Auntie Katherine," Tucker called. "Mommy said to give you this."

"I'll be right there." Katherine folded the sewing and left it on the chair. She opened the door.

Her nephew stood there, a tray of food and drink balancing precariously on his little hands.

"Thank you." As she took the tray, the boy sighed with relief.

"Auntie Katherine, are you all right?"

"Yes dear," she said, setting the tray on her nightstand. "I just didn't eat enough this morning."

"Why?" He placed his hands on his hips, imitating her.

"Because I got busy and forgot."

"That's silly. Everyone knows you have to eat."

Katherine ruffled Tucker's dark curls. "You're absolutely right."

Apparently quite pleased with his astute powers of observation, Tucker puffed up his chest and headed toward the kitchen. He was quite the charmer. Not unlike his uncle.

Katherine groaned at the thought as she bit off a hunk of her sandwich. She saw Shelton everywhere. Frightened by her growing attraction to him, she prayed she would not give in to carnality.

Chapter 6

Every inch of Shelton's body ached. He'd never worked so hard in all his life. After two days at the mill, he had blisters on his blisters and several had popped. He pulled off his work gloves to see how badly his hands bled today.

He left every morning before the rest of the family stirred. The trek to the mill took an hour on Kehoe. The stallion loved the exercise. But ten hours a day of back-breaking work forced Shelton to once again wonder whether he could ever make a living suitable enough to support his parents. The idea of running a herd of hogs to Virginia for some quick cash looked better every day.

On the other hand, going west seemed promising. People came to Creelsboro from all over, heading through on their way to the frontier. Land opportunities abounded, and rumor had it that horses roamed the plains in huge herds, with plenty for the taking.

His parents would never go that far west. His father wanted to stay in Kentucky, and his mother would want to be near their grandchildren. When he gave them some.

"Get back to work, Greene," the foreman hollered over the sound of saws, hammers, and axes.

Shelton waved and put his gloves back on. Another hour of cutting logs and he'd be able to go home for the night. "Home." He snickered and rolled the next log to be split. *I'm living in a barn.*

Eight months ago he was living in a mansion and didn't have a care in the world. His food and clothing were prepared for him every day. His only concern was how to acquire and breed more horses. *Now look at me.* He'd had to sell off almost all his stock, and he had no home to call his own. *Lord, I don't know what to do.*

The sledgehammer seemed to weigh more than it did two days ago. Shelton grabbed the iron wedge and positioned it in the log. The sharp smell of freshly cut wood invigorated him. He raised the mallet and heaved it down on the wedge.

The clang of the quitting bell rang. Shelton dusted off his work clothes and peeled off his gloves.

"You ain't worked much, have ya?" Frank Smith blustered, staring at Shelton's fingers.

"Not this kind of work."

"Humph. You'd best be putting some teat salve on them hands tonight."

"Teat salve? You mean the stuff folks use on cow udders?"

"Yes sir. Takes the bite out of them blisters like nothing else around. Check a dairy farmer's hands. They always be soft as a baby's bottom."

Shelton looked at his cracked and bleeding palms. He'd try anything at this point.

"Greene, come on over here," Mr. Crockett called.

"Thanks, Frank."

"You'd best get to Mr. Crockett right quick iffen you wants to keep this here job." Frank set a cap on his head and hiked up his collar.

Shelton ran to the main building. "What can I do for you, sir?"

He handed Shelton a brown envelope. "I'm sorry, son, but I'm afraid I have to let you go. Your work was half the amount of the others. I gave you a full day's pay. I know you tried hard."

Shelton's shoulders sank right along with his spirits. Without a word, he reached out for the envelope. Mr. Crockett didn't release it.

"You interested in selling that stallion of yours?"

"No sir."

"It appears to me you need to earn some money quickly. Why won't you sell?"

Shelton squared his shoulders. "Kehoe is my future. I might be in short supply of capital right now, but if I were to let go of Kehoe, I'd be setting back my plans by five years."

"You a breeder?"

"Yes sir. Kehoe is prime horse flesh."

"He's got good lines. Is he fast?"

"Yes sir."

"Want to test his skills against my three-year-old? If your horse wins, I'll double your pay. If mine wins, you sell Kehoe to me for a fair price."

Shelton held back a laugh. Then it dawned on him how easy it would be to fall into gambling, just like his father.

"Mr. Crockett, with all due respect, that offer is hardly worth considering. I've never seen your horse, let alone know how well he runs. If I were to blindly wager my future against yours, what profit would I have? I'd consider a friendly race between men, but I will not gamble my future away."

Mr. Crockett scrutinized Shelton with the cunning of a hawk looking over his prey. "Done. A friendly race, nothing more."

"That, sir, is acceptable."

"William," Mr. Crockett yelled. "Get Bailey."

"If you don't mind, I'll be soaking my hands while we wait for your stallion."

A smirk rose from the corners of Mr. Crockett's mouth. Shelton walked to the pump, filled the bucket, and soaked his hands in the icy water.

Feeling slightly relieved, but shivering with cold, he crossed to the holding pen, where Kehoe stood munching on some hay. "How are you, boy?"

Kehoe nuzzled his nose into Shelton's chest.

"We're going to have some fun today." Shelton cinched the saddle and readied Kehoe with some prancing around the mill yard.

Mr. Crockett's three-year-old stallion trotted into the yard. He had a chestnut coat with white boots. His muscles seemed taut and ready for action.

"Wanna race him, boy?" Shelton whispered in his horse's ear.

Kehoe raised his head and pranced in place. Shelton tightened his grasp on the reins. Kehoe loved speed, and today he'd be able to use it.

❧

Katherine didn't know what to do with herself. Prudence had prepared the evening meal. Urias and Shelton had been out of the house all day. The children were busy playing. Katherine had spent four hours sewing, but making clothing for strangers gave her little joy.

All her life, her time had been owned by others. Her own goals and desires had diminished to the point where she felt like nothing more than cattle. *But at least I knew where I fit in.* Freedom without purpose left her feeling as if there were no solid ground under her feet.

Katherine strolled to the clearing in the woods, where she'd spent a lot of private time. The circular area contained two comfortable wooden benches. The large, flowering bushes that hedged the alcove gave a person some privacy in the spring and summer, though a person wouldn't remain hidden for long in the late fall. Grandma Mac had created the little sanctuary when she was a young bride living in this new territory. Grandma and Grandpa Mac moved to Jamestown five years before it was incorporated in 1827. At that time there were only a handful of neighbors. This small area had become a safe haven for all the women of the family. Katherine felt like family to the MacKenneths.

She sat on one of the benches and glanced at the sky. A pink dusting of clouds in the west made her realize she didn't have much time to be alone.

The crack of a falling tree in the distance made her jump. *Are the men still cutting down trees for winter?* She could have sworn Urias had said they'd cut all the cords of wood needed for their three households last week.

She listened carefully. No sound of chopping. Perhaps nature had taken its course on a lone tree in the woods. Katherine peeked her head out of the sanctuary and looked for any signs of the men. She saw no one.

Settling back on the bench, she prayed. It was in this garden she had rediscovered God and become acquainted with the concept of Jesus as her friend. A smile spread across her face as she remembered Grandma Mac telling her how foolish she'd been to blame God for her mother's actions or for the way she'd been treated by the men who had owned her. She'd never been able to tell Grandma Mac, or anyone else for that matter, the sordid details about her life as a bond servant. Grandma Mac was too godly of a woman to hear such things, she reasoned. Katherine wanted to shield all the family from such horrors.

Earlier that day, when memories of her horrible past had bubbled to the surface with intense urgency, she'd almost told Shelton the truth about her life. But she couldn't. No one should know. No one would respect her if they knew.

"Oh God, why?"

Another memory floated to the surface. Shelton holding her in his arms, his loving touch on her skin. The sweet caress of his finger on her face when he brushed the strands of her hair away from her eyes.

"How can this be, Lord? How can I desire a man when. . ." Tears spilled into her lap. "Forgive me, Lord. I am such a wretch."

"Child?" Grandma Mac's voice cracked.

Katherine looked up and saw the older woman shuffling toward her. She wiped the tears from her face. "I'm sorry. I'll let you have your prayer time." She stood.

Grandma Mac leaned on her cane, placing a hand on Katherine's shoulder. "I'll not hear a single word of you apologizing for praying here." She urged Katherine to sit back down, then joined her on the bench. "Now tell me, child, why all the tears?"

❧

Shelton led Kehoe to the trough. Sweating and snorting heavily from the fast run, the horse greedily lapped up the water.

"Fine horse, Greene." Mr. Crockett brought his horse to the water. "You sure I can't interest you in selling him?"

"Afraid not."

"I can see why you're holding on to him."

"He's sired some good stock. My mare should be foaling next month. Their mating should produce excellent offspring."

"Will that one be for sale?"

"More than likely, when the time is right. Interested?"

Mr. Crockett extended his hand. "Absolutely. Send word and I'll examine the foal."

Shelton shook the man's hand.

Crockett eyed Kehoe. "I've got a mare that might produce good stock with your stallion. Would you consider allowing me to hire him to stud?"

Shelton smiled. "I'm living with Urias O'Leary. When your mare is in season, send word to me through him, and Kehoe and I will come on over."

"Wonderful. Have you considered racing him professionally? Could earn you some additional income. And those events can be good exhibitions for getting the word out about the stud service."

"I'll keep that in mind." Shelton looked at the setting sun. "I'd best be getting home. Good night, Mr. Crockett."

"Good night, Mr. Greene." Mr. Crockett handed him his pay envelope.

Shelton stuffed it in his pocket. He had earned the man's respect, but only after he'd been fired. How could he send for his parents if he couldn't find gainful employment?

As he turned his horse toward home, his hands stung from the opened blisters. The idea of Katherine's gentle fingers on these fresh wounds sent a glimmer of emotion through him. But what emotion? The word *acceptance* came to mind. Was that what he was feeling? His father and mother had accepted his help with the family finances, but only after the bankers told Hiram there was no other alternative. Urias and Prudence showed genuine concern for him, but he didn't feel exactly at home in their house. The time had come for him to make his own mark in the world. But how?

Kehoe kept a gentle canter back to the farm. Shelton decided he needed to spend more time in prayer. Then he'd talk with Urias and see if he could come up with some ideas. With the pending stud fee and the sale of the foal, maybe he could convince the bank to give him a loan for his own farm. He had proof back in Hazel Green of the profits he'd made from the breeding of his horses. Would that be enough for the bank to take a risk?

As he came up to the barn, he saw Urias loading his wagon with Katherine's belongings. A jolt of concern raced through his heart. "What's going on?"

Chapter 7

Katherine sat on her bed, perplexed at the events that had occurred over the past hour. When Grandma Mac found her in the garden sanctuary, she'd told the dear old woman how foolish she felt for wanting a little privacy, a place of her own. The next thing she knew, they were marching back to Urias's house and Grandma Mac was informing the family that Katherine was moving in with her. The family agreed it was a wonderful idea since Grandma Mac could use the company now that her husband had passed on.

"What can I carry out to the wagon?" Shelton appeared in her doorway, looking like an Irish warrior prepared to defend the honor of a maid.

"The quilt can go, but the rest of the bedding will stay here."

He held out his hands for the quilt. "Anything else?"

"Shelton," she cried out when she saw the wounds on his wonderful, sensitive hands. She ran to his side and examined the blisters more closely. "What happened?"

Shelton shuffled back and forth on his feet. "I've been working at Crockett's mill for a couple days. My hands aren't used to that kind of work."

"Let me cleanse them."

"They'll be fine." He tried to stuff them in his pockets, but quickly pulled them out again. "Why are you moving?"

"It was Grandma Mac's idea."

Prudence walked in. "And when Grandma Mac gets her mind bent on something. . ." She started folding up the quilt. "Well, let's just say folks respect their elders here."

Katherine returned her attention to the wounds on Shelton's hands. "Did you wear gloves?" She took a cool compress and drizzled water over the wounds. Dirt and grit had worked their way into some of the open sores.

Urias appeared in the doorway. "He's a sensitive boy," he said with a smirk. Prudence giggled.

"I am not a boy," Shelton seethed. "And yes, I was wearing gloves."

"Just teasing. I know you've been working hard. Mr. Crockett makes a man do an hour and a half's work in an hour."

Shelton's shoulders relaxed. Katherine fought off the desire to rub the tension from his back. "He needs some udder salve. His hands are raw."

Urias stepped into the room and peered at Shelton's fingers. "You said you had blisters. You didn't tell me they looked like ground meat. Prudence, take care of Shelton. Katherine and I can finish packing. Grandma Mac will have my hide if I don't get Katherine's bed over there in the next fifteen minutes."

ða

By the time Katherine arrived at Grandma Mac's house, the rest of the MacKenneth family had set up one of the rooms for her. She couldn't imagine a more supportive family, or one that feared the matriarch so much.

Over the years Grandma Mac had spent a lot of time with Katherine, teaching her to read and schooling her in much of the education she'd missed growing up. Would rooming with her solve her desire to have her own place? She didn't think so. But a break from the late-night awakenings of baby Elizabeth would be a welcome relief.

After the rest of the family left for home, Katherine found herself sitting on her bed in a strange room. She loved Grandma Mac and looked forward to helping her. It was becoming increasingly difficult for the dear woman to get around these days. Besides, for the first five years of Prudence and Urias's marriage, Katherine had been a part of their household. It would be nice for them to have time alone as a family. At least, that was what she kept telling herself.

A light tap on the door drew her out of her musings. "Yes?"

"May I come in, dear?"

"Of course."

Grandma Mac sat in the rocking chair beside the bed. "I suppose I acted a bit rash to have you move in with me this very evening. But there was a reason for my insistence."

Katherine clamped her mouth tight.

"The barn is not a fit place for Shelton to live. And adding a room on to Urias's house right now would not be wise because of the new baby. I proposed that you move in with me so Shelton can move into your old room."

"I see." She felt a bit embarrassed at not having thought of that herself.

It made perfect sense.

"Also, Urias is quite concerned about your fear of Shelton. Although I haven't seen it myself for the past week or more."

"No, I'm not afraid of Shelton."

"Good. Because I'm hiring him to work for me while Mac takes his family fur trapping."

Katherine nodded. She wasn't frightened by Shelton any longer. At least not in the same way as before. Now she was just afraid of the emotions she felt toward him.

"Do you love him?"

Katherine's head shot up. "No."

"Hmm. That's an awfully quick reply for a woman who was crying out to God about her feelings for a man just a few hours ago."

"I can't love him." Katherine glided her hands over the quilt. "I'm not fit."

"Nonsense. You are a redeemed child of the King. You're as fit as any woman to marry a man."

"I can't. Besides, Shelton doesn't think of me in those terms. He knows who I am, who I was. After all, I was his servant."

"Tell me this, Katherine. Does Prudence treat you like a servant?"

She shook her head.

"Does Shelton?"

Did he really? "No, I suppose not."

Grandma Mac leaned back in the rocker and swung back and forth for a moment. "Then perhaps you should trust God and pray for His guidance. You've healed tremendously since you arrived five years ago. You no longer blame God. You've trusted Him with your soul. Why not trust Him regarding your future, too?"

How could she argue with that? "I will pray," she agreed.

"Good. Now, this old woman has stayed up way beyond her bedtime." Grandma Mac lifted herself from the chair and leaned on her cane as she shuffled out of the room. "Trust God, dear. And don't argue with Him."

Was she arguing with God? Did she truly trust Him? Trust was an issue she felt she'd never overcome.

Shelton's bloody palms came back to her mind. What about Shelton? Was he working in his own strength?

❧

After a couple of days, Shelton could work his hands with minimal pain. And a good thing, too. For today he would begin working for the senior

Mrs. MacKenneth, feeding her livestock and doing some odds and ends around the place. Knowing his own limitations in farming, he'd insisted on a low wage, and thankfully, she agreed.

Planting and harvesting hay and other grains would be the hardest part. But if he were ever going to get his own place, he needed to learn how to maintain a farm. Maybe then he could get a banker to secure a loan with him to purchase his own farmstead.

The idea of working for Mrs. MacKenneth pleased him, but the thought of seeing Katherine every day increased his joy tenfold. *Father, help me win her heart.*

He rode Kehoe up to Grandma Mac's farm. He found Katherine in the yard, hanging linens on the line. A smile creased his lips. A desire to see her doing the same for him and their family one day gave him pause. He pictured her with two children hanging on to her skirts and a round belly full with another. Shelton shook off those thoughts. She wasn't ready. And although he was, he needed to keep focused on slowly building a relationship with her, one in which she didn't jump at his very presence.

"It's good to see you, Katherine."

A light blush rose on her cheeks. "How are your hands?"

"Much better, thank you. How's Mrs. MacKenneth?"

"Good, all things considered. I didn't realize she was having so much trouble getting around."

Shelton dismounted. "Did she fall?"

A gentle smile creased Katherine's face. "No. Just old bones, she says."

As much as he wanted to stay and talk with Katherine, that wasn't why he'd come. He couldn't afford to lose another job. "Excuse me, Katherine, but Mrs. MacKenneth is waiting on me."

He took the porch steps two at a time.

Half an hour later he was out in the barn with a list of chores. He couldn't imagine how Mac and Urias kept up their farms as well as Mrs. MacKenneth's. Perhaps this wasn't a token job offer after all. She really could use a part-time workman around the old house.

"Shelton," Katherine called from the barn door, "Grandma Mac says she expects you to join us for lunch."

"I take that to mean there isn't an option."

Katherine chuckled. "For an old woman she sure has some spit and fire."

"I believe you're right. Do you know where she keeps the whetstone?"

"No. I'm afraid I know little about the barn. I've only been in here a time or two. But I'll be glad to help you look."

"Thank you. I'm sure we can find it. If not, I can borrow Urias's."

She stepped inside and helped him search the barn. "Do you like farming?"

Shelton didn't quite know how to answer that question. "Truthfully, no. But there are a lot of things in this life that we have to do that aren't pleasant."

Katherine went rigid.

Shelton mentally kicked himself. He'd done it again, reminded her of the past. A past he prayed he was wrong about. He wanted to ask her straight out if she'd been abused but that would be rude. "I'm sorry. I didn't mean to speak insensitively. Forgive me."

She knitted her eyebrows and cocked her head. Her lips parted slightly, but she closed them again.

"Are you all right?"

She pressed her eyelids closed, then opened them slowly. For a moment he lost himself in those powerful green eyes that had captivated his dreams more nights than he could count.

"I'm fine. I apologize for responding so dramatically to a perfectly natural statement. What is it about farm life that you don't appreciate?"

He thought about her question for a moment. "To be honest, I guess I'm a bit spoiled. I was raised in a house where servants did my bidding. I'm not afraid of hard work, but my body hasn't done much of it. My hands protest every time I try to do something physical. I can't wait until the day when I can hire a man to do these tasks for me."

She peered at him, as if trying to determine what meaning lay behind his words.

"It's not that I find the work beneath me. I just don't like doing it. I will because I must, but it doesn't give me the same joy I find in training Kehoe and Kate."

Her eyes flew open. "You named your mare after me?"

Heat rose up his neck and covered his ears. "Yes," he confessed and went back to searching for the whetstone. He wanted to confess his love for her, but held back. Now was not the time.

"Shelton?" Her voice wavered.

He looked up at her. "Yes?"

"It's not possible." Katherine ran out of the barn.

A strong drive to run after her captured his heart. But his head kept his feet firmly planted. There would be opportunities in the future to speak with her, to convince her that they did in fact have a future. But he could not provide that future, not just yet.

❧

Katherine trembled as she yanked a large pot out of the kitchen cupboard. Why did every encounter with Shelton make her long to be in his arms? How could the simplest things he said make her want to confess her past to him? She wanted a future with him. But Hiram Greene had made it clear that she was not fit for his family. No, a relationship with Shelton was impossible.

"With God nothing shall be impossible." The fragmented piece of scripture rang in her head. "Lord, You don't understand." Katherine let out a mild cough. "That didn't come out right. But Lord, You have no idea who Hiram Greene is." She cleared her throat again and set the pot on the stove with a clang. "Lord, I know You know all, but even You have to admit that man is. . ."

"Is what, dear?" Grandma Mac asked.

Katherine looked up and saw the older woman standing in the doorway.

"I didn't mean to interrupt your prayers, but if you keep banging those pans, there won't be one fit to fry in."

Katherine looked down. "I'm sorry."

Grandma Mac sat at the kitchen table. "Tell me what's on your mind, child?"

Katherine took a tin measuring cup out of the drawer.

"Has Shelton Greene acted inappropriately toward you?"

"Shelton? He's the only man who's treated me like a woman."

"So you do love him."

"No," Katherine replied, a bit too quickly. "I respect him. Probably too much."

Grandma Mac narrowed her gaze. "Not all men behave badly, you know."

Katherine's hands shook. She put down the measuring cup and turned away from Grandma Mac's knowing gaze. The past blazed through her memory as quickly as a bolt of lightning in the sky.

Holding back tears, she faced Grandma Mac again. Her pale brown eyes spoke volumes.

Katherine sat beside the intuitive woman. "You know, don't you?" she whispered.

"I've suspected from the start. Whenever any man got within ten feet of you, your back stiffened. But you let your guard down around Shelton. At first I thought it was because he was family. Now I suspect you love him.

But because of your past you don't feel you have the right to have a blessed union with a man. Am I right?"

Katherine nodded. "Yes. But there's more to it than that."

Grandma Mac lifted her chin. "You can tell me, dear."

"If I could ever truly love a man, it would be Shelton. But. . ."

"But what, honey?"

"When Shelton's father owned me, before I came to move here. . .just before Urias found me, five years ago. . .Mr. Greene made it very clear that he would never consent to a union between me and his son."

"I see. So because you were once their servant, you aren't allowed to love Shelton? Or do you think Shelton's father would disown him if he married you?"

"Family is very important to Shelton. I don't think I've had one conversation with him in which he didn't discuss his commitment to provide for and help his family. I could never stand in the way of that." Katherine stopped herself from saying more. Some things were best kept hidden.

"You are not Hiram Greene's servant, nor any other man's. You are God's child. And He loves you. He forgives you. His heart aches for the improprieties that have fallen upon you. But you are redeemed, Katherine. You're free to pursue a relationship with Shelton if that is what you wish. Is it?"

Katherine stared at the tabletop. "Honestly, I don't know. I do like Shelton, and I enjoy talking with him very much. But I don't know if I could ever trust a man enough to love him in. . .the way that God designed."

Grandma Mac patted her hand. "Unfortunately, other women have been in situations similar to yours. Some were able to move beyond the pain of the past and have good lives with loving husbands. Others have turned to wanton ways, believing they are worthless. Please don't think that about yourself. Walk in faith and trust God."

"I could never live a life of ill repute. But I don't see how it is possible for me to live with a man."

"By God's grace, dear." Grandma Mac rose from the chair and left Katherine alone with her thoughts.

Perhaps one day I could live with a man. But the likelihood of it being Shelton was slim. Hiram Greene stood like an ox in the barnyard—huge, strong, and stubborn to the point of being immovable.

Chapter 8

Shelton worked at Mrs. MacKenneth's farm every morning. During the afternoons he rode into Creelsboro to procure stud fees. He arranged for the setup to take place in the livery stable in Creelsboro. The client would bring in a mare, then Kehoe would come into the narrow corral and do his part, after which he returned to his own pen. Unfortunately, Kehoe had suffered once or twice. After the last service, Shelton had found him bleeding. The mare had bitten him hard on the neck.

After a couple of weeks, he had earned enough money to speak with a bank manager about securing a loan for purchasing his own property. He hoped there might be a foreclosure he could pick up for a reasonable rate.

Shelton left Kehoe in the public stable and headed for the bank. The streets were filled with travelers heading west. The excitement in the air promised hope and freedom. Shelton felt its powerful tug as an easy answer to his financial problems.

He stepped off the dusty street into the dark paneled confines of the bank.

"Good afternoon." A bald, middle-aged man extended a hand to him. His pin-striped business suit draped over a stout figure.

"Afternoon," Shelton responded, accepting the handshake. "I was wondering if I could speak with the manager."

"That'd be me, sir. Reynolds is the name. What can I do for you?"

"I'd like to talk about getting a loan to purchase some property in the area."

The man lit up like a full moon. "Why don't we step into my office."

Two hours later Shelton came out with a smile on his face and a lightness in his heart. Mr. Reynolds had said that once he verified Shelton's past financial dealings with the banks back in Hazel Green, he didn't see a problem giving him a loan. He even recommended a two-hundred-acre farm where the owner had passed away and the widow hoped to return to family in New York.

Two hundred acres seemed like more than Shelton required. Then again, the horses needed grazing fields and long, open runs for strength and development. He had a lot to think about and a lot to pray about.

He sent a letter to his parents to let them know of the recent turn of events. Soon he'd be able to write and tell them where their new home would be. A desire to share his news with Katherine spurred him on. He urged Kehoe to move a bit faster. He looked at the wound on the horse's neck. It had begun to bleed again. Shelton pulled back on the reins and let the stallion trot at a nice even pace.

As he neared the outskirts of the MacKenneths' farm, the sun was beginning to set. Katherine would have to wait until tomorrow to hear his good news. He enjoyed seeing her every day at the elder MacKenneth's farm, but he missed spending time with her and the family at Urias's. The way her face lit up when she played with her nephews made his heart soar. *I think we should have a large family.*

"Whoa," he said out loud, quickly reining in his thoughts.

Kehoe pulled to an abrupt stop. Shelton clicked his tongue to encourage the animal to continue. "Sorry, boy. I wasn't talking to you."

He chided himself for allowing his imagination to stray into foolish territory. He couldn't convince her to open up to him, let alone kiss him, and here he was picturing having children with her.

When he arrived at Urias's barn, he removed Kehoe's saddle, brushed him down, and carefully washed the wound on the horse's neck. Then he checked on Kate. He gave the mare a good brushing.

"Do you always spend this much time with them?" Katherine asked.

Startled, he raised his head suddenly and nearly crowned it on the side of the pen. "What are you doing here?"

"I was invited to dinner, and Urias sent me out to fetch you to join us. The children have all eaten, but Urias is getting hungry and cranky."

Shelton chuckled. "I'm sorry. I didn't know they were holding dinner on me. I had to tend to Kehoe's injury."

Katherine came up to the stallion. "What happened?"

"A frisky mare bit him."

"Oh." A gentle blush covered Katherine's cheeks. "Is Kate almost ready to foal?"

"Any time now." Shelton put down the brush and washed his hands at the pump. "I have some good news."

Katherine smiled. The glow of her green eyes and the gentle rose pink of her lips warmed Shelton deep within.

He switched his focus back to the ice-cold water from the pump. "Mr. Reynolds at the bank said that if my references and facts concerning my bank records in Hazel Green check out, I'll be approved for a loan to purchase a farm in the area."

"Oh Shelton, that's wonderful news." Katherine wrapped her arms around him, then immediately pulled away.

He knew he couldn't pressure her to show affection, but inwardly he rejoiced that she had reached out to him. "I sent a letter to my parents and let them know it won't be much longer before they can plan on moving here."

All the energy in Katherine's face disappeared. "I'm happy for you."

If that was happy, what would describe her earlier reaction? "Katherine, Father's changed. He's a humbled man."

She gave a weak smile and a nod. "Dinner is ready whenever you are."

Shelton watched her walk off toward the house. He kicked the pump with his foot. His toe throbbed. That would teach him to take out his anger on an immoveable object.

"Father God," he prayed, "am I so blinded by love for Katherine that I'm ignoring the problems our union would create for my parents? And for her?" Shelton sighed. "Your will, Father, not mine." He hoped he meant his prayer, because he knew his heart would be destroyed if he and Katherine would never be together.

❧

Katherine sat numbly through dinner. Shelton's news flooded the conversation. Urias spoke of some farms in the area that might be available for a good price. Shelton mentioned one where a woman was recently widowed. Having lived with Grandma Mac for a short time, Katherine realized how hard it would be for an elderly woman to live alone and maintain a farm, even a small one such as Grandma Mac now owned. Rather than a farm, Shelton wanted a ranch, where he could breed horses.

The conversation moved on to other news from the area, but the lively chatter didn't engage her. She wondered how big a ranch he would have. And whether he would feel so compelled to provide for his parents that they would live on the property with him.

Urias's voice broke through her jumbled thoughts. "I read somewhere they moved Daniel Boone and his wife's bones to Frankfort on September thirteenth. The town had a parade and everything."

"Seems odd to move a man's bones after he's been laid to rest," Prudence said. "But I imagine the state is happy to have the man who blazed the trail to Kentucky back home."

Prudence peered at Katherine. "You're awfully quiet tonight."

"I suppose I don't have much to offer in a discussion about local affairs."

"I'd be interested in anything you had to say." Shelton set his fork on the table. "What were you thinking about while we were discussing Daniel Boone?"

She'd done it this time. She should have known Shelton would be able to tell she was distracted by her own thoughts.

Everyone at the table stared at her, waiting for her response. *All right,* she thought. *If he really wants to know. . .*

"I just find it hard to understand why you feel the need to provide for your parents. I suppose not having my own parents any longer, I don't understand your loyalty to them."

Shelton wiped his lips with his napkin. "It's a question of honor. I don't approve of my father's actions, but I am duty bound by God's Word and my conscience to honor my parents."

Urias reached for his glass of water. "I have to agree. Hiram Greene isn't one of my favorite people in the world, but he is Prudence's father, and I choose to respect him because he raised my beautiful wife." He looked at Prudence, who smiled lovingly at him. Then he returned his attention to Katherine. "What would you do if our mother showed up one day? Would you curse her and throw her out, or would you forgive her and provide her with a place to stay?"

"Seeing as how I don't own my own home, I couldn't make such an offer." *And I probably never will be able to anyway.* "I honestly don't know what I'd do if Mother were to show up."

"I'd have a problem with that as well," Shelton acknowledged.

"I think we all would," Prudence offered. "While my parents had their problems, they did love us and raise us well."

Katherine sat back in her chair and thought on that for a moment. The Greenes did love their children. And that was more than she could say about her mother.

Prudence reached for Urias's hand. He wrapped his fingers around hers. "Father knows he tricked us and used us. I don't think he will ever ask for forgiveness, even though we gave it to him long ago."

Katherine forked a piece of meat but couldn't raise it to her mouth. "Forgiveness is one thing. But taking care of them? Hiram Greene is not so old that he can't take care of himself."

"Father's gambling is like a sickness. He can't seem to stop. And Mother shouldn't suffer for his transgressions. So I will provide for them. In my mind it isn't an option; it is an obligation I must fulfill to be an honorable man to God."

Katherine nibbled her lower lip. "I guess it's my own bitterness that can't allow me to see why you feel so strongly about this. I don't know if I'll ever get over being owned by others."

"If Hiram Greene hadn't acquired your bond," Urias interjected, "I wouldn't have found you. I wouldn't have found my beautiful wife either. And I wouldn't have three of the most adorable children on the face of the earth. I wish things had been different for you, Katherine, but they weren't. Even though you lived through harsh times, you need to accept the facts and move on with the blessings God has given you."

"I guess," she added with a sigh, "if it wasn't for Hiram Greene, I wouldn't have my freedom and a cherished family."

Shelton smiled.

And I wouldn't have Shelton in my life, she added silently. Was Grandma Mac right? Could she have a future with him? Katherine picked up her fork and ate the now-cold chunk of meat. "Forgive me for being so rude, Shelton."

"You're always free to speak your mind around me."

She appreciated the freedom he gave her. But to live under the same roof as Hiram Greene again? That would take a double portion of God's grace.

The conversation shifted to Grandma Mac. Prudence served a delicious apple pie for dessert.

Stuffed, Katherine pushed back from the table. "I'd better help you with these dishes and get on my way or Grandma Mac might wonder why I was gone so long."

"Nonsense. Urias promised to help me in the kitchen."

Urias's eyebrows shot up. "Shelton, would you be so kind as to escort Katherine back to Grandma Mac's?"

"Be my pleasure." Shelton wiped his mouth with the cloth napkin and placed it neatly next to his dish.

He is such a gentleman, Katherine thought wistfully. "I can go by myself."

"Indulge me," Urias said. "I saw some bear tracks earlier this morning."

"All right." Katherine knew about Urias's encounters with bears. His first had occurred when he was thirteen. A smile edged her lips as she remembered the tale of her frightened brother sitting backward on the horse while the bear made itself at home in Mac and Pamela's wagon.

Her smile disappeared when she remembered another occasion. Mac had barely survived the attack from the bear that killed his first wife.

"Should we secure the livestock?" Shelton asked.

"You might want to close up the hen house and bring Grandma Mac's pig into the barn for the night," Urias suggested.

"Absolutely. What about Mac and Pam's place?"

"I secured it before dinner." Urias got up and carried some dinnerware to the kitchen. "Good night, Katherine. It was nice having you at our table again."

Katherine smiled. "It was good to be here."

They said their good-byes and Shelton escorted Katherine out the front door.

❧

Shelton placed his hand in the small of Katherine's back as they walked down the porch stairs together. He felt a slight flinch from her, but she relaxed a moment later. It had been a forward move, but it felt right.

"Look at all those stars," she declared with awe and wonder, gazing at the sky.

"God sure knows how to paint a pretty canvas, doesn't He?"

"It's magnificent." Katherine tightened her coat a notch. "I'm sorry if I offended you tonight."

"I love your straightforward honesty."

They continued to walk in the direction of Grandma Mac's house. "Shelton, there are things you don't know about me."

He weighed whether or not to ask, but decided to wait on her. "There are things you don't know about me, too, Katherine." *Like how much I love you. How much I want to wrap you in my arms and protect you. And what happened when I was sent away from you.*

"Name one thing," she challenged.

He decided to change the mood. "When I was seven, I ran away from home."

"How far did you get?"

"The neighbors' house. I didn't know how to get anywhere else."

Katherine laughed. "What did your parents do?"

"My father tanned my hide. My mother hugged me until I thought I'd break in two. Personally, I preferred my father's response. It was quick, and over in a minute. My mother kept hugging me for the next three days. At seven a boy doesn't want to be hugged a lot." *Unlike the man now standing beside you.*

"I have seen that same reaction in Mac and Pamela's boys. appreciate the affection?"

"Of course. But I couldn't let Mother see that."

"Did you ever consider running away from home again?"

"No, not really." He slowed the pace. "Remember when I was s right before Urias found you?"

"Yes." She stiffened. He kept his hand in the small of her back.

"If Father hadn't sent me away, I might have run off then. I was s with him. He was being totally unreasonable. But looking back, I was being unreasonable as well. I was only sixteen at the time. Th pretty young to. . ."

"To what?"

"I told him I loved you and that I would marry you the next tim parson came around."

Katherine stopped in her tracks. "You did what?"

He gazed at her face, bathed in the moonlight. The sight made his pound and his palms sweat. "You're even more beautiful now than w you were seventeen."

"Shelton, please don't."

"Don't what? Tell you that I love you? That I've always loved you, fr the first moment you came to my home?"

Tears ran down her cheeks. She trembled.

He stepped toward her, opening his arms, willing her to come to hir Katherine eased forward and leaned into his chest.

"My dear, sweet Katherine." He held her gently in his arms. He inhale the wonderful scent that was hers alone. *Lord, give me strength.*

"I'm damaged," she sobbed.

He held her tighter. *Lord, I wish I could take away her pain.* "Do you want to tell me about it?"

She shook her head.

"That's all right, sweetheart. Whenever you're ready." Shelton closed his eyes and held the woman he loved. For the first time, she'd come to him, willingly, openly. He would cherish this moment for as long as he lived. He kissed her gently on top of her red curls.

"I thought I was nearly free from the past," she choked out. "But since you came back I've been having nightmares. I never completely stopped having them, but they've been more frequent since you arrived."

"I'm so sorry. I never meant to hurt you."

"I feel dirty for liking you," she confessed.

Didn't you

his hands and encouraged her to look at him.
e, I love you. What happened in the past couldn't

y. "You don't understand."

e pleaded.

nt away,

nd bolted toward Grandma Mac's farmhouse.

ushed too hard. "Katherine, stop. Please!"

o angry
hink I
at was

caught her. He held her gently, fighting the desire
on to her until she saw and felt how much he loved
u're ready, you can come to me. I will not force you. I
ch to make you do something you don't want to do."
ea," she mumbled.

e the

eart
hen

m

1.

1

Chapter 9

Katherine kept to herself for the next three days. Spending time with Shelton was dangerous to her soul. She desired to be in his arms. She ached to kiss him. But she couldn't give in to such temptations, even if Grandma Mac did say God gave those desires for the holy purposes of marriage. She knew in her mind that was the truth. But she had no way to know whether she would respond positively to his kiss or if the ugly past would come back and taint the love she felt for Shelton. She didn't want to soil something as precious as his love for her and hers for him.

Not that she'd confessed her feelings for him yet.

She sat in her bedroom, working on her sewing. She'd sold several shirts to the mercantile and had an order for a dozen more.

"Katherine," Shelton's voice called out from behind the door. "May I come in?"

She set aside her sewing and opened the door. "What can I do for you?"

"I could use a favor, if you don't mind."

"What is it?"

"I'm wondering if you can take care of Mrs. MacKenneth's livestock for the next two days."

"I could try." She wanted to ask why he couldn't do it, but didn't feel she had the right to.

"Thank you. Can I show you where I keep everything?"

"Please." She followed him out of the house.

In the barn, Shelton showed her the sacks of grain and instructed her in how Grandma Mac liked to mix her pig slop. "Any questions?" he asked.

"Nope. Looks pretty straightforward."

"I appreciate this. I'll be happy to pay you for your time."

Katherine placed her hands on her hips.

Shelton laughed. "I didn't think so, but I was duty bound to offer."

"You have a strong sense of duty and honor, don't you?"

"I get that from my father. I know it doesn't make sense, with his gambling and all, but he wasn't always irresponsible. He taught us that a man's word isn't worth anything if he doesn't back it up with his actions. I know you've only known my father when he was gambling, but there is another side to him."

"Urias made sense the other night when he said you and Prudence wouldn't be the people you are today if not for how your parents raised you."

Shelton opened his arms but she didn't step into his embrace. "Katherine, I've missed you."

She looked at the hay on the floorboards and brushed it aside with her foot. "I've missed you, too."

"I apologize if confessing my love for you made you uncomfortable."

"There's precious little you can do that won't make me uncomfortable. But it's not you; it's me. Eventually, I will not be as uneasy around you."

Shelton's smile sent her heart beating faster.

"So, where are you going that you need someone to help with the livestock?" she asked, eager to change the subject.

"Urias is taking me fur trapping. He's going to show me how to set traps, how to maintain them, and how to skin and prepare the hides. He and Mac bring in a little extra income that way. Once I purchase my own land, I'll need to know what I can hunt and what is marketable."

"Any more signs of the bear?"

"Not that we've seen or heard about. Hopefully it went back to the woods." Shelton leaned against a post supporting the upper loft and chewed on a piece of hay.

"You're looking pretty relaxed today," she observed.

"I am. I feel like my prayers are finally being answered. I should hear from the bank soon. I've been looking at some properties, but so far I haven't found one I'm excited about."

"What are you looking for?"

"Enough land for the horses to run and graze. Also enough to grow the grain for their feed. Hopefully a property with a house already built on it. Otherwise, my parents won't be able to move out here until next spring. I'm not sure they'll make it through the winter in Hazel Green."

Katherine stiffened. A knot the size of a feed bucket tightened in her stomach. "I still find it hard to believe that your father squandered away all his money."

"You're not the only one. It's so out of character that he'd get caught up in gambling. He taught Prudence and me to be wise with our money. I guess sin is an all-consuming thing."

"How does one know the difference between sin and love?" Katherine covered her mouth with her hands. She hadn't meant to say that.

"Are you ready to talk about the past?"

She shook her head.

"Then let's not attempt to answer that question now. Later will be soon enough."

"Shelton, it's not you."

"It's not you either, Katherine. It's sin that's been done to you."

Katherine balled her hands into fists. "Do you know?"

"I suspect—because of how afraid you are of men—that one or more. . . took liberties with you."

Katherine nodded and choked back tears.

"When you're ready to tell me about it, I'll be here. In the meantime, know that I'm praying for you, that I love you, and that nothing that happened to you will change my love for you."

"I don't deserve you." She sniffed.

Shelton opened his arms. She snuggled into his embrace. "You deserve better than me, Katherine. You're sweet and precious and I love you."

"I love you, too," she whispered into his chest.

⁜

Shelton didn't want to let her go. However, Urias was waiting on him. He hated the thought of leaving, especially now that Katherine was opening up her heart to him. But he had no choice.

He pulled slightly away from her. "So, have you ever helped a horse deliver a foal?"

"No." Her gentle curls brushed under his chin. She stepped out of his embrace. "Are you concerned about Kate?"

"She's showing signs that she's about to deliver. She's done it before, so there shouldn't be any problems. But if it happens while I'm off fur trapping. . ."

"Perhaps you should tell Urias you'd prefer to go another time. He'll understand."

"I'm certain he will. But I want to have enough money—"

Katherine finished his sentence. "—to purchase your land."

He shrugged.

"What's of more value to you, the foal or a few furs?"

"If you put it that way, the foal." He looked out past the open doors of the barn.

"You need to be near Kate, just in case."

He looked back at her. "You're right."

"Remain focused on the overall plan."

Shelton smiled. "Besides being beautiful, you're a smart woman. I like that."

Katherine wagged her head back and forth. "You're impossible."

"Me?"

"And a real charmer. I bet all the ladies back in Hazel Green found you quite appealing."

His own past flashed before his eyes. As much as he wanted to tell Katherine about it, the time wasn't right. He decided to keep the moment light. "I can turn on the charm when I want to. But those women all bored me." He winked. "I've been stuck on an Irish lass from my youth."

Katherine blushed. "How can you be so certain about. . ." she whispered. "Us?"

She acknowledged with a nod.

"I wasn't, until I saw you again. I've been praying for five years, Katherine. I didn't know if my love was simply a child's fantasy or a real connection. Now that I've come to know you, I'm convinced this is real. However, I don't believe we can rush into a courtship. As much as I'd love to take you in my arms and rush off to the parson, there is a time and place for us. I'm willing to wait. Are you?"

Katherine took in a deep breath and let it out slowly. "I don't know how to answer that. Until last week I honestly didn't believe I was fit for marriage. Grandma Mac is challenging me to remember God's redemption and His forgiveness. I'm trying to hold on to that. I've lived a long time thinking I was worthless."

"My sweet Katherine, you are worth more than rubies or finely spun gold. You are precious in God's eyes and in mine, and I cherish your wisdom. I like discussing my plans with you. No one has ever listened to me and my ideas the way you do."

"I find your plans fascinating."

"You're the first person I wanted to tell about the bank coming through on the loan. Not my parents, not Urias and Prudence, but you. I want you to be a part of my future. Would you do me the honor of looking over the land and properties I'm most interested in? I'd very much like your opinion."

"You want me to help you decide on your property?"

"I'm hoping eventually it will be our property. I'm not looking for a commitment right now. I am planning for you to be my wife one day. But

I believe we have a lot of work ahead of us before that can happen."

"What kind of work?"

"Things like my being able to take your hand without you pulling away from me. Time is the best healer, and you have to learn to trust me, slowly and surely." *In much the same way that I tame an unbroken horse.* "I'm willing to wait. We have time. Just be honest with me, and share your heart when you're ready to."

"I've never met a man so honest about his feelings."

"I've never been this honest before. You bring it out in me, Katherine. You're good for me in so many ways. I just pray I'm helpful to you as well."

A single tear fell from her eye. "You are."

He opened his arms and waited for her to walk into his embrace. Slowly she leaned into him and he cradled her in his arms. He inhaled that fresh scent that was uniquely hers. One day he'd be able to reach out and capture her in his arms. But it would take time to earn Katherine's trust. And with God's grace, he could wait.

ଈ

Katherine wiped the tears from her eyes as she rose from her knees after spending time with God, talking to Him about all that had happened that day. Shelton wanted to marry her. She'd known it before. In fact, she wanted it herself. But some part of her didn't. *How long before I can trust Shelton, Lord?*

Katherine dressed and went down to the kitchen. Preparing breakfast for herself and Grandma Mac didn't take half the time it took to prepare for Urias's family.

"Good morning, dear. Did you sleep well?"

"Yes, thank you. How are you today?" Katherine placed the eggs in boiling water to poach them.

"As fit as a woman can be when her bones ache just walking. Feels like a storm's brewing. An early winter storm, if my joints are correct."

"Anything I can do to help prepare?"

"I don't think so. We've been keeping the chickens in the coop at night since Urias spotted those bear tracks. Mac'll take care of things. Now tell me how your conversation with Shelton went yesterday when you two were in the barn together."

Katherine chuckled. "You don't miss much, do you?"

"Not much. You looked happy, but as if the world was resting on your shoulders."

"He wants to marry me."

Grandma Mac's eyes twinkled. "Well, praise the Lord! Did you say yes?"

"He didn't ask me." Katherine pulled the toast off the grill and strained the poached eggs, placing one on each slice of bread. The smell of the wheat toast stirred up her hunger. Grandma Mac's favorite morning breakfast had become Katherine's as well.

"I'm confused."

"You're not the only one." Katherine explained how Shelton hoped they would marry one day, but he expected it to take some time before she was ready.

"Does he know about your past?"

"I haven't told him any details, but he figured it out, just like you did. I must be wearing a sign around my neck that says DAMAGED."

"Hardly." Grandma Mac shook some salt and pepper over her egg. "It's clear to those who love and care about you."

She knew she would one day have to tell Shelton the horrid details of the past if they were going to have a future together. She'd deal with that later, and with God's grace she would somehow manage to tell him.

"Tell me, have you and Shelton kissed?"

Katherine sat back. Heat spread across her cheeks. "No. I can't even hold the man's hand yet."

"I see."

Did she? Katherine certainly didn't understand her own fear. "I've sought comfort in his arms though," she confessed.

Grandma Mac beamed. "And it was comforting?"

"Like nothing else I've experienced before."

"Ah, child. I do believe Shelton is right; you will be married one day. Now eat up. You've got to deliver those shirts to Creelsboro today. I asked Mac to send Shelton over to escort you."

"You are a matchmaker."

"No, dear. God is the matchmaker. I'm simply providing moments when the two of you can talk and get to know each other." She gave the table two light taps.

As Katherine ate her eggs, peace covered her like a blanket. God's peace. Forgiving peace. Contented peace, like she'd always hoped to feel one day.

"You know, holding a man's hand is mighty satisfying if it's the right man." Grandma Mac grinned. "I loved my husband with a passion that grew as we aged."

Katherine blushed. "How can you talk about such things so freely?"

"God spoke about married love in the Bible. I figure if the good Lord saw fit to write about it, I might as well be willing to speak about it when the occasion arises." She sighed. "After Nash—Mac, as you know him— had his first marriage fail, my husband and I decided we should be honest and open with our children about love and relationships. Nash's first wife married him for his money, or the money she thought he had. They never got along. Over the years, she became a different person. Oh, I'm sure Nash did some things to provoke her. I'm not saying my son was totally innocent. But that woman, God rest her soul, could never be happy."

"Thank you, Grandma Mac. You're helping me a lot."

"You're welcome, dear. Now finish your eggs. Shelton will be here shortly."

Chapter 10

S helton stretched. He'd been up all night with Kate. If the foal didn't crown soon, he'd have to reach in and take it out.

"Shelton," Katherine called from just inside the barn door.

"I'm in Kate's stable." In a flash, he recalled promising Grandma Mac he'd pick Katherine up and take her into town that morning. "Oh no. I forgot about our trip today. I'm sorry."

"Don't worry about it." Katherine leaned over the rail of Kate's stable. "How's she doing?"

"She's been in labor all night."

"How can I help?"

Shelton glanced at her vivid green Sunday morning church dress. "Not in those clothes."

"I'll go back into the house and change. Anything else you need while I'm there?"

"Hot water for me to wash with."

A sudden deluge poured out of Kate. The mare stomped her hoof and her eyes grew wide. "It's all right, girl." Shelton patted the horse's flank.

"I'll be right back with that water."

As Katherine fled for the barn door, the foal's nose emerged. "You're doing fine, Kate." The front legs emerged. Shelton gently pulled the foal out.

"It's a boy!" The colt had Kehoe's black coat and Kate's markings. He was a good blend of the two horses.

The mare shifted on wobbly legs. She stared at the foal for a moment, then continued to pace in the stall. "What's the matter, girl?"

Her belly seemed too extended for having just given birth. Was there a problem with the placenta? Just then another nose crowned. "Twins!" Shelton smiled, then moved the newborn out of the way of Kate's determined pacing.

By the time Katherine returned with the bucket of water, Shelton was rubbing Kate down with some clean rags.

"Twins," she squealed. "Oh Shelton, they're beautiful."

"They sure are. And Kate is a wonderful mother."

Kate cleaned up the foals and nudged them to their feet. Shelton finished washing down the new mother and then sponged himself down.

Katherine watched in awe. "I can't believe they both came out of her. It doesn't seem possible."

"It's amazing, isn't it? The miracle of birth fascinates me every time I witness it. God certainly chose an interesting way to bring new life into the world."

"Are they boys or girls?"

"One of each. A colt and a filly."

Shelton watched Katherine stare at the twin foals. He wondered if she were thinking about they might have children one day. *Don't push it*, he reminded himself. As easy as it was to tell Katherine he could be a patient man, he knew he'd have to fight impulse after impulse. Like right now. He wanted to come up beside her and wrap his arm around her. But he had to wait on Katherine. He would not spook her, no matter how much he wanted them to share every precious moment of life together.

He groaned inwardly. He was beginning to sound like a philosopher or poet. His father would have a few words about that, no doubt. No matter what he told himself or Katherine, he had to face the reality that their union would bring a harsh response from Hiram Greene. *Lord, please continue to change him, to soften him.*

"What's happening?" Urias asked from the doorway of the barn.

"Twins." Katherine beamed.

Urias ran to Kate's pen. "God's blessing you, Shelton. You've just doubled your income."

Shelton grinned. "I'm thinking of keeping the filly and selling the colt. On the other hand, the sale of both might be beneficial. I should pray on the matter."

"Ah yes. The quick dollar or the long, slow profit. Hard choices. How's Kehoe doing?" Urias glanced at the stallion's pen.

"His neck is healing well."

"Excellent." Urias leaned against the barn wall. "Mac says that bear was back on the property last night. Got one of the sheep my nephew was raising. Unless Mac and I can find him today, we need you to stay close and protect the women and children tonight."

"Be happy to."

Urias slapped him on the back. "Keep up the good work." He nodded at the newborns, then sauntered out of the barn.

Shelton yawned and stretched his weary muscles.

"If you're going to be up guarding the houses tonight," Katherine said, "you'd better get some rest."

"I'd like to, but I have chores to do."

"I'll take care of them for you. What do you need done?"

He started to protest. But she wouldn't hear of it. He succumbed to her willingness to help him and went to bed. The last thought in his mind was how Katherine's face had glowed while witnessing the new life of the foals.

≈

Katherine rushed around the barn, taking care of Shelton's chores. She enjoyed watching the new mother with her young. She still couldn't get over twins. She fought the desire to wake up Shelton to talk with him, but he needed his rest.

As she worked she prayed that Urias and Mac would find the bear today. This time of year bears ate anything they could get their paws on to build up for their hibernation period. The children would have to stay close to the house, and the twin foals would be a huge temptation. She was glad Shelton now had her old room in the house.

A renewed desire to be a mother one day surfaced with such intensity that she could no longer remain in the barn. She worked her way back toward Grandma Mac's house as soon as she finished Shelton's chores.

She didn't really want to face Grandma Mac and her perceptive ways. Things Katherine had kept hidden for years came out in the presence of that woman, though Katherine wasn't sure why. She considered going to the garden sanctuary, but fear of the bear kept her away.

Katherine stopped midstride. *Where can I go?* Again, an overwhelming desire for her own place took root.

Then she recalled Shelton's comment about his hope that his property would be hers one day. *Is that really possible?* There was no denying the sense of security she felt in his arms—a calmness she'd never known. There was something about laying her head on his chest that was so. . .relaxing.

"Lord, give me strength to overcome the evils that have befallen me. You know my pain and my shame. Please help me love Shelton the way You designed a man and woman to love each other."

She took one uncertain step forward. Fear over the desire she had just confessed circled around like a vulture waiting for the kill. Katherine collapsed onto her knees and wept. Bondage still held her. "Father God, please," she cried, "remove this fear."

She cupped her hands to her face and repeated the prayer over and over. Exhausted, she waited in the stillness that surrounded her. A gentle peace slowly began to fill her. Katherine wiped her eyes and stood. The fresh earthen scent of rich soil and pine needles invigorated her. The world around her seemed suddenly bright. Was she finally free? She took a tentative step forward, then another. Her back straightened with a surge of confidence. Her strides sure, she marched up to Grandma Mac's house.

She told the old woman the news of the twin foals and let her know that she would be going to Creelsboro that day. Grandma Mac questioned her, but Katherine found the inner strength to firmly yet politely tell her that she simply had business in town. An hour later she was on the road with the newest order for the mercantile.

"Good afternoon, Mr. Hastings," Katherine greeted the shopkeeper as she entered the store. The wooden shelves and bins were full. Various tools hung on the right-hand wall. Perishable items were close to the counter in the back part of the store. A basket of fresh eggs sat near the register with rows of glass jars filled with brightly colored candy sticks. "I've completed the next order."

"Wonderful. I'm down to the last shirt. I'll need a dozen more as soon as possible. And could I get a few blouses for the ladies?"

"Do you have the material?" Katherine no longer paid for the fabric. She and Mr. Hastings had bartered. In exchange for free fabric Mr. Hastings paid a reduced price for the finished products.

"There are some light yellow, pink, and white cotton bolts over there. Take whatever you need."

"Thank you." Katherine walked to the fabric area. A bolt of beautiful ivory satin stood against the wall.

Mr. Hastings came over with his sheers. "Do you believe they sent that? I can't see me selling more than a yard or two for christening outfits. Brides don't marry in fancy getups here like they do back East. My supplier didn't even charge me for it. Would you like some?"

Katherine's eyes sparkled. "You wouldn't mind?"

"Not at all. In fact, why don't I keep four yards and give you the rest? I honestly don't think I'll be able to sell even the four yards."

"Thank you." Katherine thought of all the things she could do with that fabric. She could use some to make beautiful pillows for Christmas gifts, adding a special touch with some embroidery.

Then an image floated into her mind. Herself in a wedding gown made of this very material. Katherine's foot faltered.

Mr. Hastings reached out and caught her. "Are you all right?"

"I'm fine. My heel must have caught on the floorboard."

He released her.

"I'd like three yards each of the white, pink, and yellow cotton for the women's blouses you spoke of. Also, twenty yards of red flannel for the men's shirts. And as much of the ivory silk as you'd like to give me."

"Very good. Take your time and browse through the store. I just received some new shipments. Took in some wares from the folks heading west, too. Most of those items won't sell, but I feel sorry for those women who packed all their precious china, only to discover how impractical it is for the trip."

Katherine glanced over the myriad assorted wares. The mercantile carried a wide variety of things, from heavy tools to dainty teacups.

"How about some spools of thread?"

"Yes, please." Katherine eyed a set of china dishes with a pattern of a horse and a lady. She thought of Shelton. "How much for this set?"

"Fifteen dollars. But for you, I'll call it even with the shirts you brought in today."

"Are you certain?"

"Absolutely." He raised his right eyebrow. "For your dowry, perhaps?"

Katherine blushed.

❧

Shelton woke up just in time for dinner. He couldn't believe he'd slept the day away. He checked on Kate and the foals, ate dinner with the women and children, then prepared his rifle for his evening watch of the property. Once the family was secure for the night, he began his rounds, keeping watch over the pens close to the houses.

Katherine had seemed preoccupied at dinner. Apparently the shirts she'd been making had been selling so well that Mr. Hastings increased his order to include women's blouses. The ladies went on and on about them all night. As far as he was concerned, one blouse was as good as another. He'd seen plenty of finery in Hazel Green; it didn't impress him much. He had never really fit in with "high society," as his father liked to call it. There was something refreshingly honest about people who worked off the land. Clothing was functional. Back home, women had closets larger than some of the bedrooms here. He definitely liked this simpler life.

Shelton guffawed out loud at the irony. *Life is not simpler out here. Whoever coined that phrase should have his head examined.*

There was one thing about life in Hazel Green that he did prefer, however, and that was the use of coal for cooking and heating. It lasted longer than wood and didn't require all that chopping.

He decided to sit in a central location between the three houses to listen for any trouble. He leaned against a large boulder that marked the borders of the three properties and waited.

The sky darkened quickly after the sun went down. A chilly wind licked the back of his neck. Shelton pulled up the lapels on his woolen coat.

Crack. A twig snapped behind him. He reached for his rifle and turned.

"Shelton, where are you?" Katherine called softly.

Shelton lowered the rifle. "Over here."

She slowly emerged from the darkness.

"What are you doing out here?"

"I wanted to talk with you."

Shelton wagged his head. "Sometimes you do very foolish things." He pointed to his rifle. "Don't you realize how dangerous this is?"

Her eyes widened. "I'm sorry. I couldn't wait until morning."

"You're here now. What did you want to talk about?"

"Nothing specific, really. We just haven't had any time since this morning and. . ." Her words trailed off.

"I missed you, too." He opened his arms. "Come here."

She stepped into his embrace. He inhaled deeply. *Lord, I love this woman.*

She pulled back slightly and looked up at him. "I had a revelation. Well, I think it was a revelation. I was crying out to God today about my fear of love, and I decided to walk in faith. Then, as I stepped forward, I felt incredible crushing fear, like I have in the past. I prayed for God to remove it, and after a few moments, a gentle peace washed over me."

"Praise the Lord! That's wonderful."

"I've done that before, but this time God's peace felt a lot stronger. Or maybe I'm more confident in trusting it. I don't know. But the oddest thing happened at the mercantile this afternoon. While I was there, my footing slipped and Mr. Hastings reached out and caught me from falling. In the past, I would have jumped out of my skin. This time I didn't react at all. It seemed perfectly natural. I knew he wasn't trying to take advantage of me, but simply offering a helping hand."

"Oh Katherine, I'm so happy for you. God is healing you."

"Yes. And for the first time, I feel worthy of it. Thanks to you."

"I'm glad. Now tell me about the twins. I missed their first hours. How did they respond to their mother?"

Katherine leaned beside him against the rock and told him about the first hours of life for the new foals. Kate was a good mother; she'd raised a foal before. Shelton knew she'd do well with the twins.

He wanted to ask Katherine how many children she would like to have one day, but reminded himself that he had promised to take their relationship slowly.

"Katherine, would you be willing to look over a piece of property with me tomorrow?"

"I have a lot of sewing to do."

He felt her wall of resistance spring up again. "That's fine. I just thought I'd ask."

They sat together for a while in silence. "Shelton, I'd like to go with you, but I'm afraid."

"Of what?"

"Of believing all this is possible."

As much as he wanted her to help pick out their future home, he understood her concerns. "I tell you what. I'll go ahead and purchase my ideal for a farm. . .one I can afford of course. And when we are ready to get married, you can ask for whatever revisions you'd like on the house. Is that fair?"

Katherine stared at the ground. "It's too much too soon," she whispered.

"True, and I said I wouldn't rush our relationship. All right. How about this? What if we set a time from when we become engaged to when we will marry. Let's say six months. . .or a year. . .whatever amount of time you feel comfortable with."

Katherine said nothing for nearly ten minutes. He prayed the entire time that she would open her heart to him.

Finally, she whispered, "I'm not being honest with you, Shelton."

Chapter 11

Katherine braced herself for anger. Hadn't the men in her past been angry with her when she spoke her mind? Instead, Shelton was patiently waiting for her to speak. She let out a pent-up breath. "I purchased some items for my dowry." She'd carefully wrapped the horse-pattern china dishes in a bundle of gingham cloth and slid them under her bed beside the linen tablecloth and matching napkins she'd made earlier. That's where her wedding dress would go, too, when she was done with it.

Shelton's smile lit up his face. "So you *are* hoping we'll get married one day."

"Yes," she confessed, and stepped back.

He didn't move. If his heart was anything like her own, he must want to kiss her. And he would, she knew, with the slightest encouragement from her. But she didn't trust herself, so she let the chilly night air separate them.

"I'm honored, Katherine. I see it as another sign of God's healing."

"Me, too."

"What did you purchase? If you don't mind my asking."

She felt the heat of embarrassment and looked down, not wanting him to see her flushed face. "May I keep it as a surprise for you?"

"I love surprises." Shelton chuckled.

Katherine looked up and faced him. "I have another confession."

"Try me."

"I. . ." She couldn't do it. *I want to tell him I love him, Lord, but. . .* Just buying the china for her dowry had taken huge amounts of courage. "I'm sorry. I can't."

"That's all right. When you're ready to tell me, I'll be here. What's your favorite color?"

"Where did that come from?"

"I just want to get to know you better."

Katherine laughed. "You're incorrigible."

"Yes, but you love that about me. Now, what is your favorite color?"

"I love a rich, vibrant green for clothing, but my favorite color for decorating would be light purples and pinks."

"Hmm. Pink is not my favorite. But purple I could live with. In moderation."

Katherine joined him back on the rock. "How do you feel about yellow and blue?"

"If it's a mild yellow, I'm fine with it. Bright yellow, like a canary, would be too overpowering. But the yellow of a daffodil could be nice."

"I agree."

"I think we'll find we have a lot in common. But we'll also find we have a lot of differences. I like differences. I like mating my horses with ones that complement each other."

"Like Kehoe and Kate?"

"Absolutely. Kehoe is fast, has good lines, and runs a race well. Kate is light on her feet and has a fire in her eyes when pushed. I hope the twins will inherit all of those qualities from their parents."

Katherine mulled over the seriousness with which he treated his horses, especially in choosing which ones to mate for the outcome of new stock. She realized he might feel the same way about his future wife and children. "Shelton, I don't come from good stock."

"Nonsense. Look at your brother; he's an honorable man. That same quality is in you. It has to be."

"No, you don't understand. Urias got that from the MacKenneths, not from our parents. I'm not like him at all. I'm self-centered. That's why I can't commit to you. I can't trust myself."

Shelton's chest rose, then slowly deflated. She'd noticed him doing this often before he spoke. "You've given your life to help others. You sacrifice your own wants for the sake of others all the time."

"Not really. I do things for people because they give me a roof over my head and food in my belly. I love them of course. But my first desire every day is for me. For my own place. My own freedom."

"Sounds normal to me."

She started to interrupt. He placed a finger on her lips. The gentle touch seared her heart.

"Let me explain. As much as I love my family and will do whatever I can to provide for them, my first thoughts are always for myself. It's how I respond to those thoughts that make me selfish or not. I'll wager, if you ask anyone our age—perhaps even a bit older—they would say the same thing. I don't know if our elders are beyond that. But I suspect most people are like that."

"Like what?"

"We feed, clothe, and take care of our bodies. Like the Bible tells us, no man hates his own body, but cares for it. We have to choose to put others first, before our own desires. Sure, I feel obligated to help my family. But I do it from my love for them and my love of God and my desire to serve Him. You, probably better than anyone else, understand what it means to be a servant, to obey without question. I struggle with that all the time. I have to fight off my desires and seek the Lord's desires every day."

Katherine didn't know what to say. She'd never liked the scripture verses about being God's servant, because servitude caused a bitter taste in her mouth. But did Shelton have a point? Did she respond to God in a different way because of her past? Was that a blessing? How could it be?

She gazed up at him. He waited patiently for her response. "Why do you always wait until I've processed what you're saying before speaking more to me?"

A slow smile rose on his face. "You're not going to like my answer."

Katherine braced herself.

"I've found that treating you like I would a skittish horse has been the most helpful approach."

Katherine frowned at him. "You're treating me like a horse?"

"Not exactly, but somewhat. However, I don't think putting reins on you would work." He chuckled at his own joke.

Katherine laughed with him. Then, with the intensity of a lightning bolt, a memory seared her mind. The image of her hands bound, ropes cutting into her wrists, holding her down. . . She shook her head slightly.

"Katherine, what's wrong?"

Her body trembled. She leaned into Shelton and let him envelop her in his love.

"It's all right, my dear, sweet Katherine. I'm here." His loving words massaged the mounting tension unleashed by the triggered memory.

%

He'd done it again, said something that sent her back to that dark place. "What happened just now?"

Her body shook. "There was a time when I was tied to the bed. . ."

As Katherine poured her heart out to him, he fought back anger at what had happened to her while relishing in the joy of realizing she finally trusted him enough to expose the horrible events of her past.

"I'm so sorry you went through that."

She sniffed. "Can you still. . ."

"Love you? How can you even ask? I love you even more."

She caressed his face. "You're such an amazing man, Shelton. I do care for you, deeply."

He wanted to tease her into admitting that she loved him. But now was not the time. Her emotions were raw and exhausted. She had exposed the darkest, deepest secrets of her life to him. "I love you, Katherine."

"I want to kiss you, Shelton, but I'm afraid."

"I want to kiss you, too. But we'll wait. Give yourself some time." He took her hand. "Can I pray for you?"

She nodded.

He closed his eyes. "Father, fill Katherine with Your cleansing blood and peace. Protect her mind from the memories of the past; strengthen her to walk in Your strength and grace. Thank You for the healing You've done so far in her life. Thank You for allowing me to be a part of it. Bless us as we move forward in our relationship, and may it be founded in You." He opened his eyes and gazed at her. "God's been moving in a mighty big way today, Katherine."

"I know. It's terrifying."

"I have to admit, I would love to get my hands on those men who hurt you and do some serious bodily harm to them. But I know that's not what the Lord would have me do."

She cocked her head sideways. "Why?"

"Why would I like to harm them, or why is that not what the Lord would have me do?"

"Both, I guess." She nestled into the crook of his arm.

A whiff of her freshly washed hair caught in his nostrils, calming his raw nerves. "If I were to beat the stuffings out of them, they would have a momentary pain, but they'd heal quickly from it. While it would make me feel better, it wouldn't change them. But God's Word tells us of His vengeance against those who hurt His people. That vengeance would make your attackers realize the profound effect their actions had on you, and on others they've treated so horrendously." He still wanted to pulverize them, but he kept that piece of knowledge to himself. That was a part of him she didn't need to see.

The sound of a gun firing made them both jump.

"That was close," she said.

"Too close," he agreed. "Mac," he called out in the dark. "Urias!"

Hearing nothing, Shelton lifted his rifle and scanned the area. Nothing stirred. "I'm going to walk you to Grandma Mac's house. Stay inside. I'll come back when I know what's going on."

"All right," she whispered.

He crept slowly through the dark, conscious of every movement and sound. They reached Mrs. MacKenneth's house in ten minutes.

Back at Urias's place, he scanned the perimeter of each house and pen but found no disturbance.

Urias appeared out of the dark. "We got him!" he announced. "Mac's hanging him on a tree to make him ready for eating. Have you ever had bear meat, Shelton?"

"Can't say that I have."

"It's good, but the gristle can break your teeth."

Bear meat and gristle were the furthest thoughts from his mind. "I need to go tell Katherine everything is okay."

Urias narrowed his gaze. "Are you and she. . ."

"She's safe with me, Urias. I love her, and I'll take care of her."

"She's been through a lot. I don't want you to hurt her. If you're not serious, I suggest you back away now."

"I'm very serious, and I will be patient and wait on her. Tonight she told me everything that happened to her."

"She told you?" Urias leaned on his rifle. "She's never even told me."

"You don't want to know. I don't want to know. But it had to get out in the open between us for our relationship to go forward."

Urias stood up straight and grabbed Shelton's shoulder. "You'll give me your word you'll be honorable to her?"

"Yes sir."

"Then you have my blessing."

"Thank you."

Urias left without saying another word.

When Shelton reached Mrs. MacKenneth's porch, he took the steps two at a time and knocked on the door. Katherine opened it right away.

"They shot the bear. Everyone is safe."

"Am I?" Her voice trembled.

"Your secret is safe with me, Katherine. And we don't need to talk about it again. . .unless you want to. I will keep praying for you and for God's healing to continue. Just remember, you are free and clean from all that has happened to you because of God's grace and the sacrifice His Son made for you and me on the cross."

"I know. It's just hard to accept sometimes."

"Yes, it is." *Someday I'll tell you about my life journey. And hopefully you'll forgive me the way God has.*

Katherine read Shelton's note for the fifth time. It said he'd purchased the land he'd mentioned to her two days before. He also wrote that he had gone back to Hazel Green to talk with his parents, with all indications that he would be telling them about his new relationship with Katherine.

She felt betrayed. She'd opened her heart to him about her past and he had run off. Each day he was gone she tried to convince herself that he hadn't run away, that he was doing as he always said he would do—preparing a place for his parents. But old fears continued to plague her.

He'd been gone ten days before she received another letter from him.

My dear, sweet Katherine,

I love you and miss you terribly. I'm packing up my parents' house for their move to Jamestown. I had to let the last servant go, but I secured work for him with the Rawlins family over in Mount Sterling.

I'd hoped my parents would come on their own so that I'd be able to quickly return to you. However, the situation has become unbearable for Mother, and they wish to return with me. I will be back as soon as possible.

I hate to ask, but I need a favor from you. I'm wondering if you can have Urias and some of the others help clean the old farmhouse on my new property. Mac and Urias know where it is. You are familiar with my mother's tastes. If you could oversee the painting and curtains for the larger bedroom, I'd appreciate it. I know I'm asking a lot from you, but you're the only one I trust to do right for them.

Yours forever,
Shelton

Katherine read the letter three times before running to Urias and asking him to take her to Shelton's new house.

She and Urias's family did a thorough inspection of the place. Urias found some structural issues that required immediate attention.

The farmhouse was in such disrepair Katherine wondered if Shelton had ever seen it in the daylight. For the next three days, the MacKenneths, the O'Learys, and other neighbors cleaned, painted, and fixed the interior of the house. Urias said they'd have to wait until spring to paint the exterior.

Katherine made curtains for the larger bedroom, living room, dining area, and kitchen. Prudence washed the kitchen, scrubbing through layers of soot until she could see the yellowed wood of the knotty pine cabinets and the cast iron of the stove gleamed black. Pamela scrubbed the walls and floors. The men repaired trim, doors, windows, and a serious problem with the center beam of the foundation. Then they cleared the drive from the road to the house.

Katherine wondered why Shelton had purchased this place. Until she saw the view from the second-story bedroom window. Spread out before her was a clear view of the Cumberland River at one of its widest points. It was so expansive she could have mistaken it for a lake.

She peeled off the bedroom's wallpaper and applied a fresh coat of paint. If the bed were positioned against the wall opposite the window, one could look out over the river. She'd love to wake up to that view every morning. But Shelton had said this room was for his parents. He was giving them the best view in the house. Katherine remembered Shelton's determination to honor them. He certainly was doing it now. If she and Shelton were to marry, she would have to honor them as well. She wondered if she could do it.

From her own savings, Katherine had purchased fabric for the curtains and pillowcases for the bed. There was enough to reupholster the chair and ottoman. . .if Mrs. Greene would like.

At the end of the first week, the house seemed habitable. Everyone went back to their daily responsibilities. . .except Katherine. She wanted to make the house as fit for Shelton and his parents as she could.

In her heart she knew that, even if the Greenes could never see her as anything other than a bond servant, she should love them in the same way Shelton did. From everything he'd said, that would at times be a choice, not a feeling.

She tried not to think about what it would be like to have the Greenes living so close. There were plenty of other issues to deal with. Perhaps the fact that the house was in such disrepair was a good thing. It made her concentrate on work rather than on foolishly meandering through the past.

She had no idea what items of furniture his parents would be able to bring along. Would Shelton restrict them to a single wagonload?

Katherine stood on a stool to hang the last of the curtains in the front sitting room. She spotted Shelton with a wagon full of furniture coming toward the house. He was alone.

She jumped off the stool, raced out of the house, and ran across the field to greet him. "Shelton!" she called, waving as she ran.

He pulled up a few yards from the house and stared at her. "Katherine, you're a sight for sore eyes." He nodded at the house. "Please don't tell me you're still working on the place."

"You don't know the half of it."

"I'm afraid I do." He hopped to the ground and dusted off his trousers. "Where are your parents?"

"I dropped them off at Prudence's house so I could unload some of their furniture first. Mac told me how bad the house was. I'm sorry. If I'd known it was that bad, I wouldn't have asked you to help fix it up."

"Nonsense. I saw the view from the larger bedroom. I would have wanted the house, too."

Shelton's blue eyes danced with merriment. He brushed away a curl that dangled over her right eye. "I've missed you so much."

"I've missed you, too."

She reached for his hand. "Come, let me show you what we've done."

He held her hand and gave it a quick squeeze.

Chapter 12

Shelton couldn't believe the transformation of the house. He held Katherine's hand and caressed the top of it with his thumb as they looked out over the river from the bedroom. The sun sparkled on the little ripples of water. It was a splendid sight, even more enchanting than when he viewed it a few weeks ago.

"Katherine, this room is marvelous. I can't believe you did all this. Mother will be thrilled."

"I saved some fabric to cover her chair and ottoman. Were you able to bring them?"

"I did. We have two wagons full of furniture and other belongings. Father drove one wagon, and I drove the other." *And hidden deep in my wagon is the family heirloom I hope to give you one day.* He prayed the precious family heirloom, a china vase, hadn't broken during the trip.

"Was it difficult for them to leave their home?"

"It was horrible. Apparently news traveled fast about Father's financial situation, and the reason for it. Mother said none of her friends would even speak with her."

"I'm so sorry."

"Father has lost his will to go on. I don't know how to reach him. I'm praying this new house will be just what he needs to get back on his feet."

"I hope so."

"I managed to sell the house rather than have the bank acquire it. That produced some much-needed funds. And we earned a profit from the coal mines. I sold that land but retained the mineral rights, so we'll receive a percentage of the profit—if the mine makes a profit. It will give my parents a small income each year."

"You're a wise businessman, Shelton. I'm so proud of you."

He beamed at her praise. "So, what do you think of the place?"

"I haven't looked over the land, but the house will be wonderful once it's done. Urias said we have to wait until spring to paint the exterior."

"I hope my parents come visit the place in the dark first. Then they'll see the exterior after they've seen what everyone has done on the inside. Still, it won't be like their old home. I hope they can adjust to it."

She nodded.

"Do you think you can adjust to them?"

Her smooth forehead crinkled. "I've tried to honor your parents the way you do, simply for being your parents. But it's hard."

"I'm just pleased that you've tried. You're an incredible woman, Katherine. I can't believe you did all this for them. Urias and Prudence told me you did all the work in their room. I wish this room was ours."

A slight smile creased her lips. "I do, too. But they deserve a room like this for their sanctuary."

"And you've made it into one. Thank you."

"Come." She took him by the hand. "Let me show you your room."

"My room?"

"Well, the room I thought you might enjoy as yours."

"Lead on." He marveled at the softness of her hand. Soft but sturdy, hard-working hands, unlike his own. Then again, he reflected, his hands were not the same as when he left home months ago.

She gripped his fingers a bit more tightly as she led him inside the room. She had decorated it in masculine earth tones. A painting of a horse hung on the wall. She had placed a rustic bouquet of dried autumn flowers on the nightstand. A dark green spread draped over the bed.

"Where did you get this?"

"I splurged and purchased the fabric. It's only a cover. I didn't have time to make an actual quilt, but I thought this would do."

"It's beautiful. Thank you."

"You're welcome."

"Katherine, it's too much. Let me pay you for your time."

She stiffened and released his hand.

"I'm sorry. I didn't mean to offend you. It's just that I know you've been saving for—"

She placed a finger to his lips. In spite of his firm resolve, he gave in to the powerful desire and gave her finger a light kiss.

Her breathing became ragged. "Shelton, I. . .I. . ." She pulled away.

"I'm sorry. I promise not to kiss you again until you ask me to."

"You don't understand. I want to so much, I ache. But I don't think. . .I mean. . ."

"You're worried you'll cross the line from a chaste kiss to the kind of passionate kiss reserved for marriage?"

"Yes."

"I understand, and I respect that. I'll wait until you're ready. Until we're both ready."

"I feel horrible about this. I know what God designed. It's just that. . ."

"Shh." He placed his finger to her lips. "It's all right. I know. And God will give us the strength to deal with the wait."

"I don't deserve you." Katherine turned away from him and held her sides.

"No, Katherine, you deserve better than me. But I'm confident of God's desire for us to become one someday. We will get past this."

He glanced around the room one more time. "Let's unpack before my parents arrive."

"Too late," Hiram Greene announced from the hallway. "Which room is ours?"

Shelton walked out to the hallway. "That one." He pointed to the doorway on the opposite end of the hall.

Hiram nodded and bent to pick up a heavy-looking wood crate. Shelton helped him carry it into the bedroom.

"Oh my," Elizabeth Greene crooned as she entered the room. "Shelton, this is beautiful."

"You can thank Katherine for that."

"You mean Kate?"

"She prefers to be called Katherine, Mother."

"I didn't know that. I'll try to remember. Where is she?"

"I'm right here, ma'am." She hovered in the doorway, her face pale.

"You did an exquisite job. But won't you and Shelton want this room for yourselves?"

Katherine glanced at Shelton.

He shrugged. "I told them we hoped to get married in the future."

"Oh." Katherine cleared her throat. "Shelton and I felt this room would be a good place for the two of you. There's a great view of the river."

"Are you sure, son?" Hiram asked.

"Yes sir. This is your room. Katherine did everything you see here."

"Thank you," he mumbled.

Shelton's stomach tightened as his father looked at the floor.

"There are fresh linens and pillows in the closet," Katherine said. "When the men get your bed put together, I'll be happy to make it up for you."

Elizabeth Greene smiled. "Nonsense, you've done enough."

❧

Katherine didn't know what to think. These people were a faded image of who they once were. Her heart went out to them in a way she'd never dreamed possible. She took Shelton's hand. "Come and help me."

He followed her down the stairs and out the door.

"Shelton, what's happened to them?"

"This move has been very hard on them."

"They're definitely not the same people."

"No, they're not. But I'm worried. Father doesn't seem to have much of a will to live. I know he disapproves of our union, but he doesn't have the strength to fight me on it. If he starts feeling better soon, I imagine we'll exchange a few words on the subject."

Katherine let out a pent-up gasp of air. "I'll be praying for him." A part of her liked that Mr. Greene was not acting boisterous and arguing. But another part understood that something was wrong.

"Hopefully one day he'll regain his strength *and* approve of our marriage."

Katherine chuckled. "Did anyone ever tell you you're an optimist?"

"Yes. My father. You two are quite alike sometimes."

Katherine bristled at the comparison, but then realized that maybe Shelton was right. She had very strong opinions, although most people didn't know it. If anyone did, it was Shelton.

He pointed out the living room window. "Here come Urias and Mac with the rest of the furniture."

Katherine pretty much stayed out of the way while the men moved in the various pieces. So many treasured items from the house in Hazel Green had not been packed. Katherine hated to think about all that the Greenes had lost. Items she had spent hours dusting, cleaning, arranging. Possessions that set their home apart from all others in the area. She particularly remembered the old china vase that had belonged to Hiram's great-grandfather, who used to captain ships around the world. Katherine wondered who now owned all those things, did they cherish them as much as Mrs. Greene once had?

It didn't matter. Now was the time to rebuild. With God's help, and with Shelton's, perhaps one day the Greenes would live a gay life again.

❧

Katherine spent the next day helping Grandma Mac. Her house had been neglected since Katherine had taken on the project of fixing up Shelton's home.

"It's such a shame." Grandma Mac rocked back and forth in her rocker. "But at least the Greenes have their health, and they're back with family. With God's grace, they'll get through this change in their lives."

"I hope so."

"I hear you did some mighty fancy work in that house. Tell me about it."

Katherine went into great detail about all the remodeling and sewing she'd done for the place.

"My, my. Have you been able to fill your orders for Mr. Hastings as well?"

"Not yet. I have to make one more shirt tonight. Then I can take everything in tomorrow morning. I have to purchase more needles with my next order. The ones I've been using are getting worn down."

"I don't doubt it. Now tell me, have you and Shelton kissed yet?"

"You're far too preoccupied with other people's romances."

"True. But I sense you and Shelton have grown closer."

"Yes, we have. But no kisses yet. Although he did kiss my finger. Does that count?"

Grandma Mac laughed out loud. "It's a start. I think that boy has spent too much time with his horses."

Katherine chuckled. *I wonder if she knows how very much I wanted to kiss him.*

૨૦

Shelton spent the first month after his parents' arrival getting the new barn ready for Kehoe and Kate. Katherine helped build a fence for the corral, but other than that, they spent precious little time with each other. He ached to talk with her. While he was certain she wanted to be with him, he had to help his parents adjust to their new living environment.

Tonight would be different. He planned to spend the evening with Katherine and Grandma Mac.

Shelton cleaned up from his work, dressed in his Sunday-morning trousers, and put on a crisp white shirt with a black bow tie. He opted to leave the suit coat at home and wear instead the warmer leather jacket Prudence and Urias had given him. The first snowfall of the year had provided a light dusting on the ground. The air would be crisp come evening.

As he ran a comb through his unruly hair, he thought about the twins. They were doing well, their bushy winter coats growing in nicely. He'd purchased a half dozen chickens and a piglet to raise over the winter. Urias and Mac had provided fresh meat and winter vegetables for the new household.

His father seemed to gain strength every day, but he still lacked focus and purpose. His mother was blissfully happy with her grandchildren nearby. Katherine's infrequent appearances to his home concerned him. She told him on many occasions she had no purpose being there, and she had chores and obligations elsewhere. He prayed that was true, but in his heart he knew she was avoiding his parents. This, like everything else, would take time.

"My, you're looking handsome this afternoon," his mother said when he joined her in the living room.

"Thank you."

"How's Kate?"

"Katherine," he corrected.

"Forgive me. She answered to Kate for so many years, it's hard to remember."

Didn't she realize that was the reason Katherine preferred her proper name?

"Do you know where your father is?"

"He said he was going to Creelsboro today to look for work."

"Oh, that's right. Well, I'm visiting with Prudence and the children this evening. We're going to make Christmas gifts after the children go to bed."

"Would you like me to pick you up after my dinner with Katherine and Mrs. MacKenneth?"

"That would be lovely, dear. Thank you."

Shelton bid his mother good-bye and headed off to Mrs. MacKenneth's. He'd been contemplating for days what to get Katherine for Christmas. He wanted just the right gift, but kept coming up blank.

He arrived fifteen minutes early and settled Kehoe in the barn for the evening.

"Hi there, handsome." Katherine's green eyes sparkled.

Shelton's heart pounded. "Hi, beautiful. You look real good." A rich evergreen dress cascaded down her body, accenting her feminine form. A white lace collar framed her glorious face.

"Grandma Mac sent me out to fetch you. Frankly, the old woman is a matchmaker above all matchmakers. But I like having the chance to be alone with you for a few moments."

Shelton cherished her acknowledgment. How long had it taken her to come to that point? *Thank You, Lord.* "I'm glad we have a few minutes alone, too."

She reached out and he took her hand. She pulled him closer. "Shelton," she whispered, "I want to kiss you."

He fought off the desire to swoop her up in his arms and kiss her with all the passion he had for her. "Are you sure?"

"Yes. But we must promise each other not to let our desires run away from our self-control."

"I promise." He gently caressed her face. His fingers tingled from the closeness.

She closed her eyes.

He brushed her lips with his thumb. "You're sure?" he asked in a whisper.

Her eyes sprung open. "If you don't kiss me now, I won't be able to kiss you for a very long time."

He could see the fire of passion in her eyes. *Lord, give me strength.* He moved in slowly. "I love you, Katherine." He placed a slow, soft kiss on her lips. She relaxed and returned the kiss. Her hands ruffled through his hair.

Shelton pulled back and counted to ten in an attempt to gain self-control. It wasn't working.

Katherine leaned into him. Shelton kissed her neck. "I have to stop, Katherine."

She pulled away, her eyes wide and glistening.

He held her in a gentle embrace. "I will always cherish our first kiss."

Her lips curled upward. "Me, too."

Shelton chuckled and stepped out of the embrace. "You're right. We have to keep the promise not to give in to our desires."

"That will be difficult."

She has no idea. Or perhaps she did. Either way, he knew that her kiss sent a spark of desire through him that was so strong it would take all of his willpower to remain an honorable man.

And he still hadn't told her about his past yet.

Chapter 13

Two weeks and ten kisses later, Katherine felt like she could handle her emotions when she was with Shelton. He'd been the strong one, and she was grateful for it.

On her way into Creelsboro, she couldn't stop thinking about him. Day and night, he was always on her mind. Grandma Mac had told her the best way to handle those kinds of thoughts were to turn them into prayers for Shelton, for the Lord to bless him and strengthen him. She'd prayed the entire two hours to Creelsboro.

"Good morning, Mr. Hastings." The scent of oiled leather filled the store. Every time Katherine entered the place it had a different smell. It all depended on what new merchandise had come in.

"Good morning, Miss O'Leary. Have you got my order?"

"Yes sir. I also made a couple of dolls. With Christmas coming, I thought you might be able to sell them."

"I'm sure I can. But I probably won't be needin' any more clothing until spring. There aren't many folks traveling west this time of year."

"I understand."

"I'll send word to you once I need more." He scribbled a few notations in his ledger book, then walked to the cash register. "Have you and Shelton set a date yet?"

"Not yet. He wants his parents to settle in first."

The cash drawer opened and he pulled out a piece of paper. "Would you give this to Shelton?" The store owner handed her a slip of paper. "His father's been charging, and he's run up quite a bill."

Katherine clamped her mouth shut. Hiram didn't have a job and was living off his son's income. What could he be purchasing? It wasn't her place to ask. "I'll be happy to." She took the paper and slipped it into her purse.

She glanced over the housewares section of the store. "Where's the tea set?"

"Sold it last week."

Katherine's heart sank. She'd been saving for a month to purchase the

350

service. It was a full set, with teapot, sugar bowl, creamer, and a silver serving tray, rare in these parts.

"Forgive me, Katherine. I didn't realize you wanted it."

"That's all right. I'll just get some more linen to make a tablecloth and matching napkins for Prudence's Christmas present." She had plenty of time to sew now that she'd finished making her wedding dress. The task had seemed presumptuous since they weren't officially engaged yet. But Shelton had promised they would marry one day, and she believed him.

She moved to the leatherworks section. Shelton would love a new bit and brace for Kehoe. "How much are these?"

They settled on a fair price and she put off the linens for another time. Next, she purchased some flannel to make undergarments for the family for Christmas. It was a practical gift; she knew how thin those undergarments would get before a new set was made.

Her money spent, she loaded her packs and headed for her horse.

A ruckus down the street caught her attention. Katherine looked over her shoulder and saw a drunk being kicked out of the saloon. She didn't see such a sight often, but knew all too well the evils of drink.

The drunk landed face down in the mud of the street.

"And stay out!" she heard the barkeeper yell. Inside, a roar of laughter followed.

Katherine shook her head and prayed the man's family could help him.

She mounted her horse. The way home went past the saloon. When she passed the drunk, he lifted himself out of the mud.

"Oh no."

☙

Shelton handed his Christmas gift for Katherine to his mother, asking her to polish it to perfection. He'd found the silver tea tray in the mercantile, and Mr. Hastings had told him that Katherine had her eye on it for weeks. The store owner had conducted a healthy bartering session. Finally Shelton agreed to sell him some of his grain harvest next year, provided he had a surplus. Not being a farmer, he had no idea how well his crops would grow.

He sat at the kitchen table while his mother examined the silver set. "This is very nice, Shelton. Katherine will love it."

"I hope so." Shelton shifted in his seat, then mustered up the most casual voice he could. "Have you seen Father?"

"Not since this morning. He said he had some business in town."

This was getting to be a habit. His father had been going to Creelsboro every day for weeks, but he hadn't come back with a job or any legitimate-sounding explanation of what he'd been doing there. One time Shelton smelled alcohol on his father's breath, but Hiram passed it off as having brushed up against a man with an open flask. Back in Hazel Green his father would have an occasional drink. But as far as Shelton knew, he drank in moderation and only during social visits.

Concerned that his father might be gambling again, he rode Kehoe to Creelsboro.

Near town, he saw a horse with a sickly looking rider on it. A woman walked beside the horse. With a start, he recognized her face. "Katherine?"

"Shelton! Thank God you're here."

He got a good look at the man bent over the saddle horn. "Father?"

"He was kicked out of the saloon," Katherine explained. "I'm afraid he's not doing well."

Shelton dismounted. He came up beside Katherine's horse and took the reins. "Father, are you all right?"

Hiram leaned off the other side of the horse and vomited.

"Do you know what happened?" he asked Katherine.

"His breath reeks of liquor. But my mother didn't get this sick when she drank. Is he used to alcohol?"

"I've never known him to be a heavy drinker."

"Don't be talkin' 'bout me as if I wasn't here," Hiram scolded, his words slurred.

"What happened, Father?"

"I got drunk."

Shelton shared a look of frustration with Katherine.

"You still plannin' on marryin' that tramp?" Hiram sneered.

"You will not speak of Katherine that way."

"I ain't talkin' 'bout her. I mean the other one." Hiram started to slide off the saddle.

Shelton caught his father and looked at Katherine, who was staring back at him, a huge question in her green eyes. "Later," he told her.

He could see her nostrils flare.

"Ride Kehoe to my house and tell Mother I'll be back as soon as I can."

She nodded, mounted his horse, and left without saying a word.

He knew he should have told her sooner. Now his father had spilled his past in a drunken stupor. He walked beside the horse, steadying Hiram on the saddle.

After a couple of hours, his father's words were less slurred, and he began to make sense.

"What happened, Dad?"

"I can't say."

Shelton balled his fists and slowly released them. "Have you been gambling again?"

Hiram nodded.

"Wonderful. I move you to a new place to make a clean start, and this is the thanks I get? How many people do you owe now?"

"I'll take care of my affairs, son. You can mind your own business."

"You can't take care of anything. How are you planning to pay your debts?"

Hiram coughed, then vomited again.

"Mother's going to love seeing you like this," Shelton quipped.

"Don't tell her."

"There's no way to keep this from her."

"I beg you, please don't tell your mother. She'll leave me for sure. You don't know how bad things were in Hazel Green. How bad they still are between us. She hardly speaks to me. Please, you can't tell her."

"Dad, it isn't a question of my telling her. You need to be honest with your wife. About your insecurities, your failures, everything."

"Like you've been with that wench." Hiram spat.

"Don't you ever speak about her like that again. Or so help me, I'll. . ."

"You ain't got the guts."

Shelton curled his fingers into a fist.

"Go ahead, hit me. I dare you."

Shelton relaxed his hand. "No. I won't hit a man when he's down. You have a decision to make, Dad. Either you change or I'm kicking you out of my house."

"You can't do that!"

"Can't I? You're living on my land, Dad. My property. You have nothing left."

"You can't treat me like a child. I'm your father." Hiram slurred.

"You have three days to make your decision, Dad."

They traveled the rest of the way in silence.

Shelton helped his father down from the horse. Hiram wobbled a couple of steps, then fell to the ground.

"Shelton!" his mother shrieked as she ran to them from the porch. "What happened?"

"He has a serious problem, Mom. And it goes beyond gambling. I gave him three days to make a decision to change. If he doesn't, I'm kicking him out. You can stay if you want."

Shelton mounted Katherine's horse and headed to Grandma Mac's house.

a

Katherine paced in her room. Hiram Greene's comment made her question everything Shelton had ever said to her. Apparently, he wanted to marry someone else. Katherine held her sides and tried to brace herself for the truth.

Was Hiram confused because he was drunk? Did she look so different that he was thinking of her in the past? Maybe that was it.

She wouldn't know until she spoke with Shelton. She didn't want to confront the situation, but knew she had to.

She went to the kitchen to prepare for the evening meal. She found Grandma Mac there, putting on her heavy winter coat.

"I'll be spending the evening with Mac and Pamela," the older woman said. "Nash Jr. is coming to fetch me." Nash Jr. was the oldest of Pamela and Mac's children. At nine years of age, he was so proud to be old enough to drive the wagon by himself, he offered rides to anyone who wanted them.

Katherine took down a couple of the canned foods Grandma Mac had prepared earlier in the year. Her hand trembled and one of the jars crashed to the counter.

"Are you all right, dear?"

"I'm fine."

Grandma Mac snickered. "If you're fine, I'd hate to see what wonderful is like."

"I'll be okay. I just have to calm down."

"From what?"

Nash Jr. knocked on the door and came right in. "Hi, Grandma, I'm here." He gave Katherine a slight bow. "Evenin', Miss O'Leary."

"Evenin', Master Nash." Katherine tilted her head slightly to the side and smiled. "Have a good night tonight. And don't beat your Grandma too badly in checkers."

Nash Jr. chuckled. "Grandma doesn't allow me to win anymore. I have to win on my own now."

"You're too smart," Grandma Mac chimed in. "You win about half the time. Next year I won't be able to play with you at all."

Grandma Mac and Nash said their good-byes and left her alone. She had craved solitude for so long, yet now that she had it, she wasn't sure she liked it. She'd prefer to have someone in the house with her. It seemed more comfortable. "What's wrong with me, Lord? I beg for my own place, and now I can't stand being alone. Will I ever be normal?"

All in good time, a gentle whisper spoke inside her head.

She wondered how Shelton was dealing with his father. *Will there ever come a day when his parents aren't his first priority? When I am?*

The door rattled in its jamb as a knock resounded through the house. "Who is it?"

"Shelton. May I come in?"

She opened the door. He looked weary, beaten.

He stomped the dirt off his boots and came inside. "I'm sorry you found my father in such a state."

"I'm glad I was there to take him home. Did he tell you what happened?"

"Not in words, but I'm certain he was gambling. Probably lost a lot of money he didn't have and then drank too much." Shelton took off his coat and sat on the sofa.

Katherine sat across from him in the rocking chair.

"Katherine, we need to talk about what my father said."

She began to shake. She didn't want to believe it was true. She couldn't speak, so she gave a simple nod for him to continue.

He swallowed. "I've tried to tell you this a few times, but never found the right opportunity. Forgive me."

She nodded again.

"When my father sent me away at sixteen, I was very angry. While I was away from home, I took advantage of a young lady. She conceived."

Katherine squeezed her eyes closed. *No, this can't be. Not Shelton. He's a gentleman.*

"Father offered her family money to go away. They were so upset, they refused to listen to him or me. I was banned from ever seeing her again."

Bile rose in her throat. Her head was telling her this wasn't the man she wanted to marry. Her heart felt like it was tearing apart.

"A while later, I heard she lost the baby."

Tears edged her eyelids.

"I offered to marry her, but her family refused. So I snuck into her house one night, planning to take her to a preacher. The family found me and beat me. Someone pulled a knife—" He pulled up his shirt and pointed to a large scar under his right arm.

Her heart tightened. She wanted to reach out and touch him. She laced her fingers together, keeping her hands folded in her lap.

"Why didn't you tell me about this sooner?"

"I tried to. But I was afraid if you knew I'd been less than honorable in the past, you wouldn't trust me."

"You're right. I wouldn't have trusted you." Sadness and anger swirled in her mind. This had to be a bad dream. "Did you love her?"

"No. That's even more shameful. I used her. I'm not worthy of your love, Katherine. I've told you that before, but I don't think you believed me. Now you know."

"What else have you not told me?" She rocked back to get a better look at his face.

"Nothing. Well, I'm sure there are moments when I must have done other wrong things, but nothing so serious."

After all this time thinking he was so perfect, hearing this about him sent myriad emotions coursing through her heart, all vying for supremacy. Anger quickly won. "I felt so dirty compared to you."

Shelton hung his head. "I know. I'm sorry. You were innocent of what happened to you. I was the guilty person. But I also know of God's redemptive power. He has forgiven me for my actions." Shelton knelt before her. "Can you?"

She closed her eyes. Could she forgive him? Could she trust him? *If he lied about this. . . Well, he didn't actually lie, he just omitted this part of his past. But can I believe that there isn't more to tell?* "I don't know."

Shelton's hands shook. He stood, stared at her for a moment, then left the house in silence.

Katherine's heart broke and she wept. The man she loved was not the man she thought he was.

Chapter 14

Shelton split more logs than he had use for. Katherine had not spoken to him for three days. Today was the deadline for his father to decide if he was going to change his ways or pack his bags. Shelton found himself not caring what his father decided. Nothing mattered if Katherine wasn't going to be a part of his life.

"Shelton?" his mother called from the back door of the kitchen.

"Be right there." He swung the axe into the block and left it there. He grabbed his coat and walked back to the house.

Inside he found his mother and father sitting at the table. Parson Kincaid sat next to them. "Parson." Shelton extended his hand. "What can I do for you?"

"I'm here at your parents' request."

Shelton took a seat.

"Shel," his mother said, "your father and I want to stay."

Shelton stared at his dad. "He knows my conditions."

Hiram kept his gaze away from Shelton.

"That's why I'm here," Parson Kincaid offered. "Your father has told me he is willing to change. But he didn't think you'd believe him."

"He has a tongue. He can speak for himself." Shelton continued to stare at his father.

"And who made you lord and master?" Hiram growled. Squinting his right eye, he glared at Shelton. "You're not perfect yourself."

"And thanks to you, Katherine knows all about it. I was going to tell her at the right opportunity. She didn't deserve to hear it from a drunk."

"What on earth are you two talking about?" his mother cried.

Shelton inhaled deeply and counted to ten before exhaling. "I'm sorry, Mother. But when I was sixteen and Father sent me away, I took advantage of a young lady. Father tried to pay the family off. They didn't appreciate the offer. They refused to even let me talk with her and wanted me to have nothing to do with the baby."

Elizabeth Greene's eyes widened. "I have a grandchild I don't know about?" she whispered.

"No. I received word that she lost the baby. I've repented and God has been gracious to me ever since."

"And your pious attitude has been destroying this family," Hiram accused.

"Hiram," the parson said, "do you really blame Shelton for your gambling problem?"

Hiram coughed. "No."

"But you don't like your son telling you what to do, right?"

"Precisely."

"Parson," Shelton said, "I've heard his vows to change before. I've been dealing with this problem for nearly a year now. I don't trust his word."

The parson turned toward Hiram. "What do you have to say about this?"

He pushed the chair back and stood. "I'll be moved out in an hour."

"Hiram," Elizabeth cried. She turned to her son and the parson. "Could you give us some privacy, please?"

They left the room and stood out on the porch.

"You're forcing your father to make some hard choices," Parson Kincaid said.

"I know. But I don't think he'll change if I keep providing for him and bailing him out of all the jams he gets into."

"You mean like he did for you when you were younger?"

Shelton thought back on that time. His father had tried to help. It wasn't the right kind of help, but at least he did try. "Every time he tried to step in, he made the wrong choice. Money doesn't solve all our problems. It's the heart that matters."

"And has your heart hardened toward your father?"

"No, Parson. I still love him. That's why it hurts so much to see him like this."

"Has anyone threatened to have him arrested for his debts?" Parson Kincaid asked.

Shelton sat on the rail. "Not here. But back in Hazel Green he would have gone to jail if not for me. I took care of things for him. But I see now that didn't really help. Perhaps I made things worse for him. I don't know. I just know that I'm not doing him any favors by letting him live here for free."

"Then may I suggest another alternative?"

"What do you have in mind, Parson?"

❧

Katherine felt miserable. She couldn't imagine life without Shelton. But now she knew she couldn't trust him. In her mind she'd gone over what Shelton said again and again, but couldn't get away from the fact that he should have told her sooner. His confession now led her to be suspicious of him. If she hadn't heard the words of his father, would he have ever told her?

"Lord, this is nonsense," she moaned.

"You got that right." Grandma Mac had a way of sneaking up on a person. "Tell me, child, what happened the other night?"

Katherine took in a shaky breath. "Shelton has a past."

"Don't we all?" Grandma Mac sat down on a nearby rocking chair.

Katherine continued to press the pleats of the outfit she'd made for Elizabeth Katherine for Christmas. "Hiram Greene is a beast."

"What did he do?"

"He's a horrible drunk."

"That isn't so extreme."

Katherine put down the iron and took the little dress off the board. She folded it neatly and set it aside. She wasn't nearly as mad at Hiram Greene as she was with Shelton. "Shelton had an. . .indiscretion."

"What did he do? When?"

"When he was sixteen."

"I see. And that makes you feel, what? Foolish because you felt so sinful compared to him?"

"Yes." Foolish. Betrayed. Katherine had so many emotions swimming around in her heart she couldn't trust her own thoughts, much less her words or actions.

"Tell me, my dear, before you became comfortable with Shelton, didn't you think of yourself as being more sinful than most people?"

"Well, yes."

"So Shelton becoming a part of your life had nothing to do with how you felt about yourself."

"His presence made it worse. . .at first."

"Did it? Or did it simply force you to deal with unresolved hurts, pains, and matters of trust between you and the Lord?"

Katherine thought for a moment. She had to admit, her relationship with Shelton had helped bring her to a place of genuine healing.

"It seems to me that you've been unable to trust for a long time. You've held on to the bondage of past sins rather than go through the painful process of letting go and letting God free you. When Shelton came along, you forced yourself to face those painful memories and give them over to the Lord once and for all. Am I right?"

Katherine groaned. Did Grandma Mac have an ear horn against the door every time she poured her heart out to the Lord? "I don't like it when you're right."

Grandma Mac gave a hearty laugh. "You mean when God's right. Child, I'm an old woman. I've seen a lot of things in my life. Age and experience have given me a perspective that's more straightforward than I had when I was younger. Oh, I made mistakes when I was young, and I've had to battle with my emotions until I completely surrendered them to the Lord. After I did, I wondered why I took so long to do it. Foolish pride, I guess. Only the good Lord knows. But our God is a God of action and change. He's forever moving, and He wants us to move forward in our lives. You've broken through the bondage of the past. The question is, are you going to forgive and move forward into the relationship God has designed for you?"

Had God really designed Shelton for her? Were they meant to have a life together? A couple of weeks ago she wouldn't have questioned it. Did it really matter that Shelton did something he was ashamed of, that he repented of? "You don't mince words, do you?"

"I'm glad it hurts, dear. Giving up our ability to retreat and lick our wounds always hurts. We must allow God to dig deeper and help us rid ourselves of all the memories that will fester and become ugly unless the Lord lances our wounds. Think about it, pray about it. But most important, do what is right and holy in God's eyes. . .not yours, mine, Hiram's, or Shelton's."

She didn't want to admit it, but Grandma Mac made sense. If she gave in to all her anger and embarrassment, she would be right back where she'd started.

Grandma Mac stood and patted her shoulder. Then she shuffled out of the room without saying another word.

Katherine went back to ironing her Christmas presents. Working with her hands seemed better than dealing with the words Grandma Mac had just spoken. But she couldn't stop thinking about them. She replayed the conversation over and over. Then she remembered Shelton saying that one day he would tell her about his past and how unworthy he was. *He had said that.* He wasn't trying to hide this from her.

"Dear Lord, can Shelton and I have the kind of relationship You designed for a man and woman? Can we ever have the completeness that will make us one? Or will our pasts always get in the way?"

&

"Katherine, I need to speak with you," Shelton called from outside her bedroom door. He'd waited for three days to talk to her. Now, after the recent visit from Parson Kincaid, he had no choice. "Please, Katherine. Something has come up."

"I'll be right there." He heard her scurrying about in her room.

Shelton stepped back and waited. When she peeked out the doorway, he felt thrilled to see her crown of red curls. "Do you have a minute?"

She looked into her room, then back at him. "Sure. Wait for me in the sitting room." She closed the door.

Shelton nearly skipped toward the sitting room. *At least she didn't throw something at me.* He grinned. He sat on the sofa, then jumped up and paced before the fireplace.

Katherine came in with her hair straightened.

"Katherine, I'm so sorry."

"Shh. I'm sorry. I overreacted."

"I don't think so. One day soon we'll discuss what happened in greater detail, but right now I want to speak with you about something Parson Kincaid just suggested."

She sat on the sofa. "All right."

"I know we talked about waiting to get married until we were ready, but Parson Kincaid thinks we might want to change those plans."

"Why?"

"He thinks I was being less than generous to give my father only three days to make a decision about how he was going to live his life. But he had an alternative."

Shelton sat beside her. "The parson believes that if we marry now, we may be able to help Father stop his gambling habit. It would take a long time and a lot of work. We'd have to watch over him constantly and not let him out of our sight."

"And what does that have to do with our getting married?"

"Parson Kincaid knows we're planning on getting married eventually anyway. His suggestion is that we do it sooner rather than later. Between the two of us, we can keep a better eye on him. And we could find strength in each other."

"But Parson Kincaid doesn't know about my past. He doesn't know how difficult the adjustment will be, especially in our first year together. I think adding your parents' issues and your father's gambling habits into the mix would be foolhardy."

Shelton leaned back in the sofa. "You're right, he doesn't know about you. But he knows about me."

"How?"

"My father, in his anger, blurted it out in front of my mother and the parson."

She took his hand.

"Father's blaming me for his problems."

"Then he's not ready to stop gambling."

"No, he isn't. So he's going to have to move out of my house. Mother insists on going with him."

"Does she know how bad your father's problem is?"

"Yes. That's what perplexes me. Why does she want to stay with him?"

Katherine smiled. "Because she loves him."

"Well, there is that." Shelton's shoulders slumped. "What should I do?"

"They're not children. You can't order them about. You have to let them make their own choices—right or wrong."

"But he'll gamble again."

"No doubt. But isn't there a church right down the street from the saloon?"

"Yes."

"Maybe if your parents have nowhere to go and no one to fall back on, they'll make the right choice."

"I still don't like it."

"I don't either. But maybe that's what it's going to take. We're not so far from town that we can't keep tabs on them."

Katherine stuffed her hands in her pockets to warm them. She felt the piece of paper Mr. Hastings had given her. "Oh, I almost forgot. Mr. Hastings gave this to me the day I found your father. Apparently he's been charging at the store."

Shelton took the crumpled piece of paper and read. "My father charged fifty dollars' worth of merchandize to my account."

"Oh my. I think before they move into town, you should advise the businessmen that you are not responsible for your father's debts."

"You're a wise woman, Katherine."

"I've been around a lot of gamblers."

He placed his hands on her shoulders. "Would you go to my house and tell my parents they can stay for another night? I want to go into town and talk with the business owners right away. If I go speak with my parents now, I know I'm just going to blow up at Father. I need to know how far he's put me in debt before I speak with them. Ask them to stay for one more night. I'll see them in the morning."

"All right."

Shelton took her hands into his. "Katherine, will you still marry me?"

"Is that a proposal?" she asked.

"I just want to know if you're ready."

"Not quite yet, but I'm getting there. With you in my life, I don't care what other nonsense I have to deal with. I just want you by my side."

He smiled.

"Kiss me before I say something foolish," she encouraged.

And he did.

Chapter 15

Katherine prayed the entire trip from Grandma Mac's house to Shelton's. She had no idea what she would find when she arrived, or how Hiram Greene would respond to her.

"Hello," she called out as she entered the front door. "Is anyone home?"

Elizabeth Greene came from the front parlor, her eyes puffy and red.

"Mrs. Greene, Shelton asked me to come over and let you know that you can stay for one more night."

"We'll not be taking any more charity from him," Hiram gruffed as he entered the room. "As soon as the boy tells us which wagon is ours, we'll be on our way."

"Shelton will be back late this evening. That's why he suggested you leave tomorrow."

Hiram turned to face his wife. "Let's just take one, Elizabeth. I can't stand to be in this house another minute."

Before she could answer, Katherine said, "I'm sorry you feel that way, Mr. Greene. Shelton worked very hard to help you."

"What do you know about it?" he sneered.

More than you want me to know. "Mr. and Mrs. Greene, why don't we make some tea while we wait for Shelton?"

"Hiram, please." Elizabeth placed a loving hand on his arm.

"Oh, all right."

Katherine went to the kitchen, followed by the Greenes. "Have you packed away your kitchen belongings yet?"

"No," Elizabeth said. "Since we don't know where we're going to stay, I thought we'd leave them here for now. I hope Shelton won't mind."

"I don't think he will."

"What gives you the right to tell us what our son is thinking?" Hiram spat.

Katherine squeezed her eyes shut and prayed for God's grace to help her say something that would reflect God's mercy and grace. "Mr. Greene, I took your abusive tongue when I was your servant. But I am not a servant any longer, and I will not be spoken to in that tone."

"And who made you—"

"God did." Katherine placed her hands on her hips. "Now, sit down before my temper really starts to rise."

He sat.

Katherine filled a kettle with water. "You do know that Shelton and I are planning on getting married one day."

Hiram mumbled.

Elizabeth smiled. "Yes, dear, Shelton made that clear when he came back to Hazel Green."

Katherine put the kettle on the stove. "He and I have spoken openly with each other. He loves you both and respects you tremendously. He's hurting terribly having to make this decision, but he can't support your gambling habit, Mr. Greene."

"Who's asking him to?"

"You are," Katherine stated.

Hiram Greene blanched.

Katherine wasn't sure where she'd found such boldness. Perhaps living with Grandma Mac was rubbing off on her.

"We haven't asked Shelton for any money," Elizabeth interjected.

"True. But your husband has been charging to your son's accounts in town."

Elizabeth stared at him with wide eyes. "Hiram?"

He buried his face in his hands. "I was going to pay it back."

"With what?" Katherine asked.

He sat up straight and squared his shoulders. "With the money I'd earn."

"How? From gambling? How much have you won so far?" Katherine stared at his blank face for a moment before continuing. "That's the problem. You can't think straight when you're gambling. It controls you. I've lived with enough gamblers to know how it works."

"Hiram, is this true?"

He turned his face away from his wife.

Katherine felt sorry for them. "Mrs. Greene, I'm sure your husband didn't set out to become a gambler. It may have started as a gentleman's wager over a horse race or some such thing. He probably made some money in the beginning. Then it began to control him, forcing him to make unwise choices. Fortunately, or unfortunately, you had enough money that he could hide his gambling from the family for years. Shelton says he only learned about it six months before he came here. But I know he's been gambling for at least seven years."

"How do you know that?" Elizabeth asked.

"That's how I came to work for your family. Mr. Greene won me in a poker game."

Tears pooled in Elizabeth's eyes. "Hiram, is this true?"

Hiram pulled at his collar.

Katherine poured the hot water into the teapot and let the tea steep. "Mr. Greene do you really want to throw away your wife, your children, and your grandchildren for a deck of cards?"

He shook his head.

"You have the perfect opportunity to make things right. You can start over. Work with Shelton and help him breed horses. A man with your business sense must know legitimate ways to make a profit."

Hiram Greene cleared his throat. "He wouldn't want me."

Katherine chuckled. "He knows all about my past, and he wants me. You both raised a wonderful son who has become a man with such respect for his parents that he wouldn't listen to me when I said you should pay for your own mistakes. Instead, he convinced me that the right thing to do was to love and honor you by helping you and by having you move into this house."

Katherine poured tea into each cup, then added milk the way she knew the Greenes liked it. She was serving them now as a free woman, out of love for God and gratitude for what He'd done for her, not out of a debt that Hiram Greene once held over her. Katherine knew beyond a doubt she was totally free from the bondage of the past. *Thank You, Lord.*

"Mr. and Mrs. Greene, there's something else you should know." She sat across from the couple. "I love Shelton, and I know now that I can truly love him without fear from the past." She looked Hiram straight in the eye. She could tell from the look on his face that he realized she was recalling the night when he threatened her. "I thank you for all you've done to raise my future husband. I will be honored to have him as my partner in life. Even your mistakes have made him strong."

Katherine pushed the chair away from the table and stood. "Mr. Greene, this is your house, if you choose to let the Lord rebuild you." Katherine laid a hand on Elizabeth's shoulder and gave a gentle squeeze. "I'll see myself out."

❧

Shelton found he owed more than a hundred dollars in town, thanks to his father's charging. He had money left from the sale of the property in

Hazel Green, so he made arrangements to pay off each debt. But he made it clear that he would not accept any further charges on his father's behalf.

He didn't know whether he'd find his parents at the house or not, but he hoped he would. He'd spoken harshly with his father earlier, and he wanted to make peace with the man before he left.

He'd hoped Katherine would agree to marry him since Parson Kincaid had suggested it. But she was right; a new marriage was hard enough. They shouldn't start with his parents and their problems weighing them down. He couldn't be his father's guardian any longer. Until the man's heart changed and he repented of his sin, nothing would be different.

When he arrived back at the house, he sighed with relief that his parents were home. But the conversation he had with them took an unexpected turn.

"Shelton, I need to apologize to you," Hiram said. "I've made a mess of my life and squandered my family's fortune. Katherine opened my eyes, with a little help from your mother." He glanced at his wife, then turned back to Shelton. "She doesn't let a man off the hook, does she?"

Shelton chuckled. "No, she doesn't."

"You'll have your hands full with that one, son. But she's right. I do want to change."

"Katherine told me your father's been gambling for at least seven years," Elizabeth said. "He confessed that it's been nine. Does that sound right with what you saw in the financial books?"

"Yes," he reluctantly admitted.

"Your father has agreed not to touch the finances. I'm going to pay all the bills and he'll help me decide how and which ones."

"Dad, are you aware of the debt you've incurred in Creelsboro?"

Hiram hung his head in shame, then lifted it again and faced Shelton. "Yes. About a hundred dollars, give or take a few."

Elizabeth gasped. "Do we have that kind of money?"

"I do," Shelton acknowledged. "I've made arrangements with the businessmen in town. I should have it all paid off in time for Christmas."

Hiram's shoulders slumped. Then he lifted them and looked directly into his son's eyes. "Shelton, I know it won't be easy, but I'm willing to work at changing."

"It'll only happen by God's grace, Dad. You can't do this in your own strength. Trust me, I've tried."

Hiram nodded.

Elizabeth took her husband's hand. "Shelton, your father and I have a lot to talk about. Will you excuse us?"

"Of course. Good night." He stood. "I'm glad you're going to stay."

&

Shelton was restless all night. Unable to sleep, he took an early morning stroll through the woods and down to the river. Ice-covered rocks lined the river's edge.

He turned up the collar on his coat and walked north around the peninsula that stuck out into the Cumberland. It felt good to own property. In spite of all his father had done to waste the family's wealth, Shelton had the potential to earn it back again. The problem would be keeping that from becoming his primary purpose in life.

As he rounded the peninsula, he found an inlet with calm water and an embankment that climbed up twenty-five to thirty feet. Shelton climbed up the steep terrain. From the top, he could see his house to the left. The breathtaking view was spectacular. "This is where I'll build, Lord. Katherine deserves a beautiful house with a wonderful view. She'll love it here."

With single-minded determination he set about making his plans. He would build a cabin with a loft. Upstairs would be their bedroom. From there they could see water all around them.

Shelton walked to Urias's house. By the time he arrived the sun was up over the eastern ridge. "Urias?" he called as he entered the barn.

"Over here."

Shelton stepped into the darkened barn. The smell of freshly spread hay made him realize he needed to do the same in his own barn. Urias sat by the cow, milking her.

"Have your parents moved out?"

Shelton filled Urias in about the latest turn of events. "If Father follows through on his promises, it looks like he and Mother will be living in the house permanently. Of course, if Katherine and I get married, it'll be tough living under the same roof with them. But we'll have to. . .at least until I can build a house for the two of us."

Urias leaned back and raked his hair with his fingers. "Before you and Katherine started developing a relationship, Mac and I were building a log cabin for her a little to the west of Grandma Mac's house. She wanted so much to have her own home."

Shelton knew about that desire.

"We got as far as putting up the sides, but haven't put a roof on yet. What do you think about you two living there for a couple of years while you build your own home?"

"My parents could use the privacy."

"And so could you and Katherine." Urias described the cabin's location and the work they had accomplished so far. The weather was too cold to put on the roof right away, but come spring, it could be finished within a day or two. Shelton wondered if Katherine would be ready to marry by spring.

As he made his way to Grandma Mac's house, he wondered if he should take Urias up on the offer of the log cabin or if he should just build his own house on the peninsula overlooking the river. He couldn't wait to consult Katherine.

"Good morning, Mrs. MacKenneth," he said when she opened the door to him.

"Morning, Shelton," she said, escorting him into the living room. "You're up early."

I haven't gone to sleep, he held back from telling her. "Is Katherine up?"

"Haven't seen her yet this morning. What happened last night?"

"I'm not sure. That's why I need to talk with her."

"I'll go fetch her. You set for a spell. You look exhausted."

Shelton paced in the sitting area until Katherine entered, wearing her robe. "Is everything all right?"

"It's fine. I didn't mean to worry you."

"What's the matter? Why are you here so early?"

"I have to ask you a couple of questions about your conversation with my parents last night."

Katherine tensed.

"Honey, relax. Whatever you said did wonders. Father is repentant. Mother is in shock. They both want to stay. Is that all right with you? I mean, it's your house, too, or at least it will be."

"Shelton, sit down." Katherine coaxed him to the chair and she sat in the rocking chair. "It's not my house, Shelton." Tears formed in her eyes. "It never will be."

"Why? What's happened?"

28.

"I can't really explain this," Katherine said, "but yesterday, when I was speaking with your parents, I realized the house would never truly be mine. It's theirs. You probably think I'm missing some mental capacities, and I probably am, but—"

Shelton placed a finger to her lips and smiled. "I know what you mean.

I was out this morning exploring my—I mean our—property, and I found what I think will be the ideal place for us to build our home one day. Unfortunately, it will be a couple years before I have the funds to build the kind of house I'd like for us."

Katherine blinked. "Two years?"

"Yes."

"We have to wait two years?" she repeated. Didn't he know she'd be happy living just about anywhere with him? *Except in his parents' house*, she amended.

Shelton flushed. "Well, we could get married in the spring if you don't mind living in something temporarily."

"What are you saying?"

"Apparently, Mac and Urias started building a log cabin for you a while back. Urias told me about it this morning. The roof isn't on, but we could put one on in the spring. It's small, but it would be big enough for us to use for a while. What do you think?"

"I think this family tries to help each other a little too much."

Shelton chuckled. "You're probably right. But you didn't answer my question."

"I'm not sure. It sounds promising, but. . ."

Not wanting her to talk herself out of getting married next spring, he changed the subject. "So, what did you say to my parents?"

Katherine gave a detailed account of the things she'd said to the Greenes. "We still have some issues to deal with regarding your parents. We can't be paying up every time your father slips up and gambles."

"We have to trust them."

"I can't, Shelton. Not yet. I need more time."

Chapter 16

For two weeks Katherine found various ways to avoid Shelton's parents. The Christmas season provided an excellent excuse. She had gifts to make and embroidery and needlepoint to finish.

She knew Shelton no longer believed her excuses. He hadn't pushed her, but he stopped inviting her to come to the house and have dinner with him and his parents.

But on Christmas Eve, meeting with the family was unavoidable. The O'Learys, the Greenes, and the MacKenneths were all getting together at Urias's house tonight. Katherine packed the last of her gifts in the satchel.

"Katherine?" Grandma Mac called from the bottom of the stairs.

"Yes?" Katherine tied the bag closed and placed the strap over her shoulder.

"Shelton is here."

Katherine stood at the top of the stairs and looked down at the elderly woman. If she and Shelton got married in the spring, Katherine realized, Grandma Mac would have to move in with Mac and Pam. "I'm ready."

Shelton stepped up behind Grandma Mac and placed his hands on her shoulders. "She's mighty pretty, ain't she?" Shelton winked.

"Isn't she," Grandma Mac corrected with a light tap on his knuckles.

Katherine held back a giggle.

"She's very pretty, isn't she?" he amended.

Grandma Mac smacked him on his backside with her cane. "Go load those packages by the door into the wagon."

"Yes ma'am."

After he left, Grandma Mac whispered to Katherine, "Two can play at that game. Notice, he didn't get a chance to kiss you yet."

"What did I do to deserve such treatment?" Katherine said, enjoying their little repartee.

"You encouraged him. I saw the twinkle in your eyes. I may be getting on in years, but you can't fool me."

Katherine giggled. "No ma'am."

Outside, they climbed into the carriage. Shelton provided several wool blankets and a large bearskin to wrap around Grandma Mac.

"Mac sent this, didn't he?"

"Yes ma'am. He didn't want you getting too cold on the way to Urias's."

"Humph. I dressed in layers."

Shelton draped the bearskin around her anyway.

"Can I join you under there?" Katherine asked, shivering.

The old woman clucked her tongue as she lifted the blanket for Katherine. "You young folks don't know how to weather the elements. Why, back in my day. . ." Grandma Mac instructed them on cold weather survival all the way to Urias's.

Shelton brought the carriage to a stop at their destination and escorted Grandma Mac to the front door.

A hint of jealousy swept over Katherine at the sight of someone else in Shelton's arms. How long had it been since she'd been in his embrace? She sighed and managed to wiggle her way out of the bearskin covering and retrieve her satchel from under the bench.

Shelton came up behind her and wrapped her in his arms. "I missed you." He kissed the nape of her neck.

Katherine turned in his arms and faced him. "I've missed you, too. I'm actually jealous of Grandma Mac."

"Really?" Shelton chortled. "She's a great old woman, but not my type."

"Grandpa Mac must have had his hands full with her."

Shelton released her, and an instant chill washed over her. "No doubt about it." He reached behind the bench and gathered Grandma Mac's packages. "What did she make?"

"I don't know. She's been rather secretive."

He eyed her satchel. "What about you?"

"You'll have to wait and see," she teased. "But your present isn't in here."

"It's not?" He grabbed a third package.

"I saved it for later, for just the two of us."

A smile spread across his lips and lit up his blue eyes.

Lord, I love that smile.

"Then you'll have to wait to receive your gift, too."

"When can we slip away?"

"Honey, if I had my way, we would have slipped away ages ago." He leaned over and gave her a quick kiss. "We need to talk, but it's freezing out here. And if I don't take Grandma Mac's packages inside she'll skin me alive."

Katherine relaxed again and chuckled. "Aye, that be your lot for sure."

They scurried into the warm house. The family members sat in the living room while the children ran up and down the hallway. The air seemed alive with excitement. . .until she caught a glimpse of Hiram Greene's eyes.

Katherine's back tightened and she felt the color drain from her face. How could she live like this for the rest of her life?

%

Shelton leaned against the living room wall. He noticed Katherine's demeanor change as soon as she walked into the house. *Why?*

Everyone else seemed full of cheer. Even his parents were enjoying their grandchildren. He gently rubbed the back of her neck. "Are you all right?" he whispered in her ear.

She turned and looked at him. Her lively green eyes reflected a deep sadness. He pulled her into his embrace. "Whatever it is, it will be all right."

Katherine shook her head.

Lord, help me. I don't understand what has Katherine so upset. His mind flickered back over the moments before they entered the house. Everything was fine. She had been happy, excited, playful. What could have changed?

The rumble of laughter and merriment dissolved into an expectant hush as Mac cleared his throat and stood. "Grandma Mac, as the matriarch of the family, would you please read Luke's account of Jesus's birth?"

Grandma Mac's weathered face lit up. "I'd be happy to."

Shelton slipped out of the family room with Katherine in tow. "Come on. We should talk."

Katherine planted her feet. "Not now," she whispered. "Later."

He didn't want to wait. He wanted to deal with whatever was bothering her immediately. But he also didn't want to make a scene and have the entire family in on their discussion. He let her go back to the living room. But instead of joining her, he left by the back door and headed to the barn.

For the past month, since his father had decided to quit gambling, Shelton's time with Katherine had become almost nonexistent. His parents, the house, the barn, and the horses all needed him. He'd been working with his mother on their finances, trying to teach her how to keep records and ledger sheets. Father had never let her be a part of the financial picture, and there were many little details she had to understand. In addition, Shelton was busy every day working on the land, preparing it for next year's planting. If only he had more time.

Kehoe stood in his stall, noisily munching on oats.

"Hey boy, how you doing?"

Kehoe's silence emanated unquestioned loyalty and acceptance.

"I can't stay in here." Shelton patted the animal's neck. "Katherine and I need more time together."

Kehoe shook his head and snorted.

"You're right. I should be inside with her. I don't like it much when she shuts me out."

Kehoe took half a step sideways, leaving little room for Shelton.

He chuckled. "All right, boy, I get the message."

He turned toward the barn door and found Urias standing there, his hands draped across his chest. "Pru sent me out to get you to come back inside and join the festivities. What's the problem?"

"Nothing."

"If I believed that, I'd be dumber than a stump. Are you and Katherine having trouble?"

Shelton clapped Urias on the back. "Nothing that can't be solved with time and a little conversation."

Urias's green eyes fixed on Shelton. He squared up his shoulders, his posture like a soldier standing at attention. "Fine, I'll trust you. But don't hurt her. She's had enough trouble in her life."

They made their way back to the house. As he entered the living room, Shelton smiled at Katherine. She turned away. His heart sank. *Dear Lord, don't let me lose her.*

ટ

Katherine buried herself under the covers. A chill nipped her nose. The house creaked against frequent gusts of wind.

Christmas morning had arrived. But she didn't feel much like celebrating. All night she'd battled conflicting emotions. Her love for Shelton. His love for her. Hiram Greene's disdain. Would she ever be free from the past? The bondage she'd been in for so many years was gone. But the anger in Hiram Greene's eyes led her to believe she'd never be able to marry Shelton. How could she bring children into this world when their only grandfather hated her so?

"Why do I have to keep going over the same things, Lord? When will I be truly satisfied and accept myself as someone You cherish? As someone Shelton cherishes? Why does it have to be so hard? Will I ever stop overreacting when people like Hiram Greene glare at me?"

Katherine threw off the covers and jumped out of bed. Her fur-lined slippers, a gift from Mac and Pam a couple of Christmases ago, gloved her feet. They were getting thin on the bottom and she could use a new pair, but she'd never felt the freedom to ask for anything for herself.

"Katherine?" Grandma Mac called out. Her voice sounded weak and shaky.

She bolted out of her room. "Where are you?"

"In my room, dear. I'm all right. I'm just a bit unsteady on my feet."

Katherine ran to Grandma Mac's room and saw the older woman holding on to the tall bedpost. "What's the matter?"

"I'm just old, and stayed up too late, I suspect. Would you help me get ready for Christmas dinner? I want to wear my red dress and white lace shawl, the one Pam and Mac gave me last year."

Katherine offered a steadying hand. "Why don't you sit in the chair and I'll get your things."

"Thank you," Grandma Mac sighed as she sat.

Katherine's heart pounded in her chest. She'd feared something like this would happen one day. Age had a way of creeping up on folks, but Grandma Mac never seemed as old as she really was.

She moved to the closet and glanced back at the old woman. Grandma Mac's chest moved up and down in slow, labored breaths. "Are you certain you're all right?"

The woman's brown eyes seemed darker. "Perhaps I should rest."

"We've got plenty of time, Grandma Mac," she said, returning to the woman's side. "Here, let me help you back into bed."

Blue-veined hands patted Katherine's arm. "Thank you."

Katherine helped Grandma Mac settle into bed. *Father God, please be with Grandma Mac and heal her,* she prayed over and over. She hoped someone would come to call on them. Last night, the group had decided that each family would spend the early morning hours at home, then gather at Urias's house for a late breakfast while they waited for the Christmas dinner to cook. Not that she wanted to spend any more time with Hiram Greene and his accusing scowls.

Katherine paced and nibbled her fingernails. "Lord, please make Grandma Mac well."

Tea! The idea hit her hard. She ran to the cabinets and looked through the various tins and glass jars. Mac always claimed tea helped a person get going in the morning. Personally, she didn't care for the stuff. It tasted too much like the roots and dirt it had grown from. But she had to confess, it did give her a boost when she didn't feel quite herself.

She pushed things around until she found the little blue tin. She positioned the kettle on the stove and added some wood to the cooling embers, found a tea rag, and measured out a rounded teaspoon. She placed the spoonful of leaves in the center of the tea-stained cloth and tied a thin cotton string around it. Then she set it in the china teapot that Grandma Mac claimed came from England as a gift from her grandmother, who had received it from her mother as a wedding present.

Katherine put a tray together and rummaged through the room for things to decorate the tray for the festive holiday. She placed the tip of a pine branch in the corner with a hand-painted red glass ball that Grandma Mac said had been a gift from Grandpa Mac on their fifth Christmas together.

With the tray set, she carried it to Grandma Mac's bedroom. When she pressed the door open, she saw Grandma Mac sleeping comfortably. Her breathing was even, less labored.

A loud rattle at the front door echoed through the house. Katherine set the tray on a table and went to the front door. When she opened it, Hiram Greene's eyes locked with hers. Katherine shrank back against the wall.

Chapter 17

"Merry Christmas, Katherine," Shelton said as he worked his way around his father. Her stance reminded him of a frightened filly plastered against the back wall of a corral. "Honey, what's the matter?"

She looked at the floor. "Grandma Mac isn't feeling well." She slowly lifted her head. "If you stay with her, I'll get Pam and Mac."

He laid a reassuring hand on her forearm. "I'll go. You stay here and take care of her."

She glanced at his father. Her shoulders squared off as if bracing herself against some unseen horror. Shelton's mind flicked back across the stories Katherine had revealed about her past. Had his father abused her? No. Katherine had been clear on that. Then what had he done or said that made her so leery of him?

"I'll go." Hiram stepped out of the doorway and back onto the front porch.

Katherine visibly relaxed.

As his father climbed into the wagon, Shelton inched closer to Katherine. "Hi." He lightly brushed his lips against her satin cheek. "Merry Christmas."

"It hasn't been merry so far," she mumbled.

"Katherine, we have to talk."

"Not now," she protested, and slipped past him into the living room.

"When?" He reached for her. She flinched from his touch. He debated removing his hand, then waited a moment longer, hoping she would relax under his grip. Thankfully, she did.

"Shelton, I can't marry you."

"Pardon?"

"Your father will never accept our relationship. I won't put myself in a position of wondering every day of my life if you will begin resenting me because of your father's disdain for me and who I was."

"I don't care what my father thinks."

"Yes, you do." She cupped his cheek. "Your entire existence revolves around making certain everything is all right with them. They are your top priority."

He opened his mouth to protest. Her fingers on his lips stopped him.

"You should see the anger in your father's eyes whenever he looks at me. It's just like that time. . ." She cut off her words and walked away from him.

Shelton came up behind her and held her in a loving embrace. "What did he do to you?"

"Nothing."

Shelton spun her around to face him. "I don't believe that."

Tears welled in her eyes. She looked at her feet. He bent his knees and lifted her chin. "Katherine, look at me."

The tears fell and streamed down her face. "In your father's eyes, I will always be a servant. Think about how your family has treated servants in the past. We were possessions, cattle. We were not people with our own thoughts and desires. You're a part of that. You've treated your servants like that too—even me."

"You were never. . ." He let his words trail off. She was right. He had treated her like a servant. He had ordered her about the way he did all the others. Until he fell in love with her. "I can't accept that it's not possible for us to marry, Katherine. I admit there will be hardships at times, but God is the Lord of our lives. He'll help us."

"Perhaps. But Hiram Greene will always stand in the way," she said with a boldness he'd never heard from her.

Shelton's heart pounded. How could this be, after all this time of being patient, gently coaxing her like a skittish mare? "I love you, Katherine. Nothing should stand in opposition to that. Except God. And I believe He brought us together."

"I'm sorry, Shelton. I just can't."

He wanted to argue, but what would that accomplish? Instead, he gave her a passionate kiss. "If you ever change your mind, you know how to find me." With all the strength he could muster, he left.

God, he prayed as he climbed up on Kehoe, *move in Katherine's heart. There's nothing more I can do.*

≈

Three long days had passed since she'd pushed Shelton out of her life. Katherine craved his touch and affection.

She'd burned a lot of wood since Christmas, trying to keep the house warm for Grandma Mac. The wood boxes by the fireplace were nearly empty. She grabbed her winter coat and braced for the damp chill that had blown in from the north last night.

Arriving at the woodshed, she noticed there were only two cords under the protection of the shelter. She loaded the canvas carrier and took it into the house. She repeated the process three more times until the wood boxes in the house were full.

Rubbing her hands together for warmth, she ventured back outside and moved a cord of wood from the elements to the protection of the woodshed. "Oh, how I miss Shelton," she moaned. *Father, I don't understand. Why did I let myself fall in love with a man I could never be with?*

"Good morning, Katherine." Urias stepped up beside her. "Let me take care of that."

She gratefully stood back to let him handle the heavy bundle.

"So tell me," he said, putting on his leather work gloves, "what's happened between you and Shelton?"

"There's nothing to tell. We've simply agreed we aren't right for each other."

Urias peered at her. "Interesting. He said you broke off the engagement."

Katherine felt the sting of her reddened face. She knew it had nothing to do with the northern winds, but from her own shame of being slightly deceptive with her brother. "Yes, I suppose I did."

"Do you mind if I ask why?"

Katherine took a step back. "Urias, how do you deal with Hiram Greene?"

"Like I told you before, I honor the man simply because he is Prudence's father."

"I tried that, but it didn't work."

"It isn't just about honor. You need to forgive Hiram."

"I did," she said.

"Then what's the problem?"

"Did you see the way he looked at me on Christmas Eve when I walked into your house?"

Urias hauled an armful of logs to the shed. "No. How did he look?"

"Like I was the cause of all his problems."

Urias dropped the wood onto the floor. "Fact is, you are a major part of his current situation. Thanks to you, his wife now knows the full details of his gambling habit."

"That's not my fault," she defended.

He placed a loving hand on her shoulder. "Katherine, we are called to forgive those who have sinned against us. You should pray and ask God if you really have forgiven him."

"I can't make Shelton decide between me and his parents."

Urias massaged her shoulder for a moment. "Katherine, you do needle-point. What's on the surface is pretty. The tangled mess of threads under-neath is not. Being a bond servant was a horrific experience. I understand that. But God is weaving you into a new tapestry. The redemptive power of His blood is like the piece of fabric you sew on. The finished needle-point is what you're becoming. But that doesn't negate the tangled mess that's under that cloth."

Katherine sighed.

"Forgiveness is a process. Hiram Greene must go through his own process as well. But you can't live your life based on the changes going on in another person."

Urias's words grated. She knew her fears were to blame for her decision, but she couldn't see any other choice.

"You have to decide whether or not you think Shelton is a gift the Lord is giving you. If he is, grab on to him and don't let him go."

She wanted that with all her heart. But it couldn't be that simple, could it? "I'll think about it."

"Good. Now, why don't you go on inside and make some coffee while I finish up here. I'm going to need something hot today. Mac says we could be in for a cold snap."

Back inside the house she prepared Urias's coffee, then went to check on Grandma Mac. The woman's illness had been a blessing, in a way. In her weakened condition, Grandma Mac hadn't been able to chastise her about calling a halt to her engagement with Shelton.

Grandma Mac sat in her rocking chair next to the window, reading her Bible.

"How are you feeling?" Katherine asked.

"Better. I don't know what came over me. I was fit as a fiddle one moment and worn out like an old shoe the next."

Katherine smiled. "Can I make you some breakfast?"

"A poached egg on toast would be nice."

"Would you like to eat in your room?"

"No, dear. I think I'd better start moving or these old bones will set in place."

"I doubt that." Katherine chuckled, then bid a hasty retreat to the kitchen. She busied herself with the breakfast preparation, trying to ignore

Urias's words, which echoed over and over in her head.

What angered her more than Urias's advice was that Shelton hadn't stopped by for the past three days. She missed their times together. She missed being in his arms.

Urias and Grandma Mac took up most of the conversation around the breakfast table, giving Katherine some relief.

"Thank you for the coffee and the eggs," Urias said as he pushed his chair back and stood. "But I must be off. I'm working on the cabin this morning."

"Why?" Katherine asked.

Urias placed his coonskin cap on his head. "Because you want a place of your own, remember?"

"Yes, but. . ." She and Shelton were supposed to have moved in there after they married. But that wasn't going to happen.

Urias gave her shoulder a loving squeeze. "Even if you and Shelton don't marry, I want you to have your own home."

Katherine swallowed her emotions and simply nodded.

Urias patted her shoulder and left. Grandma Mac rose from the table and took her plate to the sink.

"Let me do that," Katherine protested.

"I'm fine. But it appears you're not. Want to tell me about it?"

"There's not much to tell. Shelton and I agreed it wasn't wise for us to get married."

Grandma Mac peered at Katherine in a way that said, *"Fess up."*

"All right. I told Shelton we couldn't get married. I can't live with Hiram Greene's attitude toward me."

"You know, I did notice Hiram's appearance change when you entered the house on Christmas Eve. But I don't believe he was reacting in quite the way you think. That man is a troubled soul. But from what I hear, he's working hard to get right with his family and, I dare say, his Maker. You, on the other hand, seem to be living in fear again. Am I right?"

&

"How is she?" Shelton asked as Urias joined him at the log cabin.

"Miserable. Same as you. Why don't you go talk to her?"

Shelton pounded the nail harder, sinking it with one swing. Taking another from his nail apron, he tapped then sank it deep in the wood. The cold temperatures made working this time of year hard on a person, but he needed to burn off his anger so he could wait patiently. "Katherine has to come to me. I think it's important for her to step out in order to get past all she's been through and know she has the right to approach me."

"This isn't about you. It's about your father."

"I'm aware of that." Feeling the tension rise, Shelton moved over to the saw and cut the next plank. "And he knows what he's done. He wanted to apologize to her on Christmas morning, but Katherine overreacted. Honestly, I thought she was afraid he'd beat her. Urias, if she can't conquer these fears, our marriage really would be a mistake."

"You're probably right. But you're as stubborn as she is, you know."

Shelton chuckled.

Urias picked up a plank for the window frame. "If you two aren't going to get married, why is it so important for us to get this cabin ready right now? Katherine seems to enjoy living with Grandma Mac."

The cut end of the board fell to the floor. Shelton wiped the sweat from his brow. "While I was praying about our broken engagement, I felt like the Lord was impressing on me to give Katherine what she's wanted for so long. I don't believe she wants to be alone. She only thinks she does. But she won't know that if she's never given the chance."

"I reckon you know what you're doing. But why couldn't we wait until spring?"

"I'm hoping she'll come to her senses by then and marry me."

Urias grinned.

They worked long and hard until noon. "I have to go," Urias said. "I'll be back tomorrow."

Shelton extended his hand. "Thanks for the help."

"You're welcome. It should be ready by next week."

"I hope so. I still want to bring in some wood or coal for heat."

"We can help with that." Urias pulled a small pouch from his pocket. "Pru and I set aside a small amount to help you with the expenses."

Shelton didn't want to take the money but knew it would come in handy. "Thank you."

After a quick meal Shelton went back to work on the log cabin. He had filled all the joints with clay, the roof was on, and the only remaining things to be done were small.

Mac joined him for three hours in the afternoon. By dinnertime Shelton put away his tools and headed for home.

As he arrived at the old farmhouse, he couldn't help but think of Katherine. She'd gone out of her way to work on the place and get it ready for him and his parents. *Lord, she has a wonderful heart. Please help her get past this overwhelming fear.*

In the barn, he checked on Kate and the twins. His gut tightened another notch as he remembered the night Katherine helped with the delivery. He brushed the dust off his clothes before entering the house.

His mother stood by the kitchen stove. "Did you have a good day, son?"

"We got a lot accomplished."

"Good. Your father's in the den. He'd like to speak with you. We'll be eating in thirty minutes. Be sure and clean up before you come to the table."

"Yes ma'am."

Shelton collected his thoughts as he walked to the den. His father sat in a high-backed stuffed chair that Katherine had refinished. "Mother said you wished to speak with me."

"Yes. I must confess I've been rather displeased with your desire to marry Kate."

"Katherine," Shelton corrected.

Hiram Greene nodded and motioned for Shelton to take a seat. "And when you pushed me to apologize on Christmas, I admit I was doing it to please you, not because I agreed with it. But your mother and I have been doing a lot of talking lately. She's a wise woman."

Shelton could imagine his mother giving his father a piece of her mind. He'd been on the receiving end of her lectures many times. It seemed strange that she'd never spoken to her husband in the same way.

"I'm a proud man, Shelton, so this isn't easy for me. But. . ." Hiram stopped.

"Father?"

"What I mean to say is, what can I do to make things right between you and Katherine?"

If only Katherine could hear this. "I still think you should apologize to her. But as for our relationship—it's in the Lord's hands." *And Katherine's.*

"Very well. But if there's anything else I can do, let me know."

"Thanks, Dad. Mother said dinner would be ready in thirty minutes. Guess I'd better wash up." Shelton excused himself and went to his room. He poured water into the basin, then stripped off his soiled clothes and tossed them in a heap.

Washed and refreshed, he dressed in a clean set of white flannels, dark trousers, and a white shirt. With his hair semi-dry, he combed it back. After a quick examination in the mirror he decided he looked more like he was heading for Sunday morning vespers than for dinner with his family. Dressing up for the evening meal had been a regularity back in Hazel

Green, but since moving to Jamestown, the occasions had been few.

He went downstairs and was about to enter the dining room when a knock on the front door distracted him. He pulled the door open. His heart stopped.

Chapter 18

Katherine didn't know whether she was shaking more from fear or the cold, but seeing Shelton standing there all dressed up made her want to leap into his arms.

"Katherine."

She fought the desire to jump into his embrace. "Hi."

Shelton beamed. "Come on in."

Katherine squeezed her eyes shut and braved the step over the threshold of Shelton's home. Her legs wobbled but somehow managed to move forward. *Why does it have to be this hard?*

"We're about to eat dinner. Would you like to join us?"

"No, no. I can come back." Katherine spun around.

Shelton grabbed her wrist. His light touch crumbled her resolve.

"I just came to say I'm sorry, Shelton. And I miss you. But. . ."

"Honey, I told you I would wait." He inched closer.

Katherine wanted to nuzzle into his embrace. But she hesitated. She'd felt guilty all day. She couldn't change her feelings toward his father, or calm her fears. They came from a place where she had no control. They sprang up in her even when she didn't want them to.

Shelton caressed the back of her neck with his fingers. "I love you."

She collapsed in his arms. Tears ran down onto his shirt. She inhaled deeply, taking in the scent of his cologne. "I wish I could love you back," she mumbled.

"You will. Give it time." Shelton pulled back slightly. "Your log cabin will be ready by the end of the week. You'll have your dream home, Katherine, a place all to yourself, just like you wanted."

Katherine wept so hard she couldn't speak.

"Mother," Shelton called out, "you and Father go ahead and start the evening meal without me."

Katherine sensed his parents watching from the next room. She should probably stand up straight and remove herself from his shoulder. But nothing mattered at this moment except being in the loving embrace of the man she loved.

Shelton drove her back to Grandma Mac's home. They didn't talk. She knew Shelton was a patient man. She'd watched him work with his horses, firm yet never getting cross. A quiet strength seemed to emanate from him.

She drew on that strength to help her gain the courage to leave the wagon and enter Grandma Mac's home. He walked her to the door and kissed her lightly on the cheek. "Good night, Katherine. I'll see you soon."

She entered the darkened house and went straight to her room. She couldn't face Grandma Mac tonight. She couldn't face herself. She'd gone to Shelton's house to make things right between them. But how could she when fear wrapped its stringy threads around her heart?

⁂

Three days later Katherine moved into her own house. Every member of the family came to help her settle in. She found traces of everyone's handiwork around the new log cabin. It had been a labor of love.

She had received the desire of her heart. But after her first night in the log cabin, she felt more alone than ever before.

A knock on the front door sent her running. She smiled excitedly, expecting Shelton. She opened the door to Hiram Greene. Her smile dropped.

"May I come in?"

She held on to the doorknob. "What can I help you with, Mr. Greene?"

"I came to apologize."

"Pardon?"

"Please let me come inside, Katherine. There are some things you should know."

Katherine took in a deep breath and stepped aside. "Can I get you some coffee? Tea?"

"No, thank you. I'll get right to the point."

Hiram admitted his guilt with regard to her position in society and asked her forgiveness for every inappropriate thing he'd ever said to her. "Please forgive me. I see now that you and Shelton have a special love. I hope it's not too late."

Katherine's voice caught in her throat. "I forgive you." What else could she do? God required it. She told Urias she had done it. So why did it seem so stiff and forced?

Hiram smiled and gave a curt nod of his head. "I'll be on my way, then. Thank you for your time, Miss O'Leary."

Katherine followed her unexpected guest to the front door and watched as he climbed into the saddle and rode away. Her world seemed to spin. One moment she thought she was doing what was best. Then it all fell back in her lap. She had to decide if she could truly forgive Hiram Greene and trust Shelton and his love enough for them to build a marriage.

But she hadn't seen Shelton much since Christmas morning. Had she gone too far? Would he still take her back? *Lord, I've made such a mess of my life. Please help me.*

ઢ

The next month was the hardest one Shelton had ever lived through. Every fiber of his being wanted to be with Katherine, but he still felt the Lord was asking him to wait. And he had, even after he knew that his father had spoken with her and apologized. Still, she didn't come. For days he tried to conjure up ways they could "accidentally" meet, but he knew he shouldn't.

Urias and the others checked on Katherine in her new home from time to time, and she visited with Grandma Mac nearly every day. Yet she still kept her distance from him. *Why?* It didn't make sense, at least not to his way of thinking.

He spent a lot of time with his horses. The twin foals were growing every day. Mr. Crockett purchased the colt, although Shelton would continue to raise them for a time.

Shelton saddled Kehoe and rode to the spit of land overlooking the Cumberland River. "Forgive me, Lord, but I can't wait any longer. I have to know what she's thinking, what she's feeling." He turned Kehoe in the direction of Katherine's log cabin. He saw her a little ways ahead, sitting on a large boulder overlooking the river.

"Katherine!" he hollered.

She smiled and waved.

Shelton jumped off Kehoe and hustled up to the side of the rock. "What are you doing here?"

"I come here to pray sometimes." She looked at her folded hands in her lap. "Your father came to see me."

"He spoke with me after he visited you." He sat on the rock beside her.

"I've missed you," she confessed.

Renewed hope surged through his heart. "I've missed you, too. How's your new cottage?"

"Horrible."

"Horrible? What's the matter? You should have told me sooner. I would have come and fixed whatever the problem is."

She let out half a chuckle. "No, you can't fix this, Shelton. It's me. I've found that I don't like living alone."

Shelton raised his eyebrows. "Ah Katherine, I can fix that. Just give the word and we'll marry."

She took his hand. "I know. That's why I didn't come to you. God gave me the desire of my heart to have my own home. I felt I should live there for a while and make peace with my mistakes."

"Mistakes?"

She raised her fingers to his lips. "I wanted my own place for selfish reasons. I wasn't appreciating everything the Lord had already given me. I was taking it all for granted, complaining, murmuring like the Jews on their way to the Promised Land from enslavement in Egypt. I've been trying to learn to be content with what I have and what's been given to me. I can't be a good wife to you if I'm not content with myself."

"I respect that. But wouldn't it be better if we spent time with each other, and with my family, in order for you to be comfortable with them and with me?"

"That's exactly what I've been trying to get up the courage to ask you."

Shelton pulled her to himself. "I love you, Katherine," he whispered as his lips captured hers.

As the passion rose, she placed her hands on his chest and pushed back some. "I love you, too."

"Then tell me you'll marry me." *Please don't push me away again.*

Slowly she raised her head and leveled those incredible green eyes with his. "I will."

He pulled her closer and held her so tight he feared he'd break her ribs. He relaxed his grip. "When?"

"As soon as possible."

"Today?"

"If you wish."

"Really?" He jumped up. "Come, let's tell the family." He reached down to help her up.

She continued to sit. "I have something to ask you first."

Please, Lord. Don't let her doubt and fears take over. He sat back down. The rock seemed colder this time.

ଵ

Lord, I hope I'm not being too forward here, she prayed. "Shel—can I call you that?"

He let out a nervous chuckle. "You can call me anything you'd like."

"If you don't mind, I'd like to get married privately. I'm not opposed to your family being a part of our special day, but I've thought about this for a while now. It seems you and I have always been involved with the family. Every holiday, every big event, we're surrounded by them. Not that it's bad, and after a month of living on my own, I really do appreciate the people who care about me. But. . ."

"I think I understand, and no, I don't mind. We could leave tomorrow for Creelsboro, get the parson to marry us, then take a steamer along the Cumberland River. What do you think?"

"Can you afford it?"

"I sold the colt to Mr. Crockett. That should more than cover the cost."

The idea of being alone with Shelton for several days thrilled her. "I like it. You don't mind?"

"No. But if my sister learns of our plans, the whole family will come running down to the church."

"True." Was it right to be so selfish? "Perhaps we should invite them."

"No. But we should probably tell someone of our plans. I'll swear Father to secrecy. If anyone can keep a secret, he can."

It seemed odd to trust Hiram Greene with any part of her future, but she knew she had to get over those lingering doubts. She nodded her agreement. "Do whatever you think is best."

"Tomorrow it is, then."

"Yes."

"Pack a trunk. I'll ride into Creelsboro and make arrangements with the parson and check on the steamer schedules."

With a boldness she'd only seen in herself once before, she pulled Shelton into a kiss. His arms wrapped around her. *Thank You, Lord, for this tremendous gift.*

❧

The next morning Katherine dressed in the ivory satin wedding dress. The problem was, how to keep Shelton from seeing it until she met him at the altar? There were definite disadvantages to not having a family wedding, she mused. But she was still convinced that their union should be just between the two of them. And while she knew from Hiram's own mouth that he would not oppose the wedding, she still wondered if he would be having second thoughts during the wedding service.

When she heard Shelton's wagon drive up to the house, she covered the dress as best she could with her woolen coat and put her ribbon-and-pearl headpiece, ivory silk gloves, and lace veil into a large cloth purse. Then she reached into the hand-carved box she used to keep under the floorboards of Urias's barn. Since moving to Grandma Mac's and then to her own place, she no longer kept it hidden.

She pulled out the note she'd written last night, in which she opened her heart completely to Shelton. She planned to give him the letter as a part of her wedding gift to him. She also removed a thin gold band she prayed would fit Shelton's ring finger.

She opened the door before he knocked.

"Good morning." His smile filled his handsome face.

"Have ye come to fetch me?" she said in her best Irish brogue.

Shelton chuckled. "Absolutely. All packed?"

"Trunk's there." She pointed to her left.

"What's this?" He nodded at the dining table. She'd set it with the fine linen tablecloth, matching napkins, and the horse-patterned china she had bought what seemed like ages ago.

He lifted a china plate. "This is very nice."

"It's one of the dowry items I purchased."

He put the dish back on the table. "I love it." He picked up the trunk and hefted it into the wagon. "I've made arrangements with the stable to house the buggy and horse for the few days we're aboard the steamer."

"When's the next ship?"

"Not until tomorrow. We'll spend tonight in the hotel. I reserved a room and I've made arrangements at the tavern for dinner."

"You've thought of everything." She reached up to climb into the carriage.

"Allow me." Shelton swooped her into his arms and lifted her, brushing his lips lightly across hers.

"You're such a romantic."

He winked. "I can be."

"I have a surprise for you, but you'll have to wait," she teased, patting the gold ring that sat in her pocket.

Shelton made his way around the wagon and got in on the other side. "I think I'm going to enjoy our marriage." He snapped the reins.

"I hope so. Where are we going to live after we get back?"

"At your little log cabin. I figure we'll build our own home on that peninsula overlooking the Cumberland as soon as we have the funds."

All the way to Creelsboro they talked about their future, the desire for children, and their hopes and dreams. At the church, Katherine sequestered herself in a small room to get ready for the ceremony.

A gentle knock on the door was followed by Parson Kincaid's wife poking her head in. "Can I help?"

"Please. I'm so nervous I can't get this headpiece in my hair."

The plump, middle-aged woman came into the room. "Your dress is lovely. Did you make it yourself?"

"Yes."

"Gracious, you are an excellent seamstress. No wonder Mr. Hastings can't keep your shirts in the store for long. Did you make this headpiece as well?"

"Yes." Katherine fought the instinct to nod as she allowed Mrs. Kincaid to adjust the headpiece. "I can't believe I'm so nervous."

The woman gave her a conspiratorial wink. "Mr. Greene has just about worn a hole in my husband's office floor."

Really? The information helped her relax.

Mrs. Kincaid placed the veil over Katherine's red hair. "You're beautiful," she gushed.

She glanced in the mirror. Her reflection did look beautiful. She felt beautiful, too, knowing Shelton loved her no matter what her past held. She felt covered in his love and in God's cleansing love. "Thank you."

"Come down the aisle when you hear the music, child."

"I will."

A few minutes later Katherine heard the music. She reached for the crystal doorknob and took in a deep breath. "Help me, Lord." A gentle peace washed over her. Confidently, she pulled the door open and walked to the aisle. Down at the front stood Shelton, dressed in his Sunday best with his black trousers, white shirt, and black dress coat and tails. His deep blue eyes sparkled and his smile brightened his whole face.

Katherine took a tentative step forward. It seemed to take an eternity to walk down that aisle, yet in a moment she was standing by his side. He reached out and held her hand. They turned and faced Parson Kincaid.

She repeated the words the parson asked her to say. She heard Shelton proclaim his love. But she didn't feel married until their lips met. Her arms slipped around the man she loved, cradling and holding him with all the passion and love she had. And in that moment, she found what she'd been looking for all her life. In her love for Shelton, in being one with him, she found the place of her own that she had always longed for.

Their kiss deepened. Parson Kincaid cleared his throat.

Shelton pulled back. "I love you, Katherine."

"I love you, too."

LYNN A. COLEMAN was raised on Martha's Vineyard and now calls Miami, Florida, home. She has three grown children and seven grandchildren. She is a minister's wife who writes to the Lord's glory through the various means of articles, short stories, and a Web site. She also hosts an inspirational romance writing workshop on the Internet and serves as advisor of the American Christian Romance Writers organization. Visit her Web page at: www.lynncoleman.com

If You Liked This Book, You'll Also Like...

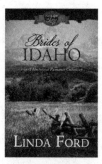

Brides of Idaho by Linda Ford
Three historical romances from bestselling author Linda Ford take readers into the rough mining country of Idaho. The three independent Hamilton sisters struggle to make a home and livelihood for themselves, and they don't have time for men they can't trust. Can love sneak in and change their stubborn hearts?
Paperback / 978-1-63409-798-7 / $12.99

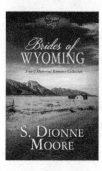

Brides of Wyoming by S. Dionne Moore
Author S. Dionne Moore takes readers onto the Wyoming rangeland of the late 1800s. In this historical romance collection, three strong men work ranches against the untamed forces of nature, outlaws, and feisty women. Can faith and love grow where suspicion and greed roam the range?
Paperback / 978-1-63409-799-4 / $12.99

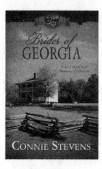

Brides of Georgia by Connie Stevens
Author Connie Stevens travels back to 1800s Georgia during pivotal changes in the history of the Old South. In this historical romance collection, three men are on the verge of losing all hope for their futures, until they meet women who profoundly affect their hearts and faith.
Paperback / 978-1-63409-800-7 / $12.99

JOIN US ONLINE!

Christian Fiction for Women

Christian Fiction for Women is your online home for the latest in Christian fiction.

Check us out online for:

- Giveaways
- Recipes
- Info about Upcoming Releases
- Book Trailers
- News and More!

Find Christian Fiction for Women at Your Favorite Social Media Site:

 Search "Christian Fiction for Women"

 @fictionforwomen